NEW MOONS

NEW MOONS

Contemporary Writing by

NORTH AMERICAN MUSLIMS

ᴠ

EDITED BY

❧ Kazim Ali ❧

Red Hen Press | Pasadena, CA

Book design by Mark E. Cull

Library of Congress Cataloging-in-Publication Data

TBA

ISBN· 978-1-63628-006-6

The National Endowment for the Arts, the Los Angeles County Arts Commission, the Ahmanson Foundation, the Dwight Stuart Youth Fund, the Max Factor Family Foundation, the Pasadena Tournament of Roses Foundation, the Pasadena Arts & Culture Commission and the City of Pasadena Cultural Affairs Division, the City of Los Angeles Department of Cultural Affairs, the Audrey & Sydney Irmas Charitable Foundation, the Meta & George Rosenberg Foundation, the Albert and Elaine Borchard Foundation, the Adams Family Foundation, Amazon Literary Partnership, the Sam Francis Foundation, and the Mara W. Breech Foundation partially support Red Hen Press.

First Edition
Published by Red Hen Press
www.redhen.org

Acknowledgments & Permissions

The editor would like to thank and acknowledge the journals and publications in which some of these works have previously appeared:

"A dream is a merciful thing" by Mahdi Chowdhury was originally published in *Popula* (2019). Reprinted by permission of the author.

"Portrait of My Father Drowning" by Tariq Luthun was originally published in *Crab Orchard Review* (2019). Reprinted by permission of the author.

"Quebec Was The Semi-Colon" by Haroon Moghul was originally published in "Stranded In Between: An American and a Muslim," *Haaretz* (2016). Reprinted by permission of the author.

"The Summer My Cousin Went Missing" by Tariq Luthun was originally published in *Michigan Quarterly Review* (2020). Reprinted by permission of the author.

"Upon Leaving the Diamond to Catch 14 Stitches in My Left Brow" by Tariq Luthun was originally published in *Mizna* (2017). Reprinted by permission of the author.

"Woman-Crisp" by Mohja Kahf was originally published on the *Thirteen Myna Birds* Blogspot (2017). Reprinted by permission of the author.

"You Care More About Me Being Black Than I Do—Reflections on an Interracial Marriage" by Mahin Ibrahim was originally published in *Amaliah* (2019).

Contents

KAZIM ALI

Introduction

At the outset, I want to suggest that the project of this anthology may run counter to the most common purposes of such anthology, which would normally be to suggest an arc or trajectory or a range of common interests of Muslim writers. But it is hard to say what a "Muslim" is. There are, of course, a multiplicity of Islams, a range of perspectives and schools of thought about the way to practice, what the religion means, and how to access the divine. This plurality is historical: nearly immediately upon its founding, there were already multiple streams of Islams, lineages that continued, in the first generation of Islam's founding, to diverge. As Islam spread, within the two centuries following the Prophet's death, across the Maghreb to the west and then into Spain and France to the north and into the rest of Africa to the south, and along the Silk Roads into China to the east, and on into South Asia and Oceania, and eventually to the Americas via the slave trade, Islam continued to develop, change, and grow, and to influence and be influenced by the cultures it encountered. Islam as it's practiced in the Middle East bears only some similarities to the culturally distinct South Asian Islam and so on. This flowering found what many scholars consider to be its first "Golden Age" in the medieval Arab Mediterranean, including the Levant, Italy, North Africa, and, particularly, in the Western Caliphate whose capital was in Al-Andalus in the southern Iberian Peninsula. It was there in cities like Granada, Toledo, Seville, and Cordoba, that Muslim scholars, artists, and artisans were pioneering astronomy, chemistry, mathematics, architecture, garden design, poetry, bookmaking and illumination, the study of languages and translation, physics, engineering, music, and dance.

My point is that that this plurality is neither modern, postmodern or contemporary—or if it is "modern," it is modern in the sense that Syrian poet Adonis used the term: that modernity came to the Arab world in the seventh century with the spread of Islam across the region and the conversion of the political institutions of the day. This plurality has been part and parcel of Islam since nearly the moment of its founding.

I wanted to put together this archive of writing precisely because I wanted to begin to shape a new definition of "Muslim," of "Islam." Maybe it is a strange thing for someone like me — someone at odds with the tradition, someone who struggles with the expectations of what it means to be "Muslim" in the first place—to be editing an anthology of writing by North American Muslims. On the other hand, maybe that is precisely the reason why I can.

Muslim writing in North America is older than anyone supposes. Most, if not all, of the first Western Africans who lived here—brought as enslaved labor—were practicing Muslims and had been for hundreds of years before their capture. The Islam they practiced was generational, sophisticated, and infused with a deeply African spiritual and philosophical framework. To my mind, the theology of liberation that drove Southern Black Christianity as it was practiced among enslaved African populations, from their arrival through to the Civil Rights movement and the present day, has its roots in the deeply foundational liberation theology of original Islam.

In fact, Islam, at its heart and at its foundation—at its "fundament," I might dare say—is cosmopolitan, multicultural, multilingual, anticapitalist, feminist, friendly to alternative family and community structures, and radical in its approach to questions of religious and political authority. So radical, in fact, that within years of the passing of the Prophet and the original generation of teachers, what Muslims call his "companions," the ruling classes of the era had fully co-opted the teachings, eliminated the democratic oral transmission of scripture by canonizing a written version of the Quran and destroying all variants, and marginalized or murdered most of the teachers who taught alternative doctrines to that which was approved by the political elite ruling from first Damascus, then later Baghdad and later still Cairo. It wasn't until the ascendance hundreds of years later of the more socially liberal Western Caliphate in Al-Andalus that Islam began to once more resemble the Islam of its earliest days.

I was raised a Shia Muslim. Depending on who you listen to, the essential difference between Sunni and Shia Islam is that upon the Prophet's death, the Shia followed what they believe to be the oral transmission of the Prophet regarding succession by following Ali, his son-in-law, while Sunnis followed the more dominant group at the time (and since then) when the collective of chieftains elected Abu Bakr, one of the Prophet's companions, to succeed him as Caliph. While the Shias revere the imams, the Sunni revere the first four of these Caliphs, referred to "Rashidun," or The Rightly Guided.

For a time the Rashidun, the political rulers of the empire, were elected (by the elite, granted, but still a rudimentary form of democracy)—after Abu Bakr, the general Umar took the reins; he was followed by Osman, who codified the Quran into a written canon and collected and destroyed all variants, and finally the Prophet's son-in-law Ali took the Caliphate. Upon Ali's assassination by a rival power group, the Caliphate began a steady transformation into a hereditary monarchy of various dynasties. Meanwhile, on the margins of the government that came to rule in the capital, the Shia followed a lineage of teachers descended from Fatima, the Prophet's daughter—first Ali, then his sons, and then in a patrilineal line to the last of the Twelver Shia imams, Al-Mahdi. There are numerous other branches of Shi'ism which follow different lineages descended from Fatima, including some with women teachers, even in the earliest days of Islam. That's why the term "Muslim fundamentalist" is a supreme irony. Because almost as soon as breath left the body of the Prophet, the Body of Islam fractured, and within a single generation there were countless factions and factions within factions. The movements now commonly associated with the notion of a fundamentalist—the Wahabi and Salafi movements—are twentieth-century movements founded in response to continued European aggression and colonization following the fall of the Ottoman Empire in the early part of the century.

To be sure there existed in the rough center of this matrix an outline of a figure—to this day in paintings and images his face remains blank, mere outline—called "Mohammed," but one Mohammed has very little to do with another. In fact, classical Islamic arts, such as calligraphy, geometry, and architecture, center nonrepresentation and visual abstraction. As Cairo-based art critic Lilian Karnouk writes,

Islamic art is an adventure in nonfiguration dictated by a rejection of the Pythagorean idea of man as "the measure of all things." The Islamic artist opts for an aesthetic process rooted in religious transcendence: an art based on harmonies of the formal elements of line, surface, and color arranged to a mathematical perception of time and space. His intention is to attain the visualization of a thought which does not represent man or nature but life understood as energy and motion.

Islam as a system of belief, like poetry itself, incorporates doubt and questioning into its fiber because even though one can be considered Muslim by birth, one still has to recite the *shahada* to embrace Islam and declare oneself a believer. In fact, in Twelver Shi'ism, this choice is codified further: since Al-Mahdi is absent—or at very least, unseen—each Shia person is required to select a contemporary scholar to be their own spiritual leader. It is not uncommon for different people in the same household to have different spiritual leaders.

One significant verse of the Quran appears near its beginning "This is the book. In it there is no doubt." Growing up under the shadow of such an author-itarian dictum, I continually wondered at my own doubts, engagements with faith, forays away, through, and within dogmatic teachings. Only recently, in a new translation by Muhammad Sarwer, I read a different rendering of the same verse: "There is no doubt this book is a guide for the pious." It's not just the wording, but also the punctuation (in fact Sarwer's is closer to the original Ara-bic), which opens the meaning up. There is space in the book—for engagement, for conversation, for interpretation.

My father told me once about the story of "one hundred and four" books revealed by God to prophets through the ages to all the various peoples of the world. For each people, throughout time, there was a different revelation, in a form that they would be able to hear and understand. Four of these books are mentioned by name in the Quran—the Taurat, the Quran itself, the Injeel of Isa (considered to be a lost text), and the Zubuur—the Psalms of David—but a Muslim would believe there a hundred others out there whose names we do not know—that perhaps the Bhagavad-Gita is one, or the Heart Sutra, or the Yoga Sutras, or the Popol Vuh, who can say?

The hundred books of course call to mind the "hundred names of God," of which ninety-nine are named in tradition, the last one being secret. Always this dark place, the place of unknown, the place you cannot go. A place where you are not sure what is what.

This sense of unsurety is even built into the very way we celebrate the reve-lation of this Quran. During the month of fasting—Ramadhan—we celebrate Lail-at-al-Qadr, the Night of Majesty, on which the scripture was said to be first revealed. But scholars do not agree on the actual historical date, saying only it is an odd-numbered evening in the last third of the month. So traditionally we celebrate the occasion on three separate evenings—the nineteenth, twenty-first, and twenty-third evenings. It sounds manic and amazing and it is. It's a miracle of unknowing and allowing the mystery of that subsume the centralization or systemizing of a single day.

The beginning and ending of the lunar months of the Islamic calendar are similarly fraught with disagreements. Many people believe the month itself has not started unless the very first sliver of the moon is officially sighted. For those of us who live in the West, we more often than not depend upon the visions of those living far away, on the other side of the world. In the final days of the fast-ing month, I can still remember my father on the phone with Iran or Pakistan, waiting to hear if the moon had been sighted there. Had it been, it would signal the end of our fast, thousands of miles away.

The tricky moon was also the site of one of the Prophet's major miracles. While Jesus fed the masses and Moses parted the sea, Prophet Mohammed's miracle was, appropriately, centered upon the night sky—he pointed to the moon once and it broke in half.

The written scripture itself was revealed to a man said to be illiterate. He was commanded to read by the Angel Gabriel and protested that he could not read, and so came the first revealed verse of the Quran: "Say: in the name of Your Lord Who created you." And so the angel coached the Prophet into memorizing those lines of poetry a few at a time. Rather than elide the role of the text as text told from one being to another, the exhortation "say"—in Arabic "qul"—occurs hundreds more times across the Quran.

The chronology of the Quran is similarly disguised in its written form. The Prophet came down from the mountain and dictated it to scribes; eventually these verses were organized into chapters, and the chapters themselves were given a canonical order. This order, unlike the long deliberative process surrounding the compiling of the Bible as we now know it, has not changed from that first arrangement under Caliph Usman and is the one thing that all of the sundry sects of Islam do share in common and agree upon.

It's the word and not the man or his flesh or even the definitive understanding of the word itself that reigns supreme in the Islamic consciousness. There hasn't seemed to have been the same kind of lively tradition of commentary and cross-commentary on Quranic scripture as there as been in Judaism. The real heart of the controversy around Rushdie's novel The Satanic Verses was not after all on the caricature of the Prophet, but rather on the triggering plot device—that Satan had managed to corrupt the scribe taking dictation of the Quran, inducing him to introduce false verses into the scripture.

In such a fundamentally decentralized religion where even the satellite in the sky could break into pieces, when the one thing that everyone could hold onto was called into question, even fictionally, all hell broke loose. Literally. The great shame is that the novel remained widely unread in the Muslim world, when it is the one book that comes so close to describe the fever and fervor of Islamic thought, the "art based on harmonies of the formal elements of line, surface, and color arranged to a mathematical perception of time and space" of which Karnouk spoke.

It remains the province of poetry, an art made for the doubting and the doubtful, to create structures for meaning, to privilege and plumb the notions of bewilderment, doubt, and interrogative spirituality. Though Islam requires five daily prayers and an obligatory pilgrimage, the Prophet also said, "one hour of work towards attaining knowledge is worth sixty years of worship."

And what is that worship towards? The five daily prayers are performed in the direction of the qibla—the direction toward the Mecca Masjid, more specifically to the Kaaba, a black square structure at its heart. The famous hajj, obligatory on every adult Muslim, takes one to this same building, called colloquially the House of God. The house itself—like every mosque—is empty inside.

What I mean to say is that what makes an anthology like this interesting are precisely the reasons it would seem on the surface to be irrelevant. Each of the writers contained in this anthology brings their own relationship with Islam to the page. It is not always apparent from writer to writer how they are positioning themselves within the context of Islam. This collection includes the religious of all stripes; practicing and nonpracticing; the cultural Muslim; the secular Muslim; the feminist Muslim; Muslims of various gender identities, sexualities, and national origins. The writers within are converts, reverts, "good" Muslims, "bad" Muslims, born Muslim, ex-Muslim, and trying-to-be or failing-to-be Muslim. I choose to refute any ghost of a "trajectory" by structuring the anthology in alphabetical order. In this sense, the architecture that is created will be by chance divination—the alphabet being as magical and ordinary an ordering system as any other. My goal with this anthology was to represent that full range of contemporary expressions of Islam, as well as a full range of genres— poetry, fiction, essay, memoir, political writing, cultural writing, and of course plenty of texts that mix and match and blur all of these modes.

Not only is the figure of the editor effaced, but the trajectories between the pieces—like that of kismet—will be multiple, nonlinear, abstract. The Muslim community is plural and contradictory. This collection of voices ought to be symphony and cacophony at once, like the body of Muslims as they are today.

Kazim Ali
San Diego, California
April 2020

NEW MOONS

NEW HOOKS

DILRUBA AHMED

Choke

Was there a beanstalk, a golden-egg-laying hen?
No. Just a magic seed.
A courtyard of crooked men.

Was there a giant?
There must always be a giant.

In how many ways did the giant try to choke you?
He did not attempt this with bare hands.

In how many ways did the giant try to choke you?
He didn't choke me. He choked
the competition. Flooded
the market with magic seeds.

Was magic involved?
How else could he ensure economic
chokehold? How else the power to ban
sales of nature's seeds?

Was magic involved?
How else could he choke off
a normal trade flow?
How else, in revitalization's name—
a new-world economy.

What life were you doomed to live?
Must there always be doom in the developing world?

What life were you doomed to live?
Lifetime poverty, I was told.

How did you pay 1,000 dollars for your first bag of seeds?
A loan, a loan, a loan, a loan.
Forgive me my children my wife a loan.

How did you know the seeds were enchanted?
They only grow once. My pockets
emptied without end.

And what of the pesticides?
The giant implied the magic seed
has little need—save
your rupees, save your children.

What did the seeds grow?
Nothing, every time.

How many times did you try?
Too many, then I took my life.

Who weeps now over the blighted fields?
My wife my children my god what could I do.

How many witnessed you drinking the pesticide?
On our first date, we secretly strolled
and tossed scraps to birds.

What did the giant say when you died?
From his heights will he notice
the smell of blood?
"Be he alive, or be he dead, I'll grind
his bones to make my bread."

Who'll pay the loans now that you're dead?
Please tell the world what is happening here.

The Feast

My father is hosting the final picnic.
      He rolls a melon back and forth
on the slate table to steady it

and slice, each piece bleeding
      onto a white plate. The coals turn
gray but still flicker and burn, with raw

meat slung on top of the grill, oozing
      blood red to clear. In the river
bordering the grove, a lone man paddles

his arms, stomach pressed
      to a blue surfboard.
Black and white ripples

radiate from him while boats knock
      against the pier. The children
gather their Frisbees from grass,

their volleyballs and racquets, appearing
      and disappearing
in bright shirts like confetti.

Their voices rise and fall. It is late.
      The sun shines, but not
for much longer. The golden hour

has begun. For a moment
      the moss-covered trees glow
lime green, frozen in their looming

heights. My father: white shirt,
        gray pants, silver wristwatch,
glasses. He always cut the melon.

The plates are ready, the food
        is hot, the watermelon cold
and seedless. And our lives,

for a moment, are an untouched
        meal: perishable, and delicious,
one we've barely begun to taste.

GOOGLE Search Autocomplete

God who sees
who wasn't there
who created hearts to love
who strengthens me
God who is rich in mercy
who saves

God how can I serve you
how do I let go
how can we forgive
God how do I change
how do I lose weight
how long must I wait
God how can I make money
how I hate you
how do I hear you

God of carnage
God bless America
God bless America movie
God gave me you
God gave me you lyrics

God why
God why meme
why are you doing this to me
why am I here
why am I alone
why did this happen

God when will I find love
God when he's drunk

when will it be my turn
when are you coming
when will I die

God who heals lyrics
God who gave fire to man [sic]
God who provides
God what should I do
what should we do now
what is our purpose

God what to do with my life
what is your plan for us
God what is your name.

Snake Oil, Snake Bite

They staunched the wound with a stone.
They drew blue venom from his blood
        until there was none.
When his veins ran true his face remained
lifeless and all the mothers of the village
wept and pounded their chests until the sky
        had little choice
but to grant their supplications. God made
        the boy breathe again.

God breathes life into us, it is said,
only once. But this case was an exception.
God drew back in a giant gust and blew life into the boy
and like a stranded fish, he shuddered, oceanless.

It was true: the boy lived.
He lived for a very long time. The toxins
were an oil slick: contaminated, cleaned.
But just as soon as the women
kissed redness back into his cheeks
the boy began to die again.
He continued to die for the rest of his life.
The dying took place slowly, sweetly.
The dying took a very long time.

HINA AHMED

Oxygen

"What do you think about the X-rays, Dr. Smith?" Dr. Zoya Khan asked him over the phone. "I think we should remove that tooth, especially since she has been complaining about its pain for so long. It just needs to come out."

"No, I do not foresee any complications with this procedure," he added, before hanging up.

Text message

Zoya: I scheduled your procedure with one of the best oral surgeons in the area. The appointment has been made for exactly two weeks from now, at 8:00 a.m. Make sure you show up on time and don't eat or drink anything four hours before the procedure. You will be just fine, trust me. There is no reason to be nervous.

"Hi, I would like to see Dr. Smith to talk to him before my procedure," Zareena said to the secretary over the phone.

"We are so sorry, but he is booked solid each day of the week. We even have him working through his lunch. Why don't you come in a little earlier on the day of the appointment?" Zareena agreed.

Zareena's father sat beside her on her bed. "I can take you to your appointment."

"Thanks, Abu, that would be great."

"Don't worry, this seems like a routine procedure, and it has been bothering you for some time. Certainly this is the wise choice."

"Yes, you are right."

The night before the procedure, Zareena came downstairs and chewed on half a loaf of bread, sliced tomatoes, and parmesan cheese. "It is *just* a tooth Zareena, get some sleep, you will be *juuuust* fine," her mother said.

Zareena made her way upstairs into her comfortable bed but was unable to sleep as the strong winds crashed against her bedroom windows. The night erupted in a noisy storm, as blood poured profusely between her. While approximately 7,000 miles away, ghastlier winds targeted innocent bystanders, with heavy shelling and explosions of countless missile attacks causing an outpouring of bleeding veins in dying bodies, while enormous dust clouds captured the desert sky, scattering darkness upon an entire city.

Zareena woke up at 6 a.m. to the reckless wind that blew outside her bedroom window. Recalling that her sister had said not to drink anything before the procedure, she did so anyway. She washed her face with lukewarm water, brushed her teeth, and got dressed. She put on fitted, black jeans and threw on a sweater. She took her tincture of rose-hip oil and dabbed it around her bare chest. She looked at herself in the mirror, her skin glowing, her black, thick hair tousled. She thought back to the last time she had met Dr. Smith, who had told her that she was 'a pretty little thing' whose presence in his office 'added sparks' to a boring day. On the one hand, his remarks had angered her, making her feel like the objectified brown woman. Yet, on the other hand, his comments fed her craving for a man's attention, enabling a kind of femininity within her that she both loved and hated.

When Zareena walked downstairs, she saw her father dressed and eating breakfast. Zareena sat on the steps waiting in front of the door. The rain poured, and the wind blew, crashing against the house. Zareena gazed out of the glass door waiting like she would at an airport before a flight.

"Ready?" her father asked, putting on his coat.

"Ready." In the car, Zareena inserted her headphones and listened to NPR as they drove through the dark, desolate streets of the early morning.

"The United States, along with Great Britain and France, bombed Syria last night, hitting three targets, all related to what the United States believes is Syria's chemical weapons program," the commentator said.

"This war in Syria sounds strikingly similar to the narrative that was used in Iraq, doesn't it Abu?"

"Yes, it certainly does."

"The United Nations and Arab League have estimated that the total death toll since the start of the war is around 400,000, of which over 500 have been children," the commentator continued. Zareena turned off the radio and looked through *The Independent*, where she saw an image of a little boy wearing an oxygen mask.

Zareena turned off her phone.

They arrived at the office. A solid structure made out of red bricks sat on top of the hill, overlooking the entire city. Although it was the beginning of spring, snow continued to fall, and the wind howled like a werewolf, pushing Zareena and her father through the entrance doors.

"Please have a seat over there," the secretary said. The room reminded Zareena of a fancy ski lodge with its wooden interior, sleek leather couches, and Pottery Barn–style décor. The room faced a shiny black, flat-screen T.V. and a remote-controlled fireplace that was next to a fully stocked Keurig machine.

"Hi, are you Zaa-riiin-a?" said a woman with the kind of freakish smile one would see if a circus clown was doing a Crest whitening commercial, with skin that looked too taut to be real, and orange enough to resemble Donald Trump; a woman with bleach-blond hair that had been hair-sprayed to a stiff perfection.

"You will come with me. Everything you need to know will be on the blue sheet that we will give you after the procedure," she said, smiling. "You can leave all of your belongings right here."

Zareena looked at her father. "Ok, Abu. I will see you in a bit."

She followed the nurse down the long hall into a fluorescently lighted room with a mint-green leather chair that was waiting for her arrival.

"Go ahead and lay down. Let me take your glasses," the nurse said, while she turned on a machine that sounded like a humidifier.

"I am going to place this mask on you. Just inhale and exhale like you normally would. Just relax into it . . . *breeeeeathe* deeply."

Zareena pressed her head deeper into the cushion of the chair, her eyes slowly closing. As she breathed into the mask, her fingertips tingled, while her legs began to feel unattached to the rest of her body.

"Yoo-hoo, are you okay over there?" Zareena heard the voice of the nurse and giggled. A few minutes later, Zareena began to move her head from side to side. Her eyes fluttered, and her hands dangled off the armrest.

"Ok . . . I am going to turn this down from a five to a three," the nurse said, dialing the knob to the left.

Zareena bent her neck further back, her chest moving up and down. The images of war-ravaged children flashed before her eyes. She swung her hand to her mouth and ripped the mask off her face.

"I am not doing this!" she exclaimed.

"Okay . . . Okay . . . ! We need to get the doctor in here!"

The doctor emerged. Zareena could see the foggy shadow of his tall, burly silhouette.

"I don't know if I can do this."

A momentary silence filled the room with the weight of toxic fumes.

"There is nothing to be afraid of. But I will tell you this; I won't be rescheduling this, not after the effort I made to get you here."

"Well, it's not my fault I feel afraid. Don't you understand? I need ten minutes to myself."

The nurse stood behind her frantically unwrapping plastic packages.

"I will be back in exactly ten minutes," the doctor said.

"I am sorry. I just don't know that this procedure is necessary . . . I am just not convinced that this pain will be worth it," Zareena said to the nurse.

"Well, it has been causing you pain. If you don't get it out, it *will* get infected."

"Well—I just—I just don't know that I can do this."

"Oh, you can. You can do this."

Ten minutes later, the doctor re-entered the room.

"Ok, I will do this. But, I do not want that gas mask on my face."

"Open your mouth nice and wide," he said, inserting his hand in her mouth. Zareena watched his large, rough hands move in and out of her mouth, her hands clenched, her body frozen. From the corner of her eye, she could see the nurse's leg covered in navy blue pants. Images of her sweating hands grabbing her leg flashed before her eyes.

"That's it, that a girl," the doctor said, inserting his big hands in her delicate mouth. The residue of her chiseled tooth flickered like sawdust in the air. The nurse held Zareena's head still with her hands covered in red acrylic nails, the tips of which pressed down on the sides of her brown temples.

"Now, I am going to just stitch this up," the doctor said, taking a long, black string and weaving it in and out of her.

"That's it, the procedure is all done!" he said.

"That's it? It's over?" Zareena said, springing up in the seat.

"Good job, kiddo," he said, taking out his fist and bumping it against hers. As she walked out of the room, she saw her bloody tooth lying on the white paper towel.

The doctor stopped her in the dark corridor, where he stood at the entrance of a room with a manila envelope in his hands. "Everything you need to take is in this envelope right here. Take all of these today and your pain will be completely gone. It will be as if nothing ever happened."

Zareena left the surgical room and arrived in the waiting room. The room was completely full now. It seemed as if each seat held the body of a white man wearing a camouflage jacket and a baseball hat. The channel of the television had been switched from CNN to Fox. The reporter said, "The United States has successfully conquered the Islamic jihadists."

Zareena's father walked toward her and placed his hands on her shoulders. "Were you able to hear my screams?" Zareena asked.

"The procedure will be three hundred dollars," the woman at the checkout desk said.

"I thought my insurance would have covered this," Zareena whispered to her father as he took out his wallet.

"Do I need to schedule a follow-up appointment?" Zareena asked.

"No, there will be no need for that."

Zareena grabbed her coat and followed her father out of the office. Outside, the wind gushed harder, with a thin layer of snow covering the ground. Her father opened her side of the door. When he got in the driver's seat he did not insert his keys. Zareena silently stared out the window. Her father did the same.

When they arrived home, Zareena called her sister.

"I just hated that mask. All I could see was the image of war. The Syrian war, the Holocaust, the gas chambers of war . . ." but before she could finish, her sister interrupted.

"Ok, you are so crazy. Of course someone like you would make those comparisons! It is not the oral surgeon's job to help you with your trauma, or the trauma of the world. You know time is money in this world. Why can't you just act like a grown-up and carry on in the world like normal people do?"

Zareena sat in front of the bay window in the kitchen with her cat next to her. The wind had stopped swirling, and the snow had settled crisply onto sharp edges of green blades of grass. The sky was clear with white, puffy clouds fully settled within it. Zareena's father stood next to her, slicing a soft pear with a sharp bladed knife. "These are for you," he said, placing the plate in front of her. But Zareena was unable to eat them. Instead, she looked on at a world that stood still before her.

TANZILA AHMED

Muslimah Fight Club

"For instance, I know by your stance right now that if anything happened, you'd be ready to defend yourself," he said with dark, calculating eyes.

I looked down at my forearms, trying to stifle my surprise. An arm casually rested against the bar, and a hand was placed on my chin. We were both leaning on the wooden bar while talking closely to each other. My shoulder was angled to him so that even though I was talking to him, neither of us were facing each other straight. I also made sure that I was facing in the direction of the front door.

I wondered what other signs my body was giving off and betraying me. I wondered if the reason I was single was because my body language was always defensive. I wondered if he could tell that I was avoiding eye contact because I was intimidated by him but drawn to him. Maybe this was why I was a terrible flirt. Maybe I was never really signaling vulnerability.

We were in a bar talking about the latest events of the apocalypse. I had seen him around town. B___ was a friend of friends. A regime change had just occurred the day before, and a bunch of us from our community were drowning our grief in the local sausage spot. Inside, it was all bright lights and industrial décor and fusion foods—nothing had changed, but it felt like everything had changed. There was a dark cloud that had been pulled over everything. People walked in slow motion and talked in hushed, deep octaves. We were all commiserating with our drinks at the bar—discussing the lives that would be lost on the frontlines in this political strife that would ensue. We didn't know how or what would happen—but given the lead up to the political turnover, we anticipated which communities would have targets on their back and be sent to concentration camps, or worse, genocide. The dramatic verbal attacks in the theatre of political media gave permission to the supremacists to act out physically. People had been bullied, attacked, and stabbed. People were going to start dying soon. With this regime change, the fear would be sanctified, and the attacks honored.

I felt it too. My skin was brown, my hair was dark, and my faith was villainized. To them, my mere existence was a threat. I could tell my people would have to prepare for annihilation. There were survivor skills I would need to gain if I was going to be able to battle for my community, my family, for myself. I both felt incredibly helpless and an incredible need to shift all my resources to help everyone, using whatever means necessary.

Outside the bar, we could hear chants down the street. A protest had erupted, and people across the city were taking to the streets, letting their voices of dissent against the current regime change be heard.

I gave him a sideways look.

"Your arms are up to protect your face, and you won't be caught off guard," he continued. "I've been thinking about how we are entering these dark times and how we need to be resources for each other. But I'm an artist, you know? I don't have money to donate to the resistance. I have edge weapon skills; I could train people in that, at least. It's what we can anticipate that our community will need to keep safe. To be able to think on defense—"

"Edge skills? Do you mean like, knives?" I interrupted.

"Yeah, sharp-edged weapon." He evaded saying knife.

"So, what, can you like grab a knife flying at you from the air?" I asked.

"Yeah, potentially. It takes a certain type of skill. I could show you. I probably can't train you to grab a knife out of thin air, but I could train you in combat concepts with edge tools, and we can take it from there."

"That's definitely a skill I could use. Brown-skinned women and women with their hair covered are often the ones who get attacked first." I paused heavily, thinking about how this conversation had suddenly become a candle in the darkness. "If I brought together a group of Muslim women that are going to be on the frontlines of this war . . . do you think you could train us in edge skills?"

"Yeah. I primarily teach concepts and navigating contexts of engagement. But get a group of Muslim women together, maximum of ten. And if there's interest, we could do something. But I have two rules—you can't tell anyone who I am, and these classes have to be completely secretive. Nobody can know."

A secret fight club. But with knives. And for Muslim women.

He stood on the sidewalk as he watched me walk to my car—for my safety, he said. In the distance, I could hear helicopters in the air. I looked over my shoulder and saw him smoking a cigarette nonchalantly, and at the intersection just beyond, a protest of a massive mob of people taking over the streets. Maybe this was our new normal.

۵

I never learned how to hold a knife until the summer I sold knives door to door.

Silly now, to think what neighbors would say to a young Brown Muslim girl going door to door with a briefcase full of knives. But this was before the towers had crumbled, before the latest iteration of the fear-mongering industrial complex had kicked in, before I knew not to feel fearless. The world was my oyster, the streets paved in gold, and I could pull myself up by the bootstraps. Anything was possible. It was my first summer college break, and I was determined to go back to school with money in my pocket. I had found a job out of the black and white pages of the PennySaver and for the interview, I showed up to a beige sterile suburban office complex. The guy interviewing me wore a chocolate-colored suit that matched the walls and a smarmy smile. He explained to me that I would need to buy a full set of knives so that I would be able to sell them. The gimmick was to cut through a penny with our high-grade steel rust-proof extra sharp scissors. I got hired on the spot.

"So, this is a pyramid scheme?" my uncle asked, as I showed him my knives.

"No, it's not," I insisted, as I pulled out a cleaver that I had just bought to sell to him.

"Why do you have bandages on your fingers? Did you cut yourself on the knife?"

"A sharp knife is a safe knife," I responded with confidence.

"Maybe you aren't cut out for the job."

He was probably right. By the end of summer, I had bandages and scars on all of my fingers. The only people who had bought any knives were family members, only out of obligation. Knives and I didn't really get along.

ॐ

We would meet in dirt-filled backyards and empty warehouses. We'd meet weekly, a mishmash of Muslimahs who all felt the need to prepare given the current regime change. In the group, I had secretly gathered the leader of a Desi rock band, an activist hijabi, an amateur fighter-writer, and more, about ten women in total. These were all people I adored. Most I'd met through organizing on community causes, many I stood side by side with at protests. These were my ride-or-die in this fight. It was the first time though, I was sure, that B___ had been surrounded by so many Muslim women. He was unfamiliar with the customs and the culture, but he didn't care. He was here to provide a service.

"Here, take this," the instructor, B___, handed me a rubber blade. My fingers tingled as I grasped the handle. It was black, about four inches long, with a blade that would bend. In my hand, it felt heavy, weighted. I glanced around—she was holding a flashlight, and she was holding a two-foot-long wooden stick. We were all holding different types of weapons as we prepared to train. I pretended to stab myself with the rubber blade in my arm—it might not cut, but it would bruise. It felt real. It was real.

We Muslimahs stood in a line, breathed into the ground, and then breathed into the air. Deep breaths, grounding our existence. Then we walked side by side, taking steps in a triangle as we found our center. And then, we learned to fight.

I had never felt so alive.

⟡

I wasn't the kind of kid that got into fights. I was the kind of kid that always imagined what it'd be like to get into a fight as I walked away. The closest I remember to getting into a brawl was in kindergarten; I got mad at the girls in the playground who wouldn't let me play with them. So, I kicked sand in their faces. I got in trouble with the teacher, and I promised I would never do it again.

I was raised to not make trouble. My parents were immigrants in this country and were vigilant about not wanting to rock the boat. We were not to cause problems. Whenever I felt confronted as I grew older, I'd just put my head down, wrap my arms around my chest, and pretend like everything was okay.

After the towers fell, it felt different. I felt all eyes on me in a way I never had before. I would hear whispers and rumblings as I walked on the street. My Brown skin set me apart.

What the boy at the mall did was ostensibly a hate crime, and I wish I knew how to fight then. He told me my uncle was a terrorist, but he'd do me still. I ignored him as he followed me around making lewd comments until I ducked into a store. I breathed deep while hiding between the racks with my fists clenched. I didn't know how to fight. I wish I knew how to fight. If only, to learn to defend myself.

There would be many more subtle and obtuse hate incidents over the years. But after a while, who even remembers all of their microaggressions anymore?

⟡

It's so intimate, knife fighting. To stab someone, you need to feel their breath on your skin, their fingers on your arm, your waist in their grasp. You can feel their heat evaporating off their body. You can smell their scent. You can see the tears in their eyes. You can feel their blood rushing through their veins. And then you can feel your own blood.

"I want you to approach me aiming here, in slow motion." B___ pointed at his side. "We are going to practice this move five times."

I breathed in deep. In slow motion, with the rubber blade in my left hand, I felt his bare arm run against mine. I pinned B___'s arm under my elbow. We were uncomfortably close, and I could feel my breath catch in my throat. I could feel his heat on mine, and I wondered if he could hear my rapid heartbeat.

"Trust yourself," he said.

He was teaching me how to disarm someone holding a weapon. But in slow motion it felt like an intimate dance.

I took a deep breath and did the move again. This time I could feel his muscles shift and heard the knife drop from his hand.

"They can't scare us into being silent unless they can scare us for being loud," he said.

In the days of fear, I rarely experienced human touch. I had isolated myself from romance, from physical friendships, from hugging people too long. My fingers sparked when getting change from the cashier and my skin tingled when I accidentally bumped into strangers. Every skin touch made me want to cry. In these days, the only time I experienced real human touch was in fight club.

It was the oxytocin that rushed through my system each week after fight club that made me think I was falling in love with everyone I touched. At least that's what I told myself.

ﺵ

The regime change meant people that looked like me were on the news a lot. The Nazis were emboldened by the anti-Muslim dog whistles of their leader. Through the encrypted text messaging app, in secret groups, we'd share links to stories of Muslimahs getting attacked.

There was the story of the young hijabi woman on the subway in Portland, where two men died from being stabbed protecting her from an Islamophobe. There was the elderly Bangladeshi auntie that was walking on NYC streets who was stabbed as her husband walked behind her. A woman's hijab was pulled back before she was attacked with a knife.

Each secret fight club session felt more urgent than the last, as these incidences were fresh on our minds. Each class was adjusted based on the trauma in the news that week. After the hijab pull hate crime, we learned how to turn quickly so that we would use the scarf as a weapon. There were rumors that the Nazis were going to show up at protests protecting the rights of Muslims. The class after that, we learned how to wield the protest sign as a weapon.

I didn't want fear to drive me. But I didn't know what being driven by love looked like. All I knew was that I was scared and my friends were scared, and people that looked like us were scared.

What I didn't expect was how full of love and adoration I felt for the Muslimahs in fight club after each class. I loved them so much that I knew I'd wield a knife for them if they needed me to. It was Assata Shakur that said, "We must love each other and protect each other. We have nothing to lose but our chains." In this time of strife, though this started as a mission to combat fear, I found myself in the depths of a different kind of falling in love.

~

It was different than holding a knife when cutting a tomato or cucumber. You had to feel the weight of the knife in your hand, hold the center of balance. I got into the habit of holding pens, sticks, and scissors in my hand like they were weapons. From hand to hand, I'd toss them, trying to find the center. Holding things in my hands like they were weapons became second nature. It made me feel stronger, confident. I played with the pink folded pocket knife in my pocket when I walked on the streets, artificially brazen.

~

A secret sisterhood of the Muslimahs had been formed. When we crossed paths in public—like at parties or protests—we didn't acknowledge how we were secretly meeting each other weekly. Other people could sense the bond that had been created between us, but no one knew why. How could they? A Muslimah girl gang learning to knife fight was beyond their comprehension. Muslimahs were supposed to be meek, objects, submissive. But we didn't need them to know otherwise—this was our little secret.

~

I grabbed the fighter-writer, K___, by her tattooed shoulders and tripped her behind her knee. She was solid muscle, and when she fell back, we both collapsed into a pile of giggles. The exercise was to push each other, then to catch each other. But we couldn't stop laughing. We took a breath, stood up to try again. But as K___ reached for my waist, I cringed into another fit of giggles. She pushed me down—but I pulled her down, and we couldn't stop giggling. We turned into tangled limbs on the floor mat in a laughing fit.

"That's good, laugh it all out now, so that you are better prepared if you get into a situation. You'll know your instincts," B___ responded. He was always so serious, but I saw him crack a smile at the giggles. It was infectious.

It was part of his learning as well. In teaching a posse of Muslimahs to guard ourselves, B___ learned he had to let down his own guard. He started smiling more, was less driven by fear, and even laughed at our dumb jokes. He was always serious, but by summertime, we giggled all the same.

ॐ

It crept on slowly. This one morning, when we slashed at the sky, I noticed a thin strand of air glimmered behind it. I blinked, and just as quickly, it faded away. I thought I had been dreaming.

I practiced figure eights in my living room, with the plastic blade I had bought online. The more my fist circled, the more it seemed the blade was slicing magic into the sky. With each *whoosh*, a glittering silver aura started growing around me. I stopped and blinked, and then it would be gone, instantaneously. I thought, for sure, I was seeing things.

The next fight club, as we Muslimahs practiced stabbing the blades through the sky, I saw glitter spiral out of each blade, and a glimmering smoke encased us all. Each slice would mute the sound of the world, making it feel like no one else existed outside of us. We all saw the glittering silver aura around us, but none of us said anything about it—worried we'd break the spell. We had manifested something incredible—the swing of our blades crafted prisms and glitters. Maybe it was love. Maybe it was Allah's protection. Maybe it was a guardian angel. Maybe this was what a prayer looked like. Whatever it was, we had found within us the power to be invincible.

We didn't speak of what we had seen that day. Who would have believed us, anyway?

We descended on the airport to disrupt travel and to protest against the vicious policy the regime had just enacted. A powerful executive order that stifled the civil rights of Brown people, preventing the free travel of people at borders and airports. Across the nation, airports were being shut down as the rebels mobbed the streets and prevented flights from going out.

I showed up with a protest sign in my hand and a switchblade tucked in my boot. I walked up slowly and noted the counter-protest supremacists across the street—a mob of skinheads and white shirts and White men holding flags. No weapons were drawn, but I knew these men weren't there to play.

I marched back and forth on the sidewalk with the other rebel protesters, screaming chants at the top of my lungs. Out of the side of my eyes, I spotted the rest of the Muslimahs—we made eye contact with each other and gave each other a knowing nod. We positioned ourselves spaced on the outskirts of the protest, creating a circle that could only be seen by our own.

A knife flew through the sky; the blade came down pointed at the rebels. And then another one, and another one. It was raining blades. The rebel insurgence was under attack by the supremacists.

I looked up to the sky and saw a hand reach up and grab a knife out of the sky and drop it on the ground. I saw K__ on the outskirts of the crowd giggling as she reached into the air, grabbing two knives at once. Hands kept grabbing the knives, one after another after another. The rebel chants became louder. The glimmering aura created a dome over the protest laughter and erupted the crowds. The Muslimahs made eye contact across the crowd; our giggles could hardly be stifled.

Love would protect us all.

KAVEH AKBAR

Learning to Pray

My father moved patiently
cupping his hands beneath his chin,
    kneeling on a janamaz
            then pressing his forehead to a circle
                of Karbala clay. Occasionally
                he'd glance over at my clumsy mirroring,
    my too-big Packers T-shirt
and pebble-red shorts,
        and smile a little, despite himself.
                Bending there with his whole form
                    marbled in light, he looked like
                a photograph of a famous ghost.
    I ached to be so beautiful.
I hardly knew anything yet—
    not the boiling point of water
            or the capital of Iran,
                not the five pillars of Islam
            or the Verse of the Sword—
    I knew only that I wanted
to be like him,
    that twilit stripe of father,
                mesmerizing as the blue-white Iznik tile
                    hanging in our kitchen, worshipped
            as the long faultless tongue of God.

Every Drunk Wants to Die Sober
It's How We Beat the Game

Hazrat Ali son-in-law of the prophet was martyred by a poisoned sword
while saying his evening prayers his final words *I am successful*   I am
successful I want to carve it in my forehead I've been cut into before
it barely hurt I found my body to be hard and bloodless as
glass still for effect I tore my shirt to tourniquets   let me now be
calm for one fucking second let me be open to revision eternity looms
in the corner like a home invader saying *don't mind me I'm just here to watch you nap*
if you throw prayer beads at a ghost they will cut through him soft
as a sabre through silk I finally have answers to the questions I taught
my mother not to ask but now she won't ask them   as a child I was so tiny
and sweet she would tuck me in saying *moosh bokhoradet* a mouse
should eat you I melted away that sweet like sugar in water like once-fresh
honey dripping down a thigh   today I lean on habit and rarely unstrap
my muzzle it's hard to speak of something so gauche as ambition
while the whole wheezing mosaic chips away but let it be known
I do hope one day to be free of this body's dry wood   if living proves
anything it's that such astonishment is possible the kite loosed
from its string outpaces its shadow an olive tree explodes
into the sky dazzling even the night I don't understand the words
I babble in home movies from Tehran but I assume
they were lovely I have always been a tangle of tongue and pretty
want   in Islam there are prayers to return almost anything even
prayers to return faith I have been going through book after book pushing
the sounds through my teeth   I will keep making these noises
as long as deemed necessary until there is nothing left of me to forgive

Being in This World Makes Me Feel
Like a Time Traveler

visiting a past self. Being anywhere makes me thirsty.
When I wake, I ask God to slide into my head quickly before I do.
As a boy, I spit a peach pit onto my father's prayer rug and immediately

it turned into a locust. Its charge: devour the vast fields of my ignorance.
The Prophet Muhammad described a full stomach as containing
one-third food, one-third liquid, and one-third air.

For years, I kept a two-fists-long beard and opened my mouth only to push air out.
One day, I stopped in a lobby for cocktails and hors d'oeuvres
and ever since, the life of this world has seemed still. Every night,

the moon unpeels itself without affectation. It's exhausting, remaining
humble amidst the vicissitudes of fortune. It's difficult
to be anything at all with the whole world right here for the having.

Heritage

Reyhaneh Jabbari, a twenty-six-year-old Iranian woman, was hanged
on October 25th, 2014 for killing a man who was attempting to rape her.

the body is a mosque borrowed from Heaven   centuries of time
stain the glazed brick   our skin rubs away like a chip
in the middle of an hourglass   sometimes I am so ashamed

of my sentience how little it matters   angels don't care about humility
you shaved your head   spent eleven days half-starved in solitary
and not a single divine trumpet wept into song   now it's lonely all over

I'm becoming more a vessel of memories than a person   it's a myth
that love lives in the heart   it lives in the throat we push it out
when we speak   when we gasp we take a little for ourselves

in books love can be war-ending   a soldier drops his sword
to lie forking oysters into his enemy's mouth   in life we hold love up to the light
to marvel at its impotence   you said in a letter to Sholeh

you weren't even killing the roaches in your cell   that you would take them up
by their antennae and flick them through the bars into a courtyard
where you could see men hammering long planks of cypress into gallows

the same men who years before threw their rings in the mud   who watered them
five times daily   who shot blackbirds off almond branches
and kissed the soil at the sight of sprouts   then cursed each other when the stalks

which should have licked their lips withered dryly at their knees   may God beat
us awake   scourge our brains to life   may we measure every victory
by the momentary absence of pain   there is no solace in history   this is a gift

we are given at birth   a pocket we fold into at death   goodbye now you mountain
you armada of flowers   you entire miserable decade in a lump in my throat
despite all our endlessly rehearsed rituals of mercy   it was you we sent on

in which Nisa bargains unevenly

he spits her vowels like a maiden name
and she sags unpunctuated

over an empty sink. a plate to her right
overturned
fruit peels cascading across the metal

the ransacked (room) (plate) (air) unbearable
she gathers and packs
the drain with their gauze

under her breath, she gardens:

AL-JABBAR, the Compeller
"one who recites this will be protected
from violence
severity
or hardness"

                    i will use my right hand if he lets me keep my left
                            i will beat myself into rightness   if he leaves
                    if i make myself right   who of me will be left

AL-KHALIQ, the Creator
"recitation of this at night
will create
an angel"

                    i will beat myself into rightness   i will feather
                    my back saccharine   i will drown out every voice
                            of his with flapping

AL-HAQQ, the Truth
"recite this to regain
what was lost"

i will garden   i will garden a song,
paradise   orchard of feminine orthography

self portrait as body written for God

if he cuts off my fingers i will count your names   eyelash
by eyelash, breath by breath   how can i pretend i am blameless,
unsullied   with this body of clay   the dirt there beneath
my nails for all to see?   Nisa is working on folding her tongue
proportional to truth   as is, my body is adjacent-earnest, reluctant
to bend, but perfect in form for those fleeting moments of humility.
God gave Man a script but still   I pull words from air
beg in some vernacular   curve everything but my spine
Nisa writes of the Beloved   but forgets to write to Him
she says   in our abandoned tongue,   *forgive me,*   *I tell*
everyone else   what I hide from you

THREA ALMONTASER

Spray Of Citrus and a Month-Long Suffering

I want my stomach to growl like a fearsome animal,
to follow the rise and fall of the sun, suffer

willingly with the believers, offer myself fully—small head
resting on a silver platter, ruby-red apple in my mouth, body

glistening with satay sauce, ready for God's teeth, burped
up His long throat, deemed delicious. *You're too young to suffer,*

Baba says. Yet I refuse to eat like the rest of them, thought *siyam*
made me righteous. Sunday school Sisters starve themselves, bodies

slight as bamboo reeds. I hunger to be as holy, be part of the martyr
pack, become an empty echo of a girl, bone and flesh only, suffering

into a sinless white sheet. *When you fast, act kindly and think*
of those less fortunate, the Sisters tell me. And I think of small bodies

from my balcony in Yemen. They rang doorbells for trash bags,
the scraps they'd salvage there, old bones whittled down, suffered

deep scratches scrambling with street cats for leftovers,
feral and famished in their hunt. I listened to their bodies

begging to be fed. When I bit into a Mars Bar knowing they ate it
with their eyes, that they'd never feel this fuller suffering,

the stretch and sick of it. All month, the Sisters move like sharp-angled
ghosts in their worship. I, too, starve my way into God's good graces. Embody

a hungry divinity, dry-mouthed as I chant. I'll dwindle down to the thinnest
thread, empty of food and fickle habits, flossed between God's teeth

after He peels me like a blood orange, squeezes my pulp and seed
straight onto His parched tongue, spit into the sink as daybreak.

Raghead Gains Enlightenment

Bikes corner me, their steel-glint skinning me to the core.
My veiny tongue flaps, exposed. One bike *moos* like a cow

when saying *Muslim*. Another bike opens its seat-cushion mouth
to spit gum-wads like a stoning. I want to chew its cushioned handles

so sundrenched metal burns the tender palms that grasp it.
I could do the same thing to their ankle bones so these white boys

fall on stinging concrete, crying, pink flesh between my teeth.
I'm the lunch box that smells of goat gizzards. Who never goes

to school dances. Mama says I should refine my accent,
smile more. *You have to fit in.* Makes my siblings and I recite,

With liberty and justice for all, correcting our fumbles
like survival. Bikes heave my hijab from behind, tug-of-war.

I leak spittle, claw at my blazing throat, thrash blue-faced.
I'm reminded of the couple who tied bundles of thorns,

placed them along paths the Holy Messenger took.
Their fervid intent to harm a mystery to me until now,

like this, naked, seared raw. *Guess she's not blonde after all,*
dollars from the bet swapped between tires. I'm ogled like a slug

they want to slice open and salt. Black braid sliced from my tailbone
with their father's hunting blade. Tossed like a hot potato,

Mama's daily diligence scattered beneath Reeboks like unearthed
roots, my hijab a banner for their handlebars. I walk home

like a persecuted prophet pelted from dawn to dusk, left with a newborn
knowing, a small dark sense spreading like spilled ink inside me.

Mama sees me cut, almost sighs with relief. Tired of twisting wild
locks 'til the ends go solid with raw shea. I refused to straighten.

She didn't know what to do with hair fending for itself. Nobody
on Steinway Street did—Arab mothers afraid to touch parts of their daughters

left undomesticated. Their first view of America: White women
on the other side of Queens, honeyed hair flat, in place. The rest of my hair
is sheared, exposed without ceremony. *Hush, it's easier to manage this way.*
Mama's own 'fro buried in a tight bun, greasy sheen held back

with bobby pins, silky doo-rag. I braid phantom hair in my sleep. Sit alone
at lunch for months. Classmates can't make sense of the scarf on my head:

*Does it support 9/11? Are you bald? What are you really hiding
underneath?* I want to lie. Say my hair is too striking to show.

I go to sleep dreaming of gordian knots, bristled brushings.
Endless hours of oiling, smoothing, stringing with beads. Of brown water

from hair playing in dirt. Wind-waving curls like seaweed underwater,
tickling cheeks. Hair you can lose a hand in, hair you can cry into.

And the bees—when one buzzed too close, ensnared in my black
forest, wings against scalp, the panicked tangle of us.

HALA ALYAN

A Good Penance

The olive-eyed waitress sets down the *cafe con leche* and smiles at Abdullah. "You sure you don't want breakfast?" Her accent is thick, rolling the r's.

His own smile is hesitant. Flirty women rattle him. "This is my breakfast."

"You're missing out." The way she wears her braid over one shoulder reminds him of Inez. She turns to Colin. "Tell him."

Colin grins down at his plate of omelet, tomatoes, and chorizo. He pats his stomach. "He never listens. More for me." After she walks away, he winks at Abdullah. "Nice pair of legs."

"Your consistency is comforting."

They had been roommates at Oxford. Both new doctoral students when they met nearly a decade earlier, but their similarities ended there. Colin hailed from his native London; Abdullah had left Amman, where he'd been raised, for graduate school. Abdullah spent his days in the library, reading books on caliphs and Al-Ghazali and mysticism, taking the bus every Friday to the mosque. Colin was the handsome one. He stayed out late on weekends, went to pubs in Cowley, and twice was arrested for public urination. He dated smart, attractive girls named Kelly and Olivia, whom he'd promptly lose interest in.

More than once, Abdullah would wake to a girl on their couch, crying. "That asshole," they'd weep, and he'd brew some tea, try to console them. Still, Colin had magnetism, a frank need for pleasure that could be disarming.

Since graduation six years ago, their friendship has been tethered by occasional emails. When he wrote to Colin of his sabbatical in Seville, they planned to meet for a few days in Barcelona before Abdullah's return to Amman.

"When are you seeing your sister?"

They are in the neighborhood of Gòtic. The restaurant is two blocks from their hotel. The outdoor tables are sheltered by canvas umbrellas, many covered with tapas and carafes. There is a Mediterranean atmosphere, unhurried and casual—the antithesis of most big cities.

"At two. She texted me the address of some café."

Abdullah is dreading it. The last time he saw her, Hena was still flighty, making jokes about dropping out of college. He'd missed the family's yearly gathering with other relatives last summer, instead going to Petra with Alma. It's been nearly two years since he has seen Hena.

Her jokes turned out to be prophetic. A few months ago, he overheard his mother speaking distraughtly on the phone. He could hear his sister's stubborn voice on the other line. Hena had decided not to register for fall classes; she was moving to Barcelona. Nobody could budge her. Her mind was made up.

Abdullah went to Seville—ostensibly—for research. The university in Amman encouraged him to go, found replacements for his classes. They loved his proposal, an expansion of his Oxford dissertation, an interminable manuscript titled *Islamic Representation and Influence in Western Institutions.*

Only later did he realize his error. After Alma, he needed crowds, noise, the stir of a city. Instead, Seville was quiet and enchanting, his afternoons spent in archives of the university library, poring through academic texts on Islam in Andalusian culture. He was constantly alone.

That's where he met Inez: in the aisle of religious tomes. She was carrying a stack of books, and when she saw him, she dropped her chin to her chest and remarked, "These smell like rotten eggs."

He liked her voice. There was something caustic about her, an irreverence that he found bracing. She was a decade older than he, a Seville transplant from Girona. They began to spend their evenings together, Inez taking him to bars where long-haired men played flamenco music and everyone drank wine with Sprite. Sometimes they spoke, sometimes they didn't. It was what he needed, he realized: companionship without the cost.

His rented apartment was in Triana, overlooking the Guadalquivir River; in the mornings, he walked along the bridge. More than once, he sent Alma a long, sentimental text messages. *Please, I've made a mistake Alma you have to speak to me.* She never responded.

Barcelona is faster than Seville. It reminds him of a post-modern Arab city, with insouciant, tattooed women and narrow streets leading nowhere. After breakfast, Colin leaves for the beach, and Abdullah walks along La Rambla, the shops beckoning to tourists. The streets are clogged with families, children tugging at their mothers' hands. It is cool, cooler than it was in Seville, the air pleasantly nippy. Like most coastal cities, you never forget the water is nearby.

He sidesteps to avoid a man on rollerblades and walks down an alley. It winds and turns into a dead end. There is a shop there with a fat man sitting on a stool.

"Come, friend," he calls to Abdullah. "Pretty things here."

The store is cramped, shelves cluttered with kitschy gift objects, ashtrays and candles and picture frames. An aisle is devoted to Gaudiesque figurines, colorful salamanders alongside flamenco dancers mid-twirl. A large map of Turkey hangs above the cashier. Muslim, Abdullah thinks.

It comforts him, finding other Muslims in foreign countries. In Seville, he spent long hours in the *Alcázar palace*, drawn to the Moorish architecture, the calligraphy of Quranic verses etched into the walls. *The Arabs used to rule half the world*, he tells his students. Alma liked to tease him for orientalism, the wistfulness of elderly men. He never told her it wasn't nostalgia; he wanted the students to feel pride. His classrooms were a sea of Coldplay T-shirts and cell phones. *We are something too*, he was trying to say. *We were kings once.*

The shopkeeper ushers him through the store. He holds out a jewelry box, the inside plush velvet.

"Buy this," he advises. His English is broken. "For your lady. She will like."

"What if there's no lady?" Abdullah is overcome with urges to confess these days, to divulge everything to strangers. It is unlike him.

"Ah." The shopkeeper's face falls. "This is sad. Very sad. Not good to talk of sad things on beautiful day," he admonishes.

Abdullah can't help smiling. "You're right."

The shopkeeper gives a satisfied grunt. "See this? Keeps bad things away." He points at a rack of miniature evil eye pendants hanging from leather straps.

"I have one." Abdullah gives a little wave at the doorway. "Thank you."

"Come back later, yes?" The man calls after him. "I'm always here."

Barcelona had been his mother's idea. "You're going to be so close," she'd told him.

"You can check up on Hena, see how she's doing." When he hesitated, she sighed. "Habibi, you know how she is."

"Why don't you go?" he asked. "Or Baba?" But he knew the answer. Hena didn't want their parents there.

His wayward sister. Even when he lived in London, he felt close to his mother; they Skyped on the weekends, and he flew back home twice a year. But then Hena, she seems to have taken departure to heart—barely returning yearly, talking to their grandparents only on holidays. Sometimes, Abdullah pores through her Facebook photographs, fascinated with the unfamiliar lives grinning back at him. House parties, beer gardens, road trips across Midwestern cities.

When he told Hena he was coming, she sent him an email peppered with exclamation marks, talking about *finally catching up* and *the most amazing city in the world.*

He is afraid that she'll ask questions. Hena's chatter can be tactless. How to explain the last few months, his time away from Amman, the abrupt upheaval in his life.

Well, I came here to get away from Alma. You remember Alma, right? You met her once, a couple of years ago, at Teta's house during Eid. Yes, the night you and that friend of yours, Samar or Sara, snuck out and got drunk on rum. No, not away from her. I actually came because I made a mistake. I did some stupid things. Anyway, it doesn't matter. I used to be afraid, and then I wasn't anymore. But it was too late. You sound like Mama. I know I'm afraid, I just said that. You know what, forget it. I came here to do research. I came for the Alcázar Palace.

He's tired just thinking about it.

He kept seeing Alma in Seville, all those dark-eyed women, as though she'd multiplied herself. In the end, it was Inez he found, the opposite of Alma—small and fair, a scar near her hairline. She studied art in cemeteries. She had been married twice; the last husband left her for her younger sister.

"They live on a farm near Girona now," she told him during one of their walks. "Raising pigs. It's like something out of a bad movie." She shrugged. "But then, life often is."

She asked about his family, Amman, his years at Oxford.

"The closest thing I came to love was God." It felt irreverent, hearing himself say it aloud.

"Was that enough?"

It wasn't. He told her about his childhood, their spacious house, with the little shed in the garden that they all called the Fixture. About his father—a doctor with a kind heart—who used the Fixture to treat the refugees who flooded Amman during wars and uprisings, the ones too poor to go to the hospital, the ones with furtive pasts. He told Inez about his father's worn face year after year—Saddam's invasion of Kuwait, the war in Yemen—as he tried to heal all who came to him. About how his heart would constrict when he heard the men beg, their desperation as repulsive as their illness, his own fear, an avid, watchful creature. He was afraid of everything—the dark, his mother leaving, refugee children taking over his bedroom, the sound of men coughing in the gardens. Sometimes he'd wander out there, when the Fixture was empty, and sit in that dim space that smelt of perspiration and decay no matter how much the maid scrubbed. He'd sit on the cots, feel the heat of the men that had lain there.

What would you think about?"

"Death." *This is what we are*, his younger self would think: the fleeting scent we leave behind in rooms. The brevity terrified him. "I stole from the men."

Inez looked rapt. "What would you take?"

Buttons from jackets, little combs, a plastic pillbox. Once, he took a strand of hair left behind on the pillowcase. He arranged these objects in an old pencil case, then hid it beneath his mattress, a place he knew nobody would look. He kept them like talismans; they would protect him, he believed, from some un-named dread, his own mortality. When he took them out, they seemed to pulse in his hand.

Inez asked, predictably, about Alma. He explained that he met her during a trip home from Oxford; she was the daughter of his father's old colleagues. He saw himself in her dependability. She was bookish and clever and unadorned, the kind of woman that disliked attention.

"She sounds a little dull," Inez said once. The comment stung.

The night before he left Seville, he and Inez snuck into a small garden and sat watching the stars. The air was cool, and around them, wind swished the leaves. Inez leaned on him, her cheek against his shoulder.

He tried to kiss her. But she smiled sadly and said, "Ah, *mi corazon*. Tell the truth."

The restaurant Hena chose is shabby and colorful, at the edge of Raval. There are several plastic tables on the sidewalk, and inside, the walls are painted ma-genta. He had expected to wait for a while, but she is already there, sitting next to the window. Catching sight of him, she claps.

"The prodigal son." She hugs him, her shoulders bony beneath his arms.

"It's good to see you." He realizes this is true. She wears a loose dress, her legs and arms tanned. Her lips match the walls, and her hair is unkempt as ever, parts of it hanging in short, fuzzy dreadlocks.

"What do you think?" She motions towards the table, restaurant, Barcelona. "Unreal, huh?"

"It's beautiful," he says truthfully.

"So." She rumples her hair with her fingers, a gesture he recognizes from childhood. He was a teenager when she was born. He remembers her dark wispy hair, tiny nose. She used to call him *Da-la*. "How are you?"

"How are *you*?" He hopes the deflection will work.

It does. She wrinkles her nose. "Let me guess. You've been sent on a fact-finding mission. *Abdullah, ask her how she's doing. Is she eating? Who are her friends? What time does she go to sleep?*" She adopts their mother's voice.

"Maybe a little. *Are* you eating?"

She laughs. "I'm alive, aren't I? I bet they didn't tell you why I left. Shocking. Have you ever read Plath?"

He shakes his head.

"Okay, so there's this girl, Esther's her name, and she's thinking about her life, and she sees it like a fig tree. It's full of fruit and she sees them as her choices, right? Like the figs are all the different lives she could have. But she can't pick one. So they start to rot. And it's like she's wasting her life, year after year, sitting around, watching the figs drop."

"The figs are university?"

"They're everything!" A flutter of her hands. "The riots, the shutdowns. Fucking Beirut. People getting high before raves. Every few weeks, someone's beat up for saying stupid shit about some politician. It was just . . ." She struggles. "So *pedestrian*."

"Right." Abdullah thinks *she* sounds pedestrian, but he doesn't dare say it aloud.

"And I realized I'm under that tree. I can either keep sitting around and become another pissed off college brat, or I can get up. Yank one of those figs."

A boy, Abdullah thinks. *There must be a boy.* "Why Barcelona?"

Hena blushes, confirming his suspicion. "I have friends here. Baba lost it, saying it's too far. But it's not like I'm in America."

She continues her chatter, Abdullah half-listening, distracted by the silver dots studding her earlobe, her clanking bracelets. She looks like a Spaniard, and when the waitress comes, she rattles off in Spanish with her for several minutes.

"That's pretty good."

She shrugs, but he can tell she's pleased. "You pick it up."

"Where do you live?"

"Not far." She sounds distracted, looking around the restaurant. A waiter walks by and they smile at each other. "How was Seville?"

"Fine." He talks about his time in the library, how he'd leave biscotti crumbs on the windowsill of his rented flat, so the birds would come. One had flown inside, and it took Abdullah hours to coax the panicked creature out. He doesn't mention Inez.

"It's heaven out there. I went down with a friend." A small smile flits across Hena's face. "We slept on the roof every night."

The waitress brings them plates of fish and meat. His sardines are garnished with cilantro and eggplant. Hena's plate is filled with something braised and maroon, draped over potatoes.

"What's that?"

"*Pulpo*," she grins.

They eat for several moments, the silence suddenly uncomfortable. They have rarely been alone together, Abdullah realizes.

Hena clears her throat, remembering. "So." She tries to keep her voice bright. "How's Baba?"

Abdullah pictures his father's new, sunken face, the blue irises—his favorite—he asks them to bring during his treatments. When Hena left for university, the cancer had just been found, and Abdullah had a feeling that his mother didn't tell Hena everything. "He's okay. The doctors . . ." A few months ago, he'd soiled himself in the hospital. Abdullah and his mother stood around, useless, embarrassed at the smell, as a nurse helped him to the bathroom. Abdullah's mother followed them; he could hear her soft voice speaking. She came out afterward, her face drawn, saying *Let's go home*. "He's okay," he repeats.

"Good." They stare down at their plates. "I miss him," she says unexpectedly. "He calls me every Sunday, right before dinner."

"Really?" His father hadn't mentioned it to him. He felt an old, familiar nip of resentment. His sister, baby of the family, could do whatever she wanted and still be adored.

The waitress clears the table and tucks the bill between the salt and pepper shakers. Hena reaches for her purse, but Abdullah waves her off.

"You seem well," he admits.

"I'm great." She grins. "Living clean. Actually, are you free tonight? There's a small gathering in Barceloneta, at the beach. Just some friends I've gotten to know here. You should come."

"Maybe."

"Come on!" She reaches across the table and slaps his hand. Her eyes are clear and mischievous. "I'd like you to meet them."

"I'll try."

Hena nods at someone behind Abdullah. "Sorry, I've gotta go. My shift starts in five minutes." It isn't until Abdullah has paid the bill, Hena kissing him on the cheek, and walked outside, standing alone on the sidewalk, that he realizes she works there.

Abdullah wanders the streets of Raval, crossing La Rambla once more, glancing at the map on his phone until he reaches the Sagrada Familia. It takes nearly an hour. The only other time he visited Barcelona was when he was living in Oxford; the cathedral was still under construction, ensconced in scaffolding and cranes. Now, long spires pierce the sky, the Gothic design imposing and at odds with the sunny day. Intricate sculptures of trees and animals are carved in the stone; a gaggle of tourists pose for a photograph below the Nativity façade.

He waits in line and buys a ticket. The interior is dizzying. Tourists swarm.

"Gaudí's vision," he hears a man whisper to his wife "Isn't it magnificent?"

"I think the word's *psychedelic.*"

The space pulsates with looming columns, stained glass windows, a ceiling that looks like a stone forest. There is the heady smell of incense, sandalwood. People kneel in the burnished pews, their eyes shut while they pray. A group of priests in swirling robes move down one of the aisles. They keep their eyes downcast as they walk, a silent dignity about them.

There was a time Abdullah wanted to be an *imam*. That life beckoned urgently to him, discreet, sparse, filled with afternoons in the mosque, sermons, and prayer. He liked the idea of being a lighthouse in a messy world, someone others would turn to for repair. He felt safest next to his grandfather as a child, Atef smelling of peppermint and smoke, listening to Abdullah recite Quran *suras*. Atef gave him a dinar for each one he memorized.

The boy knows more Quran than I ever did, he'd tell people proudly.

"*Perdóna!*" A little girl whizzes past Abdullah. She strolls to the central nave. Her dark hair is cut to her chin. She turns back to Abdullah and giggles.

He couldn't tell Hena the truth about their father. At the last visit, the doctor told them about the lungs. The cancer had metastasized. While the doctor spoke, Abdullah pictured plump, hateful cells fucking each other, angrily splintering, embedding themselves in his father's organs.

His phone vibrates. A text from Colin. *Tapas?*

There is a line of tourists at the votive candles. Abdullah waits until his turn, then lights one. He admonishes himself to pray, to say a name, anything, but his mind blanks.

The dreams began when he was ten. He would be walking alone in an abandoned village, rows of houses with empty windows. Suddenly the voices would start, refugees calling from attics and kitchens. They were wailing. He'd rush to the houses, but the doors were always locked, the terrible pleas getting louder.

He'd wake panting. He wanted to run to his mother, but something kept him in bed, shaking and clammy. The refugees in the Fixture upset her as well. He could see it in her tense smile whenever one arrived.

"They need us," his mother would say. "We have so much, and they have none."

But Abdullah was jealous of them, hated that his father spent hours in the Fixture, stitching strangers' skin until they howled. In his blacker moments, he wished himself disfigured, an accident leaving him crippled or scarred, something to bring his father to him.

He became convinced the dreams were punishment for stealing. Still, he took a pair of eyeglasses, someone's broken wristwatch. He'd lay out his plunder on the floor and touch them one by one like treasures.

A man died in the Fixture. Although Abdullah never saw him, he knew what he looked like. Gray skin, sunken cheeks, untrimmed beard. He knew because he heard his mother sobbing about it on the telephone. Soon after that, Abdullah took his pencil case to the garden after everyone had fallen asleep. He found a spot next to the jasmine shrub and dug until his arms ached. His body stank of sweat. One of his fingernails broke, and he licked the blood.

"Please," he whispered in the dark. He pictured the dead man, eyes glassy as coins at the bottom of a fountain. He dropped the objects into the hole, the buttons, the eyeglasses, the bobby pin that had once belonged to someone's wife. He peered into the hole at the things he had taken. "Forgive me."

He piled them with dirt.

A decade later, the dreams returned. Abdullah was twenty, doing his undergraduate degree in Amman, his evenings spent in smoke-filled living rooms, with men who roared about God and politics. Some of these men were classmates, others the older brothers and uncles of his friends. When the older men joined, the atmosphere changed: the others became more attentive, hanging on the elders' every word.

The older men spoke of occupation, maps that had been drawn by foreign hands, the fickle borders of their land. Of the filthy refugee camps and Netanyahu's megalomania, the hollow promises of Clinton and Blair, the necessity of martyrdom to mend an impure world. Their voices quaked with anger. *The West has ruined us. If a snake bites you, you don't beg it for the cure. You slice its head off.* Listening to their talk, Abdullah would picture how the Arab landscape had looked before the foreigners came: the clean, stark desert, the oil quietly brewing underground, generations who'd lived and died on the same soil.

When the men printed brochures and pamphlets, Abdullah took them, though he was too shy to hand them out at university like everyone else. Instead, he stuffed them into his backpack and hid it at home, pretended that he'd given them all away. The brochures were sleek, bordered in green and gold, pages filled with instructions on prayer and the Prophet's teachings, the true practice of Islam. Abdullah quoted them and grew his beard out, wore dishdashas mimicked the way the older men crossed their arms, but deep down, he knew he was unlike them. They never flinched from their ideas, their conviction of what the world needed, and Abdullah envied them. He wanted that kind of certainty, the ability to assign himself a life and live it, without hesitation or question. He knew it alarmed his mother and father. They watched him with alert eyes during those years. But he never explained what it was like, listening to the elders' visions, being part of something profound and beautiful, a version of himself—Abdullah, *visible*, man of loyalty—he never saw again.

Everything changed abruptly. One autumn day, Abdullah was leaving university when a classmate ran up to him.

"Something's happened."

Abdullah watched the towers fall every day for a month. They were remade each time, like some Greek myth, silver and whole and alive only to collapse again and again. It was a lie Abdullah ached to believe: that what was could be undone, that there was some way to reverse the specks of bodies falling against the blue sky, the streets charged with dust so heavy it looked strangely beautiful, a prehistoric fog through which people ran, weeping and holding their hands over their white-streaked heads.

Some people celebrated. There were fireworks, people dancing in the streets as American flags were burnt. His own mother wept.

"Look what they've done. Look." He didn't ask which *they* she meant.

He hungered for the elders like a love. They who made faith of everything, who had assembled their loyalties into a truth. He needed them to explain, illuminate, to find Allah in this for him.

But the men sat solemnly in their living rooms, eyes opaque and heavy. Some spoke of justice, of America's sins, the inevitability of decline; others spoke of clemency. Voices were raised. One man hit another. They began to shout at each other from the depth of their own fear, spitting blame at one another.

"Why is their blood better than ours? Are *their* dead more dead than *ours*?"

"Butchery is butchery!"

"You think they ask these questions? Watching Iraq, *Falasteen*? You think they lament our murdered?"

Abdullah didn't speak for fear of weeping. Something was happening to him in that airless room, those towers collapsing once more on the television screen, the men's bodies angrily reeking. He felt the plummet of those tiny specks. He felt the human ache of watching their fall. *What does it mean*, he wanted to ask, *what does any of it mean?*

For weeks, he slept like someone whose heart had been broken. He dreamt of the refugees stealing rubble from the towers—a sapphire choker, someone's thermos of coffee—while he screamed at them to stop. He dreamt of white men in army camps, stamping around lakes in boots, their breath white as snow.

There was hell, his mother said, and someone was going to pay it.

"I turned to the books for shelter," he told Inez. He read Averroes and Ibn Khaldun. He read about Al Farabi's soul-city, the intricacies of devotional law. At Oxford, he listened to his professors discuss fatalism, had late-night debates with his classmates in cafés about the divine purpose of human suffering. But it was theoretical, removed. There were no answers, and so the world hurt him less. Iraq was invaded and wrecked. Militants bombed Jordan, slaughtering a wedding party. In Southern Beirut, American bombs fell from the bellies of Israeli planes. He still felt anger, disgust, sorrow, but at a distance, as though from a part of himself miles away. He no longer wanted the surrender of unfettered faith. He wanted a god who coolly patted his hand, a god that had better things to do.

By the time Abdullah arrives at the bar, the sun is nearly set. The pink light makes the streets radiate. The restaurant is crowded, open to the street. He likes the name—*Champañeria*—how it rolled off the tongue of a man he stopped for directions. People spill onto the sidewalk with their glasses, conversing with each other in Catalan, Spanish, German. There is a jovial air to the crowd, men bustling behind the bar, sliding small tapas plates towards the customers, loudly counting out euros.

Colin is leaning against the far end of the bar, raising a glass of something pink toward Abdullah. There are several plates perched next to him, olives and anchovies and bread.

"We have to go," he says when Abdullah tells him about Hena's invitation.

"They're a decade younger."

"I could always use more friends, mate."

"I think you have plenty."

"Listen." Colin's eyes turn serious. "I know we haven't really talked. About your girl, what's her name. Tala?"

"Alma." Abdullah's ears burn. Her name feels illegal in his mouth.

"Right, Alma. You don't want to talk. I get that. It's how you are. All stoic, like." His laughter is kind. "But it'll be good to get out."

The last time Abdullah saw Alma, she was yelling. By the time he reached for her, she was already putting her coat on. *Not everything's a theoretical treatise.* He stared at the door for a long time afterwards.

Colin's voice cuts through his thoughts.

"So come on, Boudi." He pronounces it *bawdy.* "Let's have a little adventure."

The gathering is at the far end of Barceloneta beach. They pass sunburnt tourists, couples swinging hands. A towering sculpture of cubes, teenagers stretched out below it. "Everything in this city's art, eh?" Colin remarks.

Every few minutes, they stop and squint in the dark at groups of people. Abdullah had expected Hena's group to be wild, full of dancing, loud music, an impression gleaned from the few times he went to clubs in London.

Instead, it is twenty or so people, a man playing guitar. There is a small bonfire in the middle. Towels and blankets are spread out. The girls are dressed in shorts, the men topless. A couple of girls practice yoga poses near the water's edge. People are passing around a cigarette that takes Abdullah several minutes to realize isn't a cigarette.

He spots Hena and waves.

"Pretty," Colin says. Abdullah elbows him, hard, in the gut. "Ai! Jesus, alright. Loud and clear."

"You came!" Hena hugs Abdullah, gives Colin a kiss on the cheek. "Hena."

"Colin." He gestures. "This is great."

She looks around like she forgot. "Oh, yeah, it is. Sorry." She gives an impish smile. "It's just another Thursday around here."

They walk around the bonfire, nodding and saying hello to people. "This is Fran." Hena nods towards a tall, black woman with tangerine-colored hair.

"Welcome." Fran gives each of them a kiss. She smells like coconut oil. Colin catches Abdullah's eye and winks. Abdullah shakes his head.

"Have you lived here long?" Colin asks.

"Five years," Fran says. "I work at the docks. For a boating company. Taking tourists out for day trips." Abdullah tries, fails, to imagine a life of beaches and sailing. "I moved here from Toronto."

"I'm thinking of doing the same myself," Colin quips.

"You'd be in good company. There's a group of us. You just wake up one morning and decide, *enough*. No more offices, no more sitting in traffic watching your life go by. Hena's the latest convert." She drapes an arm around Hena's shoulder. They beam at each other.

Someone passes Hena the roach. She takes a long toke.

Abdullah can't help himself. "What happened to clean living?"

"It *is* clean." She laughs. "Straight from the earth."

Fran takes a toke, then proffers it to Abdullah. He puts a hand up. He has never tried anything, not even a sip of alcohol. People marvel at his abstinence—even Alma had tried wine before—but it is calculated: better not to be tempted. Easier not to know what he is missing. In truth, it is a way of bypassing sacrifice.

"Beer?" Fran asks. Colin follows her to a cooler near the bonfire. The bottles she pulls out glint in the firelight.

Hena loops an arm through Abdullah's, leading him to a paisley sheet on the sand. She introduces him to people, men and women offering their cities like IDs.

"Melbourne."

'Helsinki."

"Albuquerque."

Their stories are predictable. They speak of small towns and angry families, broken hearts, moving here to wait tables and tutor. Their accents mingle together, French and Russian and Swedish. One of the Chilean girls tells a story about being detained in Madrid for an expired visa, and the others *tsk*. There seems to be an unspoken competition amongst them over whose hometown was the dullest, whose lifestyle is most unorthodox. Still, Abdullah finds himself getting bored. The group strikes him as inauthentic, a forgery of identity somehow—self-imposed exile discomfits him—but he understands what attracts Hena. She has always seemed hungry for inclusion.

Every now and then, he glances over at Colin, chatting with Fran and a wiry man in red shorts. Colin takes a hearty puff of the joint, laughs at something the man says.

One of the yoga women sits next to Abdullah on the blanket. A strand of beads hangs between her breasts.

"I'm Susan. Where are you from?" It is the first question anyone has asked him in an hour.

"Amman. What about you?"

Susan rolls her eyes. "Ririe, Idaho. Can you imagine? My parents farmed alfalfa. I was landlocked for twenty years. Is there a sea in Amman?"

"Nearby, yes."

"I'm a true thalassophile." She waits a beat. "It means lover of the sea."

She has obviously used the line before. Alma would take pity on this girl, ask her questions. Tell her about Aqaba and the Dead Sea. Inez would roll her eyes. She'd say something about the inanity of using obsolete language in conversation.

Abdullah just nods.

The guitarist starts to strum something fast, and several people sing along. Hena stands and sways her shoulders. She looks spellbound. Abdullah turns toward the cooler to catch Colin's eye, but the spot is empty.

Abdullah thinks suddenly of Inez. He thinks of her little house, her sturdy life. Art historian: even her work sounds solid. A small city, a television, ordering food in. Men enter and leave her life like seasons, carrying grocery bags for her and calling her nicknames. The kind of life you envision for yourself before you know any better. He is happy for her. Jealous, too.

Something bad happened to Alma when she was younger. She never spoke about it, but it trailed her like a shadow. He had to piece it together on his own: her stiffening at certain sounds; the way she looked faraway at times; the cousin whose name came up in conversation once, and how her mouth turned ugly like she was about to spit. She had crying spells sometimes. There were days when she slept instead of going to work. She would cover every mirror in her house with towels.

The rest of the time, she was like everyone else. She worked as a translator at the Embassy, but had always wanted to be a writer and spent her weekends at a small desk in her living room. Abdullah liked to be in her apartment while she worked, watching television or reading as the sound of her light, deft typing surrounded him like rainfall. People liked her, and were drawn to her docility.

Every few months, she would let him read a new story, biting her cuticles and watching him while he read. *Beautiful*, he always said and kissed her. The truth was that her stories felt a little thin to him; oftentimes their friends and family and—worst of all—Abdullah himself too easily recognizable in them.

They were often about women who found themselves in new lives, the men usually treacherous or absent, or both.

Sometimes the word *marriage* was tossed around, by their parents, friends, even Alma at times, but something within Abdullah resisted, though he wasn't certain why. It wasn't Alma's frailty, or even the rope of grief she coiled around herself at times. In this way. Abdullah and Alma ere alike: they were both strangers to themselves, harboring wants without understanding them.

One evening, they agreed to meet at her place after work. She wanted to cook him a meal. She called him around four, her voice trembling, to say that a stranger had yelled at her because she'd clipped his car in the grocery parking lot. She asked Abdullah what he thought. She wanted to examine the details of the encounter, the man's voice, the angle that he had been parked. She spoke for several minutes, crying, finally lapsing into silence, waiting. Abdullah hesitated before saying that he had a lot of work, that they could talk more this evening, and he knew as he spoke that it was the wrong thing. Alma's voice turned stony. *I should go*, she said. Abdullah sighed when he hung up. He knew he'd find this moment in one of Alma's stories, sometime down the road. The prospect tired him.

When he arrived that evening, he found her in the kitchen, an uncooked chicken breast on the counter. She was bent over the sink, crying.

Something snapped in him. It was too much.

It reminded him of the Fixture. Of one of the refugee children, decades ago, running in his mother's garden and the hem of his pants getting caught in the chicken wire. Abdullah had been playing tag with him. The boy had an amputated arm, and his sleeve flapped in the wind as he stood, motionless, a look of panic on his face. Abdullah froze. He watched the trapped boy. He could have ripped the fabric free, unwound the wire, but instead, he just stood there.

Watching Alma, he couldn't move. Not when her tears turned into sobbing, not when she threw a sponge at him. Her docility broke. She began to curse him.

"You don't care," she screamed, "about anything. You're a piece of furniture! *What's wrong with you?*"

They had watched their friends marry, have children. More than once, their parents dropped hints about weddings. All around them, people had uncomplicated lives, came together, and that was it. He wanted Alma: even with everything, she was the only person he'd ever wanted.

But she got it wrong. He didn't feel nothing, but rather was flooded by the enormity of what it meant to be standing in this kitchen, alive with this woman, his bare neck still perspiring from the afternoon sun. It wasn't apathy. It was love; it paralyzed him.

It is late. Abdullah is tired. The gathering has grown; people sprawl on the sand, singing songs in Spanish. The smell of hashish is strong. He listens to Susan talk about her travels in Europe. A few of the braver girls—Hena one of them—go into the water. Over the waves and music, they shriek at the cold.

Colin is lost. Abdullah can't find him anywhere. When he catches sight of Fran, sitting on one of the towels, he is relieved.

"Have you seen my friend?"

She gives him a quizzical grin. "I'm sure he's fine."

Finally, he gives up. Bathroom, then back to the hotel, Abdullah decides. He'll say bye to Hena and talk to Colin in the morning. *Tried looking for you,* he texts.

There is a toilet near the cube sculpture. The light fades away from the bonfire, and Abdullah nearly loses his balance in the sand.

The bathroom is dark and empty, three urinals and a large handicapped stall. Moonlight reflects itself on the faucet and mirrors. He pees and washes his hands. There is a sudden sound, like a sob, from the handicapped stall. *Someone's hurt*, he thinks.

He walks to the stall and lifts his hand to knock. But the door is unlocked; it swings open at his touch.

It takes a moment to understand what he is seeing. Colin. He is fighting with another man. The man he was talking to earlier. Their shirts are off. The man's red shorts are around his ankles. They are fighting. Colin's bare ass is white in the moonlight. He moves it, frantically, like a dance. Colin knocks into the man once, twice. Abdullah calls for him, but no sound comes out.

Not fighting, his mind screams. Not fighting. The other thing. The thing he has never done. Colin hunches over the man, his hands braced above the toilet. Someone emits a sigh. Their breathing is clamorous. The man suddenly pitches his head back, arching his spine. He moans. Abdullah feels a ripple, murmuring from somewhere within him, a stir his body bids. The urge to approach. It terrifies him.

He steps back. Gasps.

The men stop. Colin whirls his head over his shoulder and sees Abdullah, and the look in his eyes is immense, spanning everything, everything they have known about each other, ten years of friendship, a lifetime of crying girls in their Oxford apartment, Abdullah brewing tea, the jokes about girls' asses.

Abdullah rushes out.

He moves like he is being chased. Stumbling on the sand until he is on concrete again, away from the water. His mind races. A quartet of men amble by, speaking in loud, drunken tones. He pushes through them, walking past shuttered ice cream shops and souvenir stands.

His phone vibrate, but he ignores it. Hena is splashing in the water, telling friends about the future, stories about her dying father. Alma eats dinner alone, watching one of her Old Hollywood movies. Abdullah feels desire like a punch. His desire to be touched, by anyone.

They tried to have sex once, he and Alma. But she cried when he touched her breasts. She told him they'd get married someday. It would get easier.

Abdullah passes Gòtic and continues to La Rambla. He walks and walks. The sun will be up in a few hours, but some of the places are still open, music trickling from the bars. He did ask Alma, finally, after that evening at her house. He sent it in a text, then through a friend, then told her mother. He begged her to say yes. He never heard back.

When he reaches Plaça Reial, he is surprised by the crowd. Wakeful cities unnerve him. A few kids sit around the fountain, rolling cigarettes. One of the boys spits. Two women walk across the courtyard, their heels in hand. One of them eyes him, whispers something to her friend, and smiles.

He wants to pray. *You took something from me,* he yells soundlessly. But what was taken? His faith? The men in the Fixture? Alma? With her pain and her narrow brown eyes, the hands she placed on his forehead.

Partygoers kiss against the columns. Abdullah watches for as long as he can bear, then walks away. Loneliness is a mountain he has to climb, alone and slowly. At each archway of the plaza, streets fork into different ones, and Abdullah follows them arbitrarily. Dark men, Bangladeshi, Indian, wander the narrow backstreets, holding out six-packs of beer to him, their faces eager. *Cervesa, cervesa.* He wishes these men were at the beach right now, telling their story of exile to Hena's friends.

He recognizes a graffitied wall, a woman's face tilted to the side. Each eyelash is as long as his arm. By instinct, he takes a left at the corner, and lets out a laugh. There, sandwiched between two boarded-up storefronts, is the shop from earlier, the fat man sitting outside with a friend. A small hookah pipe is between them, the water gurgling as they inhale.

The shopkeeper nods at the sight of Abdullah.

"You come back." He says something in Turkish to his friend. The other man snorts, takes the hookah hose.

"Come, come," the shopkeeper says.

The store seems altered at night, a surreal quality to the aisles of unclaimed objects. Abdullah suddenly wants the postcards, ashtrays, even the map above the cashier. He remembers the objects from the Fixture, how he felt closer to those men by taking what belonged to them. He begins to gather things from the shelves: an embroidered fan, keychains, expensive chocolates. For his mother, a leather-bound notebook. For his father, a wooden chessboard. A shawl for his grandmother.

The shopkeeper lets out a whistle. His tone changes. "Best pashmina in the world! From Istanbul."

He picks a tapas cookbook for his mother. He'll mail it to her. Several mosaic animals—lizards, horses, birds—for his younger cousins in Amman. He wants to buy something for the man in the red shorts, for the vendors with beer cans outside. *Take it,* he'll shout. When he was younger, he would dream of raking all of his father's money into a hill, then dropping a lit match on it.

"My father's dying" he told Inez that night in the garden after he tried to kiss her.

"It was always going to happen," she said. "All along. We just forget it. When it does, we feel betrayed by it. But why? We were never promised anything." The years in cemeteries had toughened her. Death wasn't punishment, she told him. It was binding, a requisite; there was something beautiful there. She held him.

It was always going to happen.

Under the glass display, there are rows of jewelry. He picks a sapphire pendant for Alma. The prettiest one. He wants to ask her about marriage. He'll say it differently this time. Not like she owes him anything. He wants what Colin had in that bathroom. The humanity of it.

The shopkeeper begins to laugh. "You crazy man, yes?"

Abdullah exhales. "All of it," he says. "I'll take it all."

He piles the counter with gifts, stacking them atop each other, each one alive with its possibility, the stack getting bigger and bigger, the shopkeeper laughing as he watches.

BARRAK ALZAID

"The Lesson"

My collection of illustrated Islamic books shares a shelf with the mythological exploits of the Greeks, brimming with dreamers and prophets, parables of right and wrong. I had arranged the books chronologically from Adam to Prophet Mohammad, and today I was mulling over Prophet Yusuf for a religion class quiz. The cover of his volume depicted the story's climax. Two women loomed over a table of fruit. One looked horrified; the knife she held was covered in her own blood, the deep ochre of henna. The other woman bows her head, cheeks flushed.

The faces and bodies of our prophets were left to our imagination, and I imagined him gracefully entering that hall, handsome eyes flashing at the scene.

Baba and I sat side by side at my desk. His legs knocked absentmindedly into mine, and every so often, his hands. I looked over, annoyed at the constant touch, and realized I was sitting much taller compared to last spring when we studied at this table. Desire and longing define Prophet Yusuf's story. His brothers, vying for the affections of their father, cast their younger brother into a well.

My voice rose and then cracked into its lower register, "Why didn't he know his brothers would do that to him if he could see the future?" Like Tiresias or the Oracle of Delphi, this prophet was an interpreter of dreams.

It didn't matter whether Baba was lecturing me to "be nice with the people," or if he was talking on the phone, his voice always boomed.

"Allah gave him a gift. But it came after many tests to his faith. His brothers were very jealous. But he had faith in Allah, so he was rescued."

Baba pressed his finger into the spine of my religion class workbook to flatten the pages.

"Allah tested Prophet Yusuf, to give him strength."

"Strength for what?"

"For going to jail."

"But why was he put in jail?"

I pressed questions on him to stretch our study sessions out. I knew the answer, but I relished getting Baba to tell it. He stared me down for a long minute.

"Barrak." He stretched the second syllable into a reprimand, "Do tafseer for this section of the surah."

I paused, unsure how to summarize Zoulikha's salacious acts and the prophet's imprisonment at her hand. After Prophet Yusuf was rescued, he fell into the employ of a high-ranking official in Pharaoh's court, eventually encountering the official's wife, Zoulikha, the woman whose face burned with desire on my cover. Zoulikha watched Prophet Yusuf day to day, and I imagined her advancing on him, her nails clinging tight to his shirt, tearing away a fragment as he tried to escape her reach. I lingered inside this vision, as she must have lingered on the taut muscles stretching across his back as he reached for the door.

"She, uh, tried to trick Prophet Yusuf." I hurried to the safe generic answer, "But he was strong and had faith in Allah."

After rocking my knees together for a few minutes, I was suddenly very aware of the warmth gathering in the seat of my pants. I pulled at the threads of hair that had settled along my chin over the summer to distract myself. I'd been nagging Mama for a razor and shaving cream, and she kept saying I had to ask Baba. My eyes wandered to another passage in my illustrated book. Baba noticed and slammed his palm on the table, then flicked my picture book to the floor. He hadn't looked close enough to see the passages of the Quraan annotating the pictures, and my gut felt heavy knowing those verses touched the floor.

"Better you read the textbook for the exam. What do you need from these childish things?"

Baba was fluent in English, but when he got agitated, his sentences got clunky. His generation was the first to really benefit from Kuwait's nascent oil wealth, and in the 1950s and 1960s, the government sent youth abroad to learn English. But they started late enough that his tongue never fully grasped the language. He hardly ever spoke to me in Arabic though, and even when I asked him, and tried speaking to him in Arabic, he mostly responded in English. Since religion class was bilingual, Baba could get away with us reading Quraan in Arabic and doing summaries in English.

"Okay, repeat now."

I followed along with each syllable and stumbled over the vowels. Diacritic marks on the consonants were signposts to meaning, but I often missed them. A relic of jumping from government school to an American school too early in my education. "Baba, what does 'balagha' mean?"

He squinted, "He became a man."

This was my first ever real opening to the puberty conversation with Baba. I ignored my churning stomach and tried to lead into my request. I thought carefully of how to frame it. A couple years ago, Mama had tossed an illustrated guide to puberty into my room and walked off, "Let us know if you have any questions."

Which part of the puberty guide talked about how to ask your father about the changes going on in your body? I already knew the basics from studying my children's encyclopedias; the human development section featured naked illustrations of boys and girls, men and women with growing patches of hair. Someone must have noticed the time I spent sitting in the living room with that volume because it mysteriously disappeared.

The Maghreb call to prayer pierced through my windows and interrupted my tangential thoughts. The muezzin must have gotten sick from recent dust storms because this evening's athan was throaty and rattled with phlegm. My weekend was almost over, and soon, Baba would rush out to pray. If I could just shave, my hair could grow thicker. But my stomach churned, and Baba's dishdasha swished out the door, leaving behind woody notes of cologne.

⌘

I usually slept through my morning alarm, so Mama in her fuzzy pink bathrobe and slippers, hair flat from sleep, would slide my shutters open. This had been our ritual since my very first day of kindergarten, but today the sky was still dark when she cracked my shutters open.

Relics of last night's dream. The smooth back of my shirtless prophet lingered, and I felt my damp core swell. Cinderella had been there too, singing about dreams and wishes the heart makes. I thought about Prophet Yusuf's chest and pictured it covered in thick hair.

"Yalla Barrak, you have to catch your father before he leaves for salaat."

Baba's routine was fixed around three things: lunch, his post-lunch nap, and five daily prayers. It was unusual for him to deviate, and to catch him immediately before his attendance to one of these rites was to broker a tense and hurried exchange.

I pulled my covers back over my head. I'd long given up my morning prayers, preferring the extra sleep, and Baba had given me no resistance there. She yanked at my blanket.

"Mama, I'm tired—" I pulled the blanket back, praying I hadn't peeked out of my pajamas.

"Fine, I give up! If you want to teach yourself to shave, that's fine."

That passive-aggressive guilt-tripping strategy never failed, and I trudged over to my parents' bathroom.

Baba stood at the sink in white cotton boxers and wiped water off his bare chest. He's too comfortable in his own skin despite the large swathes of tight hairless membrane that stretch across his legs and upper thighs. That story is family legend. He was eight and camping in the desert with his father when his blanket caught fire. His father managed to wrench it off, but not before Baba suffered burns that melted the delicate tissue in his lower body and bound him to a hospital bed for months. When Baba hit adolescence a few years later, Baba Saud passed away. Other than some anecdotes about how energetic and naughty he was, my impoverished understanding of Baba's youth was defined solely by these traumas.

My own childhood memories are replete with Baba's playful energy and nonsense rhymes ("*singy singy songa, bingy bingy bonga!*"). I can recall our intimacies in detail, and they are well documented in our albums and home movies: the Camcorder lingers on me at age four or five. I am cradling a bottle, and my sniffling nose is red. Baba speaks from behind the camera, "Barrak is very sick, very depressed." His playful tone belies his concern. In an even older video, I am laying on my stomach and looking up at him with shining eyes. He tosses crinkled magazine pages at me in a silly makeshift game.

I just can't reconcile this father with the one I face in the bathroom. I wonder if the vacuum I feel is the same one he experienced when his father died.

"Mama says you have to show me how to shave."

"Hah?" An impatient burst of breath, a soundless chuckle. The edges of his mouth pulled apart, and his eyes narrowed when I snapped the lid off the can of Barbasol shaving cream. I feigned spraying it into my hand and accidentally squirted a large wad of cream, antiseptic peppermint notes cloyed their way into my nose. Baba glanced at his watch and yanked my wet hand across my face. It was cool and tickled the hairs in my nose.

"Be sure to use new razor. When you finish it, you throw it away." These were sanitation instructions he might dispense to nurses at his hospital. It was similar to his injunction against sharing nail clippers, even within our family.

"Okay, but how long until I grow more?"

"Why are you in a rush? Just wait, then it will come inshallah."

He swept the blade across his face, a couple centimeters from the surface of his skin.

"You do like this, then like this."

He repeated the gesture, and the blade travelled just above the grain, then landed in my hand. I strained across the length of the sink to peek at the meager hairs tucked in the crook of my neck and caught him slipping his dishdasha over his head, the white cotton flowing down his body and settling over his body. He sailed out the door without a glance backwards.

When I was a child, I had another picture book, and each page had different textured material I fondled. The duck had feathers, the quilt had cloth, and the father had dark grey sandpaper on his face which, over the course of my childhood, I had rubbed smooth. I stroked the grainy surface of my chin and felt my whole body swell.

RUTH AWAD

The Keeper of Allah's Hidden Names

When I looked up, the clouds muted the bulb of moonlight
or they wisped like scarves around the neck of a woman,
        that perfume between light and darkness,
and I was still counting.

        I counted the white-clothed canopies pinned to the mountainside,
blustering there
        as though they could drip down the stone wall

like water and wash away.
That water jeweled with blood.
        Your names like the sea's broken glass.

I was counting when
you looked down on your animals
        who leaned into your breath with wonder
at the wind stinging through their ribs,

        was counting when you pulled the moon down into the sea, a pearl
on the tongue of an animal
        too stupid to swallow your name and keep it there,

was counting from the cliffs every syllable
of light and water and leaf and bone,
        braying your names like an incantation
against the loneliness of knowing you.

Let me be a lamb in a world that wants my lion.
In the beginning, there was an angel with cloven feet who stood by me,
and the angel said, *My wings are an ocean,* and its shoulders split until
feathers fell around us. This is how you leave your country.
On the back of an ocean. Choked with feathers.

꒰꒱

If someone gives you water, drink. And if they hand you a glass of blood,
tell yourself it's water. If they hand you a lamb and say *eat,* they will
see a lion. They will call you *lion* when you walk down the street.
When the towers come down. When blood is the water they drink.

꒰꒱

When my belly sings with hunger, it's asking, *Will you die for an idea?*
I dreamt I walked the shore of my country and each wave cracked like
a bone. The sea of my childhood rattles with skulls, and their mouths—
agape with my name—drown its vowels, call me "S," say it's the name
the sea spoke when I dragged my feet across an ocean and became
somewhere new. I call my dead *Beloved,* but they have too much
time for me. If I close my eyes, I see my father on the beach,
his hands cupped for water. He says, *The dead are always thirsty,*
and I wake up in time to catch the L for work that hardly keeps me fed.

꒰꒱

Heaven, leave your light on a little longer. I looked for you on earth
and found my daughters. I looked for you and saw your stars strung
electric as sorrow and they wound my current across their backs
and carried me here, the middle of a grocery store parking lot,
the whine of flood lights burrowing into my capped head

and the black night ahead, and I think, *My god, will I ever not be surprised by what I can survive?* The long country of my loneliness stretched out before me, my hands heavy with the food I can eat—
I'm so full of honey in a time of war, winter in a land
I'm learning to love, in a land that won't love me.

Amor Fati

Our gods disappoint us so we make new ones.   Some glower like smoke. Some
wheel in suffering like dying stars.   Oh,   simple interstellar dust,

you've made us love the fate that yokes us. To be good when living makes us
mean.
Say you know what I mean, northern flicker,   small feather of a smaller planet.

God who ate everything,   did this world feed you? There were enough bodies.
There were blades that passed like a stranger in starlight.   In some worlds,
you're so

close I could kiss you.
                    In some worlds, we keep meeting.

God of six supposedly impossible things: weep of wolves, a drought of bullets,
the claws of a catalpa,   a mother's   unworry,   a wilderness of blood,

the dead keeping count.

I, too, am rich in things I never asked for.

A. AZAD

shahadah

what does it mean to be born muslim? my muslimness was taken care of at birth. literally. a father, a paper cone, and an adhan. the ritual is the same in a hospital on the east coast as a bedside in south asia. shahadah itself was abstract. we were supposed to have taken it by default, believed its message inherently. supposed to.

my parents migrated from kashmir at different stages of life, by way of my maternal grandfather. we called him abjee, because our baby tongues flattened words into as few syllables as possible until we made the typical desi title of "abu-ji" into something our own, into something wholly confused diaspora. abjee hopped off a trade ship on the east coast in the seventies leaving a wife and six daughters back home, and he came to amreeka for the same reasons everyone else does: opportunity without access. moved to the boroughs of new york city, a middle-aged brown dude without papers living in a basement with six other middle-aged brown dudes without papers. worked on a dead bengali man's social security because a laminated blue card afforded him personhood that his existence did not. this is where my ancestral appreciation for brownness comes from, but particularly these working-class brown angels who ushered him under winged roofs in brooklyn and queens for years. there was more—there was a visa shaad to a white cocaine addict, owning a crown fried chicken spot, another marriage in the quest for a son—but mostly i remember abjee for his round spectacles that have forever imprinted him in my memory as the grandpa from the simpsons. he had a gentle laugh and a sweet tooth, brought me and my sisters glasses with punch-out m&ms even when my mama refused to let us have them. he made me happy to be who i was, filled our tiny one-bedroom apartment with calm even when there was six of us bumping limbs at every corner.

and when he left, my urdu went with him. i thought it had died with him too. but at some point, i began to learn again. and at some point, i took the shahadah on my own. when it was no longer empty arabic words that i didn't understand, when there were no longer difficult urdu words i felt too scared to pronounce. that's when i began to believe.

salat

my biggest struggle as a muslim has been prayer. it makes me jealous, when others speak of the comfort they find in bowing their head to god. when others' relationships with the structure of islam comes easy. i never did do well with authority.

our masjid made matters worse. pakistani by culture and by audience, it harbored hushed whispers that echoed around dingy underfunded walls with the help of the one painfully tiny fan in the women's corner. the masjid was across the street from the housing projects, run-down brick buildings with a little playground always so hauntingly empty, projects that were eventually blown up in favor of highrises to house white gentrifiers and the spirit of occupation. this masjid was rooted in anti-Blackness, and anti-anyone not within the narrow confines of their respectability politics. my sister and i spent a couple of months in a qari's run-down basement along with dozens of other little kids. he had a hanger, or some whip-type contraption—i can't quite remember—and he used it when kids didn't pronounce their qur'anic recitation correctly.

none of us understood arabic. they had been telling us how to sound out the letters in the vaguest of terms, in terms that nearly made it a disservice to the voice of god. zabr zheir chupair became the universal understanding and the qari made me uncomfortable. he was a strange brown man whose eyes had too much free reign in the dimness of that sprawling bottom floor and i felt like jahannam could rise up through the crust of the earth into that basement. he picked on my little sister one too many times. yelled at her, looked at her in a way that made my skin crawl. and that was the first time i consciously remember throwing a temper tantrum, to get us out of a supposed house of god.

zakat

"give to the less fortunate," they told us. but what happens when you are the lesser fortunate? when your survival rests wholly on the availability of government funds for food?

charity becomes complicated when you are poor and muslim, becomes a loaded word in whatever language you translate it into. two point five percent doesn't seem like a lot until there are seven of you living on less than thirty thousand dollars in a bustling brown city. i still remember the day i realized i was poor, the day i realized blue checks and rent control from the state were not the norm—i was seventeen, deciding between attending a public university and a private college. a privilege in and of itself. and after a year of applications and standardized exams and recommendations it was money that proved to be the final barrier. the institution i ended up at had an annual price tag of double my father's salary. my english teacher, a graduate of another bougie liberal arts college, asked me how much we made, how much we could afford to pay. her eyes widened at my copy of the tax return: how are you guys surviving off this?

in the years that came, the years of predominantly white and wealthy peers, the years of thinly-veiled classism and bootstraps narratives, this question echoed around my head: how were we surviving? the thing about poverty is this. when you're in it, it's difficult to see out of it. when you're in it, it becomes the norm. it was just as much of my culture as muslim or brown or american. it's the culture of distinguishing gunshots from fireworks, of dodging the bloods in your basement, of fire hydrant sprinklers on humid summer days. it's the culture of syrup sandwiches and five-cent swedish fish, of freeze tag and wallzies, of never-ending vermin infestations no matter how clean you keep the claustrophobic apartment. it's the feeling of men on stoops with their bud light watching you, the feeling of the cops watching you, your landlord watching you, your mom—there are eyes everywhere and noise everywhere and suddenly one day everything is quiet and the community surveillance is of a different variety and you make nearly as much money as your baba did four years ago and you realize that you are no longer the less fortunate.

and still, my mama says what she always has: give in the name of your lord, for he will return it to you many times over.

sawm

the one thing that has always made me feel the most muslim is ramadan. that feeling of breaking bread with ones you love and keeping yourself from other things you love—like popeyes cheesecake on summer days and raunchy sitcoms in the middle of the night—made me feel invincible. my first memories of fasting are in middle school, the last time that ramadan fell on winter months, and i would bundle up in my favorite massive red hoodie, the one i couldn't wear outside because i could be mistaken for a gangbanger, and drag myself happily to the dining room table at a godly ungodly hour. i love it but it's always the same. mama spends a full hour cooking. eggs and parathas. i shovel a sad bowl of cheerios into my mouth. i'm happy but tired and quiet, unusual. baba takes this silence as opportunity, shattering it with some complaint or the other he has written over the tired wrinkled forehead of my baby sister. she glares at him silently over her orange juice, and his eyes spark. it's a scary look that comes over his face, something akin to glee when he finds his chance. not that he ever waits for an excuse. he smacks her across the face and everything gets even quieter. then mama begins to yell. you haven't even begun your fast yet and you've already broken it. what do you get from beating your jawaan daughters? shame on you.

but he never is ashamed. and at some point my mama loses her shame too, because it is never her body on the line. we are thick-skinned in different ways and i begin to hate her as i hate him, hate her for the one january night she called the police only because he raised his hand at her, hate the fast and the way it seems to enable this man who claims to be my baba, hate that every facet of islam becomes tainted by him. i am the besharam one. but i shudder at the man who funneled the adhan into my ear and made me muslim, the man who didn't seem to be the man he is now, or rather, the man who was adept at hiding it. the memory of being twelve years old beat into the ground for praying asr late, the memory of blood and tears escaping my body and hating my thin skin fragile bones functional tear ducts for betraying me like this. holding the sides of the sink looking into the water-stained mirror whispering to myself: you're good. you're good. you're good. and then balancing on the edge of the tub feet reaching the other wall to keep me distracted enough with the laws of physics that i don't start screaming. because i know another law of physics that tells me, once it begins, it will never stop. i can't stop shuddering at the memory of the cold tense suhoors and iftars and everything in between. and years later there comes this word—trauma—that begins to describe the shudder.

hajj

it's fucked up, but before i moved away to college i was under the impression that all black and brown people in this country were also as poor as me, didn't have access to travel even for the sake of god. then i met a pakistani girl who had been to hajj. and then another. and then another. and i began to realize why the model minority trope was so widely touted. regardless, the leaving was important. maybe the most important thing i have ever done for myself. for the first time, i didn't need a mama baba qari sheikh zakir naik youtube lecture at nine on a sunday morning breathing down my neck to be muslim. maybe i just was. and eventually i began to frequent the musallah in our little religious house, this room that smelled like rain and dust and years of muslim women surviving and perhaps even thriving.

pilgrimage is about mobility, in the end, social spiritual physical. in my family of seven, i had the good grace to be the first to move out, the first to experience white-collar racism in a white-collar workplace. firsts are exhausting and so i come back to the comforts of home every few weekends. and on this particular saturday it is my mama's forty-something birthday. i am eating leftover ice cream cake in a cereal bowl, watching as the cream melts down into a puddle of swirls and crunches. mama sits on the couch attentively watching a pirated pakistani drama on her ipad mini. she's smiling with such gentle conviction at the professions of love emanating from the screen in urdu, soft sweet piano soundtracks playing over fawad khan's voice. she does this often. sometimes i wonder if that is something she once wanted for her life, many moons ago, before her emotionally abusive husband, before her five children, before a life rooted in mundane routine. but she turns to me and says. meri jaan. this is what i want for you. a love that makes you this happy, a love that will make you believe in love, a love that will care for you so much you won't know what to do with it.

and i feel little fissures bloom in my heart, because what she doesn't know is that i already have a love like that. a love that warms me from the inside out, a love that takes care of me in ways that no one else does. my love has given my mama gifts, laughed and talked politics with my stubborn baba. my love has treated my younger siblings to chocolates, has held my hand under the blanket during movie nights with my oblivious family.

but my love is a woman. and this is not something accounted for in mama's dramas. and so my silence persists.

deen

i cannot begin to fathom how my muslimness informs every part of me, and how every part of me informs my muslimness. breaking cycles is an easy phrase but it is anything but an easy process. building a trust that was never there is even more difficult. it happens slowly, in places you don't expect. i am sitting in the minivan with my brother, a little brown boy who is ten years my junior, and he asks me why we refer to god as a he if gender is a construct anyway. i am praying in a mixed-gender congregation next to my partner, and she radiates noor like no one i have ever seen. i am waiting in a doctor's office and a somali woman smiles at me with the happiest salaam on her lips. i am standing in front of the mirror on a monday morning and for the first time in eight years i cannot bring myself to wear my hijab in this predominantly white world i am stuck in. but for the first time in eight years i don't allow the hijab to dictate my muslimness. i don't let my queerness get in the way of it, i don't let the leaving define it. because finally finally finally i trust God. and They said: be. and it was.

AYEH BANDEH-AHMADI

Arab Sheik

Ayeh wakes up to the sound of birds singing outside the balcony of her Caltech dorm room. She has an assignment to turn in and some checks to deposit into the Student Union's account at Bank of America on Lake Avenue. It's a gorgeous Friday in Pasadena. Fridays mean no class and lots of time to enjoy the Southern California sunshine.

She gets dressed in jeans and a heather gray tank top from Forever 21 topped with a turquoise blue cardigan from Express. She grabs her shiny cream-colored Dollhouse-brand sunglasses and matches her breezy, pink-and-cream headscarf to a pair of pink flip-flops with big faux flowers that were a birthday gift from Tory, her freshman roommate from West Virginia.

Outside, the sweat builds instantly in the heat, even under the Spanish-style stucco arches of the breezeway connecting the dorms to the Olive Walk. She removes the cardigan gingerly, carefully tying it around her waist, the zephyr generated by her pace gently tickling her bare arms.

Three turtles sun themselves on the rocks next to Throop Pond. Along the landscaped paths, students and professors chat as they stroll. Suddenly, a man lurches in the distance, his gaze fixed on Ayeh, his mouth stretched into a grin, his body wiggling with laughter. He walks amongst others, alone, down the paved path that points towards her. Like her own family, he looks Iranian. He seems old enough to be a professor. He raises his hand to cover the corner of his gaping jaw, gesturing how out-of-place Ayeh looks. From behind her sunglasses, Ayeh tries to narrate the story unfurling in his mind.

Are they wearing tank tops with hijab to be outrageous, now? Does she think it's chic? Is it possible this girl is truly that naïve about how a headscarf is supposed to hide your body not show it? Ayeh's bare skin prickles with exposure as he uncovers his still-gaping mouth. She focuses on keeping her facial muscles relaxed and maintaining her pace as blood thumps through her chest.

She strains to remember the list of six Iranians on campus a grad-student friend recounted to her family last year with pride in the growing small community. All she can recall is that most taught or studied electrical engineering on the other side of campus. She had seen one of them drink at parties and make a pass at Ayeh's gorgeous half-Hispanic friend, so he wasn't very religious and probably wouldn't give Ayeh a hard time, but then you never knew. Sometimes those who broke certain rules were the quickest to pounce on others for breaking slightly different ones, as if doing so would fortify their own membership in the club. Only a couple of the Iranians on the family friend's list knew Ayeh's parents directly. Behind her sunglasses, she has plausible deniability that she sees the professor, that she is Ayeh, that this episode is actually happening.

As the professor nears, his gaze lifts like a breeze from her shoulders. It glosses past Ayeh's eyes to the horizon where it remains consumed in thought, evidently less interested in questioning the source of his amusement directly than mulling the delicious story he now owns.

The birds return to singing. The other students and staff go on with their beautiful Fridays. No one has noticed the Iranian professor laughing. Their eyes don't linger on Ayeh or admit anything out of the ordinary lunchtime routine. Ensconced in this safety, Ayeh considers the professor's rudeness, then considers that he does not know how to interpret the situation any other way. Before sending Ayeh off to college, her Dad had pointed out that when you break the rules of your own religion, even people from other religions respect you less. Had she really forgotten that there were other Iranians on campus? Had she really expected she could avoid bumping into them as she strolled through greater Tehrangeles? Was it that important to know what it felt like to wear a tank top? Or, had she actually thought she didn't care?

There was a time, when Ayeh lived at home and the prospects of getting out of the house with exposed arms were nil, when she would have laughed along with the ridiculousness of a girl wearing a hijab and a tank top. As she continues across the grass in a more secluded part of campus, she thinks about how easy it had seemed to break Muslim women into groups who did and did not wear headscarves. From this distinction seemed to follow the women who felt others should and should not wear headscarves, who were more faithful or less faithful, and who would scold you if the skin above your jeans showed when you bent over or pity your effort to wear the headscarf and western clothes you'd grown up with. There were those times that she would have loaded on the joke herself, taking a measure of joy in belonging to a group, in being well-versed in its rules, in what contradicting those rules looked like.

She imagines the Iranian professors in an electrical engineering lab, relishing the puzzle of her identity, trying to deduce it through the process of elimination. Would the only other headscarf-wearing woman at Caltech mistakenly become the face of this story? But there is nothing to do. If she tracks down the professor, the story will only gain more currency, becoming even more egregious and retellable. As it stands, a committed sleuth could deduce her identity with high likelihood but not with total certainty. The cost of embarrassing the wrong girl would be sufficiently high enough that any storyteller in the community would have to acknowledge he wasn't sure who the girl in the tank top and headscarf was, lest he risk offending the wrong family. Thus, in any retelling, the uncertainty around the girl in the headscarf and tank top would increase until no one could pin this episode down on anyone for sure.

Ayeh considers putting her cardigan back on. Out of paralysis, defiance, or the heat, it's hard for her to know how much of which, she presses on past the edge of campus, up California Boulevard toward the Starbucks at the corner of Lake Avenue.

Iced mocha in hand and sunglasses on, Ayeh strolls by the tiny shops lining the Avenue: Express, Ann Taylor, the upscale Macy's where the ladies who lunch in San Marino go shopping, and Crocodile Café, where the most delicious wasabi ahi tuna sandwiches come from.

"You're not Muslim, are you?" a voice asks from the mostly female crowd of shoppers walking up and down the gold-flecked sidewalk. The sandy-blonde middle-aged woman gesturing at Ayeh is wearing khaki shorts and a worn pastel tee revealing her sunburned décolletage. A shorter woman, with pudgy cheeks and mouse-brown hair, wearing denim shorts and a white tank top, accompanies her.

"Yes?" Ayeh responds. She removes her sunglasses and studies both the women, waiting to see how she can help them.

"You're naked! I know how you're supposed to cover up. I've been over there. I've been to Saudi. You're just wearing that headscarf for show! Look at you!"

Ayeh can't believe her ears. She expects this kind of admonishment from her mother but not from someone here, like this. What right does a woman in shorts have to tell her to cover up? Her heart races. And yet, she considers if the woman might be right. If her responsibility for dressing with respect to Southern Californian norms means picking one of those sets of norms and sticking with it. She trembles with uncertainty about how to respond.

"I almost married a sheik while I was there." The woman continues as her friend looks on. "They all loved me there. They just love blondes!"

The woman and her friend look overweight and unpretty. Ayeh grasps for something, a reference point, a story, some sort of wisdom about Saudi Arabia to put a stop to this nonsense. But she has never traveled overseas. She looks down, the pink flip-flops a reminder of the story her roommate Tory told about her family vacation to Cairo, how many camels an Egyptian man casually offered in exchange for marriage to each American woman who walked past him on the street. The more stereotypically beautiful young women received the highest offers but every woman, even Tory's nine-year-old sister and her long-ago married mom, received a bid. Ayeh found the story shocking when she first heard it. Up until then, she had assumed any talk of Arabs trading camels for women had been a joke about how backwards old times were. Now, with this woman standing in front of her, she does not know where to begin.

"They have so much money, you wouldn't believe it," the woman says. "It's because of you I'm not married to one now! They all want someone who wears a veil they can bring home to mom. And you're all frauds! You think that you can wear a veil and break all the rules."

Sensing Ayeh's disbelief, the woman adds, "I was going to put on the veil and do everything by the rules once I got married. When you marry a sheik you have to follow the rules. But I'm going to go back and I will marry a sheik!"

Ayeh's chest pounds. She can't imagine someone wanting to subject themselves to all the judgment. She struggles for the words to explain how wrong the woman has it. She remembers the granddaughter of a family friend who refused a lavish marriage proposal from a Saudi prince when it eventually became clear she would have to live a double life and accompany the prince in his. It had been a shock to learn that members of the royalty did not adhere to their own rules. For the family friend, there had been too much royal debauchery in private and too much forced propriety she would have to accept in public. Ayeh wonders whether that is the kind of life this woman sought. What good was money if you could only do with it what the prince or sheik said?

"I'm not Saudi and I've never been to Saudi, and I don't want to marry a sheik."

"It doesn't matter. You're still a fraud!" The woman grabs at the cleavage spilling above her neckline, cupping it, raising her voice. "You're like this! I can see all of this!" The friend watches calmly.

Ayeh considers if she really is a fraud. Why else would her outfit draw these reactions from individuals just going about their days only moments before? She considers suggesting that the woman is showing at least as much skin as Ayeh is. Each time a sensible argument comes to mind, a sickening feeling in the pit of her stomach tells her the woman won't take it well. Maybe, she thinks to herself, she miscalculated with her outfit, with her false confidence in the idea that teenagers are allowed to experiment, or with who she is supposed to be with whom. Maybe the rules really are different for her.

"You're like this!" the woman interrupts, her face full of rage, hands grabbing at her own cleavage.

While Ayeh searches for the right words, the woman reaches into her coral tee with both hands and grasps her left breast. An aureola appears. Then Ayeh sees a nipple.

Hearing the shouting, passersby have begun to stop and watch from a distance. Ayeh wonders if someone will step in to help. She wonders if she deserves help or if the situation reads as an encounter between two tawdry characters not worth getting involved with. She wonders if she looks cheap and desperate to all these strangers. If she looks like she is trying too hard. The passersby keep their distance.

"You're like this!" The woman shrieks, jiggling her visible breast with both hands to emphasize the point.

"You're the one who's naked." The words come easily.

The statement registers first in the woman's eyes and then in her posture. The woman's hands press the bare breast back into the coral top.

Ayeh doesn't wait for more questions. She walks away, maintaining her gait for almost two blocks, then glances around to see if anyone is staring at her. The world goes on about its day. Noticing this, she slips her cardigan back on.

She continues, still trembling, toward Bank of America.

MARIAM BAZEED

pure, again

if you want to be pure again, when you are ten, and there is blood that some-
times runs down your thighs because your mom said that now you are a woman,
there are things you need to do in a specific order and with special care because
the realm of care and order is where girls go when they become women.

if you want to be pure again, when you are ten, and the blood has stopped run-
ning after a few days and you have checked and checked to make sure that there
are no tell-tale droplets after the third or fourth or fifth day depending on what
your body has decided to do that month, because a drop in this case you have
been led to understand is enough to poison a bucket a bathtub a lake the nile
the ocean the whole city of cairo and its governorates egypt the country the
middle east as in the whole region israel included africa the continent the polar
ice caps all of it somehow unclean.

if you want to be pure again, when you are ten, you will make sure to wash
your hands thoroughly and in the winter this washing will be enough to make
them raw and cracked and hurting. your mother the gynecologist the sur-
geon the woman who introduced you to umm kulthoum to art to literature
to marron glace has told you that if you are not careful and even a little bit
ends up in your eye you may go blind because even though some small part of
her knows better that is what she was told and that is what her piano-playing
french-speaking mother was told and that is what her mother before her was
told and her mother before her unto an eternity of history fading into the faint
echoes of the cracked feet of all of your distant mothers and all the lies that were
supposed to save them. if blinding to your eyes what could it do to your hearing
to your taste buds to your speech to your hairline to your ability to feel the sand-
paper of your skin puckering with new hair you think to yourself as you become
paralyzed with the image of you struck deaf dumb blind hairless harelipped
your bones hollow and your mouth empty of its teeth.

if you want to be pure again, when you are ten, you will get into the shower be-
cause you have been told only running water can purify only running water can

scrub filth away only running water can drown your shame only running water can sluice away from you what standing water would only bathe and corrupt you in. if you want to be pure again you will focus your attention on each body part and you will say the shehadah, an incantation to purity. but you can't say it out loud because you are in the bathroom and that is not where the name of allah should be spoken and so you will repeat it only in your head but because you are not pure and you are ten your mind will wander to cartoons and to classmates and to questions like whether the red that you see is the same red that other people see and you will think about space and time and dolls and g i joes and ponies and what you did and didn't do but should've done last summer. and then you will forget to continue saying the shehadah as you move your sight your attention your intention from hand to arm to elbow to shoulder to chest to stomach to unmentionable and then you will remember yourself and start over.

you will repeat the shehadah and concentrate this time until it matches the rhythm of your breathing the rhythm of your heart the ticking of your body clock ash-hado anna la ilaaha illa allah wa ash-hado anna mohammadan rasul ullah ash-hado anna la ilaaha illa allah wa ash-hado anna mohammadan rasul ullah ash-hado anna la ilaaha illa allah wa ash-hado anna mohammadan rasul ullah and with the incantation you will purify your hand which can now touch the qur'an again your arm which you can now extend in prayer again your elbow which your father can now touch without ruining his wudu' again your shoulder which you no longer have to slump your chest which expands with cleaner air your stomach which will take a break from cramping your unmentionable which you will not mention your legs which can bend your forehead to the ground as you show your devotion to the lord your god who made you an incomplete woman naqisat 'aql wa deen your feet which can walk back into islam after their banishment, the same two shehadas that bring infidels into your faith bringing bloody women into a temporary purity, until the next time you feel the trickling.

if you want to be pure again when you are ten, you will think later in the day, did i do my elbow. did i forget to do my elbow. did i do my elbow. is my elbow pure. is it pure. what about my elbow. did i do my elbow.

MANDY BRAUER

Memories of Palestine During the First *Intifada*

It has been years since I lived in Gaza, and yet, I've never really written about it. It was intense, demanding, heart-wrenching, and very special. As Dickens said, "It was the best of times; it was the worst of times." In Gaza, I saw the best and the worst of humanity on a daily basis.

I arrived in the Gaza Strip in December 1989, having just closed a successful psychotherapy practice in California. My husband had gone ahead of me to get settled in his job as a Refugee Affairs Officer for UNRWA (the United Nations Relief and Works Agency) and to find a flat, so he greeted me at the Tel Aviv airport. The airport was more or less like any other but with a larger military presence. Mainly, they were interested in the fact that I had brought our three housecats: two alley cats and one chubby Siamese.

Entering Gaza was not difficult in a UN car. The Israeli guards looked tired and bored, glad to get rid of us as we drove through the silent border crossing. Immediately upon entering Gaza, the road changed from one very much like any in the developed world to a sandy, bumpy stretch full of potholes and various barbed wire and concrete-filled barrels used as temporary and permanent barriers. Moving through the streets was eerie—many buildings had been partially or completely destroyed, and the closed shops looked like a series of garage doors painted with graffiti in various colors. Later I learned that wall-writing was a basic means of communication for the Palestinians because there was no way it could be censored. Upon first seeing it, I was reminded of an open-air calligraphy exhibition.

The date was just a few days before Western Christmas. Although this was not a significant date among the local population, the vast majority of whom were Muslims, the local Christians, like most Palestinian and Middle Eastern Christians, followed the Eastern calendar and celebrated their holiday a week later; for the ex-pat UNRWA and other international staff, however, this was a major event. So much so I felt as if I'd stepped off the planet!

Festivities were to be held at the UN Beach Club, a run-down blue and white building on the Mediterranean Sea. Once it had probably been quite nice, but when I saw it first, it resembled something out of a Graham Greene novel: in need of paint inside and out, and high ceilings with dusty fans and bamboo screens serving as room dividers. An enormous tree had been flown in from Norway for the occasion, along with cases of beer from various Scandinavian countries to "whet the whistles with a touch of home," as it was explained to me by a red-faced Swede. From the U.K. came chestnuts for the turkey stuffing and from someplace else, mistletoe had been obtained and was drooping from doorways.

Here I was, in a veritable war zone, and the tables were covered with pristine white linen tablecloths, someone had found a candelabra, and as I looked around, I almost expected to see Yule logs and Santa or a chorus of angels emerge at any moment.

My first encounter with another UN worker was a sandy-haired Canadian who greeted me with the words, "Your God-damned country has just invaded Panama!"

What? I was in Gaza, Palestine, where my country had been colluding with and abetting a nation intent on obliterating another, and now I was supposed to switch my thinking to a continent away and picture an invasion? I had been in Panama several years previously and recalled seeing a storefront blown out across the street from where I was walking. I could just imagine American soldiers in those same streets, and I kept seeing Panama, like Gaza, mired in war.

Later that evening, I was seated next to the wife of a high-up UN employee who was visiting Gaza for the festivities. She was a distinguished-looking, late middle-aged, tall woman with coiffed silver-colored hair and piercing blue eyes. As I smiled and wished her happy holidays she smirked, leaned close to me, and whispered conspiratorially, "I know who you are! You're Norgunn." Upon inquiry I was told that Norgunn was from Norse mythology several centuries ago and that she had "beautiful hair." My dinner companion continued. "No matter what I did, all our lives you were father's favorite. I could do nothing to please him, not a thing, but you, oh you," and she cackled, "you had to do nothing and he adored you!" After taking a sip from a barely-touched wine glass, she hissed, "You are dangerous. Oh yes, I know you! You can't fool your sister anymore!"

That discussion, being caught by strangers under the mistletoe and seeing people laugh too much and drink too much, was my first Christmas Eve in Gaza. I was beginning to feel that rather than being in Palestine, I had wandered into a theatre of the absurd!

The following weeks and months brought more of the sense of unreality, and yet, also more of an understanding of what the Palestinians had to cope with on an almost daily basis. Sometimes I found the goings on almost humorous but that was probably because I was an outsider and, as such, I was not "stuck" in Gaza for the foreseeable future but only for as long as I chose.

I awoke one morning and looked outside our rented villa to a large, sandy area beside where we were living and saw a herd of camels accompanied by children and two women in black, Bedouins from their dress. I threw on clothes and dashed outside toward a baby camel that was lying near our house. How adorable baby camels are with their soft fur and long eyelashes! And how fast camels can travel! Before I reached that baby, from a blur almost out of sight, the mother rushed over to protect her child!

Another morning I was having a cup of coffee on our balcony and a patrol of Israeli soldiers could be seen in the distance, the blue Mediterranean glistening behind them. They were running and stopping, turning and darting down deserted, sandy roads, going first in one direction and then another. They were in full combat gear with their faces covered by see-through masks. But there was no one around! Were they practicing the pursuit of phantoms? When they approached the house I was in, a few pointed their guns upward toward the balcony so I hurried back inside.

Impressions of Gaza run together, mingling good times with sad, clear acts of bravery and heroism along with cowardice and criminality. Overall, when I think of Gaza, I see sand, sand everywhere and poverty next to the most beautiful stretches of the Mediterranean imaginable. Children, searching for childhood every time there was a lull in the fighting, would be flying home-made kites of all sizes, wading barefoot in the gigantic puddles that would overflow the potholes in the streets, making the roads impassable for days and sometimes longer if the rains continued. Yet, they played, trying to steal a moment for normal childhood out of an otherwise extremely difficult situation. In one spot near the sea, children had found an abandoned shell of a car and, for months, it was one of their favorite playthings. It became a jungle gym, a hideout, a fort, and assumed all sorts of play functions. We would have been concerned that parts of it were sharp and parts of it had been burned so it was dirty and rusty, but for the children it was something wonderful and allowed their fantasies to be played out. Whenever I walked by this scene, I saw children playing in and around it. That old hulk of a car was the closest thing the children had to a playground in those times.

Sights, sounds, and smells fill my thoughts as I remember living in Palestine. One of the smells that is most memorable to me is of the superb cooking! The hospitality and graciousness of the Palestinians are famous, and their reputation is well deserved. Innumerable times, my husband and I were treated to the most delicious meals imaginable. A few years later, when my husband and I were living in the former Soviet Union and there was very little food and no way to cook it, we used to lie in bed, since it was the warmest place, and imagine we would be going to dinner at friends' homes in Gaza. We would even try to imagine what delicious treats were in store for us that evening.

As I think back now, I am almost sure that families sacrificed to feed us such wonderful meals, but at the time, we basked in their hospitality without the full realization of the family foods we were consuming. That kind of kindness was ubiquitous. People literally risked their lives during "lock-down curfews" to make sure we had enough food, especially if they had something fresh or considered a delicacy. Once, during a major lockdown, neighbors risked their lives by going out of their home when Israeli soldiers were in the neighborhood to bring us special sweets someone had brought from the West Bank! That was the kind of warmth we consistently experienced while living in Palestine and experienced later when we returned to visit.

Water was a real problem in both the West Bank and Gaza. It does not help a population, like the Palestinians, when another population, like the Israelis, wants all of the water, no matter where it is! In the West Bank, at the time of the first *intifada*, the Israelis were drilling wells deeper than the Palestinian wells and thus drying out Palestinian agricultural land.

At the time we were living in Gaza, we were told that all the sweet water went to the then-expanding settlements and to the Negev and Beersheba areas for the exclusive use of Israelis. We also were informed by international organizations that so much water was being diverted from the underground aquifers leading to Gaza that those ancient aquifers were filling up with sea water. The rate of kidney disease in Gaza was already very high because of such salinity.

As an example of how bad the water was, when a pot of tap water boiled over, the pot was white around the places where the water had spilled. The tap water was that brackish! People used lots of sugar in their tea, partly to kill the salty taste. Also, they would make a tea from sage which was delicious and camouflaged the salty residue.

Religion was ever-present and very important in Palestine. People would talk about what *The Quran* would say about almost anything and Islamic and Christian principles prevailed, especially as they concerned helping one another. It was practically mandatory to visit the sick and those in mourning. It was incumbent to help those in need, whatever the need and with whatever resources one had, however meager. I was presented in Gaza with an Islam that was kind, caring, and responsive to ordinary as well as extraordinary needs within the community, an Islam that stated the major *jihad* was fighting one's own internal demons above all else.

The other *jihad* was to fight for the rights guaranteed under Islam and Christianity and by such august bodies as the UN and as codified in the various conventions such as the UN Convention on Human Rights and the UN Convention on the Rights of the Child, as well as, of course, the Geneva Convention. There are many other codifications of human rights of which the Palestinians are acutely aware and which they do not have as a direct result of the occupation. One man, on a more recent trip to Palestine told me, "All we have now is Allah. No one else seems to care about our plight!"

And always there was the fighting, one side giving high-pitched whistles to know when and where to assemble to throw rocks, the other side responding with bullets and blasts. It sounded like being in an arcade except that sometimes the sounds would last, sometimes they were closer and sometimes further away. There were times we would be sitting with friends drinking tea and then the shooting would start. We would try to guess which area was "blowing up" and would hope that no one we knew would get killed. Often, if things were "bad," meaning there were a lot of dead and injured, my husband would receive a call and would have to dash off while I continued to drink tea and feel the unreality of the situation. I mean, how could I just sit there when people were getting killed? But what else could I do?

Stories abound about that time in Gaza. The toddler playing in the street in front of her home under the watchful eye of her mother and yet still run over by an Israeli jeep, crushing both of her little legs, the infant in his mother's arms on the balcony whose eye was shot out simply because the soldiers couldn't find her teenage brother at home are just two that have stayed with me. I can't help but wonder what has happened to those and so many other children whose lives were irrevocably changed in a moment in time that should have gone another way.

Once, when there was a major curfew and the streets were deserted, Israeli soldiers beat a donkey tethered outside its owner's home so badly that it had to be put down. People said that because of the curfew, the soldiers were angry they couldn't find anyone to beat up so they had to attack something. That something was an innocent donkey.

But killing was everywhere and happening all the time. People of all ages were killed and injured, many, many of them innocent children. Funerals happened on a continual basis and seemed to be a good time for the Israeli soldiers to kill young mourners actually, to kill anyone. Although forbidden by the Israeli authorities to assemble, social and religious dictates required family members and the community to attend a wake house to grieve with the family. Jeeps would circle the house where mourners were gathering and would open fire whenever they wanted. It was expected. The vast, vast majority of time there was no provocation from the mourners: they were simply and truly mourning.

There is so much more to say about life in Gaza but I shall end my reminiscences with part of a poem, *Funeral in Gaza*, written when I was living there:

> *Death, death, death everywhere in Gaza as brackish tears*
> *fall into polluted water; a nation is mourning as the young*
> *join together in daring danger, sometimes only spraying*
> *black slogans on clay walls before being gunned down by*
> *smiling soldier-sociopaths wearing litanies of historical*
> *horrors around their necks like medals of honor, those scars*
> *of sacred myth more than skin deep and proudly passed on*
> *as if sadness worn inside is a gift of love, not painful pathology.*

༄

> *while another legend is born of injustice, cruelty, obvious wrong,*
> *a new generation hurtled into hatred, scarred beyond healing,*
> *destined to look for an enemy on whom to carve redemption,*
> *remembering only death, death, and more death.*

HAYAN CHARARA

Bees, Honeycombs, Honey

Bees, thousands, and thousands,
surviving in a hive
under the soffit; bees,
honeycombs, and honey,
and dampness, and old wood
sticky in the sunlight;

and the beekeeper's hand,
carefully, and slowly,
vacuuming, and taking;
the bees tumbling, gently,
into the makeshift hive;
honeybees, and honeycombs,

and honey, glistening;
honey, the only food
that will not spoil; honey,
pulled from the pyramids,
still sticky, and sweet,
thousands of years later;

I may not believe, but
I want to; and the bees
before my eyes are now
disappearing; bees God
in the Qur'an inspired
to build homes in mountains

and trees; bees that built homes
in the trees near the grave
in Detroit; and the bees
in Jerusalem's graves;

bees in every city,
and in every age; bees,

honey, and honeycombs,
through disaster after
disaster; bees building,
and scouting, and dancing;
bees mating, protecting,
and attacking; the bees

are now disappearing,
and dying; and the bees
the beekeeper cannot
save are dying but still
guarding the empty hive,
butting their heads against

the children, who will grow
into men and women,
and build homes, now dipping
fingers into honey
darkening on the ground;
they are dying; the hive

is gone; the queen is gone;
thousands and thousands, gone;
but the bees will come back,
and the hive will come back;
if not here, then elsewhere;
and there will be more bees

making more honeycombs,
more honey, and more bees;
and one day all the bees
will be gone; gone, and gone;
honeycombs, and houses,
gone; and trees, gone; oak, elm,

birch, gone; all trees, flowers,
gone; and birds, leaves, branches,
cicadas, and crickets,
grasshoppers, ants, worms, gone;
and cities, and rivers,
big cities, small cities,

big rivers, small rivers,
gardens, and homes; and homes;
the bees will be gone, and
only their honey will
survive, and we will not
be around to taste it.

Being Muslim

O father bringing home crates
of apples, bushels of corn,
and skinned rabbits on ice.

O mother boiling lentils in a pot
while he watched fight after fight,
boxers pinned on the ropes

pummeling each other mercilessly.
And hung on the wall where we
ate breakfast an autographed photo

of Muhammad Ali. O father
who worshipped him and with
a clenched fist pretended to be:

Float like a butterfly, sting like a bee.
O you loved being Muslim then.
Even when you drank whiskey.

Even when you knocked down
my mother again and again.
O prayer. O god of sun.

God of moon. Of cows
and of thunder. Of women.
Of bees. Of ants and spiders,

poets and calamity.
God of the pen, of the fig,
of the elephant.

Ta' Ha', Ya Sin, Sad, Qaf.
God of my father, listen:
He prayed, he prayed, five times a day,

and he was mean.

What They Did

You died. And because your father
and mother were Muslims,
the next door neighbor, a hajji,
washed your corpse and prayed
over your body. When they
brought you to the mosque
on Joy Road and Greenfield
you were wrapped in green,
veiled so that only your face
showed. As was the custom
you hated, women sat to your left
and men to the right. A sheik,
knowing you were a teacher,
said that you were not a teacher,
but a school. Everyone cried,
even the father of a boy you taught
and fed once because the boy
was hungry and forgot his lunch,
the father cried although
he never met you. Forty times
the mourners read the *fatihah*
to help you out of the streets
into that place beyond prayer.
At the cemetery, they lifted
your casket in the wind and
chanted God is Great, the lid
blew open and silenced the crowd.
Dirt was poured over your eyes
and placed in each palm
while workers dug a grave
in the March earth. A woman
noticed your grave beside her

sister's and she was relieved
her sister would have company.
Even when you were in the ground,
your husband and daughter
would not believe, and your son stared
at the space in front of him,
under a widening spell.
For forty days people met secretly
to pray for your soul. And
the day the angels were to take
you away, everyone rejoiced,
in their own way. Your sisters
cried, your husband waited
for a tree to burst forth,
your school children sat quietly
after the morning bells, your
parents welcomed another daughter
at the airport, and after the first
gentle dream in weeks, your son
woke and sat down at his desk
to write you a poem.

LEILA CHATTI

Night Lament in Hergla

This is what the fearful do:
when a burning star torments them, they go to the sea.
—MAHMOUD DARWISH

There is no world in which I am not haunted,
no willing God to relinquish me.
My mother taught me death comes
wailing from the shadows, my father
all ghosts exist in smoke. I search
the sky for light long extinguished,
make wishes on their bright graves.
In the dark, I try every language you might
recognize, but nothing calls you back;
the words hang in the air, their own
brief phantoms. The ocean offers
no solace; I stand at its black edge
as it retreats, draws close, backs away again.
Like this, your memory wavers
in the threshold. How many nights
your name appeared on my lips
like an incantation, how many times
you've arrived in a dream, pale
as prayer at dawn—your absence
burns its hole through my waking.
I stalk the shores of your sleep,
which allow no entry. The moon
reveals nothing of heaven, a brined window.
You are gone, in this country and all others.

What Do Arabs Think of Ghosts?

I think the woman means Muslims—ghost
of a word mixed up with our bodies, as if they were
the same thing—but either way I have no answer.
I haven't asked around. There is too much
death—it swells our tongues. It chokes.
The soul is a bird flying; it doesn't rest long
and its language is different. There are three
nightjars preening under the evening's cloak,
by which I mean three souls. Are souls clean?
Are ghosts? If every sad death made
a phantom, my country would be thick with them,
we would breathe them like air, they would keep us living.
What do ghosts think of Arabs, I want to know—
our fires blooming like invasive blossoms, bombs
planted like bulbs awaiting the spring?
Death grows here. There are more every day.
Before she died, my grandmother could
only say her name. I don't know the names
of the dead accumulating like snowflakes, so many
the news talks about them as if they are one thing,
a mound of indistinguishable parts. Who
calls for them, who houses them in their mouths?
In skies blue as a door, the metal ghosts soar:
they have wings but are no bird, have no soul.
We know this better than anyone.

Muslim Christmas

It sat downstairs on the air hockey table,
its shedding needled branches, its copper wire arms.
With care, our mother draped its false twigs in silver
garlands, two for a dollar on the clearance rack,
and the ornaments—her mother's, long dead—
we cradled in our palms like baby Jesus might have
been held, our non-savior swathed in hay in the barn-crib, safe
and human. Before the two-foot tree,
we made our own, traced our hands on green construction paper,
cut out five-fingered fronds and taped them to the wall.
Our mother wept at its absurdity. But each December
he came for us, there were glittering gifts beneath
whatever false icon we had constructed, and I marveled at how
merciful this man-God could be, Santa Christ, Saint Jesus,
who had found our home and come before the altar
of the unbelieving, stood there in its wavering light,
and left for us chocolate, snow boots, everything we liked.

ZARA CHOWDHARY

Slow Violence

Every economically tumultuous period in history has been followed by a surge in nationalism. It happened in Germany after the humiliating Great War and the years following the Great Depression. Today we find ourselves struggling with rising right-wing nationalism across the globe again in the wake of 2008's recession.

In Gujarat, in the early 1980s, a thriving textile industry slowly halted to a grind as the power loom replaced traditional mills. This westernmost state of India was suddenly facing an unprecedented unemployment and economic crisis. To compound matters, Gujaratis had first-hand experience of war. To their northwest lay Pakistan, that most reviled reminder of the country's savage division across religious lines by the British. It also didn't help that a state once synonymous with Mohandas Karamchand Gandhi had, by the 1970s, slowly faded out of consequence from national politics.

A sense of failure had seeped into the consciousness of the average person on the street only a couple of decades after gaining their hard-won independence. In the years that followed, no matter where in India a Hindu-Muslim conflict started, Gujarat would be the first to burn. At one point in the 1980s, Morarji Desai, the prime minister of India, was caught off-guard in an interview and helplessly uttered: "Gujarat has gone mad." Because no matter who started the fight, between local divisive politics and a growing persecution complex in the average Gujarati, the fight always became about the Muslims.

Papa, or Zaheer as they lovingly named him, was Anwar and Nahid Chowdhary's first-born child. An absolute brat who arrived in the golden period of Gujarat—the 1950s. According to his sisters, in 1972 he emotionally black-mailed his parents into "investing" a huge portion of their savings to send for a master's degree to Irvine, California. He returned home four years later with an MBA and a disdain for "America's selfishness." The truth behind this patriotic story was revealed to us later when Phupu, annoyed at Dadi for always favoring the son, "spilled" his secret with something resembling glee.

"He didn't come back!" She smirked. "They threw him out!"

Turns out Papa had gotten himself deported for overstaying his visa by six months. When he appeared in front of the judge he was given an option: he could apologize, buy a ticket, and go home with no deportation stamp, or have the Department of Homeland Security sponsor his ticket and get stamped. Annoyed at the unyielding system (and perhaps more at his own stupidity), he refused to apologize. He took the free ticket.

His poor judgment effectively banned him from reentering the United States for the next ten years, the "prime years" of his life.

Papa never spoke of this and after seven o'clock in the evenings, when the drinking started, no one else dared utter it either. His version staunchly remained that he wouldn't even "spit on America," that he'd very much rather be home in Gujarat (a state which is ironically known for exporting most of its young men to the US). That my father was so delusional was natural. When he left India, his parents (a self-made senior government official and the daughter of a British-era magistrate), had all the comforts that being educated and upper-class in post-independence India could afford them. Chauffeurs to drive them to swim lessons and rummy parties, an English-medium education in private catholic schools and colleges, learning to jive and savor single malts in a secular, cosmopolitan bubble and even a mother who coiffed her hair each morning and obsessed over crystal bowls and freshly-bleached doilies.

Papa was hired at the very first job he applied to: manager in the state-owned Gujarat Electricity Board (GEB). The Secretary of the board, a high ranking IAS officer interviewed him, and couldn't believe that a foreign-educated MBA had chosen to come back to his underdeveloped home country and serve in the public sector.

His big American debacle soon forgotten, Papa settled into the world of being an "officer." He expected to continue living the life his parents had shown him, but the world as he knew it was slowly crumbling all around.

Young men, like him, but with half the education and a burning need for vengeance, were joining the government workforce, hoping to overturn thirty years of subjugation by the privileged upper caste and upper-class post-independence. And like every misinformed radical in history, they were turning their ire toward anyone they identified as "not their own."

My whiskey-chugging, MBA-from-the-US-toting, never-had-to-fight-for-a-thing-in-his-life Papa had no clue when he'd been marked for vendetta. The privileges he'd come back home for were his curse, and now added to it was a tiny, significant detail: He was a Muslim; exactly the "other" the Hindus of Gujarat had come to hate.

By the time I was born in 1986, Papa had been working for almost a decade in GEB. And the pattern of slow violence had congealed into our everyday lives: from micro-aggressions like being called a descendant of savage invaders like Ghazni or Afzal Khan or sly suggestions about why he didn't move to Pakistan and serve in their government to more direct harassment, each year Papa would receive a transfer order in the summer to a town or village where no one wanted to go. These places were called "punishment postings" because of the lack of potable water, or proper schools and roads. Sometimes there wouldn't even be a position there for him but one would be specially created just so he could be moved.

GEB was inherently political. Of the two major political parties in Gujarat, the Congress (the party that led our freedom movement) and the BJP, (a right-wing response to the Congress), the former held power for most of the late 1980s and early 1990s. Gauging the growing anti-Muslim resentment, Congress' national leaders consistently nominated right-leaning members to the state's government and public works, figures who were encouraging of the harassment and degradation of minorities.

In 1995 though, the BJP came into power on the rhetoric that the Congress, Gandhi's party, always would be pro-Muslim and therefore anti-Hindu. Given the Muslim community's low literacy, low employability, and systemic ghettoization over the years under the Congress' rule, that should have been a laughable campaign. But it worked. And with an openly anti-Muslim government now in place, people with pre-existing prejudices felt emboldened.

The humiliation that Papa went through at GEB became a daily routine. The peons would mock-*salaam* him, his subordinates would take over his cabin and ask him to wait in the hallway. At events he'd be introduced as the *saheb* whose only job was to speak good "inglees" or be the most "over-qualified" officer in the Board.

But nothing was a bigger joke to them than Papa's incorruptibility. He was so privileged, they said, he could afford to turn down a bribe. They weren't lying. Once, when we were traveling on the *Shatabdi* express to Bombay, the ticket-collector, after checking everyone's tickets randomly, chose Papa to check if he was carrying his ID. Talcum-powdered, immaculately-dressed Papa was hard to miss in a crowd of scruffy passengers. He was carrying his drivers' license which should have been enough, but the ticketcollector was looking to harass him and insisted he show the ID used to book the tickets, which was an employment card. The ticket-collector insisted he would either de-board us or fine us the full fare on each of our tickets plus the fine. We'd booked expensive last minute tickets because Papa had waited 'til his family travel funds came through, so the fine in this case was going to be over 4,000 rupees. It was all the money we had for our entire vacation. He then beckoned Papa to the area between the toilets and compartment door to discuss a "settlement." Five hundred rupees off the record and he'd leave us alone.

Papa came back to his seat fuming. He made Amma empty out her purse and his wallet, and together they counted the exact amount of the full fine, including all their change. Then with a proud smile on his face he turned and handed it to the shocked TC, who proceeded to shake his head in disbelief and write him an official receipt with Papa hovering over his shoulder making sure he filled in all the boxes. When we reached Bombay, his brother-in-law, a wealthy jeweler, shook his head in similar disbelief. "Why didn't you just pay the five hundred bucks, Zaheer? You can't live in this country like this!"

Papa chomped into his dinner grinning, "Arre, don't worry. I'll get it back. You'll see." And then raised his double-chin proudly to add a snide, "My money is hard-earned. It's not *haraam ka paisa*."

He returned to Ahmedabad and carefully hand wrote a five-page letter to the Western Railways Complaints and Redressal Wing detailing the incident in his perfectly articulate Queen's English, the kind that still tends to irritate most people in India and usually invites further scoffing.

A month later he received a check with the full amount refunded.

But being Papa whilst working in one of the most lucrative government departments wasn't easy. GEB produced and supplied power for a state of fifty million citizens, and very few at the time considered it an opportunity for public service. Papa was a constant thorn in their side, and he'd often find himself simply left out of meetings or decisions. Subordinates whom he had recruited were promoted ahead of him. Every year he would be up for a promotion, and each time he'd be superseded by someone his junior. Instead they'd transfer him to some remote place where he could rot away in a defunct role.

This pattern of daily harassment lasted twenty-two years. It became routine each summer, for our home to turn into a control room trying to avert a crisis. Papa and Dada would get on the phone, write letters and pleas, go out and meet old friends and contacts in the government with any influence to have the transfer rescinded. The scotch of his youth gave way to the cheapest bootlegged whiskey he could find, and on those days the drinking would be more intense, tempers would flare and when the order would be overruled my father would fall at his father's feet in gratitude and relief. This sentiment however, would last anywhere between a week to a month, basically until the next episode of workplace bigotry took place. In March of 2000, he was transferred for the last time to a town no one could find on a map. My grandfather, now seventy-seven, stepped up yet again to try and have the order revoked through the few bureaucrat friends who still remembered and respected him.

That night, we celebrated. Phupu baked a cake to bring in my parents' sixteenth wedding anniversary.

That night there was very little drinking.

That night, as we slept content in Jasmine apartments, my grandfather walked out onto the balcony, looked up at the sky, muttered a prayer, and slumped to the floor.

I'd only ever heard two voice decibels from Papa: loud bellowing yells or even louder booming laughter. I remember waking up the morning after Dada died, to the sound of Papa sobbing like a little child.

With his father's passing, an India he'd known and believed in died. The transfer order stayed as it was. Rajkot, where he was being asked to go, was still a dusty town with a severe water scarcity and very few good high schools. I was nearing tenth grade in a year's time. It was decided that Papa would leave us in our grandparents' home in Ahmedabad and go live by himself until they chose to let him come back home. Given his increasing mood swings, we were willing to take that choice.

But Papa couldn't take it anymore. He stopped going to work.

Every morning he would lay there on his bed in his soft, white kurta-pyjama, freshly bathed, watching the ceiling fan circle above him. On the creases of his fingers my father would struggle to pray the only two Arabic *aayats* he'd ever learned, thirty-two times each. As the words slipped and missed his lips, he'd hiss in frustration, bite back cuss words and keep going. He'd never learned to pray. He'd never needed to.

The new BJP-backed leadership of the board was pleased to finally have a real stick to beat him down with. "Take voluntary retirement and accept the measly pension. Or be fired for not showing up and have a long record of service ruined," they offered, smirking at this broken man.

In late 2000, forty-eight-year-old Papa *retired* from GEB. *Voluntarily*, his papers insisted. He had given them twenty-one years, practically half his life.

Two years later, on February 28th 2002, the killings began. But Papa had already been killed and burned and looted in invisible ways.

In 2006, at the age of fifty-three, Papa died of a cancer that chewed up his spine. He continued to insist Gujarat was his only home, even in those last incoherent days. What we never understood was why he never quit earlier. Neither the men who mocked him, nor those in power perpetuating hate, or even Papa realized what those twenty years of GEB had done to our family. When you're eight and twelve and fifteen and nineteen and you see your home and family destroyed by a system, the names and faces of the people in it blur into one entity. To me, the system became represented by these men who poked fun of, harassed, and broke the spirit of the foolish but principled man who didn't mince words and wouldn't bow down. These men didn't just take away a job, they turned his life into a twenty-year long purgatory, at the end of which he emerged alcoholic, bitter, and yet strangely still incorruptible till the day he died.

And the thing about seeds of slow violence sown in young minds is that they never blossom. They crack and prick at the insides of those they've been fed to, leaving them willing to look the other way and yet unable to ever truly forgive.

MAHDI CHOWDHURY

A dream is a merciful thing

According to the dream interpreter, Ibn Sirin, it was Adam who witnessed the first visions on earth. Figures and shapes, soft and nocturnal, filled the mind of the sleeping prophet. As an act of mercy from God, the first dream took form: the face of Eve.

In 1980, the Syrian filmmaker, Mohammad Malas, would recount this story while entering the bounds of Shatila Refugee Camp.

Malas was in the planning and research stages of his seminal documentary—*Al-Manam* ('The Dream')—when he first visited the camps. In creating the film, he recorded the dreams of over four hundred Palestinian refugees in Lebanon. After its release, Malas published a diary account of these years. In remembering *Al-Manam*, Malas's diaries help us to better understand one of the most haunted works of Arab cinema.

Viewers of the film are cursed with a particular foreknowledge: They know that mere months after these interviews took place, under the light of Israeli flares, Kataeb genocidaires will enter these camps. One may occasionally forget this fact in the tenderness of the film's images. But the knowledge cannot be entirely banished or forgotten. One will remember. The tender life of one's heart will move and petrify at different intervals. There is no answer, but one still asks: what are we to make of these images? The visions and dreams of those thereafter exterminated?

Walter Benjamin, quoting Moritz Heimann, considered the following statement: a "man who dies at the age of thirty-five [is] at every point of his life a man who dies at the age of thirty-five." What this sentence revealed to the late philosopher-refugee was that fatal claims, which "make no sense [in] real life" or in life as it unfolds, soon "become indisputable [in] remembered life." (Sami Khatib notes this too is how we have come to narrate Benjamin's own life in light of his suicide.) Massacre looms "at every point" in the film. The pain of viewing Malas's documentary is somewhere in this tension: seeing dispossessed and delicate visions unfold in front of the camera, all in the consciousness, the prescience, of a genocidal horizon.

Yet, this was not the film Malas intended to make. He did not seek to collect accursed artifacts. He sought, instead, to capture life and beauty in onerous conditions. An unsettling idea now, but from 1980 to 1981, it was within the pale of the filmmaker's expectations to enter Shatila and Sabra in search of hopeful things. This aspirational commitment is captured in his diaries and evidenced in the very subject of his film: dreams.

One of the first dreams recorded in Malas's diary comes from a refugee who describes an account of his own death. Dreams of the afterlife are common in *Al-Manam*. He is reunited, in another place, with his late father. "No one told me you died," remarks the father. The son clarifies his dream-state to his father: "I am dead but alive."

The father exhorts him to choose life: "Your time will come later. May God make you happy." At the end of the interview, the son ruminates and struggles for a final word to give Malas.

"A dream is a merciful thing," he concludes.

ℳ

In dreams, Palestine is often cast in the rosy hues of memory. Visions of reunified family life, episodes from childhood, the boredom of an Arabic literature class, dipping pieces of bread into olive oil, and ancestral farmlands no longer fractured by military checkpoints. In the middle of Malas's film, the liberation radio croons: "Memories come and do not hurt."

This Palestinian dreamscape, however, is not a 'utopia' for two reasons: First, 'utopia' implies the nonexistence of what is in fact a real place. Utopia is not just eu-topos, 'a good place,' but also, ou-topos, 'no place,' in the deliberate pun of Thomas More. Palestine is a real space on earth. This must not be forgotten. The Palestinian struggle, as a colonial struggle, harkens to Frantz Fanon's assertion of the "first and foremost[ness] of the land." In dreams, there are endless markers of place, and a geography of the transfigured: "Al-Nameh," "Jaffa," "the village," "Haifa," "Majadleh street," "Acre," "we cry for the land," "the East," "Saffah," "home."

In his 1967 lecture, "Des espaces autres," Michel Foucault proposed an alternative to 'utopia,' the 'heterotopia.' The late French philosopher described heterotopias as real and existing spaces. But at the same time, they are 'heterogeneous' in experience. They are punctured and sacralized by spatial functions, memories, and the rites of time. Heterotopias are spaces 'haunted by [*fan-*

tasme]': a word often translated from French as 'fantasy.' But also semantically connected to a more spectral vocabulary: 'phantasm,' 'phantom,' 'fantasmatic.' This comes close to capturing the painfully real, spatial, and damaged dreamscapes of Palestine among the refugee-interviewees of *Al-Manam.*

Second, 'utopia' does not capture the Janus-faced nature of the film's testimonies. These are dreams and nightmares both. (*Traum* is the common root from which we derive both 'dream' and trauma.') In one, an Israeli bulldozer stalks a woman down a street. An aerial bombardment so violently shakes the foundations of the home in a dream that the dreamer awakes to find her radio has fallen and shattered in real life. Many relate nightmares of the Tel al-Zaatar massacre. One dreamt of seeing Shimon Peres among the killing fields. Many of the refugees in Sabra and Shatila had survived this atrocity in 1976 only to fall victim to one still looming. Walls, borders, and the carnival of occupation. What kind of 'utopia' would this be?

In *Al-Manam*, the dream haunts us with impossible visions, impossible times. Dreams, to borrow a phrase from Benjamin, represent the "open air of history." Many are political. Many are intimate. In a shoemaker's dream, Gamal Abdel Nasser points his finger toward Palestine and trumpets the call for its war of liberation. In a barber's dream the late Saudi monarch, Ibn Saud, arrives to meet the Palestinian leadership. In a young guerilla's dream, Shaikh Zayed of the United Arab Emirates is told of the young man's honorific heritage: "This man is Palestinian." A tired Abu Ammar (the *nom de guerre* of Yasser Arafat) finds refuge in the dreamer's home, lays beside him in bed. Dreams are ways of nurturing political optimism—herein, the bittersweet fantasias of Arab nationalism.

The most affective stories, the most merciful visions, are those about loved ones. These are the dreams that relay memory or the restoration of family life: generations brought onto a common stage, martyrs and missing sons, late mothers and fathers. Malas asks one of his interviewees to clarify a strange discussion between the dreamer and her displaced father. Where did this take place in the dream?

"In the afterworld, of course."

Three decades since its release, *Al-Manam* continues to entangle us in the webs of memory, dream, and trauma. Echoing the oneiric stories of Palestinian refugees, the radio plays an Umm Kulthum song: "Our loved ones have once grieved for us." There is a semblance between, on one hand, how we venerate *Al-Manam* and its dreamers, and on the other, they their loved ones.

"Do they remember us, or have they forgotten?" Umm Kulthum sings.

Originally published in *Popula* (2019).

ASLAN DEMIR

My Mother's Rugs

After tilting at windmills for two months like Don Quixote, I decided to spend my time on things that would help me digest my reality before it digested me.

More than two years before, when I learned that some prisoners were working in jobs like farming, drawing, knitting, wood carving, and many other fields for making money and spending time on something useful, I talked with the principal of the prison and donated my mother's loom on the condition that I alone would use it until I was gone. I joined the rug-knitting club. On Mondays, Tuesdays, and Wednesdays from nine to twelve, prisoners worked in the company of guards. Thus, I started working in a workroom. After two hours of lessons, I was allowed to free-work for one hour more. This is when I knitted my life, motif by motif node, into the rugs.

I knitted Satan and his fiends. I knitted a corrupt system. I knitted a corrupt society. I knitted corrupt politicians. I knitted corrupt judges. None of them will know that it's their own story. I knitted angels. I knitted Prisoner seveteen's empty cradle and a pair of unworn baby booties in her palm. I knitted Aisha and her twins sleeping on a thin mattress on the ground. I knitted Prisoner thirteen's (Azad) birth certificate. I knitted Prisoner 153 crying in prostration. I knitted her standing next to a dead man's body on a bed. Nobody will know that he was her husband. I knitted Prisoner twenty-seven's thin, sick body that could fit into my tears. Nobody will know that she was my friend. I knitted Prisoner X's body hung to the high window bars with her white scarf. I knitted her black-and-blue neck. Nobody will ever know what they did to her. I knitted a woman being raped in the prison. I knitted the woman handcuffed at the funerals. I knitted the woman giving birth, handcuffed to hospital beds. I knitted babies behind the bars. I knitted the Maden family next to a capsized boat. I knitted drowned bodies around a capsized boat. I knitted fearful eyes on Turkish shores. I knitted hopeful eyes on the boats. I knitted tearful eyes on European shores. I knitted boats heading to dreams. I knitted my teacup. I knitted my losses. I knitted my tears. I knitted my fears. I knitted my dreams. I knitted all I had. I knitted all I could reach. I knitted all I couldn't reach. I knitted all I missed. I knitted my daughter. Overall, I knitted a life in captivity. But nobody will ever know for what special art form they are or what they mean. Nobody but me. An art form that I learned from my mother.

My mother knitted rugs. She was an artist. She used to teach young girls the art of knitting and embroidery. When we were kids, she embroidered lovely trees, flowers, and nightingales. Even though she denied it, we knew the nightingale was not the only bird she knew how to embroider. My father had a beautiful voice. Years after my father was killed, she started knitting again. But this time, she started embroidering dark figures, wild animals, owls, and shrubs all looking formidable like the guards of this prison. Circles into circles, windows into windows, and doors into doors, all getting smaller and smaller until your hypnotized eyes led you into a puzzled dark nothingness. The ornamental one that hung on the wall of our sitting room had an emotionally whelming art despite its red. Although she said it should remind us of my brother Ceco staining her favorite rug with tomato paste, we knew it was blood. Besides, her favorite one was ornamenting her bedroom wall with the figure of an angel with a sunny smile and eyes full of light, so bright they could save any soul lost in the shadows. The angel was rising from a cemetery full of faceless stones, but both wings were chopped lying on his gravestone. One night, thinking we were asleep, I remember her saying, "How joyous you look, how ardently you are smiling against life. Because the 'You' on the wall does not know 'You' are dead yet." She had a huge collection of rugs. But she refused to sell them even when we couldn't pay the bills. Years later, not sure whether it was time or its inflicted pain that hit her harder, her eyes repented to the colors and went dark.

Everyone and everything goes eventually. Death is just an excuse. Missing my father so dearly, my mother welcomed her excuse wholeheartedly. Or, maybe cancer did.

After my mother, the weaving loom was taken to the garage and hung on the wall like the rugs they used to weave on it. Darkness wove over the sun. Snow wove over the earth. The earth wove its way around the sun. Days over days, seasons over seasons, and lives over lives were woven lustfully, cheerfully, artfully, but nothing over the weaving loom.

I drove in and out every day from the garage seeing the weaving loom hung on the wall, untouched. The decaying rusty nails on the loom began to look like deserted dogs barking at heaven. The scattered strings on it looked more anile than the river Euphrates detour. The wooden parts, completely covered in dust, looked more ancient than any bone left in the soil. So, in time, it became like a ghost of unappreciated art, like every prisoner in this cell, invisible to the world.

The art of handicraft rugs couldn't weave a way out against rapid development of textile because they were cheaper, like the judges of this corrupt system. Thus, people bought it, used it, but never respected it, never called it art. Never ascribed any meaning or never felt any emotion looking at it. Because art carries emotion, art requires devotion, art carries meaning, and art carries memories of its artist. Like my mother's rugs, and her tears. Yes, tears are the most sacred form of art, the most honest manifestation of emotions.

Art is imitation, is the reflection of truth, of reality. On a canvas with a talented painters mastery strokes, on a mouth reciting poems enchantingly, on a paper word by word shouting thoughts and confessions that ears are deaf to, on a rug from long and beautiful fingers of a damsel knit by knit carrying emotions and reality, like a life in the prison, all in an artistic form.

Art is rare, and rare is beautiful, like my mother's rugs.

RAMY EL-ETREBY

(Muslim) Americans in Service
—A Civil Drama (an excerpt)

CHARACTERS:

LAYLA—mother, midfifties, Muslim, Middle Eastern, engineer, immigrated from Egypt to the USA thirty years ago with her husband Muhammad, grateful for the happy and comfortable life they have in this country.

MUHAMMAD—father, late fifties, Muslim, Middle Eastern, business owner, immigrated from Egypt to the USA thirty years ago with his wife Layla, grateful for the happy and comfortable life they have in this country.

YASMINE—daughter, late twenties, Middle Eastern, American-born, public defender, spends a lot of time seeking justice and fighting for people's rights, married to Jamal and pregnant with their first baby.

YUSUF—son, midtwenties, Muslim, Middle Eastern, American-born, no defined career, a lost soul who is in constant search for a purpose.

JAMAL—son-in-law, early thirties, Muslim, African American, immigration lawyer, spends a lot of time seeking justice and fighting for people's rights, married to Yasmine. (offstage)

TIME:
Present day. The first day of Ramadan.

SETTING:
Muhammad and Layla's home in the suburbs of Los Angeles, California.

SCENE 1: Shortly before maghrib (sunset)

A recording of the first part of the Quran can be heard.

Layla is in the kitchen preparing the first Iftar of the month.

She is pulling out serving platters from the cabinets while going back and forth to the stove to monitor the four pots she has cooking on the burners.

Muhammad enters.

MUHAMMAD: It smells amazing, *habibti* (my love).

LAYLA: That is because you are hungry.

MUHAMMAD: I am, but everything you cook smells amazing.

LAYLA: *Inshallah* (God willing) it tastes good too. I cannot taste it to check the salt and the spices.

MUHAMMAD: Everything you make is perfect. Your hands are blessed.

LAYLA: Wow. *Shukran* (thank you). You should be in the kitchen with me more often while you are fasting.

MUHAMMAD: I do not know how you do it. My head is aching and about to explode.

LAYLA: Mine is too. Only during Ramadan do you appreciate what I do for you all.

MUHAMMAD: I appreciate you every day *ya qalbi* (my heart).

LAYLA: The first day is always the hardest. It will get easier.

MUHAMMAD: *Inshallah.* Where are our children? They should be here by now.

LAYLA: Everyone moves slowly during Ramadan.

MUHAMMAD: I hope so. It's almost *maghrib* (sunset).

Yasmine enters carrying a dessert.

YASMINE: *Assalamu Alaikum! Ramadan Mubarak!* (Peace be upon you! Blessed Ramadan!)

MUHAMMAD: *Waalaikum assalam!* (And upon you peace!)

LAYLA: *Ramadan Mubarak, habibti*

Yasmine kisses them both on the cheek.

YASMINE: I brought the *kanafeh* from the bakery you like.

MUHAMMAD: *Kanafeh!* Now it's really Ramadan! Thank you, habibti.

LAYLA: You look good. How are you feeling?

YASMINE: I feel good. I'm sad I'm not fasting though.

LAYLA: Sad? Not fasting is one of the best perks about being pregnant!

YASMINE: I know, but I love Ramadan and it feels like I'm missing out on the spiritual part this year.

MUHAMMAD: You're growing my grandchild inside you. What is more spiritual than that?

YASMINE: You're right. Thanks for saying that, Dad.

MUHAMMAD: You still have to make up all the days of fasting that you miss.

LAYLA: Yes. You're not off the hook.

YASMINE: Right.

LAYLA: Where's Jamal? Is he coming?

YASMINE: No, he has to work late tonight.

LAYLA: But he knows the family always eats together for the first Iftar during Ramadan.

YASMINE: Yes, he knows and he's really sorry. He has a really important meeting he has to attend. About Black Lives Matter.

LAYLA: He still does that? That is still happening?

YASMINE: Yes, Mom. Black lives still matter.

LAYLA: Yes, but do they have to matter more than the first Iftar of Ramadan with your family?

MUHAMMAD: It is ok, *habibti*. We love that he is so dedicated to his community.

YASMINE: We should all be that dedicated. They are our community too. Your grandchild will be Black.

Awkward silence.

LAYLA: Where's Yusuf? The sun is setting.

MUHAMMAD: He will be here soon. He told me he has something exciting to tell us.

YASMINE: Really? Like what?

MUHAMMAD: I have no idea. Maybe about a job.

LAYLA: *Inshallah !Ya rabb!*

YASMINE: Or maybe he finally came to his senses and decided to go to school?

LAYLA: Please God, let it be something that will move him forward in life.

MUHAMMAD: Whatever it is, I want you two to try to be supportive. He has been stuck for a long time. If he found something that he is excited about, we must encourage him. We need to cheer him on.

LAYLA: It depends on what he tells us.

YASMINE: Yeah, remember when Yusuf wanted to be a professional breakdancer? What if it's something like that again? We're supposed to encourage him?

MUHAMMAD: Yes. I think we should have supported him more when he wanted to do that.

LAYLA: We should have let our son become a dancer?

MUHAMMAD: Remember how passionate he was about it? I haven't seen him have passion for anything since.

LAYLA: I will always encourage my son to be a professional with a college degree and a full-time job.

YASMINE: Let's just wait and see what he has to tell us.

Yusuf enters carrying a jug of apricot juice.

MUHAMMAD: Here he is!

YUSUF: *Ramadan Mubarak* everyone! Hi Mom. Hi Dad. Hey sis.

Yusuf kisses them all on the cheek.

LAYLA: *Ramadan Mubarak, habibi.* What took you so long?

MUHAMMAD: You made it just in time. With just a couple of minutes to spare.

YUSUF: Timing is everything. Per your request, Mom, I have apricot juice to break our fast with.

YASMINE: I'll get us some glasses.

YUSUF: No, relax sister. I'll get them. Aren't you carrying my little nibbling in there?

Yusuf goes to grab glasses.

Jamal isn't joining us?

YASMINE: He has a meeting.

MUHAMMAD: For Black Lives Matter.

YUSUF: Gotta love that guy. Always down to fight for his people.

YASMINE: That's one of the reasons why I love him.

YUSUF: I love him too, sis.

Yusuf pours juice into four glasses.

YASMINE: So Dad says you have something exciting to tell us.

YUSUF: Dad, I told you not to say anything.

MUHAMMAD: I didn't say anything. I don't know anything.

YUSUF: I was hoping to wait until after we eat.

YASMINE: We're eager to hear what it is so you might as well tell us now.

LAYLA: Yes, what is it? Did you get a job?

YASMINE: Did you decide to finally go to school?

YUSUF: Well, um, no. Or, sorta.

LAYLA: What?

YASMINE: What do you mean, sorta?

MUHAMMAD: Let him talk.

YUSUF: I decided to, um . . .

YASMINE: Spit it out, already!

YUSUF: I'm joining the L.A.P.D.

MUHAMMAD: The what?

LAYLA: The what??

YASMINE: The what?!

MUHAMMAD: The Los Angeles Police Department?

LAYLA: The police?!

YASMINE: Are you crazy?!

The athan (call to prayer) plays.

They look at each other.

Yusuf grabs a bowl of dates. He passes a date and a glass of apricot juice to each person.

They look at each other.

They all bite into their dates at the same time.

They look at each other.

They all drink from their glasses at the same time.

They look at each other.

They grab prayer rugs and lay them down.

They perform the maghrib prayer.

The prayer ends. They shake hands.

They look at each other.

SCENE 2: *Shortly after maghrib.*

The family sits at the dining table.

They are eating silently.

They look at each other.

LAYLA: So how does it taste?

YUSUF: It's absolutely delicious. Thanks, Mom.

MUHAMMAD: God really has blessed your hands.

YASMINE: Honestly, I can't taste a thing.

YUSUF: Pregnancy mess up your taste buds or something?

YASMINE: Or maybe I lost my fucking appetite.

LAYLA: Yasmine!

YUSUF: What's your problem, exactly? I finally found something I want
to do with my life. Isn't that what you wanted?

YASMINE: I never thought you would want to join the police! When did
that become a thing?

YUSUF: How many years have you been telling me to do something im-
portant with my life? To make a difference?

YASMINE: I told you to find something positive and meaningful. Something that contributes to society. The police don't do that. They enforce society's ills.

MUHAMMAD: Yasmine, the police are civil servants. They keep us safe and protected.

YASMINE: I'm sorry, Dad, but that is just . . . bullshit.

LAYLA: Yasmine! Watch your mouth!

YASMINE: The police are there to protect and serve us? That's a myth. They harass people. Mostly Black and brown people. Like us.

YUSUF: Come on, Yasmine. Not all police are like that.

YASMINE: Have you forgotten that I'm a public defender? I see this every day. My clients are all Black and brown people and they are the ones who get targeted and detained and arrested and incarcerated and deported and basically removed from society.

YUSUF: And I'm sure none of them commit crimes. They're all innocent.

YASMINE: My clients are regular people. They are not criminals. They are poked and prodded and provoked by the police and they get severely punished for the most minor infractions. My job is to make sure that their most basic human rights are protected because their rights are violated every day by the same people who you say are supposed to protect them.

YUSUF: That's great. I'm glad you do that work.

YASMINE: Are you? Because it sounds like you're ready to put on a badge and become someone who menaces those innocent people for a living, you asshole.

LAYLA: Yasmine!

MUHAMMAD: Yasmine. Be fair. Not everyone is innocent. There are dangerous people out there who commit real horrific crimes. We need the police to keep the rest of us safe from people like them.

YUSUF: Exactly. I'm signing up to keep innocent people protected from danger and to bring people to justice when they commit atrocities against each other. I'm trying to serve the people.

MUHAMMAD: We're proud of you, son.

LAYLA: We are??

YASMINE: You've got to be kidding me!

MUHAMMAD: We raised you children to be American and to be proud of that. We moved here to this country so we could have a better life with more opportunities for you. So you could choose to do whatever you want. *Alhamdullilah.* (Praise be to God)

YASMINE: I don't understand what you're saying, Dad. So all being an American means is having pride in your country? How blind is our pride supposed to be? Are we not allowed to be critical of the government and the way it wields its power over the people?

MUHAMMAD: You would rather us live back home in Egypt where you would not be allowed to do half the things you get to do here? You should not take your rights for granted.

YASMINE: I do not take any of my rights for granted! I know how precious my rights are! I fight for my clients' rights every day!

LAYLA: We're proud of you too, Yasmine. Please relax.

YASMINE: Don't tell me I'm not a proud American. I'm the one serving the people. I make sure that this government is held accountable for what it says and does to the people.

LAYLA: *Habibti.* It's not good for the baby for you to get this upset.

YASMINE: It's not good for the baby, this Black Muslim baby, to have its uncle be working for those who are monitoring Muslim communities and "countering violent extremism." It's not good for this Black Muslim baby to have its uncle working for those who are destroying families every day by putting Black and brown people in cages if not killing them directly.

YUSUF: You think I'm going to contribute to the surveillance of Muslims and the killing of Black and brown people?

YASMINE: Aren't you? By association?

MUHAMMAD: He can be an opportunity for change.

LAYLA: What do you mean, change?

MUHAMMAD: He can show his fellow police officers that Muslims can be good people too. That Muslims can be good Americans too.

YASMINE: This "good American" stuff is killing me! We have to prove we're good Americans by turning against our own people? What's next, Yusuf? After a couple of years, will you decide to become an ICE officer and detain Muslims from entering this country? How many brown people like us will you detain and deport in your lifetime you think? You, as a child of immigrants. What a good American. What a hypocrite.

YUSUF: I have no desire to detain or deport people. All I want is to keep American citizens safe.

YASMINE: How about those that are undocumented? Do they deserve your protection? Do they deserve to be safe too?

YUSUF: Like Dad said, I can be an opportunity for change. I can help change the culture of racial profiling and brutality from the inside.

Shouldn't there be diversity in law enforcement? Or should only white people be police officers? Is that what you want?

YASMINE: You think you'll change them before they change you? It's a whole institution. You know how many cops I've met who are people of color and have no compassion for the people they are handcuffing? Many come from the same neighborhoods they now stop and frisk people in. Their badge makes them so drunk with power that they think they're better than their own people now. They forgot that they are exactly the same.

YUSUF: I don't think I'm better than anybody else, ok. I'm just trying to do something meaningful with my life. I care about justice. I care about people. I'm sorry I'm not as smart as you, Yasmine. I'm sorry I never went to law school like you did and that I can't argue as well as you can. I'm sorry I'm not hard-working enough to become an engineer like you, Mom, or start my own business like you, Dad. I'm sorry I've been a slacker my whole life. I think joining the LAPD will be really good for me, you know. It will provide me with some discipline. For the first time ever. And a sense of duty. Whatever I do, I want it to matter. I want to serve the people. I really do. Yasmine, you have to believe that my heart is in the right place. I promise you and your Black Muslim baby that I will be one of the good ones. I will never do anything to hurt anyone.

YASMINE: I really want to believe that.

LAYLA: *Inshallah.*

MUHAMMAD: I think this is a good time to take a break for some *shay* (tea) and *kanafeh.*

LAYLA: *Yallah* (let's do it). I will go make the tea.

YUSUF: No, Mom, you relax. Let's you and I do it, Dad.

Yusuf and Muhammad go into the kitchen.

Muhammad gives Yusuf a hug and pats him on the back.

Yusuf grabs some plates.

Muhammad grabs the dessert and cuts it into little pieces.

Yusuf places a piece on each plate.

LAYLA: How do you think Jamal will respond to this?

YASMINE: I don't know, but I don't want to be there when he finds out.

LAYLA: I hope he can talk some sense into him.

YASMINE: Yes. I hope so too. *Inshallah.*

End of excerpt.

Abdel Halim Performs a Private Concert for My Mother

Once, in a stolen land that
wanted my name dead, I knew
nothing of drums and strings. Once,
I could not wake if Imam
did not bring the sun to my
cursed bed. If nothing else, I
listened carefully, heard Abdel
Wahab trick their colonial
asses. This is the rhythm of
unflinching, the sea as still
as night—we like it that way.
Here, I ask Mama again
what she needs but a radio
and she still says: batteries,
and well-pressed clothes for my child—
just so we look good when we
cry to Om Kalthoum. Once, in
a stolen land that wished my
tongue in the ocean, I could
not explain what it meant to
cry without tragedy. Now,
I hold Mama's hand as we
weep to his crooning. I raise
my hand; a request—سواح.
He smiles and asks me: for what?
We are here now, habibi.
Then for all time's sake, I plead,
for chorus of memory,
percussion as cool as dew.
And so me and Mama cry
with Abdel Halim, as we
did with Fairuz, and every

song that brought the breath back to
an empty chest. Once, I spent
a lifetime incapable
of drawing a map home, but
و الله
I have always known what it
sounds like.

At the Gates, Mikhail Makes Me a Feast of Rain and Dirt

For which I'm truly grateful.
I've spent a lifetime dreaming
    of cities wide enough to

                hold me. I have feared open
                    roads; the seduction of the
                unfathomable. All my

life I have prayed for a soil
    unburdened by time, say an
Eden of a nap. And yet,

                  I sit before him alone.
                  He asks me about my kin
                    and country. I say: I am

sorry if I ever spoke
    out of a mouth that was not
mine. I say "we" and hope that

                means something. I don't pretend
                  to know where "we" live. If there
                is a place for "us" I have

    known it only by name, but
never map. I have looked for
    "us" on the highway, only

                found sirens, restless screeching;
                  choir of dust, shriveled lotus
                by an empty bank. Maybe

"we" are all just in love with
    scorched temples, dead languages.
Every dry river has a

                  lake for a mother, and I
                am tired of the violence
                  of water; how it holds the

still land with its ego. Some
        where, there's history without
burden. There is an "us" I

                    don't have to wash of blood and
                            kerosene. Cut off my tongue
                    if I claim I know what it

        looks like, but hear me when I
say it does not smell like
        gated flowers, or stale fear

                    underneath a thick blanket.
                        I know I too am guilty
                    of this legacy. I have

praised the dirt I have spat on
        only when it grows what I
ask of it. I've dug a grave

                            for every nightingale who
                    sang too loud. And for that you
                            can call my mouth rotten, but

never rested. الحمد لله
        Insomnia's the only
vocab my city ever

                    gave me, and I speak it well,
                        let it overflow from my
                    open mouth unto the tired

        earth. I know "we" have all grown
weary from the taste of rust,
        how its brittle trauma makes

                    a home out of our teeth. But
                        find me a history that
                    has ever undone "us" and

I will go to bed tonight
          unfazed by the summer. He
says: it is foolish to fear

                                        the dark. I say: God gifts us
                              the night, and for that I am
                                        eternally grateful. There

were days when I wished myself
          small enough to die in the
flame of a lantern, but I

                              have settled for that music
                                        which shakes the stillness. I have
                              mocked martyrdom's allure, I

          am weak يا ربى I was
never near Bilal nor Omar.
          Forgive me my timid jaw,

                              my quiet hands. They only
                                        want to build.

TARFIA FAIZULLAH

Infinity Ghazal Beginning with Lice
and Never Ending with Lies

For Hasna Henna and the Rohingya

Lice? My aunt once drew a comb through my hair steady;
she wouldn't let what feeds on blood eat my inner tree.

Where now is the word for such intimacy? I know it still,
but all I see are jungles burnt of our rarest trees.

My point is: it takes a while to say, "I am a fire hazard," or,
"a household of rare birds" is another way to say tree.

I wrote one draft of this poem, then she died. Will I
forget her name, Hasna Henna? Let's smell a tree;

night-blooming jasmine, o-so-heavenly! A sapling
succeeds by flourishing from a tree's seed.

How else to perfume these needs we breathe? A sapling
of course = a small and soft tree (i.e. baby tree).

I grieve the rice she fed me off a palm leaf.
Only now can I fully marvel: how finely formed is a tree!

Someone I loved said to stop with the oceans in my poems—
well, oceans + oceans + oceans! We drown so many trees.

(Night blooming tree = baby tree = once and future tree.)
Lately, all I think about are trees.

Read this again to replace *tree* with *refugee*.
Tarfia = joy in the margins + one who lies to protect trees.

That One Time I Stayed Up All Night
Making Excuses to Talk to Danger

Maybe it was my old friend Fascination
who first let me know that Danger
was right across the hall, or maybe
it was the unrealized absence of pollen, or,
was it the nearness, Danger, of your hair's
blatant softness, just toweled.
Or, I wanted to stop thinking—and I wanted to ask,
Do you think God understands

                            attraction? Surely, right?

Or, I wanted you to notice my anger,
which you might not characterize as dangerous, per se,
but rather, fickle, a synonym
for "mercurial." Maybe that's typical. Yup,
there *is* a liquid sharpness in me I wouldn't unlid
except . . . damn, Danger,
there's this certain way you draw out epiphany . . .

You're messy, Danger,
baby, meaning untidy, confusing, monumental,
great in size, and also, of or serving
as a monument, which leads me to reconsider
the dimensions of sandwiches, as well as apartheid,
the aphid, and the scarab beetle.

                        Danger, can you feel
me tremble?
But I am saying nothing, dear

                       Danger, you don't already
know—you're used to being pursued
with rage, unwanted advice, riddles. That's not me,
respectfully—Joy is always waiting

to cyclone you with nothing more
than a matchbook,
a long gaze, a warm bowl.

YAHYA FREDERICKSON

What I Learn about Poetry In Syria

Homs

What I learn about poetry in Syria, I learn
in a mosque. As soon as Jumu'ah Prayer ends,

he's at my elbow, a student of mine from the university.
He wants to introduce me to the imam who just gave the sermon.

I can't say no. So he leads me through the crowd of lingering men
to the prayer niche up front. "The imam is my friend," he says,

and opens a secret door. There, in a long room lined with chairs
sits the imam, surrounded by his retinue waiting for extra inspiration.

Space is made for me next to him on the highest couch, while
my student kneels at my feet, ready to translate in case my Arabic fails.

I repeat my oft-repeated sentences of self-introduction:
I am an American professor, I teach English at the university,

I am an exchange professor teaching here for only one semester,
I embraced Islam fifteen years ago in Yemen, I like Syria generally,

though of course there are good people as well as bad people everywhere,
and I write poetry. The imam's eyes widen: "Ah, you are a poet!"

His retinue sighs with delight. "That's wonderful!" he says.
"Let us hear one of your poems!"

I feel my face getting warm. "I'm sorry," I say, "but I haven't memorized
any of my poems, and I don't have any of my poems written down with me."

Throughout the room, foreheads squinch in puzzlement. I try to explain:
"Poetry in America is different from poetry in the Middle East," I begin.

"In America, poets depend on written-down poems. The writing is important,
the reciting, less so. American poets usually read their poems;

they don't usually memorize them and recite them as you do here."
Hmmm . . . ahhh . . . the crowd buzzes, still puzzled, but polite.

The imam intervenes graciously, sparing me from the silence.
"Well, if not one of your own poems, perhaps you can

recite a poem by someone else, perhaps a famous English poet,
and then your student can translate it for us?"
I count the years that have passed since my last doctoral comprehensive exam.
Six. At that time, I memorized a Shakespearean sonnet to illustrate its parts.

Hard as I try, I can't conjure it. It evaporated long ago. There's nothing,
absolutely nothing I can provide this hungry audience,

not a single poem for the imam, my poor student, or even myself.
The retinue must think me a charlatan. What kind of poet

doesn't remember even one poem of his own? This time,
my student speaks, offering a poem by Donne that he memorized

in another professor's class, then translating it into Arabic.
Hmmm . . . Ahhhh . . . the room coos. The imam turns again to me:

"Anyway, we are most happy to meet you, our dear respected
Muslim brother from America." As he begins his lesson to his followers,

I excuse myself to meet my wife and daughter outside.
Everyone smiles.

What I Learn about Poetry In Yemen

Sana'a

What I learn about poetry in Yemen,
I learn at a sidewalk café off of Zubairi Street,
one of the main streets in Sana'a named
after the poet who fomented revolution with rhyme,

where I'm finishing off a plate of butterflied chicken,
the aroma of garlic and lemon marinade mixing
with the smoke fanned by a piece of cardboard box,
the grill right there on the sidewalk,

when a ragged old man tramps by looking
like a bedouin, a holy man in hard plastic shoes,
banging his walking staff on the pavement
and reciting poetry, which, even though I can't

understand, I know is poetry. Maybe the smell
of the grilled food catches his attention,
but he doesn't stop singing his poetry
as loud as his lungs will allow to the waiters, cooks,

and whoever else is listening, which I am
as I'm standing there paying my bill, and now
he's dancing—banging his staff in rhythm, stamping
a couple steps forward, a couple steps back,

BANG!—and I've got to admit that I'm feeling it too,
so I put my arms up in the air like his,
and he grasps my wrist, and suddenly
we're dancing together, the waiters smiling

and clapping as we go back and forth,
BANG! in front of the restaurant,
until the end nears, the big finish, and everyone
is standing and cheering, and I've got to

buy him lunch, I mean I've just got to, because
when was the last time I tasted poetry like this,
not just a cool mint swirl in the brain,
but a wash of chile in the marrow?

So I slam some *rials* down on the counter
for another platter of chicken and rice,
but he's got no time to sit and eat,
so the waiters bag it up for him, and off he goes

toward the city center, his bag of food
swinging from one hand, his staff in the other,
his hard shoes clopping away, my day
swinging from his neck like a medallion.

FARAH GHAFOOR

End of the World Poem

I love the fearsome crocodile as much as you love the fearsome sun
We both know your darling may very well be plotting our demise with its
    own in a couple million years
And all of us space missiles shy as white vans and when noticed, we wave
    like supermodels before paparazzi

So until it kills us, I will love the failed rocket of the crocodile propelling
    itself entirely out of the water using only its tail
See how it falls and breaks water and the water laughs!
Mouth mother-like at this surprising birth and takes further suggestions
    from the earth carrying us in its flesh

We must love and love and love until us dead things fall and ferment and
    decompose and grow grass as part of our new aesthetic
Goneness is charged guilty for interrupting Goodness but really this is
    only evolution

Goodness eats us up and in our abstractions we lay by the riverbed
    watching the crocodile drift closer and ask for its opinion
In its belly the phoenix recites poems of the crocodile's beauty whilst
    teaching us to stir ashes

All of us here in this moment die at the same rate, slow and stubborn as
    planets, as your funny sun dictates
And the redwoods grow to the lowest heaven of the galaxy, urging purity
    for our souls
And the scientists shout that the lowest heaven keeps expanding, urging
    godspeed to our souls

The Quran says that stars are lamps and decorations and weapons to be
    thrown at devils
And the sun infuriated says please ask for my opinion

Us deathless things eavesdrop and share our own tragic backstories and
    unremarkable futures
And sing the song of life we have yet to forget, the song of stomach acid
    and things that glint like glass to replenish
And know only of what the chambers of our hearts had learned of the
    world after completing their degrees in awe

How to Talk White

how my head was blown / blank and immobile / how my white friend turned
to me twice, her mouth filled with glee and glass / and noise splintering into
my face / how a brown boy's mouth dropped stolen sonnets of rolled Rs and
tough Ts / how they belonged to his parents his grandparents my parents my
grandparents / their clouded reflections crashing like teeth, breaking on contact
like rain in a public winter / how his grin stretched irreparably, mocking for the
white woman in front of the room / how he bowed, famished for applause like
a dog / like a matador in the ring / the room a colosseum / how loved a sport,
a game, fanatics displaying the colors they loved / on their thick skins / how a
series of spears were drawn like breath, burrowing into the bull's skin / the skin
thought to be thick / how it charges into a white open mouth / a sheet / to cover
(a determined animal (a person)) with when it died / how humiliated, naked, it's
funny / *they aren't talking* / *white* / *ah* / *I mean* // *right*

LAMYA H

How to De-queer Your Apartment

It'll come out of nowhere, perhaps intentionally so. An unexpected phone call from your parents outside the time slot in which your regularly scheduled conversations occur.

It'll start off innocuously, very much like the usual conversations you are bound by filial duty to have: conversations that reassure your parents that you, who live so far away, are still alive. Beta, have you eaten dinner, how's the weather there, have you prayed maghrib?

Then the slight pause.

"So you know that wedding we're going to in Long Island on Sunday?"

"Yes . . . ?"

"Well, we thought we'd come a day early and stay the night at your place. Is that okay?"

Exhale. Put on your dutiful daughter voice, which you've perfected over the years to hide rising panic. "Of course. When should I expect you?"

"Tomorrow, around 4 p.m.?"

And just like that, you have less than twenty-four hours to prepare for the impending visit of your family. Hard enough for any normal person to do, to pull off the feat of sanitizing one's life for display to the people who raised them, but what's a closeted queer to do?

Here is a handy guide to lead you through the process of de-queering your apartment.

First, cancel all your plans. This is serious business and will take longer than you expect. Then, take a few moments to ready yourself. Chug a Red Bull, pray two rakat nafil, do whatever it takes to rally reserves of focus and energy. *Bismillah.*

Start by scrubbing your apartment clean: your parents have sharply attuned radars for finding the one dust ball that has rolled under the rug in the darkest corner of your living room, and any dirt is a sign of moral decrepitude. So sweep, vacuum, do the dishes, the laundry. Throw out the expired food in your refrigerator. Change your moldy shower curtain. You know, the easy stuff.

The harder part is figuring out what to do with the all the queer accoutrements that you have acquired. The past decade of living on your own has led to the acquisition of paraphernalia that was impossible to accumulate and squirrel away in the recesses of your childhood bedroom. These effects must now not only be hidden from sharp eyes that know all your hiding spots, but also from the wandering hands of your two younger sisters. Little hands that fit easily under mattresses, make tiered My Little Pony castles from prime hiding space under couches and tables, little hands that casually open drawers and closets. Little hands belonging to little people who—it is flattering, you must admit—are enthralled by your older-sister things.

Needless to say, there is a modicum of creativity involved in the act of hiding. Contraband cannot be stashed together, cannot look like it has been deliberately hidden. Ideally, objects must be placed out of sight, but with an affected casualness, in case they're found.

With those principles in mind, start with the obvious things first. Your vibrator, for example, can be placed in an unassuming gift box hidden under a layer of colored tissue: no one will open a box that sufficiently looks like it is in the process of being gifted. Your signs from various protests, rallies, and dyke marches will slot perfectly, inauspiciously into the stack of outdated posters under your bed. The photographs of you and your flamingly queer best friends doing flamingly queer things? Those can be easily concealed in the inside covers of your old notebooks.

Your expansive collection of queer, Muslim, and brown books is not enough to arouse suspicion, especially since most of the books have unassuming titles and are randomly dispersed through your shelves. What may pose problems are specific books, which should be relocated, spine facing inwards, to the pile of books in the corner waiting to be returned to the library. Your well-worn copy of *Homosexuality in Islam* by Scott Kugle, for example, could potentially have passed unnoticed, but for the detailed annotations inside the text betraying your intimate relationship with the subject. All the highlights, the underlining of alternative interpretations of ayahs, hadith with question marks next to the ones you think are a stretch, the ticks next to the ones that speak to you. The definitive *yes!* and the occasional *this hasn't been my experience*. These might give away how you have carved out—from this book and others—a reminder that you're not the only one struggling with these identities, an appreciation for critical engagement with text, solace. That you are not alone.

And then there is the random queer paraphernalia. Mostly from the LGBTQ Muslim Retreat that you've been going to for the past two years that has been a source of rich conversations and community, but also tote bags and folders and glossy schedules and certificates for volunteering, all these things you can't bear to throw away. There are little knickknacks from other events too: lesbian buttons and zines, even a rainbow tie that you found yourself buying in a fit of misguided enthusiasm for symbols. Small tchotchkes that aren't special in and of themselves but evoke memories, tell the story of your life and consequently are more high risk. The certificate from the retreat, for example, with your name printed so unambiguously in proximity to queerness, will have to go. Other things can be hidden fairly easily: tote bags fold neatly into other tote bags, smaller things can be discretely tucked into different envelopes and folders. Separated from each other, a lot of these objects will be stripped of their power to narrate your queerness. But the certificate will have to go.

You're not done yet, not until you've done a last walk-through your apartment to make sure you haven't missed anything: a final sweep. And second and third final sweeps a few minutes later, just in case. And a last actual final final sweep right when your father calls to let you know that they're fifteen minutes away.

And then, when you're reassured that everything is safely tucked away, you can relax into the purpose of this trip: loving, and being loved. Your apartment will be filled in ways that it isn't otherwise: with the smell of food that your mother has spent the last twenty-four hours cooking for you; with stray toys and crayons and socks, courtesy of your sisters, that you'll find for weeks afterward, tucked into crevices that you had forgotten existed, with giggles and squeals that will haunt the place. You will give in to loving and being loved, you will let yourself love back recklessly. Because, in the end, this is why you do this, this intricate and involved de-queering of your apartment: out of a love so deep that it makes it worth it. You chose not to share this part of yourself with your family because you don't want anything to taint that love, to take this away from you, this feeling of being enveloped with love. You're not ready to test this, and you may never be, but that's okay. You're not hiding as much as selectively sharing. You do it because you care.

They're at the door now, you hear their boisterous voices and laughter and footsteps reverberating in the sterile hallway of your building. Take a moment for yourself before opening the door, and whisper a duaa. That it goes well.

SAMINA HADI-TABASSUM

Maqbool

The calls always came just around midnight. We were all asleep, so the story was told only from my parents' memory. A man with a deep, husky voice called several times throughout the night and my father had to get up and answer it each time, since the ringing from the old rotary phone was maddening. The man on the telephone would start scaring them and telling them about how dark men were going to come into their apartment and rob them at any time of the night and that this was not a safe neighborhood to live in for good Muslims like them. That they should move out of the apartment immediately. Then the man on the telephone would say that these dark men were going to break through the doors and set their apartment on fire. "Who is this?!" my father would yell through the phone, hair disheveled, half-awake in his white cotton undershirt, ready to pull the phone out of the wall.

Sometimes the calls came on the weekdays and sometimes on the weekend, but they always came around midnight. My mother would get up and stand next to my father when the calls came, keeping a watchful eye over our bedroom where all three of us slept. Eventually, my father figured out from the voice that this man must be a desi just like himself and switched to Urdu after a dozen threats. And when he spoke in Urdu, the man on the telephone paused for a bit but continued tapping those *t* sounds with that British English accent, refusing to acknowledge that they were tied to some Muslim brotherhood. My father nonetheless started cursing back in Urdu like a 1970s movie villain, sisterfucker and motherfucker, and threatened to find this man on the telephone and beat him senseless with his shoes.

My mother, my two siblings, and I had moved into that second-floor corner apartment when we arrived from Hyderabad, India in 1975. My father had been living in Chicago for a few years and came with his younger brother, both engineers. The apartment at Lawrence and Kedzie was a step up from the deplorable bachelor pad on Devon Avenue in which seven to eight Hyderabadi men all lived together before their wives received green cards. My father and uncle had both left India during the recession and trekked first to Tehran where engineers were needed and the Shah's money flowed. Once talk of revolution hit the streets, the young Indian men came back home and looked for another way out of dire poverty.

My father picked this apartment because it was near the Jewish kosher markets where we could get halal meat. The building owner was an old Yugoslavian man who brought over beaten-up furniture before we arrived: a few gray-threaded sofas, a wooden table with a loose leg, four mismatched chair, and a chest of drawers. No armoires. No charpoys. Everybody in the building was an immigrant, fleeing all kinds of horrors back home from the Koreans to the Slavs to the Muslims. None of us knew English and spoke in that lingua franca English of untethered migrants. All our mothers congregated in the courtyard and watched over each other's children while hanging wash on the lines and ironing clothes on the cement back porch near the laundry room. But the Muslim mothers kept to themselves and only smiled at the Koreans and Slavs. The children played without boundaries in the alleyways and carried on conversations from Hibbard Elementary down the street.

Every morning before school, even when there was a blizzard covering the streets of Chicago with knee-deep snow, our mothers gathered in front of the building to walk the children over, clad in summer saris over rubber boots, knitted sweaters poking out of their mid-riff winter coats, and cotton dupattas wrapped around their heads so the cold air did not seep into their ears. To protect their children's ears was even more sacrosanct and all of us looked like criminals walking down the street in windproof ski masks that left our faces wet with sweat. Most of us were pulled out during the day for ESL services and there were enough of us to also have an Urdu teacher who talked to us like our mother and asked about our day and what we still did not know and understand in English.

Sadiya Haq was my best friend in Mrs. Huntley's first-grade classroom; she lived in the same building as me and she was pulled out for both ESL and Urdu. Her family was from Pakistan, but only a generation ago they had migrated there from Hyderabad, India after the partition that split India into three separate countries. Sadiya had long, thick, dark brown hair and the fair skin that all our mothers coveted for their own daughters. The light hazel eyes were from her mother, who had worked in a factory in Pakistan so she could pay for all her sisters' educations.

We had never met a Muslim woman who had worked outside of the house. So my own mother was quite curious about Mrs. Haq because she often thought about how her own life would have been different if only my grandfather had allowed his six daughters to work instead of being pushed into arranged marriages to men in faraway places. Here, in our building, was a Muslim woman who had walked to the garment factory by herself in a sari and not a burka, made her own tiffin lunch, and smoked cigarettes on her break. None of the other women believed her until Mrs. Haq took out the tattered black-and-white photos of herself sitting under a barna tree with a puff of smoke circling about her own beautiful mane of brown, braided hair.

Sadiya looked just like her mother and had that same bravado that I did not possess. I was the introvert to her extrovert, the id to her ego. Sadiya walked with confidence in the *shalwar kameez* outfits that her mother sewed on the Singer machine that we could hear constantly buzzing from down the hallway. I coiled myself into a shell whenever my mother would make me wear the gaudy sequin outfits she had sewn, clashing against my gray gym shoes. Sadiya had learned to double jump before the rest of us and could sing *Queen Bee* while she jumped. She knew how to chase boys on the playground without our mothers ever knowing. She raised her hand in class all the time while the rest of us pressed our hands under our thighs, looking at our feet when the teacher asked a question. Sadiya was also the first one to bring sandwiches to lunch while the rest of us suffered through lamb meat dolloped inside wheat parathas that had been sitting in our metal lockers since 8 a.m. Sadiya was the All American Pakistani girl that we Muslim Indians dreamt of being.

The closer I came to Sadiya, the more her mother wanted Sadiya to stay away from me. At first, I thought Mrs. Haq did not like any one of us children since Sadiya was an only child and one child was enough for her. But every time I came closer to Sadiya, I saw Mrs. Haq whisper something into her ear and Sadiya standing there for a minute before coming over to play with me, her mother's cold hazel eyes staring back at my black eyes, greasy hair, and dark skin. Once, I told my mother about how Mrs. Haq did not like me, but my mother just thought it was all in my head and recommended that I bring a bag of candy to entice Sadiya to play with me, since after all, she was so beautiful and all the children wanted to play with her.

But there was something about Mrs. Haq that I never told anyone. It was my seventh birthday and my mother invited all the Muslim families over to our apartment. My mother and her sisters baked pans of lamb biryani, fried beef samosas in a deep vat of peanut oil, sliced and cubed onions and cilantro for the yogurt relish, and soaked the cooked rice into pots of creamy, sugared milk for the kheer. There was enough food for everyone and the Pakistani women commented on how delicious the meal was, even though it was not from their own country where raisins would have been thrown into everything.

The families brought small wrapped gifts for me, and then my father placed the gifts in their bedroom and closed the door after the last guests had arrived. Just when I was about to blow out the candles on my birthday cake . . . my mother announced that her water broke and she needed to go to the hospital to deliver our next and last sibling, the only American-born one, Faisal, my Gemini twin. In the midst of the chaos, the families decided that they would leave quickly so there would be some peace for quick decisions, but it was Mrs. Haq who said that she would stay behind and watch the children until my father came back from the hospital. I was overjoyed at first, knowing that Sadiya and I would get to play with my new toys and have time to jump on the bed in the bedroom, even though I shared it with my younger sister.

"Sadiya, let's open up my presents and play in my room!" I shouted.

"Oh no, no," said Mrs. Haq. "I will keep them in a safe space in our apartment so that none of them gets broken. You can open them when your mother comes back from the hospital. She will enjoy you opening them very much."

I watched Mrs. Haq walk into my parents' bedroom, scanning the walls and trying to measure the worth of the room with her eyes, the gifts bundled tightly under her arms. When she left the front door slightly ajar, she looked back at me with those eyes of hers. I don't remember when she came back into the apartment. My brother, sister, Sadiya, and I played hide-and-seek in the apartment until it got very dark outside, and we finally retreated into our bedroom to play board games, falling asleep on the floor. For dinner, we ate the rest of the birthday cake and avoided the biryani, and no one cared. Mrs. Haq watched television the whole time and only took breaks to smoke cigarettes on the back porch.

In the morning, we woke to the smell of my father, the formidable bachelor, trying to cook eggs on the skillet while wearing the same suit from last night.

"Come in for breakfast Sattar, Rubina, and Samina," shouted my father. "Your mother had a baby boy last night. Faisal. And he will join us soon." We were so excited and kept asking my father all sorts of questions. What did he look like? How fat was he? Did he cry the whole night? With a look of exhaustion, my father asked us to eat quietly and get ready to go to the hospital to see for ourselves. In the corner of the living room, getting ready to leave, I saw the stack of gifts from my birthday party, only it was a smaller pile with some missing. I did not think about Mrs. Haq again for quite some time.

Soon after we brought Faisal home from the hospital, my father decided it was time for us to move out of the city and into my uncle's townhouse in the suburbs. Maybe my paternal grandmother would come join us and help take care of the children, he said. And she did, but only for a few months. We left the city and came back on Saturdays to shop on Devon Avenue for all the groceries we needed for the week. We had lost touch with the Muslim families in that apartment building and only saw them occasionally when we went into the city to pray during Eid at McCormick Center, along with thousands of others.

Eventually all of us went onto colleges in the Midwest and then spread out in radial fashion to various parts of the country: my older brother Sattar went to medical school in New York, my younger sister Rubina ended up a lawyer in Beverly Hills, my younger brother Faisal was a social worker in Boston, and I ended up in Houston as a middle school teacher. When I came home for one Labor Day weekend, my mother and I decided to go to the Islamic Foundation's annual convention in the far suburbs and shop for clothes and jewelry; there was a giant open market with stalls from all over the world. At one of the stalls, a dark-skinned, stocky man kept staring at my mother from a few feet away and would not look away. I nudged my mother about the man, but she said that she did not recognize him as anyone she knew. It was too late, and the man put his *taqiyah* on his head while walking over to us. We said our salaams and he began with an apology.

"You do not know who I am, but I know who you are," he said. At this point, my mom's ears began searching for his voice and trying to remember where she had heard it before. "I am embarrassed to say this but . . . almost twenty years ago I used to call your apartment in Chicago and leave threatening messages." We were both stunned and my mother could not remember when the calls stopped but now she remembered his voice. The apartment. The late night calls. Their naiveté as recent arrivals.

"My name is Maqbool," he continued, "and I am the nephew of Mrs. Haq. Do you remember her? She lived down the hallway from you in that building on Kedzie. Well . . . my aunt really wanted me to move into that apartment of yours so I could be near her and Sadiya to help out. But she knew that you would not leave since you were pregnant at that time. So she had me make those calls . . . to scare you . . . so you could leave the apartment. I feel really bad about it now, but I was just twenty at that time and I had just come from Pakistan. So I did what my aunt asked me to do. You know how she was."

Then he chuckled. Neither one of us spoke. We just stared at this man for a few minutes and then walked away. It was the last time I would think about Mrs. Haq and the way she stared at me with those hazel eyes of hers. The same hazel eyes that Sadiya possessed and the eyes I no longer coveted.

UMAR HANIF

For Hasan Faqih on a Hat You Don't Remember

When you were born, I claimed you as my heir. At the age of six, before arithmetic had been tainted by years of calc and trig practice problems, I heavily favored even numbers. I was the second child, born in the second month of 2000, on a day that only comes once every four years, so it felt predestined. As such, the arrival of a fourth child and my second brother in 2006 could be nothing less than fate. I wanted you to follow in my steps and was constantly on the lookout for common traits between the two of us. Some of them will always hold true: you are endlessly curious, temperamental, and scatterbrained—things I hope you embrace and wield. But I never anticipated (though I should have feared) that we might share a fashion sense.

Abi's vast collection of clearance items and *SlickDeals.net* knick-knacks marked him as a foreigner. A magpie fascinated by all new and glossy around him, he was constantly seizing opportunities to obtain the latest (affordable) innovations in apparel, gadgets, and furniture in This Land of Wealth and Second Chances. His latest addition, decidedly less groundbreaking than its predecessors, was a flat cap. But before he ever wore it, you had claimed it as your own.

And when I saw it had passed from his hands to your head, I couldn't help but cry.

The thing was gray, coarse to the touch, and resembled the top half of an ugly clam. It gave the impression of a hat that was halfway to becoming that, but stopped trying when it realized it had met the basic requirements. A nondescript lump made both somehow flaccid and somehow stiff. I was reminded of the BBC show *Sherlock*. Befitting a place devoid of vibrance and hue, a place of exclusively stainless-steel surfaces, where cold and rapid calculations reign supreme over conversation, and the only boots on the slosh-dull streets are filled by skinny white men. I don't think anyone born after the nineteenth century or outside of Scotland had ever worn it before you.

Yet you loved the thing, I think. An infrequent impulse for us Hanifs, but not wholly novel.

Take ice cream. You love ice cream. We both favor ice cream sandwiches.

I'd developed this habit in third grade of pacing around the living room with the lights on deep into the night. It was meant to avoid my chronic nightmares—if I didn't close my eyes, I'd never be left vulnerable. They wouldn't come.

At some point, I don't know when, you started keeping me company. Not intentionally. Not for me. (Good.) Something about the witching hour made it primetime for pistachio ice cream straight from the bucket or vanilla sandwiched between two M&M cookies. Is it because of how loud it gets at night? When there's no one safe and awake to drown it all out? Maybe it just feels comforting. I don't know. Don't ask me.

Junior year, I starred in a sketch comedy show. For the duration of the opening skit my character ate a half-pint of Ben and Jerry's Cookie Dough ice cream. Every rehearsal (and live performance) as soon as the skit had finished, I would run down to the third floor bathroom and jam my fingers down my throat. Ice cream is the worst. Its bite is somehow brisker on the way back up.

I wrote that skit. My English teacher, wiping tears from her eyes, said it was her favorite of the show.

You love video games. Do you know where I go when I need a happy place? Summer 2012. Playing Wii with you and Hamzah. The *LEGO Harry Potter* game was next on our list. We'd blasted our way through *LEGO Star Wars*, escaped the treacherous paths of *LEGO Indiana Jones*, and vanquished every foe in *LEGO Batman*.

But they were all strictly campaign—unyielding linearity, the end was unquestionably the end. *Harry Potter* let you explore—pre-written narratives be damned. We'd spend hours roaming the halls of Hogwarts (you should know that Hogwarts was home when I was your age), backlit by the lilts and sprinkles of John Williams' score; it felt like 367 days of Christmas (extra magical for a Muslim). There were no goals to accomplish, we could wander endlessly and brickbuild our own paths. Hours flew by simply blasting luminescent red and orange bursts of *Expelliarmus* and *Reducto* at passing LEGO students. It would only ever end when we let it. That summer was one of those last occasions when we (willingly) took turns. We shared our joy. We could wait. We were free and we had time.

I can't find any LEGO games in your library anymore. Just shoot-em-ups. I like them too. I see the starfire in your eyes when you play them. I pray it stays. Keep playing.

You love YouTube. It was tailor-fit to us bounce-knee kiddos: a perpetually updating eye-candy encyclopedia. Who else could answer, "What would happen if everyone on Earth jumped at once?" or the more pressing, "What would I do if everyone in the room attacked me at once?"

You now watch the channel CinemaSins religiously—emulating me, because I watched it enough times it began showing up in the "Recommended" list on the living room desktop (sorry). Videos ranging from ten to thirty minutes, filled with a forty-something-year-old Reddit man's formulaic itemization of everything wrong with a movie of cartoons and dreams: "Continuity error." "I don't like the way they did that." "This isn't fun for me." "Not enough breasts."

Your eyes began to harden on our trips to the theater, narrowed with weary cynicism past your years. You stopped seeing the movie, only scoffed at the improbability of *Spider-Man*. Meanwhile, you absentmindedly tossed popcorn in your mouth. I try not to have popcorn. Carbs aren't great for the waistline. I do love it though. I share your taste for white cheddar seasoning.

As you grew, The Prophecy of '06 inched closer to reality. You were becoming just like me and I was ecstatic. We loved *Phineas and Ferb*—colorful animated step-brothers molding the laws of nature for the duration of an endless summer. We were excursive—never spoke in sentences, but unbroken essays on fifty-hundred wildly divergent topics. We loved Imagine Dragons—I was never well-versed in music theory, but they sounded like fight songs. You were sent home one day for calling a girl a bitch out of anger. I earned an in-school suspension for the same thing. You fought kids at the All-Arab Mosque where you were the only Asian/Indonesian/timid/let-me-do-my-thing kid. So did I.

You inherited my same condition of being alien. Ummi and Zahra and Hamzah and Rahma walk into rooms and understand the common tongue. We do not; our words cascade in a mess and we slip. They know how people in rooms look. We do not; we wear sheepishly grinning faces of mottled rainbow streamers and autumn debris collected from a rain gutter. They feel no threat in rooms. We do. They feel no need to defend themselves. We do. We are afraid, not angry (and weaker than we know).

The goal was always to have you embrace our commonalities so that we might stand in solidarity together.

You'll forgive my tangents. Another thing we share. (Keep it, if you want.) The hat, right?

See, it did not fit your head, the flat cap, the thing. It was comfortably snug, perfectly proportioned for you. But it didn't fit. Your floppy preteen-Asian-boy-bangs flung themselves out limply, protesting the newly imposed rule of the inelastic brim. The cap's crisp curves were met by the swells of baby fat on your cheeks. Unyielding grey plaid halted at mottled skin. (It happens to me in the summer too. We don't tan evenly, but in splotches, pigment patchwork quilts. You'll grow out of it like I did.)

Nor did it fit your face. This hat was meant to be worn by Calvinists. Men who know their craft, their make, their path. Set jaw and steely gaze treading through a street of eyeless marchers. Your wandering eyes (me too) and erratic limbs (me too) surely incensed the thing. Your dopey crooked smile beneath glasses that slide down incessantly. Me too. Indonesians have a word for having no nose bridge: *pesek*. A common trait among us island folk. But *pesek* is not an objective measurement—words are made with purpose (remember that). Nor is it a term of endearment. When we threw off the Dutch in 1945 (learn your history and heritage), we kept a few things: Our legal system, the word *hipotek* (mortgage), *Ceres* brand chocolate sprinkles, and *minder* (not confident). Also, the Eurocentric beauty standards, hence, *pesek*.

You were wearing it as you played *Minecraft* in the living room on the big computer that is really for everyone, but you like it the most and we love you (we do) so we let you play on it even when we want to use it and it's really actually yours. You so often stand on your chair, crouched over, legs hopping as you play. You may start sitting, but you rise in tune with the game's intensity, moving to a squat, then a bent-over stance, bouncing up and down on your chair at the utter thrill of Minecrafting. Throughout it all the cap remained on your head. I'd never known you to pay the slightest mind to clothing and style, but you loved the thing so much it clung to you.

When I saw you wearing the thing, I ran to my room. I didn't want you or anyone to see me cry. I could not have articulated why if anyone had asked. And I still don't know if I should.

That was the first time you or anyone else had ever made me feel like that. Like light—my light—had been cast into sea. I could only flail in the tide and watch inevitable waves take it, consume it, drown it. It wasn't the last time I felt that way.

I started weightlifting sophomore year of high school as a PE requirement. After just a month, someone mentioned I was looking better. Hoping more people would think the same, I pumped iron four times a week that year. I still do it now (less though because I'm more okay). I'd come home from a workout when you lamented, "You have better legs than me, Umar." I was flattered, then horrified. I stared at you but you weren't even looking at me. I don't think you even realized what you'd said. I don't know if I want you to.

I know that when you put that cap on I wanted to scream and scream at you to get out and go back. I wanted to rip the thing from off your head and splinter every mirror and camera in the house. I wanted to tell you I love you and you would be great and that there were no dreams, only futures, and I wanted to say it and say it so you could never pause and think about if it was true. And if I told you and you saw my eyes you would know that it couldn't be. And maybe you would cry too. Maybe for me, maybe for you, maybe just for later.

I was furious. You weren't the first boy I'd seen wear a hat like that. There were tons. Your age. When I was too. They looked just like you with their nervous shuffling, moon-eye spectacles, and eager enthusiastic spilling sentence fragments. Gawky little things trying to make room for themselves where they could. The flat cap fell into the same category as fedoras—a nervously staged entrance by boys-not-sure-if-but-maybe-almost-men into fashion.

They were worn by boys I would not have been friends with. I would snicker when they passed, myself too afraid to make that same entrance they had. I'm sorry for people like me. I am sorry and I am angry. Angry with myself for having laughed. But with you as well. For having put the thing on. For having thought you looked good. For seeing the mirror and not finding a beautiful bright boy and just that, unadulterated. For instead, seeing a figure with beauty and worth as variables. A form to be analyzed and critiqued as if you are not the same sack of flesh we all are. I am angry at you for seeing the mirror and seeing something you liked. Because to do so meant you could one day see something you don't.

I'm sorry to be angry with you. Hanifs are a stubborn brood. Anger is a simple default, it requires too much effort to blame ourselves, so we rarely do. I distinctly remember every time Abi apologized to me. They can be counted on a shattered abacus.

So I rarely fled, mostly fought. When they (I don't need to explain who "they" are, you'll know if you don't already) talked about my double chin and muffin top, I fought. When they pointed out how it didn't make sense for her to like me, I fought. When they sat in a circle, discussing their distaste for my mannerisms and opinions and general character (and one of them compared me to Trump not a month after he'd proposed banning us from the country) I fought. When they insisted that I shut up shut up shut up, I fought. When they delivered an itemized list of why they hate me hate me hate me, what was broken in here, what needed to change, I tried to fight. I did not realize that punching back did not block the blow.

I can't even say for sure when I had my first panic attack, because for so long I was certain I was just weak. That to freeze completely and find fear ice-trickling up my shoulders and lose control of my eyes was the overreaction of a fragile constitution and not the ungodly concoction of chemical imbalances. They came and I scolded myself. To grow up. To be something worthy of a man.

They came because I no longer held any strength to be angry. Because high school years of unimpeded direct hits had weakened my ability to respond. (The very strategies that led Muhammad Ali to victory in the ring crippled him.) I could not fight. Only freeze.

For a long time, the background of my phone was a text from Nora (now a good friend): "If this many people think there's something wrong with you, maybe you should take a long look at yourself." I relented. I made sure to never lose sight of the fact that I fell short as a man, as a person. How could they be wrong? What fool fights a room in total agreement?

So I fixed Umar. Formed him in a new image of a proper man. Quieter. Leaner. Angry at himself, never others. I gave the mirror a long look and I have yet to break my gaze. That looking glass realm of John Williams and endless summers and simple flesh sacks does not allow passage both ways, though I may peer back into it all I want.

Good luck with school, okay? It's okay if you don't do well. I was a star pupil.

When I got into college Abi talked to me. The way he does when he gives heartfelt (not angry) lectures, using his words like a man would Jenga blocks while trying to hold together a tower on the verge of collapse. Abi told me how after he'd finished his master's in computer science (which you must be well aware he has great passion for) he decided to pursue another, this time in business. He spent the better part of a decade on it and never finished. He explained how his official reason for doing so was to "support his new family," but in truth he couldn't bear to invest more time in a field he did not care for, no matter its pragmatism. That epiphany came too late. By then he'd had four kids, a wife who barely knew English, and the need to acquire a green card. It was too late for him to walk the other world trails.

When he'd finished clumsily stringing together clauses best as his Indonesian tongue could, I saw him. He looked afraid in a way I'd only seen twice before. The first time I was in the dentist's office getting my teeth pulled. Under the aggressive medical light, I glanced over at him. He was bent over, hands gripped at his face, with red wet eyes. I spotted fraying seams in that veil of parenthood and he no longer seemed invulnerable. He bought me a *Ben 10* toy right after for enduring the painful procedure. The second time I saw that look was after I told him I was bulimic.

Though he only lets us know in these few fragments, Abi's path has known pain. That look of fear, when he advised me on college, on life after youth, comes not from knowing pain—but from knowing we might one day inherit it.

So Faqih, when my face shows fear, know it is because I tried on hats when I was your age.

SHADAB ZEEST HASHMI

Ghazal for the Girl in the Photo

You became the girl with the piercing eyes when you found your country swiped
by a stranger
In Kabul snow, a missile turned your mother into coal, your last tears were
wiped by a stranger

A garden once hung from your name like the perfume of wild apple blossoms,
phantom tulips
In the refugee camp, are you Sharbat Gula, *liquor of flowers*, or a number typed
by a stranger?

Your eyes teach how cold flint ignites a flare, how a father's bones become an
orphan's roof
History writes itself clear as cornea, your green glare—no whitewashing, no
hype is stranger

Pity the empire that failed to decipher the disdain in your eyes, the hard stare
of war
Pity the first world's pity, the promise of friends who show up as every type of
stranger

Zeest, return to the arms of memory, the riddle of its minefields, velvet lullabies
To the lilt of this land, its lyrical storms, its bells and bagpipes, you're no stranger

Qasida of 700,000 Years of Love

So Death's muscle was pulp, a breeze past a
dandelion. Its hold frost, a weak clam
gripping me when the Honda fell
into a crater off the interstate.
True, the last breath was thin as a veil caught
in thorns but it was swift and I entered
Iblis's study. No river of pus,
lava or honey, no plank to walk but
the punishment of another journey:
seven hundred thousand years of service.

How Iblis loved God before the cosmos,
before our polished clay, our high brow, our
delicious sin. It must have been *Isha*
time on Earth. His room in the swirling
infinity was a closed tulip, a
peeling thing with heavy petals, windows
open with desire for the One who
teaches love even to moss, scale, concrete.
I hung from the windows, dangling in
Eternity, a prowler, playing the

role of an extra where Iblis absorbed
all energies in prayer: a magnet
for the Nocturnal garden, swarmed
with delicate scents. I hung like a thief
for his purity, and crept like an ape,
a vine, onto his roof. My town must by
this time be encircled by the amber rim
of dawn, *Fajr*, plush, tranquil, unrolling the
day. Iblis, through the cracks, was a glowing

ton of fire, immeasurably at peace,
knotted in prayer as a fruit blossom,
a perfumed navel, a fetus, impenetrable.
I hovered like a bomber's shadow; sun,
a lemon in the sky and earth a wheat
grain. How could I not recall the fragrance
of bread, the gusts of wind that came with trains,
the arrivals; *Zuhr* my most hungry time.
His posture in prayer made me long
to wipe the tears of red-cheeked geishas,
orphans of war, those tied up, spat upon.

Seven hundred thousand years of loving
God. I could not make it from *Zuhr* to *Asr*
without pangs. Every birdsong sewed me in
to the coarse cloth of the sufi's resolve.
With *Maghrib* came the sound of the key
turning in the lock, the lust of repose.
I clung to his study like a spider web
watching Iblis the steady servant with
his quietude, windows burnished with divine
light. Garlanded with lint, I looked below.

Notes: In the Islamic tradition, Iblis was a devout jinn, a creature made of smokeless fire, who
worshipped God for 700,000 years before Adam was created. He disobeyed God by refusing to
bow before Adam and from then onwards became "*Shaitaan*" or Satan, the evil one. Some Sufis
view his refusal as an act of extreme devotion to the beloved rather than disobedience.

Isha: Night-time prayer
Fajr: Pre-dawn prayer
Zuhr: Early afternoon prayer
Asr: Late afternoon prayer
Maghrib: Evening prayer

NOOR HINDI

On Language & Mourning

"I don't remember how to say home / in my first language, or lonely, or light."
—Kaveh Akbar

Two months before my grandfather died, he asked me to read him a poem of mine. We were at Summa Hospital. In some room. I did not want to read him a poem—because my grandfather was well read. Because he loved poetry. Because, as a child, he did not like me all the time. Because I would interrupt his reading with my play. Because my Arabic was clumsy—Americanized—and I wanted to communicate with him, I did, but felt that I couldn't because he insisted that I speak Arabic. Because trying to speak to him in Arabic was difficult—I'd forget words I needed to convey a certain meaning and when I'd reach for those words, they wouldn't land on my tongue the way I needed them to land, or as urgently as I wanted them to. Because eventually, we only spoke in formalities, never reaching below the surface of conversation.

Because he was dying.

And I did not want to disappoint him with my words, again.

༄

There was a poem he'd always recite: *My Dear and Only Love* by James Graham. In a whisper, he'd say the poem to me, all forty lines of it, and then crack a smile. My grandfather never knew the title or author of that poem. For a while, I thought he had written it. After he died, I remembered the poem, but not the words, and felt a deep sense of loss for not remembering. I asked family members if they knew the poem, but none of them could recall ever hearing him recite it. I wondered if I'd dreamed the poem, if those intimate moments I'd spent listening to my grandfather's voice had ever happened.

At night, I could hear his voice, the meter of the poem, its rhythm and sway, but I could not get past the first two words: "My dear."

Finally, one night, the words "My dear and only Love, I pray" were whispered in my ears, like a secret. A quick Google search yielded the poem on *Po-*

etry Foundation. I am not a religious person, but I do believe in love, and finding that poem felt like an act of love.

There is a video on YouTube of someone reading the poem. If I search "my dear and only love," it's the first result. I have always avoided listening to that recording of the poem for fear of forgetting my grandfather's voice.

کی

At the hospital, I read my grandfather my poem, *As Gaza Exploded*. It was the first poem I'd ever written about Palestine, a place that does not exist on the map, but is nevertheless my home and where my father and grandfather grew up.

It's also the first and only poem I'd ever published at that point in my career as a writer. I'd written it hours after meeting Palestinian poet Naomi Shihab Nye at Kent State University. She was the first poet, aside from my poetry instructor, that I'd ever met.

At the reading, she was beautiful and eloquent. I was dazzled. Her poems were compassionate and urgent reminders that the world could be kind. I saw myself in her words. I saw Palestine. I felt like I was home. When I met her, I let her sign my book, and then I asked her for permission to write about Palestine. The question jumped out of my mouth before I could stop it. She gave me my book back, and said, "I hope you will find a spark of something in these pages." I have never forgotten her words.

That night, I went home dancing. I decided I wanted to be a poet. I wrote *As Gaza Exploded* in a plunge.

کی

My parents named me *Noor* (نور) which means *light*, in Arabic. During my undergrad, I took three Arabic classes to learn how to write and read in Arabic. Although I was (fairly) fluent in Arabic, I was illiterate. In class, I learned the alphabet for the first time, how each letter connects with another, how there are sounds foreign to the English tongue, like the letter ق, which makes قهوة (coffee), or the letter ع, which makes نعناع (mint).

It's been two and a half years since my last class. Sometimes, when I'm driving or showering or making food, I'll realize I have forgotten how to write a letter. I try to picture it in my head—the twist of the letter و, the way ن looks like a plate with a dot, the swoop of the letter س—but I'll realize it's vanished from my memory, at least for now.

ॐ

At the hospital, the closer I got to the end of reading *As Gaza Exploded* to my grandpa, the redder my face became. I struggled through the poem, often tripping over my own words, stumbling over basic lines I'd read over and over again.

Half-way through, a feeling of anger overtook me. Later, I'd recognize that feeling as not exactly anger, but shame. I wondered if he could understand my words. I wanted him to connect with the poem, the way I was describing my father and Palestine, but I felt I had failed because the poem was in English, not Arabic, and I knew he would have preferred it in Arabic.

When I finished, he nodded his head, then fell asleep.

Months later, he died. I did not know him the way I wished I'd known him. In the months leading up to his death, he said "I love you" in English a lot. Once, while walking him around his nursing home, we sat next to a small waterfall. He loved the water. I wanted to talk to him, but he was tired, and I knew I wouldn't be able to convey my thoughts in Arabic the way I wanted, but I could also feel the urgency of his life, how close his death was, how very soon I wouldn't be able to talk to him at all.

We sat in silence. If we had spoken the same language, if my tongue wasn't colonized, if I'd grown up in Palestine, maybe I'd have known him better. In that moment, it's the language I mourned.

ॐ

The most beautiful words to write in Arabic are السلام عليكم which means hello; يقبرني, which is said to those we love so much we hope we'll die before them; يا روحي, which means "my soul;" "حرية, which means "freedom;" and عيوني, which means "my eyes."

In *Poem to be Read from Right to Left*, poet Marwa Helal writes, "language first my learned i / second / see see." In this poem, Helal creates a form of her own called The Arabic. In *Winter Tangerine* magazine, where the poem was published, Helal writes that the poem "vehemently rejects you if you try to read it left to right."

I love this poem for its beauty and protest, how it interrogates language and puts readers in a place of discomfort. I like that it forces readers to reconcile with the other. It asks readers to actively resist the way their eyes inevitably dart to the left side of the page. I like that it asks us to correct how we read, to dismantle what we see as superior.

For Arabic readers, especially, this form provides a place of comfort and grounding. A place where both languages exist, albeit haphazardly.

ݣ

language exists. and am I more. than this language and who am I. without it and what does it mean to occupy. a language to speak. in the language of your oppressor. to exist. in a country. where a white boy once asked me do you speak islam??? I am trying to occupy a space. where I can exist. where I can connect. to my ancestors what is the thing beyond language is it silence or perhaps the sound of Omayma El Khalil singing عصفور I am searching. for a language beyond language. if I keep saying the word language. language language. language it will eventually mean. nothing and every.thing. what is it. anyway and can we move beyond it

ݣ

In *Transfer*, Naomi Shihab Nye writes, "We were born to wander, to grieve / lost lineage . . ." I am Palestinian by blood, Jordanian by birth, and American by fate. But mostly, I am lost. I am grieving. My grandfather. Which is to say I am grieving for Palestine, for "lost lineage," for a man who would have wanted to be buried in Palestine, but was instead buried at Crown Hill Cemetery in Twinsburg, Ohio.

ݣ

When people ask, "Where are you from?" I want to say Palestine, but Israel has erased my country from the map. I want to say Jordanian, but I only spent my infancy there. I want to say America, but does this country want me? The news says otherwise.

In *Silver Road*, Kazim Ali writes, "To walk in the world is to find oneself in a body without papers, not a citizen of anything but breath."

I am trying to wander more. I am trying to breathe more, to love my lostness, to reject the notion that home is one place. The world is infinite. I think? So is space. So am I. So are we.

ᔓ

My grandfather was afraid of dying in America:
A country that denied his existence.

My grandfather was afraid of dying ~~in America:~~
~~A country that denied his existence.~~

My grandfather was afraid of ~~dying in America:~~
A country that denied his existence.

My grandfather ~~was afraid of dying in America:~~
~~A country that denied~~ his existence.

My grandfather was afraid of ~~dying in~~ America:
~~A country that denied his existence.~~

~~My grandfather was afraid of dying in~~ America:
A country that denied his existence.

ᔓ

My grandfather's library was his most cherished possession. He once
    fought with my mother because he let her borrow a book, something
    he seldom did, and she never gave it back.
My grandfather was only educated through the fifth grade. He is the
    smartest person I have ever known. He read voraciously. He loved
    literature. He did not like to talk to people.
Before he died, we discussed Pablo Neruda. My grandfather lived in
    Nicaragua for twelve years. He read Neruda in Spanish. He did not
    like the English translations of Neruda's work.
In hospice, when everything in his body started to shut down, doctors
    said he was "actively dying." I imagined the lights in the little rooms
    inside of his body going off. off. off.

A month after he died, I took a compass he'd left. I don't know how to use it. I keep it on my writing desk. It has a tiny magnifying glass and an arrow. I follow.

When I dream of him, we are silent. What does this say about love and loss and the beyond? There is no language for grief. I miss him. These words are not enough.

Before he died, I told him I wanted to be a poet. He considered my statement for a moment. Eventually, he said "good" in Arabic. I would like to think he is proud.

MAHIN IBRAHIM

"You Care More about Me Being Black Than I Do —Reflections on an Interracial Marriage"

Less than a year into our marriage, my husband Musa and I attended the valima (post-wedding reception thrown by the groom) of his high school friend in the Pacific Northwest dressed in matching lavender, which I insisted on to be "cute," and arriving much too early for a desi* wedding, which means we were right on time.

When we got there, the hosts (the groom's parents) were not yet dressed. It felt a bit like catching the Queen in her underpants while baking a roast. Instead, his family was running around putting finishing touches on DIY centerpieces: pine wood trays filled with seashells and sand, wide cylinder vases filled with blue marbles and water, matching the seagreen and blue ocean decor set up in their backyard.

After everything was ready and the guests arrived, we had lunch. Over chicken and vegetables on rented china, I struck up a conversation with the man across from us who reluctantly replied back, looking around, it seemed, for someone more interesting to talk to.

Minutes into the conversation, the man, a first-generation Pakistani American in his midthirties, clad in a sports coat, turned to Musa and asked,

"Where are you from?"

As a first-generation Bangladeshi American, when people ask me this question, it has different weight based on who is doing the asking. If it's a fellow minority, it's a way to address our mutual struggle and is perfectly fine. If it's a non-minority, it's a total eye-roll, implying that I am not from here and never will be. But when Musa is asked this question, it's a full-on war.

Let me explain.

My husband, now of almost three years, is Black . . . but he doesn't look Black. Or that's what the rest of the world seems very keen on telling him. He is a third-generation African American. Not Saudi, Egyptian or Moroccan, which he often gets. Or desi, Ethiopian, or Mexican. Many times, people assume Musa shares their race and are confounded when he says he does not, or they assume he is an immigrant, especially when he's with me. Every time this happens, it triggers childhood memories of being teased by his classmates for not looking or acting Black enough, and reminds him that though he is American, he doesn't look the part.

So when this man asked the dreaded question, I cringed at what would come next.

After a beat, Musa said, "I'm from here."

"No, where are you really from?" the man replied back.

Backed into a corner, he said, "I'm Black."

The man started to laugh, almost maniacally.

"Are you for real? You don't look Black. You look Bangladeshi, like your wife."

Oh boy.

We had gotten this before, but never with such pointed and oblivious delivery. Usually it was just perplexion. At this point, I kind of wanted to punch the guy in the face, if I was the type of person to punch people in the face. Instead, we both remained silent and dragged our forks across our plates until we could excuse ourselves for dessert.

After the wedding was over, I suggested we escape to a national forest nearby, known for its towering Western Red Cedars and Big Leaf Maples. I wanted to take us to a place where the only noise we'd hear were tiny black beetles the size of a grain of rice and not a single human being.

Now that it was just us, I started to rant like it was my own one-woman spoken word show. My voice got louder and louder, while my husband . . . stayed quiet.

Finally, Musa interrupted me and said, "You care more about me being Black than I do."

With those words, it was like my mic got cut off.

My husband is a good man; the kind of guy who's called "nice" when he leaves the room, and he's definitely not critical. So for him to say this, made me think.

Was it true? And if so, why?

۞

I was fifteen years old living in California when, over pullao and goat curry in a family room with plastic-covered sofas, an auntie leaned over to tell the group, "Did you hear Afreen married a Black man?" The disdain in her voice was clear.

It wasn't unusual for me to spend Saturday nights at family parties with my parents, or to hear my community voice this type of prejudice. In my youth, a

Pakistani-American friend once told me how her mom locked the car doors when she saw a black man walk across the street.

Flash forward sixteen years, I became eager, a little too eager, to fight this prejudice through my own means, and one way to do this was through my relationship. Like a bumper sticker that proudly displays your values and accomplishments ("My child is an honor student"), I used my marriage as a platform to turn my husband into a bumper sticker of his own: "Honk if you're in an interracial marriage!"

Unpacking anti-Black sentiment in the desi community starts with skin color. At the age of six in Austin, TX, I was joyfully eating dirt one day when a boy said, "That's why you're so dark." I spit out my gourmet meal and started to cry. It was the last time I would ever have that fine meal again. I couldn't blame him, as he was just echoing the drumbeat of our culture. Turn on Bangla TV, and you're guaranteed to watch a commercial for skin lightening cream. Attend a Bangladeshi wedding and you'll see white powder packed onto the bride's skin to make her "look beautiful."

Upon immigration to America, my elders passed down the advice to keep your head down and focus on succeeding. Since the eighties, they bought into news headlines linking Black people with the war on drugs and gangs without researching the systemic racism that put these headlines into place or understanding how the Civil Rights Movement benefited our own community so greatly. This lack of information trickled down to us first-gen kids. No one, least of all schools, taught us how the Immigration and Naturalization Act of 1965 as part of the Civil Rights Movement quadrupled the amount of Asians in the US after previous legislation largely banned us from coming.

Because of this prejudice, I thought interracial marriages between desis and Black people were rare, until last year when I read in Vivek Bald's *Bengali Harlem* of desis coming to America in the 1900s and defying anti-miscegenation laws to marry Black and Puerto Rican women. If this was our glorious past, we had forsaken it in our rigid present.

When it came time for my own marriage, I thought about what I wanted and how I could stick the middle finger at my elders' narrow-minded ways. Out of all my Muslim friends, I had one who married outside of her race. It was a beautiful wedding, with Pakistani and Scottish customs blended together. Perhaps if more of us had interracial marriages, we'd learn from each other and not about each other. I became more interested in the possibility, and after a decade of searching brought me the man I would marry, I called everyone to let them know the good news. When I mentioned to a friend that he was Black, she said, "Go Mahin! I'm so proud of you," knowing how taboo it still is for desis.

I felt a warm bubble and thought to myself, go Mahin, indeed, as if I had eradicated racism or brokered world peace. I have to be honest; a part of me also felt like I got voted "most cool in school."

Back in the forest, Musa's words churned in my mind once more:

"You care more about me being Black than I do."

Underneath the leafy, flat maple leaves and cool Pacific mist, I knew it was true.

I had become so entranced with the idea of what it said about me marrying a Black man, that when others didn't see him as Black, I grew angry not for his sake, but my own.

I had turned my beautiful, flesh-and-blood husband into a bumper sticker, and because of that, I treated my marriage like a form of activism. I made it about me, when it should have been about him.

I felt ashamed.

He is the one who has to define and defend his Blackness, constantly. He has to negotiate his identity every day and walks around with an experience I'll never know. My role should be to support him, however he needs. We are garments for each other, as the Quran states. Not as an edgy accoutrement, but for refuge.

John Green wrote in *Paper Towns*, "What a treacherous thing to believe a person is more than a person." In the end, my marriage is one person in companionship with another, not a political statement. My husband's Blackness should not be questioned by anyone—most of all me. And this is still a point of contention in our marriage and something I continue to work on. Friends who haven't met my husband yet ask, "What's he like?"

I've decided to forget the labels. Forget what we think we know when we hear about a female coder or a hijabi police officer. Forget my husband's race, age, career. If I tell you any of this, you'll form ideas of him, and they'll just be ideas, they won't be true. It is his actions that show his nature. So here's the hard truth: we have our share of crippling conflicts and have made our marriage about working through them together. We fight about doing the dishes and how he leaves his jeans on the floor so he can slip into them the next day. "It's efficient," he says. I say it's gross.

Here's the easy truth: he once texted me, "I can pick you up and drop you off," when he learned I planned to walk to dinner in a seedy part of town. He once pulled off on the side of the road when I was crying and held me for an hour until I felt better. He obliges my request to brush my hair after I shower, and calls it good practice if we have a daughter.

And as for me, I've stopped creating a scene when his race comes up. Before, I pushed Musa to work together to come up with an official response, like we were the President and First Gentleman. But now, I am quiet and give him the space to react and respond how he'd like.

Last month at a furniture store, a Black salesman chatted us up and asked where we were from. He was perplexed when Musa told him.

"I thought you were Ethiopian," he said.

My cortisol levels surged, but I let my husband take the lead.

"Yah, I get that a lot." He laughed nervously. "People think I'm South Asian or Moroccan . . ."

"Where are you from?" the salesman asked.

Musa went into his lineage and they continued talking. After they were done, we headed towards the display of fabric swatches.

"Are you okay?" I asked, when we were far enough away.

"Yah," he said.

I knew he wasn't. But I didn't say anything.

Instead, I took his hand, my fingers curled small into his giant, lined palm, and we stayed like that for a while.

And then we went home.

*A person of Bangladeshi, Indian or Pakistani descent who lives abroad. The word is originally Sanskrit, "deshi," and refers to someone or something native to that country.

HILAL ISLER

Never Forget

I became Muslim the morning of September 12, 2001. The night before, I slept poorly and not enough. I'd been unable to turn off the broadcast, and had watched hours of looped CNN footage of the most horrifying variety: those dense plumes of smoke, the ashes swirling like confetti, the smoldering metal, the people; so many people, launching themselves off the Twin Towers, graceful, tragic, sailing down to their deaths; leaves from an autumn tree.

I was in my second week of graduate school at the University of Pennsylvania at the time. I lived in a dorm and had this ancient, tiny television set with a potbelly and a cracked screen. I came back to my room on the afternoon of 9/11, a Tuesday, propped the door open as wide as it would go, and clicked on the TV.

My residents trickled in gradually, all sixty of them, mostly freshmen, many away from home for the first time, and together, we sat cross-legged on the floor, and watched that small screen for hours. We were numb and silent until the build-up of things unspoken would weigh down the air, and crack the atmosphere and someone would begin to sob.

When it was time to go to bed, a few asked if they could sleep in my room, and I remember getting out the spare bedding, spreading it out against the cold, industrial floor, watching the kids as they curled against each other, looking even younger than they were, huddling close, as if for warmth, as if they were small animals sharing a litter.

I don't remember falling asleep that night, but I do remember the next morning, remember very clearly opening my door and finding the front of it had been vandalized, the words heavy and handwritten in black ink telling me, in no uncertain terms, that I was to blame for what had happened, and ought to be punished for it. This is what I mean when I say I became Muslim that morning. I might have been born into a certain family, at a certain moment in time, and been raised a certain way, but it wasn't until I saw my front door after the Twin Towers collapsed that I began to understand who I might be in the world and what sort of place I would occupy. I realized, in a way I hadn't before, that I was being seen as different; and not a good, harmless kind of different, either. I was a suspect. We were all suspects now.

I don't think I could have understood the full extent of it then, could have anticipated what was to come in the months and years that followed: the wars entered, the dictators toppled, the hunt for weapons of mass destruction, the profiling, Guantanamo, all the crimes of hate—thousands upon thousands of them. But even still, even in that new, deeply unfamiliar moment for which I had zero personal precedent, I could sense the ground I'd been standing on was neither steady nor guaranteed to me anymore. I could sense things would be different from now on.

I came to America as a student, to attend college. My family is Turkish. We wear our Islam loosely and sometimes not at all. One of the first thoughts I had after seeing my front door was: *But how did they know I'm Muslim?* Followed closely by: *If this happened to me, who knows what will happen to the others, to the ones who pray and cover.*

In the days following 9/11, I continued to unravel emotionally. Feelings came to me suddenly, in waves, rushing and unbidden: rage, disbelief, guilt, sorrow, confusion, and other strong, foreign feelings I didn't yet have the skills to identify. I had enrolled at Penn to get an advanced degree that would help me earn lots of money. Now, money didn't seem that important anymore. My classes didn't seem that important anymore, either.

I approached my (Jewish) House Dean soon after the incident, and when I told her about the door, she understood immediately what was happening. She encouraged me to organize. *See if others want to talk about what they're going through,* she said. So with her blessing and House funds, I ordered a bunch of pizzas, sending mass emails out across campus, asking for others, similarly targeted, to gather. *Come to Hill House!* I enthused. *I've ordered tons of pizza!* But nobody showed up, and I had to give the pizza away by the boxful.

Eventually, I would come to write my dissertation about being brown on campus and would unearth many stories of hate in the process. I would come to learn of the Sikh kid whose head was cracked against a flowerpot, would go to see the nearby houses of worship torched beyond recognition, giant swastikas spray-painted thick and still visible behind the soot.

At the time, such things weren't discussed that openly, or regularly, or enough. That you could, let alone *should* be an ally wasn't a conversation being had, at least not on the large, public scale it is today, nineteen years on. Nineteen years on, and even though things are different now, I tend to forget that. I forget that I don't have to be so scared, to come so undone anymore. I forget about the allies, vocal and strong and many. Sometimes I forget the feeling of security I should have, of protection, now that I am finally, legally American and can lay claim to certain rights.

There was one day in particular, three winters ago, when I forgot. My family and I had taken a flight down from the Midwest for a few days of sun in Florida. The weekend had ended and it was late, our last night there. We were in the parking lot of a grocery store when, on a whim, I flicked the radio on and heard the news: President Trump had just issued an executive order banning Muslims from traveling. Or maybe he hadn't done that. Maybe it wasn't a "travel ban" on Muslims or maybe it was but either way the news of it coated my insides with a heavy, grubby layer of dread. A familiar feeling.

Instinctively, I powered up the windows, for privacy, and turned to my family. *We don't have our passports on us*, I said. *We don't. We can't prove we're legal.*

Motor running, we wondered out loud whether traveling inside the country was okay and was Turkey on the "evil" list? We wondered whether we would be asked to produce documentation. Would we be held at the airport or questioned or singled out and who should we call if detained?

I stared down at my thin, flimsy sandals and wrapped my hand tighter around a cold bottle of Kombucha, which suddenly seemed extravagant and pretentious and strange. *I* was strange. An alien. Not fully American. A person who turned Muslim on September 12, 2001, and so, whose legality, whose belonging could be called into question—*would* be called into question, indefinitely and independent of the firm and fierce loyalties of her heart. I turned the radio off and we drove back to our hotel in complete silence.

The next morning, we were among the first to show up to the airport in Fort Lauderdale. It was still dark when we rolled the rental car into the airport-sized carpark, leaving the keys in the ignition. We were nervous and quiet, but we were together. I had saved the ACLU's number in my phone, and deleted several Tweets critical of President Trump. At security, fingers trembling slightly, I handed over my driver's license.

A cheerful, round airport official glanced casually at it, at my boarding pass. *Minneapolis!* she smiled. There was a slim gap between her front two teeth. *You'll miss our Florida weather.*

I said I would, and managed a shaky smile, and that was it. She ushered us through. The flight was smooth and when we arrived in Minneapolis, another surprise awaited: thousands had gathered at the airport, waving signs and holding banners: *No Ban* and *No Bannon* and *I stand with Muslim Travelers*. It was glorious. Glorious and unexpected.

Even still, it wasn't until we were inside our house that it finally felt safe. We were safe. *It's over,* we said to each other in the living room. *I love you so much.*

That night, I peeled off my clothes and stepped into the shower and it was only then I began to cry. *We're okay,* I told myself. *It's okay.* And then, I said it out loud. Because sometimes, I still forget.

MOHJA KAHF

Woman-crisp

Can we speak together over time and space
as if we swam naked of our names?

This is crazy
I am crossing the boundary of rationality
I'm growing fins to swim out and meet you

Say yes: this is what writing is,
this is transformation, this is poetry
My skin is slipping away
Yesterday, I misplaced my Self

Say yes, you have been entrusted with a packet,
a word to give to me
I am ready

Text me from your galaxy
Message me from inside the sun
in your apartment of fire

Hurry! answer me
I need a voice to jump toward
so I won't break in two
from the middle of my spinal cord
to dangle in the sky, a broken crescent

Here I am now,
shaking off the lie
Blue sparks are flying from my hair
My fingernails are curling off
leaving my fingers spouting a blood called poetry

This state I'm in may not repeat itself
You know about these states

I am sizzling
in the round black frying pan of space and time
Hurry! before I fry
into a burnt woman-crisp

There is not enough
blank paper in the world
for what I need to write
and all that needs to be written
is a single word

Off Your Ars Poetica

A poem should not lie on its ass all day
A poem should get up and make coffee
for the mourners trooping in and out of the sitting room
Yes, I want a poem to climb a cherry-picker
and, with the tools hanging from its belt,
to repair the power outage for the neighborhood
What is a poem if it cannot pin an amulet
to your collar so the evil eye won't bite?
Yes, I want a poem that will perform a colonoscopy
There is no time for idle poems
There is blood to stanch
I want a poem to run a rape kit through the lab
I want a poem to identify the killer
I want a poem that can rip my soul in half,
stop a war, stay up the night translating
entreaties to save you, and me, from suicide

Exile Is a Dream Like This

Fayetteville, Arkansas. March 29, 2012. US. I make tea face stiff from crying Grief and I don't know why Four-thirty, I remember the dream. Huge swimming pool toddler boy blue shorts at pool bottom. I must reach him I can't get through thick glass. Blocked. Help. Someone, help. My voice makes no sound. It is bashar al-assad's villa. His three kids sleep deep in their bedrooms. Fifty children pool bottom now. I see them drowning. I pound and pound. No sound. Fifty children, all ages, ten, seven, girl boy, laid out on white stone terrace. Some twitching—still alive! Must get through. Pounding makes no sound. Blocked. Screaming makes no sound. No no no. bashar his three kids on a ledge legs dangling boy girl overlooking bodies. Bodies stop twitching. One by one. Look again: sunk at the pool bottom toddler boy blue shorts baby brother. Mine. My real brother real. I sob wake forget. I make tea.

SHEBA KARIM

The Last Mix Tape

In Ruby Mirza's favored fantasy, she was in New York, dressed up, feeling good; she walked into a party, a bar, a reading, a mythical Smiths reunion show. Marcus was there. Their eyes met across the room, that moment in a romantic movie when your heart begins to swell. Their gaze contained everything, the immediacy of passion and romance, the promise of longevity and stability. The conversation flowed like before, their connection unchanged. They talked and walked around the city, stumbled upon a small club with good music and ample room to dance. There wasn't much beyond this, because she usually came before they even kissed.

It had been two months since she'd masturbated. She'd recently turned forty-four and deleted her profile from all the dating apps. She felt hung-over before she even finished her first glass of wine, and to get ready and take the train into the city and meet a stranger for a drink, who, nine times out of ten, she couldn't be bothered to meet again, was far less appealing than laughing with her daughter, smoking a joint, watching Netflix, and going to sleep. Her life was not going to be a heart-swelling romantic movie, a feature in The New York Times Weddings section, Ruby Mirza and Marcus Wolff, Vows: *Falling in Love All Again, Many Years and Mix Tapes Later.*

Then one evening, Marcus Wolff entered her inbox. *I hope this is still your email.* He'd been thinking of her and was going to be in New York next weekend and he'd love to catch up. She paced, breathed through her racing heart, returned to her desk, and opened the bottom left drawer.

"Mom?"

Ruby slammed the drawer shut.

"What's in there?" Noreen asked. "King-size Snickers wrappers?"

"I don't do king size. Guess who emailed me? Marcus."

"Mix tape Marcus?"

"The one and only," she said, though her Spotify daughter would never truly understand the power of the mix tape, the thought and planning that went into the songs, their order, the cover art, the feel of it in your hand, weighty and compact.

"You know, you've never *really* told me the story," Noreen said. "Wait—let me get comfortable."

Her daughter sat cross-legged on the recliner, tied her dark brown hair back, pushed up her glasses, hugged a cushion to her chest, prepared to listen carefully and dispense advice as needed. "Okay, shoot."

Her therapist had asked her, *You've had two boyfriends since Noreen was born, but you only introduced her to one. Why?*

Because only one was worthy. And they had broken up shortly after, when it became obvious the three of them would never be in sync.

The story of Marcus carried its share of trauma, and Ruby knew Noreen would nurture this hurt, that it would cause her to worry about the past and now the future. Already she feared she was the reason Noreen was wary of romantic love. In telling your newly teenage daughter about your teenage past, where was the balance between what to share, and what to keep?

"I mean," Ruby said, "like most things, it really begins with my mother."

Ruby's mother, Azra, had many things to say about boys, distilled into this: Avoid boys almost entirely, then marry one of our choosing.

As a precautionary measure, her parents had sent her to an all-girl's K-12 school, but it had a partner boy's school, and as puberty commenced, so did the dances. For her Pakistani parents, gathering twelve-year-old girls and boys together in a gym and encouraging them to put their arms on each other and sway to Whitney Houston was a certain path to dishonor and lust and corruption. For Ruby, who from a young age maintained a steady interest in all three, it was a lost opportunity. She had crushes on Morrissey and Robert Smith and Johnny Depp, but she wanted it for real, wanted to know what it was to have a guy's arms around you, to be held, kissed, desired. She wanted the love of *The Thorn Birds* without the Catholicism, the passion of *Flowers in the Attic* without the incest.

But how? For a long time, it could be summed up like this:

Seventh Grade Slam Book

Girl Most In Need of a Makeover

Ruby! Someone please shave that mustache!

Duh she needs to wax, shaving will make it thicker

This question is so dumb, everyone knows it's Ruby

But by seventeen, Ruby was finding her painful path to beauty, excelling at academics, buoyed by the promise of freedom through college. She signed up for co-ed woodshop class because she wanted to meet boys, and also because she considered herself a feminist, and it seemed empowering to gain familiarity with tools. The first day of class, she was assigned to the same workbench as Marcus. In a daring flaunting of uniform rules, his shirt was partially unbuttoned, and she recognized the black T-shirt he wore beneath, the bright pink letters, an S, an M, the top half of I.

"Nice shirt!" she said. "'Cemetery Gate' is my current best song of all time."

"That's a great song," he agreed. "My favorite is 'The Boy with the Thorn in His Side.'""Oh, the whole album is total perfection," she said. "It almost makes me feel sad, like, how can you get better than that? It is all downhill from now on?"

"It also depends on you," Marcus said. "Where you are, how you're listening. Maybe, five years from now, you'll like a different Smiths album better. It's less about downhill or uphill but more about where you are relative to the album."

"You're right," she agreed. "But no matter where I am, it'll be pretty hard to beat *The Queen is Dead*."

Marcus laughed, and the instructor called the class to attention. Ruby was glad for the interruption. In spite of her strong beginning, she was crushing on him too hard not to be nervous, the sexy, hint of goth juxtaposition of his pale skin and pitch black hair, the way his eyes, exactly like Andrew Ridgeley's except deep emerald, sparkled as he laughed.

The instructor didn't mind that they talked non-stop as they measured and sawed, sanded and stained, as long as they kept working with wood. It stayed strictly woodshop until the last week, when Marcus told her he liked her and asked for her number. She'd made references to her situation before, but now she had to really explain: Marcus couldn't even enter the friend zone, they couldn't hang out, talk on the phone, because you see her parents were Muslims, from Pakistan, which was right next to India, which thankfully Marcus already knew. She explained to him how Azra listened in on every call, how she'd try to be stealthy but Ruby was attuned to that slight click when she picked up, could feel her breath traveling through the wires, how her and her cousin Sonia spoke in code.

She hated explaining the complications of her life with white people. They'd usually pity
her and make dismissive generalizations about her parents which she'd then

end up defending. But Marcus didn't criticize or offer his deepest sympathies. Instead, he asked, "So what should we do?"

We, she thought. *Him and me, we are worth the risk.*

"My parents are going to Home Depot Saturday," she said, "and they never take me because I whine the whole time. Here's my number. You can call me exactly at 11 a.m. If it rings more than twice and no one picks up, it means abort mission."

"You sure?"

"Yeah."

"Here," he said. "I made you a mix tape."

In the romantic movie version of her life, this was another major, heart-swelling moment. "The Boy with a Thorn in His Side" would play, shots of her rushing home to the Walkman in her room, listening as she lay in bed, dancing in place with a lovelorn grin.

At the end of their epic Saturday phone call, to relay the undying depths of her affection, Ruby played him "Song to the Siren" by This Mortal Coil, holding the phone to the stereo as she mouthed the words. Elizabeth Fraser singing . . . then, now, could she ever say it better than this?

Ruby was subject to random backpack searches, and Azra conducted one that Monday. Azra, seeing Ruby's consternation as she removed the Walkman from the bag, looked inside. The cassette was labeled *Songs for Ruby, from Marcus*, side 1 and 2. Ruby thanked Allah her own tape for him was still unfinished, hidden in her room. One mix tape was plausible denial, but a return mix tape was incontrovertible proof.

"Marcus *kaun hai?*" her mother asked. "*Kaun hai, yeh Marcus? Rubina?* Answer me!"

For Ruby, extemporaneous lying had become a necessary skill for survival.

"He's nobody," Ruby said. "I've hardly spoken to him, I swear. He just walked up to me and gave me this tape, so I took it and put it inside my Walkman because he has no friends and I feel sorry for him. I was going to throw it away."

"I know you very well," her mother said. "You're lying!"

"I am not!" Ruby said, feigning outrage.

"You're not getting your driver's license."

"What?"

"You will go school, come home, and only go out with me or Abba. And I am calling the school and telling them no co-ed classes next semester."

"I have to take a few! AP Biology is co-ed. I need to take as many AP's as I can if I'm going to get into the Brown Eight-Year Medical Program," Ruby argued.

Her mother had two moral compasses, separate yet intertwined, what she believed Allah wanted, and what the community would think. For both of these, academics was the Achilles Heel.

"Only the AP classes, nothing else," she said.

The following semester, with the exception of ten minutes between the end of lunch and fifth period on Wednesday, it was nearly impossible for Ruby to see Marcus. They started exchanging weekly mix tapes, Ruby careful to hide them well. The tapes included talking, before and in between songs, what they loved about a particular track, the week's highlights, rambling about life at school, at home, Marcus's practical optimism a good counterpart to Ruby's measured despair. Eight weeks and over fifty broadly interpreted love songs later, they were officially boyfriend and girlfriend.

Her mother remained vigilant and Ruby remained in her room. Before sleeping, she'd listen to the tapes in the dark and pretend they were making out. She wanted desperately to kiss Marcus, to feel his breath, his body, but needed a way.

It came through the mailbox, a thick, glossy envelope, an invitation inside, a calligraphic *bismillah* embossed across the top. Ruby was not invited to the *valima*, and her parents couldn't bring her, as the wealthy parents of the groom were doing this particular wedding function white people style, strict invite list, fancy country club, no kids unless closely related, formal seating arrangements with name cards. For this one night, Ruby would be home alone. On her next tape, she let Marcus know.

The plan went off perfectly; from her parents leaving around the time Ruby had guessed to Marcus's discreet entry, parking down the street, slipping into the garage, through the side door into the kitchen. His presence in her bedroom, once unthinkable, was a sudden reality, and she wasn't even that nervous. She showed him her photo albums, bared her history of horrible haircuts. He took in her posters, Morrissey, Robert Smith, The Jesus and Mary Chain, Wham, all white men, Ruby realized as she cast her memory back. They sat on the floor for a while, a bed's length apart, and Marcus looked at her and said, "You want to dance?"

He put on "Plain Song" by The Cure, which started out quietly, more of a song for falling than dancing. Her heart swelled and swelled, the axis of her minor universe permanently shifting as they fell together, kissing long and deep inside The Cure's primordial lovesick sea.

Marcus said, "I love you."

"I love you, too," Ruby said.

That night, after Marcus left, Ruby played "Plain Song" and cried as she danced in circles, arms out wide.

That night, after the party, Azra went straight to Ruby's room. She turned on the light and went straight for the desk, her gold-embroidered dupatta slipping off as she yanked open a desk drawer.

"Mom?" Ruby said.

Her mother said, "*Besharam beizuthi ladki!* I know you're hiding something."

Ruby didn't know how her mother came to suspect, if it was instinct or something tangible. Looking back, she wondered what else, what childhood trauma, what subconscious inheritance from Partition, what untold secrets and piercing heartaches helped fuel her mother's fury. Whatever its sources, it was Ruby who burned.

Her mother went through every drawer, opened every pen box and change purse, and flipped through every notebook. Ruby watched silently from the bed, her father from the doorway. After searching the chest of drawers, the nightstand, underneath the bed, her mother switched gears and began attacking the posters, Morrissey first. Ruby prayed that this would satiate her enough to abandon the search.

Having bared the walls, her mother began walking toward the closet.

It took all of Ruby's training not to give it away.

Her mother tossed out the pile of clothes in the corner, unearthed the shoeboxes underneath, found the two at the bottom filled with Marcus's mix tapes. Ruby cowered as her mother read the titles aloud, disgusted, as if they were the verbal equivalent of pork.

Love Songs for Ruby. My Week in Review, courtesy of They Might Be Giants. Selections from the Noble Wolff. Songs for the Ides of March. For: Ruby From: Marcus.

Weird Lover Wilde on My Mind

The word "lover" threw her mother into a violent panic. She came at Ruby, ready to land a *thappar* across her face. By now, Ruby was the taller one, and she suddenly became brave, a "fuck it I'm in deep shit anyway," kind of brave, fearsome, fleeting.

Ruby yelled, "Go ahead! Hit me! I'll call the child abuse hotline and they'll arrest you!"

Though her mother knew she wouldn't actually call, she lowered her hand.

She was too wary of the authorities, who would only see that she'd hit Ruby and not all the reasons why.

It didn't matter. She knew how to hurt her worse.

"This is for your own good," she said, picking up a tape, opening the cover, yanking out the cassette's reels, one by one, their songs and stories reduced to black ribbons, twisted, tangled, beyond repair, forever lost.

Better this, Ruby told herself, *then her listening*.

Once, looking backwards during therapy, she realized her father's complicity hurt almost as much as her mother's destruction, the way he watched from the doorway, not saying a word, not trying to stop Azra, getting her the garbage bag she asked for, the garbage bag that her mother later dangled in front of Ruby, her fist around it like a noose.

She said, "If you ever communicate with him again, a word, a call, a tape, anything, you are moving to Pakistan," and Ruby realized she was serious, that she was ready to upend her comfortable American existence to salvage Ruby's *izzat*.

She was so close now. She could not risk college, the rest of her life. She broke up with Marcus, withdrew, wept, studied, felt black inside, wore it outside, listened to a lot of Depeche Mode. When she was actually accepted into Brown's eight-year Medical Program, more prestigious than even Harvard in the eyes of the community, her mother said, *See? Everything we did was for your own good*.

She got back in touch with Marcus during college. He was on the opposite coast, had a serious girlfriend. It seemed too painful, and pointless, to stay in touch.

ᔓ

Ruby hadn't lost every mix tape. The night her mother found them, the latest one from Marcus was still inside her backpack, which she'd left downstairs, a rookie move turned fortuitous. It opened with New Order's "Every Little Counts" "Plain Song" the climatic track. Ruby made a slit in her mattress, hid the mix tape deep inside, took it with her to college, dorm room to dorm room, rental to rental, Manhattan to Brooklyn to Jersey townhouse, inside her bottom left desk drawer, beneath used checkbooks and old birthday cards and mortgage papers, her first love's precious remains, long spent, still breathing, buried deep, out of sight.

She and Marcus agreed to meet for dinner. Through their subsequent song exchange, they expressed nostalgia and anticipation. Noreen wanted to hear the last mix tape, so Ruby bought a boombox on Amazon. Her daughter played it from her lap as they drove to see Ruby's parents and pronounced it excellent. Ruby tried to temper her excitement over meeting Marcus, but it didn't matter. Noreen saw her crash diet, examine her white hairs in the mirror, try on outfit after outfit, witnessed her sentimental sing-alongs, walked in on her dancing circles in her room.

If you ever marry, you have to be 100 percent sure you can trust him, her mother had told her. *You have a daughter, he could sexually abuse her. If something happens, there's no going back.*

Her therapist told her she had to excavate and set free Azra's voices from her head, which was not easy when your mother kept adding to them. But in this case, her mother wasn't entirely off. How did you know if a man was truly good, and kind? Marcus was good and kind at seventeen, but what about now?

Now Ruby stood on the precipice, wearing a black dress, light make up and sensible heels. She'd chosen this restaurant because it was not too expensive or hip or loud, had decent music, was light enough to read the menu, and dark enough to touch.

Marcus messaged. He'd already arrived and was waiting at the bar.

All that remained was to go inside.

In the heart-swell movie version of this moment, *Plain Song* would be the soundtrack, would carry her fatefully across this threshold, exterior to interior continuous, here enters—Ruby Mirza, forty-four, loving mother to her own beautiful daughter, passionate fool, riddled as the tide, older, better, wiser, nursing her forever-mix-tape-heart.

SEELAI KARZAI

The Night Journey

In Sunday school, when I first read lessons
of the *miraj*, the Prophet's night ascension
and travels through the seven heavens,
I needed a sound, concrete confirmation.

On the *miraj*, the Prophet's night ascension,
there are only a few accurate, sound accounts.
And while I still needed concrete confirmation,
I clasped at closed doors, ready to renounce.

Yet I found those few accurate, sound accounts:
illuminated paintings of angels with golden vessels.
And I flung open closed doors, ready to denounce
all who threatened to sell my thoughts to devils.

Within these paintings of angels with golden vessels,
the Prophet and Buraq glide. Her silver wings soar
over those who risked unfaith becoming weapons
in the hands of a cloudy day or becoming lost to folklore.

SABA KERAMATI

Namaaz

My grandmother used to remove her teeth
and place them in a jar on my nightstand.
It was strange to see them float.
Stranger, still, to see the way her lips
would curl into her mouth.
She would come to California often,
but she would rarely leave the house,
large hips too fragile
to carry her up and down the stairs.
She was a hunched woman, and she slept on the floor.
Sometimes, she would crawl to the kitchen.
But with brittle bones and shaking knees,
five times a day, she would stand.
She would stand, raise her hands to her ears, and pray.
Green pearls in her hands and *Allah* on her lips:
what she lived for.
I never thought to ask what she prayed for.
It was difficult for me to speak to a woman with no teeth
and a different tongue.
But in the time I have lived without her,
I find myself thinking,
about five times a day,
glory be to my grandmother.

At Headlands National Park

I've borrowed my father's 1983 white Mercedes
to drive us to the dark sky
at the very tip of Michigan's hand.
I leave the engine on.
I say it's for heat, but
it's so the rumble of the diesel engine
will cover the thumpthump
of my telltale heart.
The stars are gently dusted
through the night.
I can see the moon's halo.
The car is dark,
illuminated only by the roaring fire
between our palms.
I can feel your pulse
in the very tip of your pinky finger
as it rests on my heartline.
I smell summer solstice, heat,
and love.
We are slipping into the universe.

Nightlong Longing
after Hannah Sanghee Park

Fingers intertwined,
tightly embedded
holding onto what feels like forever.

But the truth (the one truth)
the sunrise pouring through the window
illuminating

the autumn leaves
a lark,
a signal, reminding

nights belong to nightingales
(not to me) (not to
you).

Forgive me now and forgive me
tomorrow.

NAAZ KHAN

Lost in Translation between Delhi And Chicago

The city at their feet, Safiya rocked a colicky Zoha, humming a childhood lullaby. Far down below, a snow plough and a spool of CTA buses inched toward shiny, hopeful Navy Pier. In neighboring skyscrapers, red, green, and gold lights flickered, and Christmas trees glistened. Safiya's heart hurt at their promise of family, togetherness, and love; memories in the making, to be summoned to deliver hope or mend disappointments, for years to come.

If I gave you my heart today, would you still not want it? The question flitted through Safiya's mind. She gazed at the snow that lit up the night sky, even as it entombed the city; such beauty, but so cold and unforgiving.

As if sensing Safiya's thoughts, Zoha grew quiet and clenched her little fingers around the delicate gold chain at her mother's neck. Nuzzling the baby's soft cheek, Safiya took in her daughter's innocence. She gently uncurled Zoha's fist. "It'll break, sweetheart."

Eyes heavy from a sleepless night, Safiya lifted her gaze eastward. It seemed like she only had to reach out and her fingertips would touch Lake Michigan, a dream, now icy and cracked in so many places; cracked like the cocoon of familiarity woven by her parents, siblings, cousins, aunts, and uncles. India was home, yet marriage and new beginnings in America had been a suitable trade. Even trading up. Yet, nothing had prepared Safiya for what she'd slip on with that half-carat diamond wedding band. Gone was the familiarity of family and beloved neighbors—whether it was asking for a cup of sugar, sharing news of a grandchild's birth, or attending family weddings, she instead found herself sandwiched between increasingly vibrant memories and equally elusive feelings of connection.

And then there was Rafi, born and raised in the US. Self-assured, self-sufficient, a man incredibly comfortable in his own skin. Safiya sighed, her breath leaving smudges on the cold clear glass window. *If I gave you my heart today, would you still not want it?* The question grazing at the edge of Safiya's consciousness had to be nudged aside as Zoha began to fidget, rooting, hungry again. Her cries soon competed with Bruno Mars on the stereo. Padding across the floor, Safiya nestled into the second-hand couch. Lifting her feet on to the coffee table, she undid her blouse and eased the newborn into the crook of her arm. Soon, Zoha's tiny fingers rested against soft flesh.

From Delhi, one of India's biggest cities, Safiya hadn't been surprised by Chicago's awe-inspiring skyline, the pace, its ethnic mix. Before the baby, it had been all about studying for her United States Medical Licensing Examination to qualify for a medical residency at a local hospital, volunteering at an inner-city clinic, their weekend routine of dinner with Rafi's extended family or friends: a full calendar. It made life interesting. Also, she slowly realized, it was her shield against the gnawing emptiness that came when most conversations invariably stopped short of becoming a window into another's heart, hopes, aspirations, and feelings. Neighborly friendliness stalled at hello's in the hallway or elevator. And it wasn't for lack of trying on her part; a passion for food had meant gifts of freshly baked cookies, *samosas*, and chocolate bark. *Both countries had the same twenty-four hours, the same busy, demanding days. So what made people back home so open to nurturing relationships, even dropping in past 9:30 p.m. on a week night to say hello? Why were new friendships so much easier to kindle there?*

As she tried to burp Zoha, Safiya recalled the day she had discovered she was expecting. She'd been thrilled, bursting to share her happiness. She'd Skyped with her family across the continents, even before telling Rafi. Their reaction would be whoops of joy, a fountain of questions, heaps of well-meaning advice about eating well and taking care of herself, she'd imagined. An emotional, un-restrained reaction was what she'd needed, craved even. She hadn't been disap-pointed. The memory still warmed her insides, made her feel loved and cared for. Rafi had been pleased with the news, too—"That's cool!"—but where were the hugs, the jumping for joy? Where was all the emotion, the passion? Safiya couldn't help but think how well he fit the label that second generation South Asian Americans gave themselves: *ABCD's* –*American-Born Confused Desi's*.

The warmth from the fireplace tickled Safiya's toes, as the hour undulat-ed. Brushing the pink fleece blanket aside, she peered into her daughter's face, soaking in all the nuances—Zoha's wispy eyebrows, the full head of dark hair, a perfectly tiny nose, and alert eyes that roamed across the room.

Safiya had imagined a baby bridging the void. However, between an often colicky newborn, sleepless nights, and Chicago's cold, short days, the ache had only deepened. And she said as much to Rafi as he emerged from their bedroom, his hair dripping wet, a towel around his waist.

If he heard her, he showed no signs of it.

There was nothing like a hot shower, or a game of basketball, to erase the day's worries, especially after forty-eight hours on call at the hospital, he'd often say. Holding Zoha, though, was how he decompressed best.

Safiya's eyes lingered on his face. He was still as handsome as when they'd first met. A smile slipped across her face as she remembered the many times she'd pulled the towel off Rafi's body, their newly-wed days and nights when they'd made love like they couldn't have their fill.

They'd met in Delhi. Rafi had been visiting from America, an only child, looking to get married. She, one of five children, was one of the many hopefuls he was to "interview." And, yes, of course, she'd have as much of a say as him. They first met at dinner, the two of them, her siblings, his cousins. Amidst the group's non-stop chatter and the clinking of flatware against china, his measured manner and quiet humor had attracted her. His ease despite being teased for not being able to speak Urdu without a heavy American accent or jokes that he'd 'dutifully' taken the doctor path as a career, had impressed her. He'd been unruffled, obviously a rock she could lean on.

Rafi brought Safiya back to the present as he lifted a sleeping Zoha from her arms. He kissed the baby's forehead gently.

"Isn't it too warm for that towel?" she teased, pretending to yank it off.

Rafi eased onto the couch, across from his wife. Reaching for the remotes, he turned off Bruno Mars and flicked ESPN on and, just like that, Safiya knew she'd lost him.

Safiya's fists curled. *Where is my hug, my kiss? Our first in days?* she wanted to demand. Instead she tersely said, "I was listening to that song."

Rafi's attention still on the Baltimore Ravens, the comment stood unacknowledged.

Safiya shook her head, mystified. *Just how had she gone from the land of overreactions to a land of seemingly no responses?* She sometimes counted the words he spoke each day, their functional exchanges. Had she made the doctor's appointment? Had he returned the jacket he didn't want? *Did he even know what was on her heart or mind? Did he care?*

Safiya's interest in raising a family and only working part-time, her easy confidence, and gregarious personality, had attracted Rafi. They discovered their big picture ideals dovetailed – family and faith came first, education was the key to their aspirations. That both were physicians in the making meant even more common ground.

Rafi and Safiya's whirlwind courtship was conducted over family gatherings, Skype, WhatsApp, and Facebook. That Rafi was unpretentious, genuine, and transparent, was all that mattered to her. He made her smile. He noticed little things like when she'd done her nails or was wearing a color that suited her well.

She was unlike the girls he'd known in America, Rafi had said. Refreshing. Her warmth and ability to engage the young and the elderly alike endeared her to him. She was a good listener. Barefaced and dressed down, glasses instead of contacts, he loved that she had the confidence to be herself, not a girl hiding under make-up, jewelry, or brand names.

She had been the first to reveal her feelings, to say she wanted to marry him. He was kind, would work hard, and would be a gentle and loving father, she had calculated. She felt secure with him.

It all made her present loneliness and bitterness even more incomprehensible to Rafi, and sometimes even to herself. He often asked how she could feel alone, when each weekend was spent with family and friends he'd known since he was a boy. She even had the baby she'd so desperately wanted. Safiya acknowledged, even now, that Rafi was a good man, a trustworthy man, and that was invaluable. But the wound remained.

She wiped away the tear staining her cheek. *A year and a half into their marriage, where was the emotional connection? Where was the friendship, the common interests? The quiet contentment of being in each other's presence? Where were the confidences she had imagined exchanging to create ties that bound them together? Wasn't that the stuff of deep relationships, the stuff of marriage?* The questions came fast and furious. Never once did it occur to her that a man as transparent as Rafi would have no secrets, that his public and personal persona were one and the same. The more insistent her need for a deeper relationship, the more Rafi, she felt, withdrew.

As the pregnancy had progressed, Safiya's requests for back rubs and foot massages grew, as did her pining for family and India. That Rafi had two fellow residents working through their pregnancies, left him with little sympathy for Safiya. The work day's stresses never far from his mind, "Here we go again!" became his unspoken, yet clearly heard, retort. The less Safiya felt heard and understood, the more bitter she grew. Soon, she stopped choosing her battles and even abandoned curating her words.

That the two hadn't exchanged a meaningful word this evening, hurt. Safiya bit her lower lip and crossed her arms over her chest. *If her family lived in America, would they have been as restrained as Rafi and his family? Every thought weighed, edited, and filtered before being spoken? Independence and personal space defining every interaction? If she had grown up here would she, too, not care that many relationships never got beyond discussing the weather, the latest store sales and sports? Was this how Zoha would be?*

"I've made *aloo-paratha's* for dinner," she finally broke the silence.

"You go ahead. I'm not hungry." A discomfiting look came over Rafi's face. "Haven't I always said that if you are hungry, you should just eat? This isn't India where you have to wait on me."

She'd heard that response before. Between Rafi's work and whatever ESPN doled out, Safiya couldn't remember when she and her husband had shared a meal, or a conversation, that had brought them closer. Food in her new home had the flavor of a necessary evil. Safiya was certain it was robbing her cooking of its taste. Her own father had five children leaping to greet him when he returned from work. It meant a family gathering to enjoy a hot, freshly cooked meal and dinner table conversation about the food, or the news and how Papa's day had gone. Rafi, on the other hand, wanted to put his day behind him, not relive it. And it didn't help that he never tired of teasing his wife about her "living to eat" and was incredulous when she dissected the ingredients that went into a dish, or cared about stuff like the difference between onions sautéed for five minutes versus eight minutes!

Reaching for the baby, Safiya lifted Zoha out of Rafi's arms and lowered her onto the couch, between them.

Rafi's jaw tightened.

"Are we planning to do anything this evening?" Safiya asked, knowing the answer.

"You're going to bundle up the baby, warm the car, so we can plod through the snow, after a forty-eight-hour shift?" Rafi moved Zoha back on to his chest. "Why don't you watch the game with me instead?"

Safiya stifled a smirk. She'd been alone with a two-month-old, changing diaper after diaper, with no time for even a shower, let alone any adult interaction. And tomorrow would likely be the same. But he'd had the luxury of getting out of the house, meeting adults, flexing his grey cells. *Is a change of scene too much to ask for? I'm tired, too,* she thought, wondering why it wasn't obvious to her husband. "Today, tomorrow, or the day after, it will always be 'no,'" Safiya muttered. *There wasn't going to be any room for her needs, yet again.* The thought poisoned whatever little interest she had in snuggling next to him and fake-watching a game.

Safiya walked over to the charger and detaching the phone, opened up her Facebook page. There were two messages: one from her sister, the other from a woman she'd met in a Lamaze class. A sense of relief washed over her. Someone cared. Even her Facebook friends seemed available to hear her thoughts and feelings more often than her husband. And yet, the more time she enjoyed online with friends and family, the more alone her marriage made her feel. She missed the back and forth of playful banter, the soul-searching discussions about life, love and faith, the feeling that sometimes you didn't have to say anything and you'd still be heard. She missed being part of the jigsaw that was family.

A jumble of emotions, she rose to microwave the *aloo-paratha*, then jabbed at her phone. "I hope you don't mind if I eat while we talk," Safiya cradled the phone between her shoulder and her face.

"Not if you don't mind my baby fussing. The minute I get on the phone, she seems to get cranky," Sheena replied. She was an import like Safiya, albeit from Atlanta. The two women had met at a party.

Safiya took a bite of her *paratha* as she listened to Sheena lament about the hour it took to get her newborn bundled into a snowsuit and ready for a trip to the grocery store, only to need another diaper change before she'd even made it out the door. Safiya commiserated. She agreed that most days the effort was exhausting and she, too, had abandoned many a trip.

If their babies allowed it, what Sheena and Safiya would begin as a conversation about their newborns would evolve into a discussion about the price of diapers and formula, the nature of love, the emotional costs of relocating. If either of them had had any time to watch TV or follow the news online that week, that invariably became fodder for discussion whether it was US politics or international news.

"Can you take your call to the next room?" Rafi said, rocking a now whimpering Zoha in his lap. "You're disturbing her."

Maybe, Safiya longed to retort, *it's the voices on ESPN that are waking her.* She turned her back to him, reducing her side of the phone conversation to the occasional "oh no" and "uh-huh".

Even as she chatted with Sheena, Safiya imagined what Rafi would say. He had never met someone with as much capacity for self-pity. Every day, he saw people at the hospital with legitimate fears and losses. What did Safiya have to complain about?

When Safiya hung up, her plans to meet Sheena glistened, like a thin ray of hope.

"Do you have to use the phone in the same room where I'm trying to watch the game?" Rafi asked.

Safiya felt anger surge through her veins. "I feel so lonely in your company," she hissed. She felt blood as she bit her lip, hating the game, despising the TV, loathing the shared space they called a marriage. The neighbors may not discuss more than the weather with her, but within the four walls of her house she wanted to be heard, to be understood. She wanted someone to ask her how her day had gone, and to care about the answer. "If you are my husband, the very least you can do is listen to me, listen without judging," her voice rose angrily. Tears pricked the back of her eyes. *If I gave you my heart today, would you still not want it?* Once again, she had her answer. Pulling the baby away from Rafi, she rushed out of the room.

Crying, Safiya stood at the window, clutching Zoha tight against her. The snow, a cold shroud, continued falling. Above the hum of the heating all Safiya could hear was her mother's voice—Rafi was honest, a good man, she reminded Safiya over and over again. He adored Zoha, took care of her every chance he got. Yes, he wasn't like Safiya's brothers who were always a hug away and invariably had a joke to share, but he loved Safiya in his own way.

A sob caught in Safiya's throat. No marriage was perfect. All marriages took work. And, yes, there were cultural differences. They were still adjusting to each other. In her head, Safiya understood it all. *So why was it that in Rafi's company, she felt the most alone?* she asked again and again. *Where was the empathy?* Whenever they'd met in India, they'd been surrounded by a loud hearty family at every turn. Left on their own, and after the halo of their honeymoon had waned, they often were left grasping for words to share. *Was this marriage? Was this as good as it got?*

Between his silences, her bitterness, and their mushrooming resentments, neither knew they were speaking different languages, expressing and asking for love in different tongues. Neither knew even love and empathy could be lost in translation.

NASHWA KHAN

[untitled]

The self-assured hijabi best friend of Kamala Khan, Nakia Bahadir, in the long awaited and well-received *Ms. Marvel* series is underappreciated and arguably one of the most valuable Marvel universe characters of this decade. Although much fixation is on the main character Kamala, Nakia is the best friend we all needed when we ruminate on how trash we may have been as teens. Self-reflexivity is *sunnah* and, as adults recognizing that many of us as diasporic teens in North America may have made questionable decisions and faced moments of conflict between a multitude of identities, it's part of the journey. Identity formation is constant, complicated, and produced throughout our lifetimes. Like a kaleidoscope, our identities are an ever-changing view and can alter with a twist or turn, a change of scene or setting. We are an infinite number of patterns, constellations, and combinations. While our kaleidoscope patterns shift and re-configure themselves, they can embody the ruminations that occur, reflecting the negotiations many do growing up brown and Muslim in North America.

Understanding this, the desire and longing Kamala has to fit in with the popular kids who remain townies and wish they were in high school their whole lives is relatable and a snapshot of a moment of negotiating a complicated reckoning while going through growing pains of adolescence. Although many of us walk the tightrope, Kamala traverses in the *Ms.Marvel* series. Nakia is the high school friend who knew what was up before everyone; she is the racialized Muslim girl so many of us wish we were, I wish I were.

As diasporic adolescents, the snapshot of who we are in those moments, betwixt and between, it is important to have characters that counter-story the assimilation and discovery of the self-narrative arch. Nakia is underappreciated, as are many kickass women in high school and the ummah. She is WAY ahead of the curve, some of us abruptly hit during post-secondary school, where being feminist, diaspora, and different is something that can be asserted and celebrated versus muffled and set aside. Nakia is not given enough appearances in the *Ms. Marvel* comic, maybe it is her very blunt reactions to the basic whiteness of her high school, her very strong personality, or overall discontent with attempting to conform and blend in the ways Kamala does.

Within the first few pages of the comics, I found the struggles of myself and my friends leaping off the page, the scenes so palpable. Many have written about this and attribute it to the character of Kamala, and I admit for me, when I was a thinker who fixated more on warm body representations, it was about Kamala; however, on a closer read, I was hungry for more Nakia. Kamala reminded me of the racialized people I see, and don't blame, who take ignorance from others as learning as she strives to be accepted by the popular kids. We bear witness to her identity, struggle, and battle with her identity as she calls her own name weird and has disdain for aspects of her cultural identity. We witness Kamala's fixation on the tall, blonde, skinny, and popular Zoe Zimmer. Whereas with Nakia, we witness a very confident young woman who couldn't give a shit about Zoe; Nakia sees through Zoe's paternalism reminiscent of the premature stages of the white feminist savior-complex.

Kamala calls her friend Nakia by a shortened westernized nickname Kiki. Nakia asserts that she does not want to be called by that nickname. Kamala then responds by saying, "Sorry Nakia. Proud Turkish Nakia doesn't need 'Amreeki' nickname. I get it." The tone and bolding of Nakia's name for emphasis can be read as sarcasm, the line as a whole shows a dichotomy and difference between two young Muslimahs navigating similar worlds in very different ways. This lateral complication of having a name disrespected by what is viewed as a peer is one that does exist in our very real world and one we should trouble. As a child, I realized early the ease with which people bastardized the beautiful name my mother gifted me. I also recognized the ways in which people stereotype individual identities based on names. It took me a long time to be wholly proud of my name and all of the meaning and history it holds. I still struggle with correcting people and ensuring they honor every syllable in my name, the name my mother blessed me with. Many young people face this struggle and it haunts them throughout their lives, lurking in the shadows of adulthood. Nakia gracefully makes sure every syllable of her glorious name is remembered and savored. Nakia, in the aforementioned scene, is the girl a lot of us wish we were in high school. Not taking the names others gave us, not letting our names be reduced for ease of white tongues. Nakia is the true MVP of the *Ms.Marvel* cast. She got an advanced memo about shit to avoid in high school and took note.

Within this first volume, we also witness Nakia presumed to be a submissive brown daughter, who must have oppressive Muslim men in her life that are violent and overbearing. Living in the West and navigating feminism, I have often faced such loaded assumptions. Media perceptions have stigmatized Muslim men as inherently more violent, specifically when also racialized. This is an extension of the widely held belief that Muslim women who wear the hijab in the West are forced to, when in reality this is an autonomous and liberating choice that disrupts Western notions of beauty and reclaims identity in a post 9/11 society. We witness the popular white character, Zoe, nonchalantly make assumptions that are rooted in tropes, orientalism, and racism but are read by Kamala as well intentioned comments with descriptors of Zoe after the interaction as "nice," "adorable," and "happy." This is illustrated in exchanges between Nakia and Zoe with witnesses when Zoe says, "Your scarf is so pretty, Kiki. I love that color" with Nakia responding "Nakia" and Zoe countering, "But I mean . . . nobody pressured you to start wearing it, right? Your father or somebody? Nobody's going to like honor kill you? I'm just concerned." This dismissive response to Nakia's assertion of her name as well as loaded statement is one that may make other young Muslims recoil and the friends who witness it including the comic's hero watches, and, as aforementioned, also uses Kiki. Nakia, however, a true hero, responds with, "Actually my dad wants me to take it off. He thinks it's a phase," while heroine Kamala covers her face. The warm-bodied, identity politics excitement of a character like Kamala is complicated when the real reckonings and battles are with Nakia, perhaps a character that is far too fervent for the Marvel universe. Although Kamala and I share a last name, we do not share politics that places existing and merely existing as a brown person in spaces as a radical intervention, and an inadequate one in these times. Going beyond reactive warm body placeholders in pop culture, we need proactive characters built into our worlds. Nakia is a character that disrupts popular understandings and assimilation narratives, one that has implications far beyond the Marvel universe. She has a confidence in her embodiment and is fierce as fuck, she doesn't get enough cameos in *Ms. Marvel*. Maybe Nakia should get her own series, because this is the superhero I've been holding my breath for.

SHAMIMA KHAN

Fall

I can feel the remnants of that old pain, brushing my throat. Pain. Oh, I'm tired of this! Of feeling pain and not your arms, your loose lovely hugs. Where are you now? I want to be able to forgive you for not being here, for driving me to seek solace in useless things like the curling orange leaves I walked through to the library, or the whiteness of the sky, and sometimes I can. Sometimes I do find peace in them. But not today.

Now autumn is disappearing. The maples and elms are heedless of my soft, sad warnings—they spill their leaf-petals carelessly away. You showed me how the trees lining Strandherd Station look like giant blossoms now. We walk among them as if we were miniature people in a marvelous garden. You listed the names. "See that maple tree? That's really an enormous carnation." I can't remember all of them anymore. Goldfingers? Lilies? It doesn't matter.

The trees—they aren't sentient, are they? They seem to be. They seem to be standing firm in their belief that it is good to give, give, give, and keep giving. They pour out the entire contents of their hearts, caressing the ground with leaf upon leaf. They seem so sure they will always have enough, that more will come, that there is no point in hoarding. They don't worry. Or maybe they don't even think about the future. Maybe only we do. But how can we not? Every second that whizzes by is one second closer to dying. We humans are aware of death. We know we are going to die. We just don't know when.

I didn't try to catch the first early snow flurries on my tongue today. I just stood under the golden-green canopy near Mackenzie and prayed. It had been some time since I had prayed in this way. So, it took me a while to find the words, and then to search for the recipient of those words.

Usually I pray to God in the sky somewhere. Of course God is present everywhere. So this morning I looked at the ground. I sent my eyes deep, deep down into the sweet-smelling earth. The fallen red and brown and yellow leaves were starting to melt and rot. How could decay smell so good? Your parable about love—about dying brain matter smelling like flowers and creating love—haunts me. You keep cracking open my wall as if it were a thin shell. You find your way under my skin and into my aorta, my left ventricle, my heart.

I keep making mistakes, sinning even, though I try desperately to be good. I think maybe I am never going to be able to be sweet and right. No matter how much I try. So why should I keep struggling? Isn't it futile? But my lips moved anyway. I needed to pray. I held out my hands in front of me. I held them out over the earth. I prayed.

On Sunday, my friends took me to Gatineau Park. We hiked around Pink Lake. The water was so still and green and solid that I was convinced I could step out onto it. Yes, I know. I couldn't. But I thought it possible. The fall rhapsody around us, the entire forest changing, I was in ecstasy. My friends laughed at my exclamation of joy, when we turned 'round the bend to catch a glimpse of the great fire of the sun, floating in the dark green waves. They reached out and pulled me into their arms, smiling. I was glad they were with me. But oh, how I missed you. I tried to bring you to me, with the sheer fierceness of my desire. I tried to make you appear with my breath.

UZMA ASLAM KHAN

Stealth Christian, Stealth Muslim

My first time in a cathedral was also my first taste of alcohol. Rose had brought to our convent school in Karachi, Pakistan, a small bottle of vodka. As a Christian, she had legal access to it. As a Muslim, I did not. We were fifteen. With prefect gowns as screens, we tipped the vodka into 7 Up and jumped the school wall, into the courtyard of St. Patrick's Cathedral. It was 1984. A war in Afghanistan. General Zia's dictatorship at home. The 7 Up bottle green as our flag.

I understood the risks. My father was a religious man whose own father had prohibited all forms of intoxication, even tea. 'Til he got married, my father's most audacious beverage was milk. While caffeine was not forbidden for me, ditching classes and jumping walls were radical trespasses, even without the drink.

I also understood the irony. St. Patrick's Cathedral is the seat of the Roman Catholic Archdiocese of Karachi, constructed on the site of a chapel made for the Irish troops who conquered these lands. Only in Pakistan could a respite from one chain of command be another.

What I did not understand, yet, was fear.

I remember the creak of the door and the small congregation inside. No one looked twice at the two girls in convent uniforms taking seats in the back. We passed the bottle between us, the paper straw kissing our lips, the 7 Up warm. The stained glass seemed familiar, not because I had seen it before, but because I grew up reading about such things in books. Besides, by the school canteen where I lined up for lunch each day stood a life-size statue of Jesus and Mary. Christian iconography was as much a part of my daily landscape as the canteen, or General Zia's sermons against non-Muslims, women, and the countries that kept him in power.

Most of all, I remember the feel of my surroundings: restful and spacious. After that day, whenever Rose and I escaped the convent for the cathedral, the feeling was there. This was and still is my deepest impression of what it means to be in a sanctuary. A sanctuary from war, dictators, families, and the school syllabi that bored us, for it came from Cambridge University in England, instead of the environment we embodied. A sanctuary, too, from having to explain ourselves to each other. We both knew the profiling to which Pakistani

Christians were subjected—as "unpatriotic" "outsiders" sympathetic to British colonial oppressors—and the complex histories being erased through this distorted lens. Karachi's Christian community is Goan Catholic, tracing its lineage not to British, but Portuguese India, established in the 1500s. Rose's family had settled in Pakistan before the Second World War. Mine arrived later, as refugees of the 1947 Indian Partition.

Yet we never concerned ourselves with questions of national identity. Outside our sanctuary, "othering" for other reasons was more intimately felt. Though Karachi's Catholic community is wealthier than the Protestants of Pakistan's Northern provinces, Christians overall earn far less than Muslims. And while Protestants assume Muslim names and wear the traditional shalwar kameez, the Goan community has kept "English" names and attire. Rose's uniform was a dress; I had to wear trousers. Our bodies marked the boundary between "Eastern Muslim" (pure or sexually repressed, depending on who you ask) and "Western Christian" (free or sexually promiscuous, depending). Yet both communities sent their daughters to convent schools because they were the more affordable private school option, had good Victorian values, and were same-sex. Exposure to loose and poor Christian girls or stifled and privileged Muslim girls was better than exposure to any sort of boy.

What we did not know then is that these binaries were growing more pronounced at precisely the historical moment when we sought each other's company in a cathedral. While Rose and I shared bottles of vodka and 7 Up, General Zia altered Pakistan's British-era blasphemy laws to include a death sentence for anyone perceived to offend Islam. When he introduced the Hudood Ordinances that deemed adultery and fornication "criminal offenses," Rose and I shared tales of love. During one of our last conversations within the cathedral's walls, she spoke of her attraction to a girl, and of a painful war between her faith and sexuality. So we both went in stealth, each time we jumped the wall. The proof is that I still hesitate to share the story of my first drink, or disclose Rose's real name. The proof is that while I was not afraid in 1984, now I have learned fear.

Recently, I shared this story with a white American colleague. Her response—"Muslim girls do that?"—immediately landed me in a state of shut-upness. As I struggled to locate the assumptions implicit in her disbelief, it got worse. I must not be a "real" Muslim, she kept on. I didn't even "look" like one. And where did I learn to be free-spirited—is it because I live in the United States?

These were not questions. They were opinions, gesturing for validation. So I did not say that my convent schooling was before I set foot on this continent; that if I am "free" I have my chaotic, complicated upbringing to credit. Nor that in the eighteen years I have lived here, on and off, I have experienced little change in how my intersectional identities are met with. My colleague's configuration of the "East" was familiar to me even before I began hearing it in the US: I had read it in the British books taught at my convent. It was familiar, too, for being eerily in reverse to the dichotomy championed by General Zia. For her, it was "oppressive" Islam; for him, "oppressive" West. Both fixed identities in opposition to each other, denying the possibility for co-existence.

The fear I have learned stems from what Edward Said spoke of forty years ago in *Orientalism*, and what Evelyn Alsultany recalls in her essay "Stealth Muslim": "Orientalism is constructed not by 'Bavarian Beer drinkers' but by people in positions of authority—government, journalists, scholars, Hollywood films, and the like. In other words, monolithically representing the experiences of 1.2 billion Muslims worldwide is not the result of ignorance or lack of education."

The fear I have learned stems from encounters with social justice groups in the US (my colleague identifies as an "activist") with a tendency to privilege one struggle over another. For white feminists, the struggle is gender and sexuality, as though war, racism, and colonialism happen on a far-flung planet. For anti-war groups, it is gender and sexuality that happen elsewhere—not far-flung, but too-close, private, hushed. Implicit is a legitimate concern that highlighting sexism and homophobia in Muslim and "third-world" communities will reinforce racist, imperialist stereotypes.

For myself, a brown, Muslim woman from a country with a recent colonial past and a present devastated by militarization, poverty, and war, it is impossible to separate "outer" and "inner" spheres. In the words of Audre Lorde, "There is no such thing as single issue struggle because we do not live single issue lives."

Where can alternatives to the patriarchal, colonial boundaries of what can and cannot be said be found? There was a moment when it felt the space might, finally, become available.

In January 2017, after President Trump's first executive order banning citizens of seven Muslim-majority countries entry into the United States, the widespread protests were a sign of hope. Would the politicians, journalists, artists, academics, comedians, activist, and others who condemned the ban also condemn why so few of the people being heard were from the communities on whose behalf they expressed outrage?

Perhaps it was with this hope that I casually mentioned to my colleague at the college where I teach the story of Rose and I and our cathedral sanctuary, in a Karachi held under siege by an Islamist dictator. It was a moment of trust, of not needing to explain. I had known that feeling with Rose, and had been missing it. I remembered capturing that very feeling in one of my novels, *Thinner Than Skin*, back in 2010, between two made-up close friends—not women, but men—and suddenly it was exactly my own yearning in 2017, as a national rhetoric that criminalized Muslims and Arabs caused hate crimes to increase by 15 percent, surpassing those after 9/11.

There are times when reality mimics fiction, but for this to happen, the fiction has first to be written. The passage I had written was this: "I'd been missing this, the ease of being with someone without speaking, without suppressing speech. I'd grown up with it in Karachi, where groups of men will congregate in the smallest spaces—the grass between houses, a doorway, a roundabout—spaces made more generous through companionable silence. It existed between women too, this bond. My sister and her friends could spend hours reclining together on a bed, or a carpet. If secrets were murmured, it happened in a style so intuited it was pre-verbal. I hadn't experienced this very much in the West, where it seemed people had a reason for everything, including intimacy."

When my colleague responded not with companionable silence, or easeful intimacy, but with opinions masked as questions that were othering, she reminded me that it is the daily interactions with people at work and other public spaces that are the measure of whether, even among "progressive" Americans who oppose the ban—which she did—more nuanced narratives of "third-world" lives are even wanted. She reminded me that for many Muslim Americans, including myself, there has been no effort to highlight our rich and complex diversity. We are still seen as a litmus test for how far American principles extend, in an attempt to sort out where Muslims belong. And these principles involve positioning "first-world" feminists as leaders of an inclusive feminism, while in practice, a feminism that is multi-racial, multi-religious, and intersectional is disavowed.

Last summer, the US Supreme Court ruled to uphold the Muslim ban. On the day of the ruling, I was visiting Karachi. I returned to St. Patrick's Cathedral for the first time in thirty years.

As I drove to its gates, I imagined what I might say to Rose, if she still lived in Karachi. I decided that I would tell her of my recent trip to Istanbul, where something astonishing had happened. I had gone to the Tulip Mosque, just before mid-day prayer. The mosque's pale-pink carpet was soft beneath my feet and a beautiful light was streaming through the numerous windows. There were eight men inside. One glanced my way, fleetingly. I hovered behind a column, expecting to be told to leave for the side room, where women pray. It didn't happen, so I sat on the carpet. Slowly, more men arrived. They ignored me. I began to relax, to admire the mosque's curious octagonal shape, stained glass, and marble walls of red, blue, and yellow. The dome was modest in size compared to Istanbul's more famous mosques, but still vast to me, resting on eight high arches with semi-domes between them, each inscribed in languid calligraphy with the names of eminent men. As more men arrived, I counted fifty-two. Among them, a preacher. At the richly embellished mihrab, he opened a Quran. I had never before sat with men in a mosque, let alone during a sermon. That it was in a language I could not comprehend made me smile. That nobody objected to my presence made me teary. A feeling of restfulness, of spaciousness, returned. I was in a sanctuary.

And what I wanted to tell Rose, on my way to the cathedral in Karachi, was this. The preacher had glanced at me only once before continuing without chagrin. After some time, the call to prayer came. The hall was filling when a policeman arrived. Indicating the room outside the luminous octagon, he told me to leave. On my way out, I looked inside the women's room. The walls were bare, of course. I had seen this my entire life, regardless of which country I was in. No dome. No carpet. No windows. Just a tiny, separate cell.

When I arrived at the cathedral's gates, they were shut. A doorman refused to let me in. Pointing to the security cameras, he cited "high security risks," measures that had come into effect "after the December bombing." He was referring to the bomb, hidden beneath a pew, which exploded inside the cathedral in December 1998. It went off moments after Mass had ended, as the congregation was leaving, injuring one woman and partially destroying the main hall. Since then, the number of attacks against the Christian community, which comprises about 1.6 percent of the country's population—roughly the same percentage as the number of Muslims in America—has increased.

I told the watchman that I had studied at the convent next door, and I was leaving Karachi the next day. Softening, he let me in on condition that I keep to the grounds. The cathedral's doors, for the first time in my memory, were locked.

I thanked him and entered the gates. I walked along the cathedral's periphery. I touched the stone, the same color as Karachi's earth, as our markets and mosques, as the plant pots my mother tends with her abundant love. The twin spires seemed taller to me now, the Gothic architecture, more imposing. Though I was glad to be there, it was impossible to feel at rest. Nor did I feel I had any right to. Though the stained glass windows were restored after the bombing, they were shielded by heavy metal screens, and I wondered what it was like inside, with hardly any light streaming in. I wondered beneath which pew the bomb had been hidden. I wondered how it was safer all those years ago with Rose, during a brutal dictatorship. I wondered whether two girls in need of solace could ever again jump the wall in stealth. For that wall between the cathedral and the convent was now mounted high with wheels of razor wire.

I left the cathedral's gates, passing the guard. He had been watching nervously, but he had trusted me. I thanked him again.

I went to a park. Along the walking track was a marker of small, zigzag tiles the color of the cathedral. The flowerbeds were well tended and there were joggers and walkers of every gender. Children played cricket in the grass. At the park's center was an obelisk, circled by four white benches. I sat on a bench. I was rolling the word *sanctuary* around on my tongue before I knew I would write it. I was thinking a sanctuary is, simply, inclusion, and inclusion is not about giving space. For whoever gives can take away. Inclusion is not a favor. Inclusion is a right. Inclusion is entering a space as an equal, undisguised, unbeholden. Nothing less, no questions asked.

A woman approached me. She held out her palm, yet her eyes did not beg. They assessed. I told her, "I am sorry, I have nothing." She answered, without hesitation, "You have God."

SERENA W. LIN

People Here Love You

December 12, 2017

Dear Alameda,

I rented a flat near the Notre Dame de Paris, France. The Seine smells like mud, and the breeze flows like a river of perfume. When the tower bells ring, my head is a gourd. All the history of this place amplifies me, ya Allah.

History. That's what Americans only *think* they lack. You're like children who refuse to grow up and join the world. You only remember the history you want.

I holed up and read murder mysteries for the last three weeks. To cope. Maybe to heal. Since the election, I want a world where there's still a murderer behind every murder. But I can't figure whose fault it is that the world is in the state of fuck it's in.

I'm tired of us being called the crazy ones. You're in the hospital. I'm out. We're the sane ones. The ones who aren't waking up from some fantasy. As if we're drugged.

Feels like fifteen years. It's only been a year. A whole City of Sanity over here. But New York—where everything happens but nothing gets done. Time you bust out.

Maybe, Alameda, I should have been honest that I had feelings too.

Love,
Hamda

2015

It was thirty minutes to midnight on a cool fall night, a year before the fateful 2016 election, when Hamda skipped the buzzer and knocked on the door to Alameda and Penny's Flatbush apartment. Outside, somebody flushed the toilet and turned on the stadium lights in the sky. Everything was damp and grey, irradiated with the color of loss. Penny got to the door first.

"I need to talk," Hamda said, breathless from a long or fast, or both, bicycle ride.

"About what?" Penny asked.

"Don't be rude," Alameda hissed at Penny. Penny let go of the door. It bounced against the front wheel of Hamda's bike. Penny had complained before that Hamda had a crush on Alameda.

Alameda felt guilty for leaving her partner so late at night, but Penny had been clingy recently, so stepping out for a friend seemed like healthy boundary setting. Secretly though, Alameda was annoyed that Hamda had come over, stirring up trouble.

As they headed out, Alameda let the door slam shut.

They walked a few blocks against a stiff wind. Alameda's zebra-print scarf flapped in her face. Past the Mickey D's, past the gyro truck. A Doritos wrapper latched itself to Alameda's ankle. Extreme nacho. She shook it off.

Like pilgrims, they passed through the stone archway into Prospect Park. Alameda strained to keep up as Hamda clambered up a hill.

"Why are you walking like that?" Hamda asked.

"I'm out of shape. We can't all be twenty-something and fit." A week ago, Alameda had tried to impress Hamda, Isaiah, Samiyah, and Lilah in an impromptu basketball game. I may be pushing forty, but I can keep up with twenty-nine year olds, she told herself. She'd barely dribbled down half-court before she pulled her calf muscle.

Now, as the night stretched around them, the ivy climbed too, higher and higher until it scuttled along the top of the tunnel, choking and cracking the stone. A homeless man whose shadow was twice his size shimmered and reappeared as a sliver of beard and two beanies, an angel made of desperation, peeking out of a sleeping bag. His hand waved in the air, and Hamda shook her head. "I got nothing." Alameda gave him a dollar.

At the lake, Hamda gestured for them to sit on a creaking bench with peeling, green skin.

"What's the emergency, Hamda?" Alameda asked. "Penny's gonna kill me."

"I need advice. I feel like I'm going to break down. You know I've been wanting to go into theater. I can't stay in the chemistry department anymore. I can't even afford to go back to Iran. I can't see my mother and she's sick." Hamda buried her face in her hands and curled her knees up, but her eyes were dry when she raised her head. Wisps of her russet moptop rose about her like nerve endings.

"I understand how rough things are," Alameda said.

"No, you can't understand. Your family's from Taiwan. You can be a poet because you don't need special skills just to be here. People don't suspect you of being a spy when you're organizing. Even other Iranians question me, especially the ones born here."

"You're right. I can't understand." Alameda tried not to get defensive. *What would her parents say?* she wondered. *They were let into this country for their engineering degrees, like Hamda.*

Alameda scanned the park for eavesdroppers, but not another person was in sight, a rare occasion, even though it was late. The newly remodeled Lefrak ice-skating rink was empty and ghostly, lit from behind until its surface was a pale, shiny pool. It was as if there were two lakes, Alameda thought. One lake was choppy but alive. The other one was frozen.

"I can't tell you to finish your program, Hamda. When we're really close to getting something that we've worked so hard for, that has taken a long time, we get scared. We tell ourselves we don't want it anymore because it's too painful to think we won't get it."

Hamda's eyes started to water. Alameda had read that energy leapt from a crying person to the person that held them.

A voice in her head agreed. *It's like lightning from the sky to the trees.* Alameda ignored it even though she was scared. She put her arm around Hamda.

"Hamda, when we make a commitment, the person that we are changes in the middle of that journey. Sometimes the only way we'll get to know who we're becoming is to honor the decisions made by the person we *used* to be. We have to trust our past selves too. If you're no longer meant to be a scientist, you can stop in a few months when you graduate. It's not fatal, not the end."

Hamda let out a long sigh. The night tugged at Alameda, trying to turn her homeward. Gentle drops of rain began to deliver their unanswerable questions into the water.

"I used to love thermodynamics," Hamda said. "Isn't it like magic how one drop joins the whole of the water?"

As if it were never separated at all. Alameda stayed silent, not wanting to share this new voice with Hamda.

2017

In January, Alameda returned to the NYU mosque for her first Jummah since the Damp Old Runt had won. Her first Jummah since she'd returned home to an empty apartment, practically overnight. Last year, Penny had packed up and left in May. Alameda felt somehow further damaged by the election, unclean. It wasn't something she could rid herself of, the sensation that she needed to wash away the world. She'd have to burn her clothes and her baseball cap so she could feel truly and thoroughly unsullied.

Lilah and Samiyah, her closest friends in New York, hadn't even saved her a place as they huddled near the windows facing Washington Square.

The tech co-working hub that Samiyah had joined was located nearby in Union Square. She was a Jummah regular. "I was late from the office too. We thought you weren't coming," Samiyah said, catching Alameda's annoyed glance.

"I'm glad you're here. Can I borrow a scarf before the aunties bust a seam?" Lilah said as they rummaged through Alameda's backpack.

Alameda squeezed between her friends and a stern auntie with the shoulders of a baby elephant. The auntie offered a disapproving head twist and pointed toward the exit with her chin.

You're not a real Muslim, Bear said, *so you shouldn't be praying. You said you'd never follow a God who spoke through the mouths of homophobic men again.* She'd named the voice in her head Bear this summer. Her anxiety, and the voice, had intensified after Penny dumped her.

Alameda found herself shuffling along as everyone stood up and formed the line. It's wrong, she thought, to get between the righteous.

Bear shrugged and asked, *Are you an Infidel or not? Decide.*

Alameda shuddered.

When she sat back after the prayer, a curly haired baby with dusky green eyes laughed and crawled in front of Alameda as the Imam circled twice around his original point and wandered off with his Khutbah.

Nobody puts Baby in the corner, Bear reminded Alameda.

The Imam droned on about how the Prophet and his household were starving. They had one lamb left. Some travelers came to beg for food. The Prophet shared that lamb with the guests until nothing remained, except for the shoulder. His wife was upset.

"How could you do that? We only have the shoulder left," she said.

"No," the Prophet responded, "we have everything except for the shoulder."

"You only have what you give to others," the Imam insisted.

And haven't we given enough? Alameda thought, her hands trembling. Nothing was the same anymore. It was like everybody was out hunting for a safer identity. She'd been to so many protests. She'd even gone to a three-hour immigration law clinic because Samiyah wanted a useful spouse. "Has to be a trans dude, not a woman, because my family might find out," she'd hissed when Alameda had suggested herself. When Alameda had then mentioned Isaiah,

Samiyah had groaned "Are you insane? My parents would die if I married an Israeli." All Alameda wanted was to help her friends, but she'd traded in her life as a practicing attorney for a writing degree and obscure secretarial duties.

"My art makes no difference," she had argued with Bear several nights in a row.

It makes you present, Bear whispered before curling up on his side and falling asleep, drooling on the pillow. That was where Penny used to sleep. Alameda tried not to resent the imaginary creature that had replaced her girlfriend.

༄

Months ago, when she'd been about to recite the Shahada in an impromptu living room ceremony in Lilah and Samiyah's Ditmas Park apartment, she'd hesitated, causing her whole queer lot of friends to disintegrate into squabble.

"No, it doesn't technically mean you have to say he's the last, Alameda," Lilah rolled their eyes and plopped onto the couch, inspecting the hem of their poodle skirt.

"Well, do you believe he was the Prophet?" Samiyah asked, earnest, one hand on Alameda's elbow as if she could guide her to the right answer. The other hand tugged at a corner of her hijab.

Lilah jumped back in, their voice raised. "If you think you're Muslim and want to claim it, then you are. People need to stop fetishizing the Shahada. It's not some magic incantation that's the be-all and end-all of being Muslim. The Qu'ran says that it's Allah who gets to decide who's a Muslim, not some whack committee of Muslim Po-Po." Lilah was a down-to-earth scholar, and Alameda appreciated their original analysis.

"So now it's like being gay?" Hamda grumbled. "So long as you self-identify? Is everybody queer?"

"I don't know what I believe," Alameda interrupted, leaning against the flag of Palestine that covered the entire wall of Lilah's living room. Everybody stared at Alameda, their mouths dropped like traps. "For now, maybe I shouldn't say the words. Maybe it's like being queer. Oppression matters. I don't carry the same burden because of my race. So how about I just be a friend of Muhammad's, a F.O.M., 'kay?"

Alameda chuckled weakly.

Nobody else did.

"F.O.A.?"

Still, no laughs.

Have a little faith, said Bear.

~~~
⌇
~~~

October 27, 2017

Dear Hamda, why didn't you come and visit me?

~~Fuck, fuck, fuck.~~ Alameda crossed out the entire sentence. What shit. Her letter was stupid. She decided to send Hamda a copy of her latest poem, *Romantical Astrology*.

Everybody writes about the moon in Brooklyn.
My favorite astrologers are the ones who generalize about my need
for self-improvement and ask for my trust. The improvement of my
finances is pre-ordained. When I've experienced the rare let-down
that prediction entails, when I've failed to meet the right Pisces or neglected
to care for the right Cancer, I fall back on Aries. They're like a bad drug.
Your evolution on them is an entire universe. Every now and then
I'm driven out into the night, the crush of sweat and tropical punch
dance anthems overwhelms the face of a thousand lesbians. None
of whom thought once about asking me out.

My friend is certain she can find the right man to marry her. I suggest
a Capricorn because the green cards are on lock-down and people are being
sent away to places where the only phones are rotary. By the lake,
I weave a daisy chain and hand it to my friend whose eyes are the color of
sunsets that douse the gazebo in pink and crystalline. Are those for me?
would be one question she could've asked, but she asked another instead.
We're so lucky to be friends can be an appropriate reply.

I'm definitely confused about love given the way I expected the train to stop,
but the ivy has broken through the concrete. A woman with a busted umbrella
    says The MTA is repairing it tomorrow. We all react, we all jump on the R
track
    but I miss the signs because I'm reading a Neruda poem about the ocean
the rivers
    the stars. The doors open at Coney Island. I'm lonely and need to buy detergent,
    but the vendor beyond the sidewalk holds a sunflower in his fist and mouths
two for one. I gather my wits and watch the one coaster, running by itself, rattling its wooden rails, rushing to the bottom, unruined by the rain.

At the party, everyone had loaded up on plates of lentils and potatoes, rice and squash. It was a vegetarian *Thankstaking* hosted by everybody's favorite queer Muzzie mixed-hijabi couple, Lilah and Samiyah.

"Please don't bring any more food," they'd e-mailed a few days ago. "Especially not gross meat dishes."

"It'll be small," L & S group-texted Alameda. "Don't be down—she's not worth it. Come out! Have you talked to Hamda since she moved to Queens? Her mom died last week. She doesn't want to be alone and asked if you're coming too. Family + Love. See you A!"

Alameda couldn't make up her mind to say no.

You should still make something, Bear said, pointedly, taking Alameda's hand and dragging her to the kitchen.

She arrived hours late with a vegan mac, complimented Samiyah on pairing her polka dot suspenders with a houndstooth hijab, then plunked down on the couch, not feeling hungry. Her friends debated heatedly while playing Cards Against Humanity.

"Let's take a bet," Lilah said, during a game break, winking and embracing Samiyah who linked her arm around Isaiah. He self-referenced as "your friendly token neighborhood anti-Zionist Jew." The three of them leaned in. Lilah and Isaiah put their heads on Samiyah's shoulders. Alameda loved her younger friends, but she was annoyed when they all piled on each other, like puppies.

It's okay not to be touchy-feely, Bear crooned.

"I know," Lilah clapped. "Who among us is gonna have kids first?" They started calling out each other's names.

Bear hummed what sounded like: *Inshallz, Inshallz, Inshallz.*

Alameda wanted to die, but then she noticed that Hamda was red-eyed and quiet next to her, picking at a piece of bread.

"It's hard," Alameda said so only Hamda could hear. "When my father died, he'd already rejected everything that I was. But it doesn't matter what age you are. Losing a parent means losing your sense of who you are in the world. Your anchor. And you're afloat one day with no place to stop and rest." Hamda's eyes welled up. She got up and went to the bathroom without saying a word.

Alameda sat back against the couch, feeling stupid, as ten, then fifteen minutes passed. Hamda came out of the bathroom and slipped out.

"*Your friends are lost, too,*" Bear patted Alameda on the knee.

Nobody noticed when Alameda disappeared and headed toward the F train. She wrote a poem for Hamda on the train, then crumpled it up.

Bear pawed through the trashcan. *Alameda, I'm telling you, you can always start a blog.*

Wednesday, November 9, 2016

At the protest, Alameda had seen Penny sauntering around near Union Square, wearing overalls, of all things.

Strange look for her femmeness extraordinaire, Bear scoffed.

Alameda hadn't even wanted to go to the action. Her leg was sore. But Hamda had convinced her it was important to stay together and not be alone. "We're ALL in shock," her text said. "Let's #ShutItDown."

So now, even though Penny and Alameda hadn't talked for months, they were swimming together through an ocean of Not My President signs. Penny's glossy hair blew soft, touchable, like she'd merely slipped out to the bodega for a mineral water and managed to find herself in a teeming *Time* magazine portrait of thousands.

"Hey boo," Alameda said under her breath, certain Penny couldn't hear.

Don't call her boo, asshole, she heard Bear say.

This must be a goddamn joke. Running into an ex-flame was the worst. Now even the revolution was going to be tainted by Penny. A stranger jostled Alameda in the back, and she returned with a quick elbow, feeling tense.

Behind Alameda, a white woman in a pink cap walked up and screamed in her face, "Pussy Got Back!" She joined the rest of a predominantly white contingent, carrying signs of NO MORE NAZIS and FASCISTS GET LOST. Why do things always have to get weird? Alameda thought, as the white folks streamed past her chanting, "Whose streets? Our streets!"

Five Black women in front of her raised their fists in the air. Alameda raised her fist too. She noticed that Samiyah, Isaiah, Lilah, and Hamda had all done the same. The heat of the crowd caused everybody to congeal and expand. A helmeted officer stared them down, his eyes hidden behind a dirty plastic shield. High above his head, he held what resembled an 80's boombox. It blared:

Step out of the street or you will be arrested. If you are on the street, you will be arrested. Make your way to the side, you will not be arrested.

"Disperse!" Samiyah yelled, but Alameda was too mad at Penny, or the apparition of her, to listen. The crowd swarmed against her back, chanting, and she stumbled forward, her face landing somehow in Penny's chest.

Penny seized her by the shoulders, and Alameda closed her eyes. Penny's tongue in Alameda's mouth felt warm and thick. *Am I dreaming?* Alameda asked herself. She felt feverish and horny and ashamed. She was supposed to be here protesting the monster and instead she was making out with her ex, another villain. Allah knew the country was in enough danger.

Alameda had sworn she'd never sleep with Penny again. The anger flushed through her, and the throng pushed by like pounding waves. They washed up against the food truck still making out.

The vendor flashed some red sauce, and his eyes never left them, passing judgment, as he made a gyro for a hungry protestor carrying an Angela Davis sign.

Despite the passion, Alameda felt a loss that she couldn't shake or accept. Maybe it was really over—all her pretenses that it wasn't true—that the person in the world she loved most was also the one who'd hurt her. She was still kissing Penny, and she still loved her. She engulfed Penny in a hug as the anxious crowd parted like mice in the wake of the cop's directive. The crowd made their way toward the sidewalk, and Penny stepped back away from the fray. "I'm sorry Alameda, but there's more than one way to protest. You don't have to march in the cold to make change."

Then Penny was gone like so many of the protestors who'd seemed so eager to #Resist at the start. There were still shouts in the street, a clump of activists barreling from the side, past the police blockade, yelling. Ahead, Samiyah and Isaiah beckoned her to join them in Broadway, waving Lilah's Palestine flag.

"Hurry!" She heard Hamda's voice.

Bear's fur tickled her cheek. *You sure you want to do this Alameda?*

"Why?" Alameda said, tugging at the buttons of her shirt and taking off her glasses because she couldn't see past the tear stains.

Because this way is the funeral, and that way is the pyre, Bear said, pointing toward Trump Towers.

Alameda sighed as she hefted up her sign emblazoned with the words of Frantz Fanon, *We revolt simply because, for many reasons, WE CAN NO LONGER BREATHE.* Black Lives Matter. Her arm was tired, but she kept it aloft and marched past Columbus Circle.

There's no good time, Alameda realized, to mourn the past.

TARIQ LUTHUN

The Summer My Cousin Went Missing

I should have asked how our *khalto* was holding
up, but I knew where she would be: her body

weary & unkind, buried in the day's tasks; back turned
to the home she grew up in; seeds in the

farm's soil, like miracles, sprouting as
she tends to them. Is this not always the case?

Child upon child goes, and someone's mother
is no longer a mother. My aunt—a mother herself—looks,

for a moment, away; nothing she plants has roots
long enough to hold. She turns back anyway, looks

ahead. If we are too caught up in the end—like boys
fleeing from the day's news—eyes worried

about that which we cannot control,
how ever will we stay fed? How ever

will we live long enough to grieve?

Ode to Brown Child on an Airplane
for the First Time

I don't remember if I, too, was afraid,
but I do remember when the sky was
our thing—I could say the word: flight

and, in its stead, none would hear fight
spill from my jaw. The last time it took
a punch, I was in the boy's bathroom,

surrounded—by boys—as a boy
unleashed his fist into me. I returned
the favor into his gut, and ran. Moments

before, he had called me gay, but I wasn't
sure why I had to defend my glee—scarce
as it was. Hours later, a mess of tears

ran through me as I was pulled from gym
by the principal and suspended for defending
what little parts of myself I could still call

mine. I don't know why this is the story
I choose to tell, but I do know that I may
forget it once we take off; shedding the skin

that everyone fears of releasing
towards the sun. Beautiful,
isn't it, to be able to leave behind

this world, its lost and angry boys.

I Sing This Elegy for the Nameless

moon I watch in the morning before my old man wakes up
to call me on all the wrong I've done. When I used to pray,
I saw myself a dove: sun through my wings,

God lifting my back into the gunmetal-grey sky.
When I stopped calling out
to deities, some might have seen me

a crow: God beneath me and my
belly, as I cried and cried out
for anyone to take me from

my solitude, yet nobody knows
the truth. In these hours meant
for slumber, I wager that not all

creatures with wings know flight; and
there is no time for rest when
even the snakes lay eggs.

The sky is too heavy now, and what good
is the earth if the fallen is all we find
there? Those old men buried

all in the dark
with their shovels, and
called us the sin.

Upon Leaving the Diamond to Catch
14 Stitches in My Brow

You and I will never be more
brothers than we were
in the heat that summer,

in the park, when the bat,
newly painted in my blood,
lit my father to yell

at all the other kids playing baseball who
know, now, the sound of men
—darker—from a different world: hurt, ready,

and loud. Our fathers—and the off-white
noise they let loose—didn't help,
and might have

made matters worse. I wake up
in the back of an all-white room
I do not recognize, its luminescence

bouncing off the walls. I come
to know this room—place I had
never been—while you continue running

circles around the neighbors, lest their
tongues point towards our families' names;
lest they—for the first time—see us

bleed and think: prey.

Political Poem

Blessed be the Transportation Security Administration
agent for, after flagging my red duffel bag at the airport, allowing
me—who, in the winter months, is a rather light-skinned Arab-
American—upon several minutes of careful debate,
to keep my organic coconut oil so that I—despite having
bought the container from a certain Midwest superstore's
baking section—might apply this essential moisturizer to my thirsty
skin, because it is quite abundantly clear that the contained substance is
safe: solid at room temperature, and—when in its purest form—white.

I Go to the Backyard to Pick
Mint Leaves for My Mother

Today, my mouth fell
wide when I saw the light
slip into the hills, and those boys

I grew up with did not
come back. Or, so I hear. Mama
would often ask me to gather

the mint leaves from behind our home,
and so I would leave for this
nectar—without it, there is nothing sweet

to speak of. I pray that
when I am gone, my people speak
as sweetly of me as I do of them.

I see us, often, steeped
in the land and hope that
a shore remains

a shore—not a place to become
yesterday. The girls have joined the boys
now—all of them

tucked just beyond
the earth. But I know they wouldn't run
from their mothers—not without a fight,

a chase, a hunt, a honey, a home
for the tea to settle; a haven
for us to return to.

TARA MESALIK MACMAHON

A Pilgrimage to the Hives of Withered Bees

is what the gods of perfect sugar make.
And she scales a green mountain to Mexico,

to the shrine of no roof, no walls.
Where white butterflies

trace infinity loops. And the Stations of the Cross
always mess with her shadow, dealing

rummy or stud poker,
perhaps a progression of macaws.

༓

Buenos dias.
Buenos dias.

One goes up,
another comes down, and she wonders,

will she ever touch a man, the way
the gods of perfect sugar

make the mornings peach or persimmon,
even peach-persimmon.

༓

Buenos tardes.
            Buenos tardes.

And rain, and again, she a lonely firefly
in August, when she meets

a brown boy inside her yellow head,
and he speaks hyacinth, speaks blue juniper.

꒰ꗄ꒱

He even *cantas* her poetry, *cantas*
her Saturdays, her Saturday Snoopy pants

she wears all week long,
except on Saturday.

꒰ꗄ꒱

Funny, how the mind fills, fills the mouth.
How the filled mouth stretches for water-

melon, for rain. How rain fills
the calla lily, fills the belly—

button, sunbathing in August.
Akin to vodka in a votive—

꒰ꗄ꒱

in Vienna, where her grandmother was born,
before The War before The War,

before refuged to Mexico. Though no tequila
to tithe the travel. Vodka in a votive.

༄

Now repetition, just another word
for tortilla chip, another word

for train trip, her first five years
she goes to live with her grandmother.

༄

She goes to live with her grandmother because
her own mother couldn't cope. Her own mother

couldn't cope with a second child, couldn't cope
with a child born not-a-boy. A girl

who one day might bumble, even crumble,
or then again ride—

༄

the interminable train—all the places
you'd never hope to see except,

sadly, she does a thousand times
just sitting there. Movement.

Movement without movement,
without action.

Though sometimes her heart thrusts. Thrusts a rush
and she clambers back

to Grandmother's home. Grandmother's home
where the gods of perfect sugar

take their Sabbaths. Where Brother visits
on roast-chicken-Sundays and always wins

the *pan-dulce* eating contest.
But does he cheat?—

the gods and she wonder. She wonders
if Brother will return—her thoughts

clearing as after infection, after rain. Yet her words,
all fish and pine tar, and she bumbles on. Bumbles here—

here on the scales of the scales of a green mountain
to Mexico. On God's fifty-seventh floor—

somewhen between fifty-six
and after she stops yearning.

Or is it *somewhy* between fifty-eight
and how she continues to yearn?

But isn't there supposed to be
a pause, an ending? Some dark-opaque

wisdom fashioned to save her?—
to save his *cantas*?—save even a green mountain?

ॐ

     Buenos noches.
Buenos noches.

Just one swift fetch of a single flare,
and she'll open her knapsack of stars.

Even the Sky Bleeds

lilacs, chrysanthemums.

Her mouth a river, a mortar,
an anxious pestle.

Even hardwood is temporary.
So why does she keep on hurting?

How many little deaths
find a chance named remembrance?

How many accounted for? Only the ice
has ears. A marriage laid low.

Where, What, When, How
travel further together, further against,

a fast ship of inches,
these rings of questions.

Who alone swirls in the *Whylight?*
The greens so close to the blues.

Yet, what could they know?
How could anyone know?—

smoothest hands, lissome curves,
all the ways she loved him.

HAROON MOGHUL

Quebec Was the Semi-Colon

A driver's license was my chance to finally be faithful to myself. My parents' salaries provided the vehicle. An alliance with the House of Saud ensured a fantastic price for gasoline. Over ribbons of pockmarked asphalt, looking very much like my pimpled, cratered teenage skin, I raced north past Springfield, Massachusetts, and the last two skyscrapers in America. Soon the houses grew few and far between, the forests thick and haunted, the hills worn down and wizened. It would not be fantastical to say I feared I'd fall off the end of the world. Nor dishonest to say I hoped I might.

Hours more would pass, well into darkness. I could have unintentionally entered another planet. But then, abruptly, suddenly—this was before the war on terror, of course, when our politicians had the gall to call for walls to come down—Montréal. Like ending in Rivendell, long after one thought all hope had been lost. I might as well have been encountering Elves. They spoke French here, which I did not. They were beautiful, sophisticated, otherworldly, and free. None of these were me. Still farther was the Ville of Québec, an apparent castle and promontory, Chute-Montmorency, the Île d'Orléans, and then the end of the world.

I wanted to disappear to there. But I did not listen to me, and now it is too late. Québec is gone.

Though I chose New York for college, this was false bravado. Having come all the way to the capital of the world, I made the bold, uncompromising decision to study—wait for it—not even me, but who other people wanted me to be. For my foreign language requirement, I chose Arabic. (There was no Urdu, but I decided Arabic was closer to me than Hindi.) Though I briefly flirted with the idea of joining the South Asian cultural scene, largely to pretend that I could flirt with South Asian women, membership in the Islamic Center was as unoriginal as it was inevitable. For my first summer, I continued Arabic studies in Vermont, voyaged to Montréal for a weekend, and then returned to Greenwich Village still very much the same.

But when I'd gone as far as I could in the college's Arabic program, I headed to Egypt where, only twenty-one years old, I saw myself for the first time. In the sentence of my life, Cairo was the semi-colon. Rather than spend my time studying with venerable teachers in ancient seminaries, or genuflecting in supererogatory prayer, I spent my free time in the Oriental outposts of Western franchises. That, or smoke shisha, or flirt with Egyptian girls which, also, I was not very good at. I loathed what I learned about myself, even as I was incapable of fighting very hard against it. (I suspect now I never really was that interested in trying.) It was not that I disdained Islam, but that what was on offer of it had not sufficed. Though I dropped in on mosques, and not without some enthusiasm and thereafter some serenity, inevitably, I would move in another, apparently incompatible direction.

Not away from being Muslim, which I could hardly imagine.

From having to make the choice.

From the demands of an invisible, omnipresent omniscience.

Years before, after all, I had tried to convince myself Allah did not exist. My immediate response to this conclusion was to flinch. I was waiting for He-who-did-not-exist to strike me down.

My disinterest in the embodiment of standard, Sunni orthodoxy saddened me. I contrasted myself to my upbringing, to my idols, to my role models, and found myself wanting. I began to feel, for the first time in my life, that I required another kind of identity, an alternative modernity, one that had the added disadvantage of not actually existing anywhere. So, either I contribute to the construction of it, or I opt out altogether. Not from religion, but from places where the religion came from outside of me, as opposed to grew organically from within me.

Had I had the chance to do so, I may have done the second. Gone back to America. Dropped one major, added another. But then the decision was made for me. The Prophet Muhammad said that a time would come when holding onto Islam would be like holding onto hot coals. I used to think: Who burns himself purposefully? The answer: the one who is made to hold on.

I came back to America. I resumed college. A few days later, the towers were knocked down. Terrorists killed thousands. We began a war that has killed hundreds of thousands more, in an enormity so obvious in retrospect that we hide behind our culpability by calling it a mistake. The "oops" that is still unfolding. The region that hasn't even finished unraveling. When I am honest about the condition of the Muslim world, about my religion's and my country's implications in each other's tragedies, their tensions with and to each other, I am often overcome by emotions so powerful I can hardly cope. I feel myself bonded to people occupied, driven from their homes, suffocated under military rule, who have endured decades of misery and strife, even as I know another part of me is attacked, too, terrorized too, traumatized too. It is not the appreciation of a distant injustice. It is as if a part of my body itself were broken by another part of itself and I just watch.

When I'd started college, I worked with like-minded students to build another kind of Muslim students' club, something better, wider, gentler, stronger. It took me years to realize that my desires to be more Muslim and my subsequent impulses to run away from Islam were not contradictory. What brought me into the mosque was not different from what teased me out of it. Only a madman would set himself the task of repairing a house whose inhabitants seem intent on murdering themselves, condemned to a property that more and more believe should have been condemned ages ago.

Unfortunately for me, I only made this connection later, far too late, when there can be no public escape from the private burdens of identity. That is the purpose of terror: to build walls, to force us to stop where we are, to prevent us from becoming anything but who we are at one moment in time. That is the end of occupation, invasion, colonialism: to allow oneself to go anywhere, to be anything, at the expense of another people's freedom. Now, though, I must stand still, or I am made to stand still. To raise my arms. To prove I am not a threat.

Many of us thought, during the Bush years, that perhaps the world would go back to the way it was before, that this was an interregnum at most, that September 11th was a vile action which would be responded to with intelligence, courage, and foresight. Now, though, I suspect we came of age in the twilight of empire, where men more murderous than Al-Qaida have mastered the social media cycle, who know their smartphones better than they know their Qur'an, who are the detritus of a pulverized region, the dead pieces of our religion resurrected with Frankensteinian effect.

It is impossible to escape. Religion is not only belief, after all: The TSA has converted more people to Islam than any modern dervish.

We have to believe there is a better world around the corner.

Even if we know we may never see it.

At least I know now what attracted me to the Québécois, to their country, in my youth. (I do not know if I should appreciate the insight, or if instead it will burn through me with a violent resentment.) When I was still coming together as a person, those who spoke for God compelled me, but they also contained me. I could hear them better than I could hear myself. In my defense, though I did not feel fully part of their world, there existed no other world I could imagine being a part of. Enter French Canada, which was equal parts my parents and my peers, even as it was neither my parents nor my peers. The Québécois were after all Western like I was, though I was too dense to know it. They were descendants of defeated people, like many Muslims are. They were a deep south in the frozen north, except they did not fight for the right to be evil, but to be left alone.

To escape the Anglophone arc of history, which is long. And conclusive. Modernity's deceitfulness was obvious to them, and to me, even as my high school peers were oblivious to it then. Look at their blue-and-white flag with its four fleur-de-lis; the French themselves have abandoned it—these people are orphaned. Look at their license plate with its ominous nostalgia: *je me souviens*. Not only that we remember, it laments, but that you shouldn't forget that we remember, it threatens. Who is this they address with it—this white man's burden, this hierarchy of civilizations, this telos of all things, this Fukuyaman assumption, the deaf confidence of white Anglo-Saxon entitlement, still reigning now, though the hour of its hegemony grows late? I wanted to drive a car with that vengefulness assigned to me. But it is too late.

Today I am compelled by the world. I am demanded to answer for my faith. Omnipresent God has been secularized into omnipresent surveillance, not just by governments, but the vastness of our culture, the need to justify my identity, answer for it, or be limited by it. There is no escaping Islam anywhere you go. Not Islam as belief, but Islam as civilization, as threat, as peril, as crime, as guilt, as sin. Where can you go, after all, where you do not have to apologize for yourself? Certainly not to the Québec that has embraced France's Islamophobia.

When I think of Québec now, therefore, it is as a dream, a place where I could have turned into that person the world will no longer permit me to, where I can be neither American nor Muslim, a relief considering the impositions both make on those of us who are stranded in between. This isn't Stockholm syndrome. It's frustration from futilely pulling at the bars. Sometimes I sit down, close my eyes, and think back to what could've been.

I see myself in a café, faded and wood-paneled, somewhere in the towns north of the St. Lawrence delta, or on the shore of Gaspé. I'm warmed by a strong fire I can feel, though cannot find. There are singles and couples beside me, but none have yet spoken to me, and I prefer this. I see them only fuzzily, and make out snatches of mostly indecipherable conversations against the howl of a snowstorm outside, a blizzard so thick that God Himself cannot see through. I will write about worlds that don't exist, places that can be reached only with legendary difficulty. I have beside me a cup with contents I should not be drinking, in my hands a pen that has not yet been tried, and before me a notebook as open as the world was supposed to be.

FAISAL MOHYUDDIN

Ghazal for the Diaspora

We have always been the displaced children of displaced children,
Tethered by distant rivers to abandoned lands, our blood's history lost.

To temper the grief, imagine your father's last breath as a Moghul garden—
Marble pool at its center, the mirrored sky holding all his tribe had lost.

Above the tussle of his wounded city, sad-eyed paper kites fight to stay aloft.
One lucky child will be crowned the winner, everyone else will have lost.

Wish peace upon every stranger who arrives at your door, even the thief—
For you never know when your last chance at redemption will be lost.

In another version of the story, a steady loneliness mothers away the rust.
Yet, without windows in its hull, the time-traveler's supplication gets lost.

Against flame-lipped testimonies of exile's erasures, the swinging of an axe.
Felled banyan trees populate your nightmares, new enlightenments lost.

The rim of this porcelain cup is chipped, so sip with practiced caution.
Even a trace of blood will copper the flavor, the respite of tea now lost.

Tell me, Faisal, with what new surrender can you evade deeper damnation?
Whatever it is, hack away, before your children, too, become the Lost.

Song of Myself as a Tomorrow

It is not far—it is within reach;
Perhaps you have been on it since you were born, and did not know;
Perhaps it is everywhere, on water and on land.
—Walt Whitman

In America—where my face is anything
but American, I lunge for self-annihilation whenever
another set of monstering eyes double-barrels me

                              enemy
          outsider
                         sandnigger
                                        terrorist
murderer   thief
          target practice
                              less-than
dog   shitfacet   respasser
                                   imposter
          invader
                    camel jockey
                         terrorist   *Muslim*
abuser
          enemy   foreigner
                                   disembodied
                              Bedouin

But erasure—
                    what can it do when the blood's trajectory
has forever been about becoming another river, about winding its way
along some other pathway toward survival? How else
could I have come to be when

pillage

loss

civil war   Partition

        loss

displacement

                    Partition   loss

                              silence

        Partition

loss

              migration

                    heartache

    grief

              separation

        loss

                                        displacement

    Partition

        displacement   silence

migration   loss

          Partition

    Partition

                              displacement

          silence

      hunger

touched every moment
of my parents' lives
cobbled together

onto the unlived tomorrows of children?
To plunge into tomorrow requires the existence
of a tomorrow to plunge into—

I am that tomorrow, lost within the land
beyond where all rivers end,
in the barren vastness of an untethered
darkness where survival means

remembering my parents' tomorrows,
knifing new furrows through which their refugee blood
can flow—
means saying, despite the price
of standing tall and free,

        Yes

                to exile

            Yes

          to America

NOUR NAAS

Mother(land)

I was a girl who ate up hours of the night in thought. Lying on the hard floor of my father's computer shop in the storage room, I contemplated the life I was living as if it were not mine at all. That was the summer we lost everything.

Libya existed as a hope, a refuge, a swelling benediction that gripped me by the tongue. It was a place of return when America failed to keep its memory at bay; an intimate and final hope of belonging. I looked to Libya in the way I always did, rested my faith in a rumored country that I loved.

✧

I was thirteen years old the first time my father beat Mama in front of me, early in 2009. Mama shared my bed with me for the next two weeks. Every night, she held me in her arms until she fell asleep, and I would listen to her breathe, feel the heat of her whisper at the nape of my neck, always making sure to follow her pace. When summer came, we lost our home to the recession and were forced to move into my father's computer shop. That summer, my father sent me, my mother, and my little brother to Libya with a one-way ticket. It was the first time I was going to visit Libya, and Mama's first time after eleven years.

We arrived at Tripoli International Airport in July when the sun was most powerful, and I met my aunt and cousins for the first time at the baggage claim. On the way home, the country roused my tired body with *dhikr* resounding from a stereo sitting on a cart by the roadside. We drove past young men playing foosball midday on an island resting between a two-way street as women and men strolled the roads on their way to work. Muammar Gaddafi's face was plastered patriotically on billboards we saw throughout the trip to my grandparents' home. I thought of my mother's vigilant words that she repeated like a mantra: *do not say anything opposed to the regime when you are here*. Mama had stories about the life she lived in this country under dictatorship, before she married my father and immigrated with him to the United States. Stories that were buried and would not resurface until Benghazi sacrificed itself to the revolution.

The heat was wet, sticking skin to cloth, beads of sweat forming at our hairlines. The AC didn't work so we had all our windows rolled down. A thick, cool breeze brushed against our skin as the car rushed down the road, swerving potholes and waste too big to ignore. Auntie Adeba and Mama spoke and cried and laughed like they were compensating for their eleven years apart in one car ride. When we finally reached the house, I saw five kids standing on the dusty pavement in front of the gate, one slumped on his bicycle, staring at us as they opened it up: a welcome home.

꒰

Mama spoke with my father over Skype a few times while we were in Libya. He was always the one that called, and it almost always ended with Mama in tears. On those nights, she, my brother, and I would go up to the roof together. A warm breeze curled around our limbs as we looked out at the stars cradling the moon, in all its divinity. In that stillness, Mama would hold us tightly in her arms and promise things would someday change for the better.

꒰

In February 2011, Benghazi sparked a revolution. It wasn't long before the whole country was up in flames and Gaddafi made a public appearance on national television attempting to hem the revolution by threatening protesters with a bloodbath. At my father's shop, our new home, Al Jazeera was playing nonstop on the television. My family and I attended Bay Area rallies in solidarity. We shared news updates like gossip. I listened to revolutionary Libyan hip-hop artists. I wrote poetry to keep the fervor of revolution alive from my bedroom.

Mama and I never stopped speaking about breaking free from our circumstance. We both, more than anyone else, were under my father's constant surveillance. He would lend me and Mama computers to use, until she found out he had installed spyware on them. We would use the public library computers instead.

In March, a multi-state NATO-led coalition was given permission to intervene in Libya and ambush Gaddafi strongholds. In America, we grew impatient. Samra, my then-newlywed cousin who was pregnant with her first child, lost her husband to a sniper's bullet to the head. Cousins were on lockdown during the no-fly zone. In the embattled city of Misrata, my aunt and her neighbors were having their food and water delivered to their homes by the rebels while a war raged on outside. Everyone was desperate and uncertain about the future.

Seven more months passed before Gaddafi was summarily executed in late October by the rebels. Everyone was crying out freedom. Mama told me one of her distant cousins who had been in exile for more than a decade had finally returned home. The revolution intoxicated the people with hope. I recall the morning it happened, Gaddafi's bloodied body making an obnoxious appearance on every major cable news network, how naive I was to believe the transition from revolution to self-determination would go undisturbed. That naivety was one I would not recognize until I was exposed to post-revolutionary Libya.

⌇

The next time we returned to Libya, I was seventeen years old. It had been less than a year since the demise of the old regime and as we were awaiting our last connecting flight to Libya from Frankfurt, it already felt like home. There was the warmth of familiarity in the brown faces and hijab clad women seated at the gate.

The plane dropped down against the tarmac. The airport had been renamed Tripoli Idris International Airport, after the monarch who ruled Libya before Gaddafi's coup d'etat. The grass was the color of sand, long and wild, and there were barren black patches in places where fire had reached. The airport structure was riddled with dents and holes from stray bullets. I didn't notice Mama crying until she turned her head away from the window to confess her grief of returning to a homeland she recognizes less and less each time.

The airport functioned almost as lawless as the country itself. Employees blew their cigarette smoke in the faces of clients who didn't seem to mind as much as we did, and families were brought into rooms to be interrogated by plainclothes men. Huge dusty carpets were stacked against a corner of the airport for those who needed to make salah. We walked outside to the car and found men who look like my uncles striding the front of the structure with Kalashnikovs slung across their shoulders.

Graffiti had revived the old city. We didn't drive past one block on our way home without passing a mural. Gaddafi's face quashed under a boot. A name and prayer for a son was was made into a martyr. Omar al Mukhtar's image speaking the same fateful words he promised his comrades during the Italian colonization: *we do not surrender; we win or we die.* On that first day, I believed them to be a promise. The revolution will not go in vain.

꒰꒱

I celebrate my first Eid al Fitr in Libya at extended family homes. Our first stop is my mother's cousin. My Arabic is broken when spoken, but I understand it perfectly. Her cousin is holding his seven-year-old son in his lap. The boy has big brown eyes. He is shy and says little. Mama's cousin tells us about NATO's bombardment of Tripoli last year. How his son was constantly covering his ears, crying to the sound of explosives. How, after constant bombing, he learned to differentiate between the French and British warplanes. This was another moment that I realized this was not the same country I left in 2009.

꒰꒱

I visited Khoms for the first time. Khoms is Mama's birthplace, and a two-hour drive from the capital. Mama's cousin invited us to spend the day with her. My brothers and I rode in one car with Mama in the driver's seat, and my aunt and her kids took another. We drove for a long time before we reached the countryside, where Mama and auntie Ashraf raced down empty roads, taking turns passing up one another. The whole way there, we were constantly rolling the windows up and down. My brothers and I exchanged silly faces with our cousins across the lane marker, laughing heartily.

We met Mama's cousin at her home with the high ceilings. She took us to tour the place that served as a corridor to the Roman city harbored at the edge of the city. Mama paid the six dinar entrance fee, and we wandered through. My brothers and cousins found a secret staircase that ran to the tip of the ruins. They crawled up and balanced their bodies along a narrow path of stone connecting one side of the old market to the other. The rest of us looked up to see them smiling and took their pictures from below.

We moved through the ruins with the sun beating against our backs until the stone floor grew disbanded. Soon I was only walking through sand with occasional tufts of grass peeking out. In the near distance, I could hear waves lapping against each other and saw the ocean from beyond the bush leaves. The Mediterranean rests at the lip of Leptis Magna, with the pillars of Rome becoming more scattered as we approached the water, randomly prodding out of the sand like an explosion. We were the only people on the beach that afternoon, with the ancient city in plain sight. This was the first time Mama swam in the Mediterranean after twenty-three years. I watched her from the shore, twirling in the sea.

*

We left Libya at the tepid end of August. I don't know why, but the hope of return was more fleeting this time around. On the day we left, I run up four flights of stairs to go to the roof one last time and sit with my back against the wall. I scan the city sky, notice the same star I called my own standing on the veranda of my grandparents' home one night, and I suddenly start to cry.

*

During my last semester of high school, Mama was considering moving to Libya, and I had no qualms about it. She bought a plane ticket to visit alone in April to set things up and make a surer decision. When she came back, it was almost May, and my father had grown tense. I think it's because he knew Mama was planning to leave him. My father became paranoid. Some weeks after Mama returned from her trip, he had me surrender my American and Libyan passports to his possession.

The weeks following Mama's return from Libya, the tension at home swells. My father is quiet, unpredictable, like he is a hanging fire. But it is the eighth day of June when my heart sounds as if there is a dagger to my throat. I hear my parents fighting in the back room where me and Mama sleep before Mama calls my name and I am rushing my limbs to her like her life depends on it. And before I know it, we are out in the alley behind the shop—my father, Mama, and me. That's when I hear it. That's when I see it. The four bullets that pierced her flesh, though the coroner's report says it was seven. But what difference does it make? My father walking away from the body. My screams echoing through empty streets. And I run, just like Mama always told me to do. I run, run, run.

*

There are things, unspeakable things we go through as we move through this world. I cannot reconcile who I am now with the girl I was before, when I did not know death intimately, when I did not feel it carving whispers within my bones.

*

I am looking through old photographs from a box in the living room when I find one of Mama from 1999. I wipe the dust off with my fingers until it shines under the light. She is beautiful here in a way I don't remember. It was a beauty that existed separate from the sorrow that invited itself in years later, like a door left open. The room looks like a reincarnation of Libya, with traditional cloth covering the arid white walls of a typical American home, baskets woven from date palm by Tuareg, and it seems my mother is singing as she plays the riq.

ح

A lot changes over the course of three years. New passports have been issued in Libya. They are no longer the symbolic green of Gaddafi's jamahiriya, but a navy blue. It is the impulsive nature of grief, more than anything now, which makes me desperate to return. Even as I chore through the news of new deaths in Libya, new drone strikes, new policies, and a new listing as one of the most dangerous countries in the world, I am always set on return. But I never find my old Libyan passport.

In September 2015 the Department of State issued a statement warning US citizens against all travel to Libya. Two years later, with the advent of Trump's Muslim Ban, Libya passes one of their own in retaliation against American citizens. Soon, I am completely barred from entrance, unable to obtain evidence that I am a Libyan national. Without a Libyan passport, I am not recognized as a Libyan by the state. I do not exist.

LEILA CHRISTINE NADIR

Cold War

My parents competed for their children's love, measuring affection through our ethnic, religious, and consumer choices. Since we grew up in The States, my mother had the home advantage. What kid wouldn't choose her all-American fun over my father's foreign moral policing? When her favorite Top 40 songs crackled through our car's radio, she turned up the volume, and she, my siblings (one brother, two sisters), and I sang-shouted together, our blue Volkswagen van barreling down the country roads of our small town in New York State. She filled the house with the smell of chocolate chip cookies baking in the oven, pulled out her credit card for trendy outfits and ice cream sundaes at the mall, and snuck me into the hair salon when my father forbade me to cut my long hair. "Just put it in a ponytail," she said, and handed me an elastic scrunchie when the new perm curled my hair to my ears. "He'll never notice." (He did.) Baba made rules, and Mom taught me to break them. She was the normal one, I thought, just like every American in the USA. During high school football games, she twirled a baton at the front of the marching band, kicking her legs high into the air in a mini-skirt and tasseled boots. So I did my hair the way she wanted, moussed, teased, hairsprayed, and frizzy on top, so I could be normal too, like her and everyone else.

Baba was different. And not only was he hell-bent on accentuating his difference—he called it "Afghan Pride"—he wanted for his children to be different too, just like him. When my aunts sent new *perhan tumban* from Afghanistan—for some reason, they always chose the most conspicuous hues, bright red, shiny yellow, lime green—he suggested I celebrate his sisters' gifts by wearing them to the mosque, which was fine; I could do that, but he didn't stop there. Why didn't I wear these flashy baggy outfits everywhere, to the grocery store, to the post office, and—the thought terrified me—why not to school to show my friends I was a proud Afghan girl? My hometown in the 1980s was a town with limited global imagination. My classmates made sense of my brown coloring by guessing my family had come from Italy, the darkest, most faraway place these rural white kids could fathom. And I didn't correct them. When I resisted Baba's idea of interrupting my high school's parade of stonewashed jeans and white t-shirts and sneakers with an Afghan fashion show of radiant pink, he turned away, wounded, as if I had personally insulted him.

Mom gladly would have let me and my siblings plant our butts down in front of the TV all day, or chug cans of soda to quench our thirst, but Baba found these behaviors morally dubious. The icy Coca-Cola fizzing in our glasses at dinnertime, he announced one day, was actually "chemical water" and no longer allowed in his house. *Family Ties* and *The Cosby Show*, family-safe programs by most standards, were deemed proponents of a licentious American culture when the child characters grew up and began to date. One awkward teenybopper kiss and Baba was up from the couch again, shutting off the TV's power. Our time, he declared, was better spent practicing Persian writing skills, and he instituted after-dinner lessons. I drafted letters to my aunts and cousins in Kabul, whom I'd never met. I translated newspaper articles or paragraphs from novels, which he painstakingly marked up with red pen. More homework upon regular school homework, plus thirty minutes of Qur'an reading every morning and prayers five times each day. Baba exerted concentrated effort to impress an Afghan, Muslim identity upon his children, to counteract the American culture we naturally absorbed every day, the culture my mother reinforced just by being there.

Because they were engaged in a perpetual power struggle, my parents refused to tell me how, exactly, they met. They didn't want to give each other that much credit. Their relationship had turned so bitter they couldn't concede that at one time, long ago, they had actually fallen in love. Though when I was a teenager, my mother made a snarky remark I never forgot, and today I find it rich with interlocking clues.

"I was in college, and your father sexually harassed me," she quipped angrily when I pushed her on the subject. "I passed his house on my way to class. He sat outdoors smoking cigarettes and yelled at me from his porch. He said one day I'd marry him, that I was going to be his wife, and I told him to leave me alone."

My mother had followed Clarence Thomas's Supreme Court confirmation hearings closely in 1991, shaking her head at the TV, in disbelief at Congress' treatment of Anita Hill. The experience pushed her a few notches further on the feminist scale. I suspect this is when she adopted that new empowered vocabulary to describe her first encounters with my father. But her sexual harassment strategy never sat well with me, and over the years, the more I thought about her words, the clearer it became that her story didn't indict him any more than it exonerated her. I was an Afghan-American kid, I understood both my parents better than they understood each other. I knew them too well to fall prey to such easy accusations. An Afghan man in the West for the first time, my father had been unfamiliar with standard dating protocols, and though the budding-feminist version of my Mom didn't want to admit it, she'd obviously been receptive to his pursuit.

My father spent every moment he could in the fresh air. As a teen, I was driven mad by his demands that I drag myself from my horizontal position on the couch and stack wood, shovel snow, weed gardens, rake leaves, and help with all the other outdoor projects he seemed to invent for no good reason. In the summertime, when friends visited, he pulled half our living room furniture onto our front yard. Chairs, a coffee table, and a Persian carpet for "real" Afghans, like him, who preferred to sip their tea while sitting on the ground. His makeshift entertainment area included a stack of faux-wood drawers, the portable storage system for his Afghan music collection. On certain inspired evenings, when Baba popped one of his cassette tapes into his silver boom-box and pushed play, our guests would nod their heads to the beat, eyes closed, smiling nostalgically. Long-lost neighbors from Kabul, uncles who finally made it to the States, sometimes a refugee or two still living in our basement, mostly men but also a few bold women—they rose to their feet, raised their arms, flicked their wrists, and danced in that light-stepping Afghan way I've never gotten the hang of. While the voice of Ahmid Zahir, the most famous pop star of 1970s Afghanistan, crackled through my father's boom-box speakers, our guests hummed along, forgetting their exile for a moment on our lawn, remembering the optimistic days before the Soviet invasion and the mujahideen war.

So, yes, I can see a younger version of my father, outdoors on his porch, most likely sitting on his steps, foregoing the comfort of a chair. And he was a smoker back then, as my mother reported. Family members tell me a crinkled red Marlboro pack was always stuffed in his jacket pocket. And now I wonder, had he chosen the brand of the independent American cowboy because the promise of rugged independence seduced him, or because Marlboros were simply a convenient brand back in Kabul, available at all the shops? I can see him on his college apartment steps, blowing cigarette smoke into the wind, with his legs crossed, the way he sat on our stoop when I was growing up, with an elbow propped on his knee, a posture that made him appear smaller than he already was.

My father was strong-built for a relatively small man. His height was 5'6"—

just an inch taller than my Mom, but he made up for his size with agility and sturdy bones. He exhibited a sort of non-American athleticism, which he maintained with random bouts of body-conditioning. Push-ups, sit-ups, some periodic stretching to touch his toes. He began new exercise programs whenever he looked down and discovered his "stomach is too big." Jumping-jacks were the preferred regimen, wherever and whenever, sometimes while Mom fried eggs for breakfast or during commercial breaks of the evening news. A set of one hundred could even be thrown in while he waited for his carpool ride to work. In his dress-slacks, with his briefcase at the top of the stairs, he clapped his hands atop his head and his legs sprang back and forth, shaking the walls. My little sisters bounced breathlessly alongside him, practicing their Persian counting skills, *Deh, bist, si . . . sed, Baba!* For me, this was another instance of my father seeming hopelessly out-of-date, out-of-place, and improper. I wished he would put on a pair of athletic shorts or go to a gym. But his system worked. He always lost the excess weight and remained in relatively good shape his entire life.

He had begun working at the age of eight, when his father was wheeled on a gurney into a Kabul emergency room and never came back out, leaving behind three hungry daughters and a wife who couldn't work. Until his teens, my father sold newspapers, dug ditches, laid bricks, and soldered circuit boards. He did any job he could find, all while falling further and further behind in his schoolwork—until 1955, when the Afghan Institute of Technology (AIT), run by American teachers under contract with the University of Wyoming, opened in Kabul. AIT paid boys to quit their jobs and devote themselves to academics, its goal being to train the next generation of skilled, technical workers for a modernizing Afghanistan. This gift of education convinced him that the US was truly the Land of the Free. American college classrooms, he believed, were electrically charged with passionate student debates and professors who explained the ideological pitfalls of various political positions. A collective commitment to the right to free speech. He wanted to be a part.

He arrived in New York State with a full scholarship from the US Agency for International Development, and no need for a job aside from washing dishes at a local diner a few nights each week. Yet, instead of feeling on top of the world, as he had expected, he was preoccupied by his classmates' uncomfortable glances whenever he talked to them about international politics. The USSR's expansion into Third World countries concerned them, nuclear war, the war in Vietnam, and of course, communism had to be stopped. But when he pointed out the key role Afghanistan could play, he noticed them blink—"Afghani-stan?"—as if the world had fallen out of focus. He explained how the American government used to send millions of dollars to bring progress to his country, to build airports, highways, and electrical grids, but the aid had dwindled since the mid-1960s; he wasn't sure why. This left the door open to the USSR. in the north. The thoughtful responses he expected never came. Instead, his listeners said: I had no idea, I didn't know, very interesting.

Not until my father crossed the Atlantic Ocean did he realize he came from such an unconsidered place, somewhere so far away in the imagination, so alien, that it was a cliché for the most ridiculous of ideas. *"Yeah, maybe in Afghanistan!"* He heard this more than he wanted to admit, Americans' casual dismissal of his beloved home. If only he could make Afghanistan appear as a real place, with real people, not some funny idea. If he studied the books his professors assigned, the optional articles too, and typed his papers at the library until two in the morning, he could return home with an advanced American degree, become an emissary, an ambassador, represent Afghanistan on the international stage—

But he got distracted. There was another American freedom that he had not expected, a freedom more fascinating than free speech, equal opportunity, or public education: the freedom of young people to do what they want. From what he could see of his college peers, they didn't begin working as children. They weren't married off in their teens. There seemed to be no parents, no elders supervising their behavior. That's when, I believe, my father broke through the invisible wall of culture, a wall he had never realized was there, and tried to talk to the pretty blonde with the pixie haircut who walked by his house every day on her way to class.

He must have noticed his future wife's platinum hair first, hanging across her forehead, in her eyes, grazing her thin nose. Almost every Afghan man I know who came to the US to study for a university degree in the 1970s and who mar-ried an American woman just happened to fall for a blonde. These bicultural couples were my parents' best friends when I was growing up; every weekend, if their families weren't at our house, we were at theirs. I whispered my secrets to their daughters and played Nintendo games with their sons. In the kitchen, our mothers pressed *naan* onto cookie sheets and rolled their eyes about the conservative behaviors of their Afghan husbands, who were outside, oblivious, shuffling a deck of cards and sipping green tea on my father's Persian carpet on the lawn. I observed these marriages, and being a product of one, I wondered how such bickering couples had negotiated their differences when they met. The women had been interacting with the opposite sex their entire lives—as grade-school playmates, sometimes as friends, and later as lovers in that space of freedom carved out for premarital male-female intimacy in American culture. The men had attended boys-only high schools, like my father at AIT, in a society where dating did not exist.

My father's first marriage was arranged when he was eighteen. His bride was sixteen.

Perhaps, then, it makes sense that before figuring out how to invite my mother to the movies he informed her that she would be his wife.

On his porch, with a Marlboro between his lips, he shouted to her as she approached with her bag and her books.

"Ay, you! I'm going to marry you!"

NOOR IBN NAJAM

questions arabic asked in english

how she fit the life in the body? how he fit the blood in the
body? how he fit the body in the grandmother and how she fit
the grandmother in the blood? how she fit grandmother of
me
in tongue of her? how he fit gender of her in mouth of her?
how he fit mouth of her in the language? can woman she fit
gender of her in end-letters the words the arabic?
  yes, the blessing of God oh God where gender of me? no can i
  i find it in letters the alphabet, not the arabic
not the english never. no can i i read it when am i read verses
the qur'an and no when am i read the newspaper that she
drown in blood the queer.
    read me article in the newspaper about pride the queer in
    Lebanon and no found me the blood on the pages and
    returned
  her tears of me to the heart, and released her weight of the
  sorrow, and appeared her the tears time again in two eyes of
    me, and was i joyful and was her the tears without salt,
  because were we are we expect the blood and no we found
him. ~~he~~
~~fit gender of me in the language the arabic? he fit gender of~~
~~me in the language the english? why no can i i read him? why~~
~~no can i i find him?~~
am i ask questions i know her the answers indeed. no he fit
gender of me and no he translate good between the english
and the arabic because he live the gender in body of me
  and no can the body follow when he change the tongue to
  code new. am i know this. but he fit the violence very good
behind teeth of me, and all the time he wait, hidden in mouth
                                                        of me

when i speak arabic like child, no fluent.
does chair have him gender?
                        does gender chair he fit in the language
the arabic? has jam of roses
                                    gender? where he fit gender jam?
                            no, that's not the same thing
what about the roses? grandmother of me no heard me never i speak
language can she understand, never in blood on tongue of me. no i
heard grandmother of me she say word *queer,* never in blood on tongue
of her, also. he fit tongue of her in mouth of me? and is this queer?

SAMINA NAJMI

Memoir in Dust

Nostalgia is Karachi dust gleaming on the shelves of Mister Book. Watching from the balcony as lives converge in Kamran Market, the muezzin's call to prayer a periodic refrain to other imperatives: live chickens to sell from wire cages and mangoes ambering on a wheeled cart. Cumin cookies crumble in our mouths as we walk staidly to the Kodak studio for a family portrait. Nostalgia is filmee songs blaring from the barber's radio, guts on the ground, the stench of slaughter, feathers scattered at our feet.

Dust Bowl has echoes of ruin and nothingness, of land laid bare by fate and folly. Lives rendered unlivable where they had been rooted. Migration, the reset button! The toil, the journey, a new patch of eart—halien and inviting—from which to sprout a future.

"You just take care of the dusting," he says. "I'll mow the lawn." *Just?* Dusting is delicate, diligent work. Approach each piece with reverence: pick it up, caress its contours, and place it back exactly where it asks to be, a little shinier for your touch. How is that *not* heavy lifting?

Dust bin—an anomaly in my present life, on this continent. It makes my children laugh to hear me use the term; it annoys me to hear them laugh in the face of my urgency to take the trash out before we miss the weekly pickup. *Dust bin* stays, reverberates through the decades—memento of a tongue acquired in a land that wasn't mine and couldn't keep me. It holds the things I never asked for, never wanted, and the dust of everything dear.

Let me get up, then, dust myself off, and move on. From love? From motherhood? From home as I have known it for twenty years? It was dust I cultivated, dust I planted, dust that blossomed and bore fruit. Let it linger a while longer on me. I don't know how to breathe without it.

Threshold

The three-by-five color photograph stares at me accusingly from the dining room table. Down the hallway, the white door to my parents' bedroom is clamped shut. My mother emerges from it to tell me she had to calm Abbu down with a valium in the aftermath of his discovery of the photograph.

The tattling photograph shows a young woman, nineteen or so, smiling into the camera. She wears a tomato-red shalvar-qameez, her long dupatta thrown across her neck, more trendy than functional. Barrettes pull her wavy, shoulder-length hair to the sides of her temples. Light skinned for a Pakistani, her face shows the barest trace of makeup. A young man, perhaps a year or two older, sits on the couch beside her, to her right. He does not look Pakistani. Olive skin, hazel eyes, a too-straight nose and frizzy hair, he is obviously a foreigner. He wears a striped blue and white dishdasha and a dimpled smile. His head tilts toward hers, his left arm reaching around her shoulders. Their smiles are shy, their eyes aglow.

The late-afternoon Karachi sun finds Abbu seated in silence on the balcony, oblivious of the tea growing tepid in its cup. Tears stream down his face as I sit beside him, the daughter who has disgraced him.

ॐ

Maya hasn't emerged from her room this morning. Her first winter break at home from college, maybe she stayed out late with Joseph, her boyfriend of two and a half years. They came into her life the same year, Joseph and this condo, which I bought—a year after the divorce—because she loved it. While her brother took his time and I waffled, Maya's embrace of the condo was swift, decisive, and unwavering.

I must let her sleep in. Then again, she might not want to miss our yoga class together. "Maya?" I whisper outside her door, as though not meaning to be heard.

At first Maya says she doesn't think she'll go to yoga today. But a few minutes later she's in the hallway, her yoga mat rolled under her arm, long hair gathered in a ponytail.

After yoga class, we sit across from each other at Panera.

"Joseph has a profile on Tinder," she says. Her voice is gentle, her face composed.

Joseph? Sweet, soft-spoken, harmless, aimless *Joseph*?

In the flurry of texts that ensue between them that day, Joseph only digs himself deeper. But he does not want to break up.

Maya's vision is clear even where she most loves. "Maya Bina" I named her:

the Bengali for "love" paired with the Arabic for "having sight." Alchemy to dissolve the adage that love is blind.

When Joseph parked by our curb the next evening, it was for the last time. Maya met him outside with whatever belongings he had left behind. Their exchange was brief.

"Does your mother know?" he asked.

Maya nodded.

"What did she say?"

"Nobody expected it," Maya answered. And that was all.

I know not to linger at the threshold of my daughter's room. I walk by it, casting a furtive glance. Only once do I catch her off-guard, looking away, her face bereft.

ॐ

The Mourning Dove flutters between its nest in the neighbor's tree and the small, rectangular patch of my backyard brimming with grass seeds. In the early light, I detect another bird stationed in the nest, but its perch is too high up for me to see much of anything else in it. That must be the male, incubating the eggs for a few hours before he hands the job over to his female partner for the rest of the day. From among all the possible locations he showed her when he wooed her, she chose my neighbor's tree as the site of their new home. They built the nest together—he, the gatherer of the raw material, and she, the one charged with making meaning out of it.

I hear Mourning Doves are monogamous. I marvel but don't envy them.

Maybe the eggs have hatched already, and he is babysitting the fledglings up there while she gathers the rye seed below, to chew in her own mouth before feeding it to her young. They can't handle the business of living full throttle just yet. Every seed she picks is a dot of green that will be missing in the little lawn I have allowed myself this spring.

I watch her through the glass panes of the slider between my bedroom and the backyard. I see her in profile, dark semicircle under her eye. What will she do when the fledglings, plumped with grass seed, outgrow her space and falter into their own? Dizzy with dreams, and longings fueled by flight. Is that when the mourning begins?

Partition Story

I.
My father left this world
and with him some of his story.
I have small bits
but not the whole.
This is the story where we have
returned to Hyderabad together.
Back to the graves of my grandparents.
Back to things that are no longer there.
Maybe he would tell me how much has changed.
Maybe he would tell me what was here once.
The path he walked to school.
The places he loved most.
This was the story I was waiting for.

II.
I cling to glimpses of things
shared quickly over kitchen tables.
Sambar sits in silver bowls
like constellations as he
mentions long walks by cattails,
photographs of reflections in the water,
places he worked, his love of learning.
a determination to save lives.
But I never got
the full story.
It would sit there on the edge
of his lips like a small cloud.
Maybe he left that story on the Deccan plateau.
Maybe he wasn't looking back.
Maybe I never asked.

III.
In a frame is a picture of a small boy
not smiling,
post-partition India,
standing straight
with a heavy bag of books
across his young shoulder like a shield.
Holding in a story—
rain within clouds.
Kept that story
somewhere tucked in
suitcases and train windows,
buses, car rides, planes,
over oceans,
over continents,
Kept it.

IV.
This is the story you will lose
if you do not ask.
REMEMBER THE NIGHT
the police informed us
someone in our neighborhood
did not want us there
our mailbox blown up for the third time

pieces of metal box
falling across the ground
like sharp snowflakes
the year 1979
the year it was common to

blow up mailboxes of people
you want out
of your neighborhood

remember the night the police informed us
someone in our neighborhood
did not want us there
the year 1996

the year our car windows were broken
multiple times in a week
crushed glass under street lights crunching
as they said not wanted here

where are we wanted?
where is that place?

i want to be there

ZEESHAN PATHAN

Rampant, I

The day after his wedding
There is talk of un-kiss, un-touch,   un-graze,
And un-love.

There is un-fragrance (attar) in the tethered air, an un—
Raveling of hands (fingers), an undoing of skulls as in a blizzard.

My body as a letter
A defunct
Sign making-system, with snowy veins,
Inscrutable, inscrutable.

The red door of sycamore trees is closing, he says,
Like the stern voices of angels.

The febrile mind now colorless
Unhinged a little more,

Once Freud's station of the uncanny—
A creature now in the middle
Of its forsaking, in the unlit earth of the storm.
To A Mother Tongue I Can No Longer Pronounce

Protolanguage and despair
You are the daffodils given to me—
That I never plucked
From the fields of infinite pain and dire milkweed—

I hold you in my blighted palm
Sometimes at night when the horses
Are running
Feral through the pastures

When the archaeologists are sleeping amiably
Inside their tents, dreaming (with their microscopes)—
And the earthquakes, the earthquakes
Have ceased for a moment

You are the little seed I ponder, the fragment
Of a papyrus scroll, pistachio
Rust in a barrel
A bone of a ziggurat monster, with inscrutable fractures—

The broken tablet of Nimrud, a lamasu's wings of lapis lazuli
Wedded to Shiva's seventy-seven imperishable hands—
I cannot decipher you,
Not now, not ever,

No matter how many times
My tongue clenches you like Death
Between my two large teeth—
Like an earthen jug in a peasant's spent

And prostrating arm, you slip away incessantly.

Lorca, II

You are dead and I am living in the brazen
Sunlight of a day when the streets
Have been cleared of all the bones
The poets, and Shelley's ghost have finally
Been vanquished from the Thames
And under trees there are no more birds
Without broken wings or life fatigue,
This pollution in the lungs. I went into the plum field
Looking for your body and incalculable caravans
Of people followed my shadow.

I went to the olive tree and it was scarred
From an axe
Blow given by a bulldozer
Operated by a child who doesn't know what he is doing.

This is my prayer. The doors of the night
Have been eaten by termites. I am just beginning.

HANA QWFAN

Ghusl

I found myself a mystery
with the globalization,
with the name "Bint America"
with the henna across my hands
like barcodes for registries.

I found myself a mystery
when I tried to unpack the pressed
packages from Europe and now
the New America. To understand my
history of the 20k debt in matrimony.
to understand the four wives. to understand
the two female testimony.

I found myself a mystery
with what is socially constructed,
packaged and pressed down and
shipped to the Middle East. But when
the box gets delivered, the hands that open
it are called foreign. you've told me before
that you've tried by calling patriarchy
at "my Allah" in the heavens, but tell your vet husband
that he can find it under your mother-in-law's feet.

I've learned that your kind of gender divide only causes
our problems to multiply. things shouldn't
happen the way I hope to; my tribe is too barbaric,
we're still making our rounds through English
learning that what is now is "—ing" (for the indigenous)
past often has "—ed" (for the amnesia)
future always book ends with whispers of
"—will" and "—will not tolerate" (for our children)

Unowned Body Parts

READ FROM RIGHT TO LEFT

Inspired by The Arabic form created by Marwa Helal

eye evil the about worried is mother my
[1] ع aiyn
beauty youthful my for me curse will that
like more is it—witch a or spirit a not is it
will that breath deep a above currents wind
away fortune good my blow

age my about worried is father my
[2] خ oumri
both we as wither and grow will that
wali the be can he before deteriorate
price to bride a not am I—wedding my to
new a am I instead—throw to daughter a or
I pages whose chapter on a stuck reader
ending never—fold and fold and fold

be may she whoever—law-in-mother my
fertility my about worry will
[3] ع khusubti
is it instead—future my and me of because not
boy young a have to desire her and hers to due
son her smile and mannerisms same the has who
—gone is son your. inshAllah. khair. have to used
him I met before much man a was he

---

1. Evil Eye
2. My age
3. My fertility

[4] ع aiyila
weather the control cannot I
time the control cannot I
body my control cannot I

---

4. family

ANISA RAHIM

A Russian Hacked My Pinterest Account

containing images of waterfalls and fashion pin-ups
I know this because Pinterest sent me an email
that I had logged in from Moscow   and later that week the IRS called me
from an Indian call center   and when I told the man over the phone as I
    sipped my tea
that I did not believe that he was from the IRS
and that I did not owe him money   he said he would take me to municipal
    court
throw me in jail   I said he should be ashamed of himself
an Indian defrauding another Indian   imagining him and a dozen others
    huddled
together in the basement of Pallika bazaar   making these calls
where I once bought pirated CDs   I told him I would report him to the FBI
and in this way, borders permeate   their waters seep into computers and
    cellphones
I have been border-crossing all my life   not the kind of breaking
that is illegal but still a crossing,   trying now to be still and stationery
    domesticated
think of these lone figures,   specs or dots on a map   on their tablets and
    computers
trying to be like comets or shooting stars   or rather   small snipers
from the solace of a distant living room

Hot Carpets

I am on the living room floor
and my brothers and I are playing Dungeons and Dragons, slaying
as we dart from the couch to the table & I am next to a Christmas tree
in a red dress or was it white with frills   were we unwrapping
Christmas presents or were we cutting yellow birthday cake
or was it ice cream cake   and did I have chicken pox and have to stay
     home all day
did I play the piano
did my brother wander in the living room
to tell me to play Stevie Wonder's "I Just Called to Say I Love You"
or the "Entertainer," a Broadway hit but in easy form
or did I choose Beethoven's "German Dance" because
it won a competition
was I that girl winning contests,
wanting to hide in corners
was I that girl wanting to disappear as soon as I became visible
then did I fall into the ocean   fall too off a jet ski
and gaze at fresh-cut green grass from the blue of the ocean
now I am eating snow, a Chicago snow like the kind
where us roommates stayed inside for two days because there was a blizzard
and once the ice went still I wore red bellbottoms and we ate burgers
seated on red stools at Johnny Rockets   you sabotage yourself, my friend said
just as you get close to the thing you want as if you can't just
want it or have it or eat it or know it.
we are in Chicago's Hyde Park

and walking from the Shoreland dorm to the Lake but a lake is not
the sea, an endless rippling
and I am not sure what is dream or what is desertion.
I am in the desert and I wonder about the lake, the sea, the waterfall,
the stream, the river, the water,

the water. In a dream, a man chases me and I try
to run and I don't know if I escape but I think I do.
I think I know what it is to be inside hot carpets.

DUAA RANDHAWA

Bouts

On some days, I look the name of my grandfather's brother up on YouTube. The first result reads "Afzal Ahsan Randhawa—Nava Ghalughara" (New Holocaust). The video is an interview conducted in 2014 about a poem he wrote in 1984 when the Indian government attacked Sri Darbar Sahib, the holiest Gurdwara in Sikhism. My grandfather's brother says to the interviewer, in thick and fluent Punjabi, "The split of Punjab was a split of my heart, and the attack on Darbar Sahib was an attack on my body." The interviewer asks him to recite the poem and my grandfather's brother begins.

I struggle to keep up with the majesty of a language I'm only slightly familiar with. One that I hear only when my mother is mad and when my parents fight (people show their true nature when they're mad, my mother says. Her true nature is Punjabi.) One that I hear only in interactions between elders in the village and when those elders, too old and too rooted in their history to bother learning Urdu, speak to me.

Even thirty years after he's written the poem, my grandfather's brother's voice cracks when he recites it. He cries, and somedays, days like today, I cry with him. I don't understand his loss, or why the words of a man who prays in a Masjid hold such agony over the loss of a Sikh temple.

I cry because I cannot grasp my mother tongue. I cry because the words I understand knock the breath out of me with their density, their rhythm, their capacity. I cry because I cannot translate these words here on this page, because so much meaning would be lost in between. I cry because his voice sounds so much like my grandfather's and this is the closest I've been to him in so so long.

My mother tells me that when the British left India they divided up all the provinces geographically, so that when the partition happened, India and Pakistan would forever be at war. I cry for the partition that split Punjab in two, and for the elders that had to give up their tongues and adopt the language of the new land (no, the land was the same, it was the nation that was new). My grandfather's brother doesn't cry for someone else's temple, he cries for the genocide of his brothers. The people that were his home, or at least they stood for his home, before they too were ripped in two.

Mera charda suraj dubeya
Mere din nu kha gai raat

My rising sun, set
My day consumed by night

SEHRISH RANJHA

He Never Had His Own Story

Hanif's friends came to see him the day he left Lahore. His house was crowded again, and every room was full. They were sending him off—jocular patting of the back, kisses, handshakes—sending him to die. Sadi twitches at the thought. He rubs fingers through his sweaty hair. Their smiles, he thinks. He remembers then the glimpse he caught of a woman's face as she left, the way she covered her eyes, how the crowd watched Hanif, and the grimy way they said goodbye. It all comes back to him sticky with the gore of a murder, the whole company in on the action, and only two good men left at the end.

Hanif used to have a thick neck, a bullish laugh, Herculean limbs, a tremendous appetite for food, drink, and joy, the kind of sweetness and care for others that turns strangers into friends, but sickness transforms the future into a bleak, narrow tunnel, and a vital part goes with a strangled cry. Sadi heads downstairs to get water—pausing on the stairs to see if the kitchen's empty—he wants to stay away from the family. He takes a while to find the water and longer to hunt down a glass in the ill-organized cupboards. It baffles him to think they need so much china, plate on plate on plate, and tins stacked against tins. He has never understood how people live.

Northern Virginia, Sunday. Hanif wonders if this is the last place he'll know. His feet hurt. The cancer is now in his bones—it's in his hip bones, in his jaw, in his feet bones, and maybe in his brains, too. He falls asleep with his mouth open like he did as a baby. It's as if his body is trying to capture the look again of happiness. Sadi sits on the bed and watches Hanif's awkward breathing. The rise, the fall. He's here to do just that. He has come all the way to Virginia, to stay in a three-story house tucked in a quiet suburb, to watch his brother-in-law live and breathe. Sadi's fingers are abuzz with static from the carpet. "Damn," he tears up.

Wednesday. There are footsteps outside Hanif's room. He's startled awake by the sound of girlish laughter. His sisters—is it his sisters—all four of them? He imagines them as they were when he was still a child: tall beauties, already married. They're gathered together and eating *ber* they've picked from a tree by the canal. There's a picnic spread around them while they laugh and their white teeth flash in the white light and their dark hair flows in the wild wind.

Rabu sprawls down on her back, and suddenly Hanif can see what she sees. He is crouched in her eyes. He tries to sit up but falls back weakly. The pain is not in his body but has spread into the room and the room is hot with it. He's held within like a bird in a man's fist. The man squeezes down. The bird—suffocates. Where is Sadi? Sadi, the boy with thin shoulders blowing up fireworks under the shisham tree. Sadi the boy racing his bike down the street, turning too fast, and tumbling into dirt. Sadi and his constant need to be picked up and swung into air. Hanif lies back. The bed is violently shaking. The ceiling is like a projection screen. It shows a pale blue with the silver tide coming in. There's a tide coming in, a tide coming in—and if it comes in—it will wipe him away. How can he live even through this? His legs are running away and his tongue turning over. He bites it.

He can't speak for days afterwards. It's all over once you've bitten yourself. They wrap him in cool white sheets at the hospital and someone rubs his feet between their warm hands. "You've had a seizure, brother," Sadi says in the dark. It's language, isn't it? There's a secret affinity between people that only language brings out. He swings his hand out of the blanket. Sadi tucks it back in. Hanif shoves it out again and lets it dangle to the floor. He scrapes a nail against the white linoleum. They can't talk, but they know each other, don't they?

The end of July. Hanif's skin is hot against the bathroom tiles. He fumbles for the shower rail. There's a sharp note in his ears. It goes on and on until his head feels light. Sadi holds him against the wall and water sloshes into Hanif's mouth. He's panting with the effort of holding himself together. They both work to clean his body. This is why he wanted Sadi to come with him and not his wife. It's only Sadi, somehow, who could have done this for him. The cold air goes through Hanif like a needle when he steps out. His body steams white vapor as Sadi wraps towels around him. His feet are swollen red and look horribly abused, as if beaten by a mallet.

Sadi tries to beg a broom from Rabu but she refuses to have a guest clean. She promises to do it herself but forgets. She's running through her days: going to parties, cooking, driving her daughters to college, and back again. She takes Hanif to his doctor's appointments, cooks the food according to the dietary requirements, but there's a curious lack of understanding about the true nature of her brother's illness. He's not sick but dying. Rabu treats Hanif as if he has a sniffle. The family never visit the room, but sometimes they both go down to the house to eat with everyone or sit in the lounge to watch TV.

Hanif sits on the sofa with the best view of the TV. His feet are propped up on a few pillows. The curtains are open and light converges on the screen. It makes it hard to see the news. It's hard to see what's going on in the world. Hanif is cracking into halves like a tree struck by lightning. They sit together in silence. He can try to deny the passage of time but daylight pins it down exactly; light and its absence determine morning, evening, and night; modern clocks are descendants of sundials. Hanif has walked through, slept through, laughed through many sunny days. There have been so many sunny days in his sixty-something years that they slip and slide in his head. It's not death but unreasoning life that scares him now since—even weak, suffering, his bones breaking, sweating himself into a stupor—he can't do anything but live. What is his illness and how is it separate from life? The greenery outside, the warmish day, and even the insects induce real horror. There's something to be said for a neat and quiet end. He longs for existence to fold in on itself and disappear into nothingness but in Islamic eschatology nothing is quiet. There's no neat or quiet end. He has in his head all these images of mountains folding up and the ground breaking down into restless pieces. There is—instead—a clamorousness, the shout of a mourning mother, the sound of a trumpet blowing.

Northern Virginia, Friday. 7:45 p.m. The black birch trees sway. The deck is lit by late afternoon sun. It is dappled by the blooming chestnut that grows in the border between their house and the next house where their neighbor is on her hands and knees shifting through the dirt. She wears a green hat and gloves. She's always out in the garden. She sends over the things she grows: lemons and cabbages, carrots and herbs. She sometimes throws in a bit of lavender wrapped in paper. The whole house is woken by lavender at dawn like they might be by a bell in the morning or the croak of a cock. Hanif is the only one who sleeps through it. He faints into sleep at the oddest hours. He's asleep early mornings—right before daybreak—he sleeps through the morning turning to afternoon and the afternoon changing into evening. He's stubbornly awake the rest of the time. He sleeps through lavender. "He's a child again," Rabu says on the phone, but he can't stand to lean into her for comfort, as even the smallest child can do very well: sucking on the mother's shoulder when in distress, reaching out greedy hands when the need for another overwhelms them, searching in a crowded room for anyone who'll understand.

The stray cat that lives in the hedge runs across the lawn. Sadi's muscular shoulders bunch together under the dark blue t-shirt. He has the classic profile of an athlete, though he has never played sports with others but always by himself. A last orange burst before night—and the windows on the first floor reflect it back to him. He flinches like a dog brought low by a blow. He's watching Yasmin's dark hair fly as she plays a version of volleyball on the deck. She's invented it today. The sisters jump around on the wooden deck, chase the ball, laugh when they hit it too hard, and it sails over the railing. Sadi runs to get it. Yasmin thanks him. She turned sixteen today. The girls whisper to each other, shout to the sky, cry out when they lay a powerful blow on the ball and it flies further and faster than they fantasized. What a day.

They're almost boyishly strong. He's never met girls like them. They cut their eyes to him. He feels that he lives for those moments. The volleyball rolls under the deck and Sadi crouches down to reach it with his long arms. They stand behind him with fists on their hips.

The first of August. It's like a mountain in the distance, blocking up the horizon, and who knows what's beyond the mountain? Villages, cities, pastures? The mountain is everything to the person standing in front of it. Hanif leans on the window of his room and stares out. He watches a plane drift over the white sky. It leaves trails of white smoke while the trees bend down like dancers on a stage. The trees in August become thinner, denuding themselves—they embrace change. Tomorrow, they say, we'll still be here, and tomorrow, and tomorrow, but the pilot in the plane might crash, spin, flame. Hanif feels an unsettled fly whirl around him.

The pilot looks down. He spots two tiny figures by a tiny white house. Sadi has the eyes of his lonely, long dead mother. He looks melancholic, but young Yasmin welcomes him in her arms. They hold hands and disappear into the hedge. Hanif watches from his window. He can see a bare leg poking out from the green, the vulnerable curve of a shoulder, and long hair cascading out of its pins. Hanif shouts and the quiet house awakens from afternoon slumber to rush out and see what's happened. Hanif stands at the window and watches the chaos. He hacks a cough into his hand. The month of August. She's a speck of brown—a tail swishing back and forth—the stray that lives in the hedge. The neighbor two houses down owns a collection of guns he takes into the woods for target practice. He walks quietly by Dr. Yusuf on the walks the doctor takes daily, nods a hello, waves goodbye, but today some unholy impulse makes this man aim and shoot the cat (the bang, a howl). She wavers and weaves as she walks. She's all shadow in the afternoon, now swallowed up by storm and wind, by the darkening sky. The light drizzle makes her shiver and flinch. She's as sure of her own weakness as anyone can be, anything living. She's looking for a hole in which to hide.

She lays under someone's car for a few hours but then the car beeps, a man comes out holding a crying baby, and she runs out as fast as she can. She tries to crawl in a narrow pipe, so small that it barely holds her head, feels miserable when she won't fit. She's looking for smaller and smaller spaces. If it were possible, she would squeeze herself into air, but she's still body, a body in pain, and the body won't let go. It won't disappear. She is head. She is a tail. The swollen eyes. Her dry tongue. She finds a narrow window. She jumps down into a basement and spreads herself out in a corner.

A Category 2 storm blows toward Virginia. It develops from an easterly wave, moving west, a menace of thunderstorms that weakens to a tropical storm and becomes a hurricane. It blows off roofs, submerges whole cities, floods entire countries. 8 p.m. The house is plunged into darkness, but the living room is candlelit. The family and their guests are sitting together quietly. It's so quiet, so quiet, that they hear—suddenly—water swirling. It's filling and drowning the basement. Rabu rushes to the stairs with two of her daughters behind her. There's water up to their knees down there. She rolls up her *shalwar* and wades in. She has put luggage in storage here: old clothes, china, a few pieces of furniture. She wants to save what she can. Her daughters shout at her, pause, and take the plunge. The dark water ripples around them. Sadi comes to the stairs with a portable light and holds it steady overhead. He rolls up his pants and dives in. The water is another country.

8:15 p.m. Dr. Yusuf sits in the living room above and sips his coffee. He takes exception to any goal or quest his wife undertakes and opposes it as frivolous, argues against it, and never gives in. Dr. Yusuf was against Rabu's brother coming to Virginia from the start and now they've packed away a daughter to a friend's house, to protect her from the man she claims to love. The doctor thought about calling the police, but Rabu stopped him. Yasmin calls them every day. "Let me come home," she says. It's an ugly situation. "I want to come back," but they tell her to stay put. It was not the first time she was with a man, but she can't tell anyone. There's a neighbor two houses down who sometimes drives her home from school. They park the car in the wilderness by the gas station. They meet in the late evenings, while his wife is out for choir practice and walk through the dark woods. She likes his silence in the woods. "*Shh,*" he says when they see a rabbit.

What's another problem when the whole house is falling down? Dr. Yusuf hears bizarre cries coming from the basement. They sound like pain or mourning.

There's a dead cat floating in the submerged basement. She's so fat with water she seems pregnant by it. They think, at first, that the dead cat is a water snake. Sadi shines his light at it as the girls lunge for the stairs. Rabu is still stuck on the idea of the snake. She's frozen in the water. She used to picnic with her sisters by the canal in the summers. They'd bring food, a portable record player and stay for hours. They'd go swimming in the murky brown water. They stayed where the tide was low and the water tranquil because the canal took the life of a boy or a girl—sometimes an old man or an old woman—yearly. The bodies were found stuck in brambles, needles in the green hair, and eyes milky white. Snakes and tidal shifts and people said sometimes a cyclone converged on a person swimming alone.

They'd seen a little girl bit by a viper the size of a grown man's arm. It came on her from nowhere. It was black and yellow like plaque on unclean teeth. The girl was rushed to the nearest hospital and survived. Rabu still has nightmares about that snake, and that girl, but the nightmares have aged with her. They used to be about the horror of witnessing: hearing a skull crackling under a car while she sat on a sidewalk nearby, or the terror of her mother dying—those days of endless surgeries in white rooms—or a wound becoming septic when her eldest daughter turned old enough to get into all sorts of small, violent accidents. The dreams slowly gather dust now, gather oil, and vanish into a brown powder that glitters in the sun. She coughs for hours like an asthmatic.

Sadi grabs a plastic bag from upstairs and puts the cat in it. He takes it away, but the water for Rabu is poisoned. She abandons her things to it.

August 28. Sadi puts Hanif on his back, and they make their laborious way to the garage. Sadi's arms bulge with muscle, his back is strong and straight, but he's out of breath when they reach the garage door. Hanif is dead weight. Shouldn't he weigh nothing so near death? The body is mysterious. Rabu runs to start the car. Their landline died soon after the storm, and now there's no service on cell phones. The roads are damaged after the hurricane, and traffic lights are out, while emergencies are happening everywhere. They've decided to go anyway. Hanif's breathing is shallower every minute. He's had another seizure.

They place him carefully in the back seat. Sadi sits with Hanif's head in his lap. He tries to smooth down the flyaway hair as Rabu drives slowly out of the neighborhood. There are trees blown apart. They heard when the trees cracked last night. There's a car standing in a driveway with its windows shattered and the headlights broken.

Rabu brakes hard in the middle of the road. Sadi shocked out of his reverie. She's swallowing down sudden nausea. The road ahead is blocked by a huge tree. The wind must have pulled it straight from the ground and now its roots stretch on the road with clumps of dirt still on them. Its branches hold bird nests. It's covered in leaves and red flowers the size of fists. They get out of the car, look around carefully, but there's no space to drive around the tree and no way to push it off the road.

They carry Hanif to the nearest gas station—a mile or so away—and to try to call emergency services from there. Sadi hefts Hanif's slack body over his back and climbs over the narrower branches. They leave the car by the dead tree. August 28. They continue down the road. The two friends have hardly spoken since that afternoon when Rabu found her daughter—partially nude—in the bushes. She can't forget Sadi with leaves in his hair. His face was red, and he stuttered into his hand. He's hardly been in the house since then. She's caught him sleeping outside. "At least let me get you a blanket," she'd said through the porch door, feeling awful, but unable to relinquish well-worn hospitable habits. He listened to the crickets all night.

He takes care of Hanif but silently. Sadi was always home in Hanif's home after his sister and Hanif married. They moved for the first time to the city and bought their first car and had their first child. Sadi was theirs throughout that time. Hanif worked for a bank and earned enough to be comfortable. He built his own house. Sadi moved into a bedroom upstairs. Sadi got his law degree and tried marriage. He failed at both law and marriage. He was—let's be honest—a constant disappointment. He never had his own story. He was always a conical, cold-bloodied animal attached directly to Hanif's belly or back or anywhere where he could feed the parasitic need for warmth.

"Should we let that sick, unhappy man marry our girl?" says Dr. Yusuf.

"What if this gets out? How will we live with our shame?" says Rabu, but Dr. Yusuf won't have him.

There's a contrarian in Dr. Yusuf that takes pleasure in going against the wishes of his wife, his children, everyone. Yasmin has no memories of Pakistan, but it's Dr. Yusuf who has taken this place to heart. He walks for hours after work and comes home whistling. The sky is blue and inky black. The shape of the woodland behind him like a cardboard cut-out. The delicate wiring of leaves, the thin limber trees, as if ready to topple as soon as the curtain comes down.

They finally see the neon green light of the gas station. It has taken them almost an hour of walking—slowly with long pauses to rest—to make it to the gas station. The hope of a working phone is enough to get them racing to the door. It swings open. No one is inside. Rabu rushes to the payphone in the corner. It's not working. She tries again. It's not working. She shakes it, but it doesn't work. They both have the same thought then. They should have turned back after seeing that the road was blocked. They should have waited at home for the phones to work again. Hanif would have had a bed. It's strange that they both walked to this little gas station without debate. They head back on the wings of another flimsy idea. The house will be lit. They will see it from the distance. The road will surely have cleared. Their way free and easy.

The last day on Earth. Hanif talked non-stop at the dinner party after he found out he had cancer. He said all kinds of things. He remembers making others uncomfortable. He babbled all night. "Some houses burn, some merely blaze with lamplight, but I'm not allowed inside them. If the house burns, what burns, what is left?"

They lay him by the side of the road when he starts to thrash. There's an unnatural strength in his grip. His bones are so fragile that they snap under their fingers. Rabu kneels near him and bends her ear to his mouth. It matters to her to remember what he says. She wants to repeat it to all the people back home. The trumpet is blowing. "Are there things you want? Are there things you wish? Is there something I can do?" Hanif's grown mute. Rabu leans in towards him. She wants a command. He says nothing. He says nothing on purpose. The eyes are wet, they look green and verdant, and there's a virulent bitterness in them. Sadi wrestles with the limbs, grapples with the heart, breaks the ribs. He pumps his hands into the weak chest until it's dark around them. He checks the neck. There's no heartbeat. He keeps pumping, but soon grows so tired and frustrated that he strikes the body. It rolls into a ditch. Rabu tries to save her brother. She lunges for him and fights to hold him close one last time.

Sadi stands up and spits on the ground.

Nothing to do but leave. Why can't he do it? He sits on the road.

AATIF RASHID

My Racist Girlfriend

Anna and I meet in September of 2009, at a party at my friend Justin Lin's apartment. We're amongst fifty or so other Berkeley students, mostly political science majors like ourselves, all crowded in small circles in the living room and kitchen. The beige carpeting and off-white walls of the 1960s building reverberate with our laughter and our undergraduate idealism, and the warm air is thick with the smell of Trader Joe's wine and vodka.

"Hi," Anna says to me, reaching out her white hand. "I'm Anna."

"Hi," I say. "I'm Adnan."

"Adnan. Is that Indian?"

"Pakistani. Well, technically it's Arabic."

"So you're Arabic?"

"No, I'm Pakistani. Well, Pakistani-American I guess."

"So why do you have an Arabic name?"

"Well, most people in Muslim countries have Arabic names."

"You're Muslim."

"Yeah."

"Oh. Okay."

Over the course of the night, we get to know each other. Anna tells me that all her previous boyfriends ("Matthew, Mark, Luke, and John, though not in that order.") have been white, and also that she doesn't like Indian/Pakistani food ("I hate the smell."), and also that, in reference to a discussion we're all having about Switzerland's recent ban on minarets, Muslim immigrants to Europe should "stop complaining about colonialism and just assimilate." This latter point leads to a divisive conversation, and the liberal voices of Berkeley rise to the defense of me and Muslims everywhere. Afterwards, when Anna leaves to use the bathroom, Justin shakes his head and comments that "Berkeley now accepts Republicans too."

"She's not that bad," I say. "She said she voted for Obama, remember?"

"Oh please," Justin says. "You're just into her because she's white."

Anna and I kiss out on the balcony before going back to my room. After we have sex, she stands before my desk and stares at the vintage postcard taped to the wall. The room is dark, and the light that seeps in from behind the blinds frames her already pale skin in an even whiter halo.

"What's this?" she asks.

"A postcard," I say.

"I'm not an idiot, Adnan. I meant what's it a photo of?"

"Just a mosque in Karachi."

More specifically, the postcard is of Karachi's famous Tooba Masjid, a large white dome rising against a white sky, and leading up to it a Mughal-style rectangular pool lined with circular white fountains and surrounded by a white-tiled promenade. The building has a modernist, 1960s vibe, and if it weren't for the caption, it could easily pass for a museum or space station—though, as Anna's frown suggests, she is unable not to see it as a mosque.

"Are you, like, super religious?"

"No. I actually don't believe in God."

"So then why do you have this on your wall?"

"I don't know. I just like the way it looks."

Her large, brown eyes linger on the postcard. The light from the window illuminates dust floating around her face.

"Okay," she says after a long silence.

↝

"You know, my friends back in Orange County didn't want me to date you."

A month or so has passed. Our relationship is now "official," and we've put it up on Facebook. It's the afternoon, and we're sitting in Naia, on the brightly colored plastic chairs, eating gelato. The air inside is cool and smells of a mix of flavors. Outside, students amble down Shattuck, carrying books and listening to music from Apple earbuds. Across the street, a homeless man sits outside the BART station and begs for change from the indifferent passerby.

"Why not?" I ask.

"They said you'd end up going reverting to Islam, since you were raised that way, by Pakistani parents and around that kind of repressive culture, and that I'd end up with a guy who wants me to wear a veil, believes in Sharia law, and will one day go off somewhere to do jihad."

"They said all that?"

"I'm paraphrasing."

I stare at the flavors melting together in her pink plastic bowl.

"I imagine these friends of yours are white," I say, after a moment.

"Stop making this about race, Adnan." She has a habit of saying my name when she's upset, as if she wants me to understand how difficult it is for her to pronounce. "We're talking about *religion*, which, unlike race, is a choice."

"Not according to your friends."

She frowns and takes a bite of her gelato, chewing it more times than necessary before swallowing.

"They're right though, aren't they?" she says. "People do get more conservative as they get older."

I sigh and push my gelato away. The melting flavors have now congealed into an unpleasant mush.

"So why're you dating me then?" I ask.

"What kind of question is that? I like you. You're smart, you're serious, you think about things. Your dick is bigger than most white guys'."

She shrugs and scoops out the last of her gelato.

❧

A few weeks later, we go to see a production of *Othello* put on by one of Berkeley's student theater groups. We sit on black plastic chairs before a makeshift stage and cloth curtain in the basement of the Cesar Chavez Center. Before the play begins, Anna leans her head against my shoulder, and I lose myself briefly in her flowery perfume.

The play itself is mesmerizing, in spite of the misguided early nineties, *Reservoir Dogs*–style production aesthetic. I look past the toy guns and the ill-fitting suits and focus on the actor's expressions and the timeless words. I feel indescribably moved as Othello kneels by Desdemona's body and cries out to the unjust heavens.

Anna, though, feels differently.

"He's a murderer!" she says. "He kills his wife because he's a jealous asshole, and we're supposed to feel bad because he's a minority?"

We are walking through Sproul Plaza after the play. It's November now, and the air is cool and smells of recent rain. In the distance, the lights of Telegraph Avenue shimmer like lit matches against the dark blue sky.

"Yes," I say. "The fact that he's a Moor in a white society means he's been treated differently all his life."

"You're saying he suffered microagressions by the Venetian nobility?"

We reach Bancroft and Telegraph and pause at the traffic light, beside the Martin Luther King building. A beat up VW speeds by and fills the air with the sharp scent of gasoline. I imagine the sky above us turning orange with exploding fire.

"Honestly," Anna says, "I just think you're making too much of it."

⁓

Six months into our relationship, I meet Anna's parents, over dinner at Trattoria La Siciliana, an Italian restaurant in Elmwood. It's a tiny place, and our table is on the second floor, up a set of wooden stairs and tucked into a corner.

Mr. Bianchi is a barrel-chested, good natured man and wears a polo shirt and an expensive watch. Mrs. Bianchi is slim, severe, and unnervingly like Anna. We sip wine and made small talk until the waiter brings our food (Penne Arrabiata and the house Gnocchi, served family style). Mr. Bianchi likes it, but Mrs. Bianchi complains that "it isn't exactly authentic." We eat for a few quiet moments before Mrs. Bianchi turns to me.

"So you're from Pakistan?"

"My parents are. But I was born here."

"So do you speak Pakistani?"

"The language is Urdu, mom!" Anna says.

"Just English," I say.

"So then what do you think of all this Islam stuff?" Mr. Bianchi says, through a mouthful of penne.

"Dad!"

"What? I'm sure he has an opinion. I mean, for example, I read this article the other day, about how this father, Moslem guy, somewhere up near Sacramento, how he ran his daughter over with his car because he found out she was sleeping with a white guy at her school. The police referred to it as some kind of honor killing. I mean . . . God. That's fucked up."

"It is," I say, carefully. "But I don't think it has much do with Islam. This might just be one violent guy."

"Well there seem to be an awful lot of violent Islamic guys," Mrs. Bianchi says.

I turn to her and set my fork carefully on the plate. Anna grabs my arm, but I don't look over.

"There are a lot of religions which justify violence," I say. "Not just Islam.

And there are a lot of cultures in which parents don't approve of their children's romantic choices."

"Not our culture."

"No? What if Anna came home and said she doesn't want a Catholic wedding? That she's marrying an atheist and they're going to give their vows at the courthouse?"

Anna is glaring at me now. Mrs. Bianchi's eyes turn from me to her daughter.

"You're having a Catholic wedding, Anna," she says.

"Mom. You know I'm an atheist—"

"Your father and I had a Catholic Wedding, and your grandparents had one, and your great-grandparents—"

"Jesus Christ, not this again—"

Anna and her mother start yelling at each now, in Italian. The people at the neighboring tables look over, and I can see the waiter hovering anxiously, wondering whether to intervene or enjoy the theatrics.

Mr. Bianchi grabs the wine bottle and turns to me.

"More?" he asks.

ᢒ

"Adnan, can I ask you something?"

We are sitting in her apartment, a week or so after the dinner. Sunday evenings we generally spend eating calzones from Gypsies and catching up on *The Daily Show* and *The Colbert Report*, but tonight Anna just wants to eat. We sit silently on her blue IKEA sofa while above us the ceiling fan spins with a steady hum, circling the smells of tomato and mozzarella around the apartment. It's a hot day for Berkeley, and from her open window, I can see as the setting sun colors the clear sky an uncharacteristic red.

"Yeah?" I ask.

"Can we take our relationship status off Facebook?"

I stare at Anna, uncertain if I've misheard.

"Why?"

"It's just, that article my dad was talking about."

"The honor killing?"

My heart is racing, thumping in tandem with the spinning fan.

"You've said your parents wouldn't approve if they knew you were dating me,"

Anna says, "which is why we've never met them. And I'm just afraid. I mean, what if they find out?"

I feel anger flare up, like a match being lit against the inside of my chest. She's right, of course, I haven't told my parents about her, but it's not because I'm afraid of what they might do to me. My soft-spoken mother and my kind-eyed father, both doctors with benign political views (my dad voted Obama but always declared in his Pakistani accent that "that McCain fellow wouldn't have been terrible") and middle-class notions of tolerance, would never dream of turning violent. The fact that Anna even thinks they might . . .

"They're religious, right?" Anna asks, in the face of my silence. "You said they go to the mosque every Friday to pray."

"That doesn't mean they're violent," I say, trying to control the violence in my own voice. "It's just, if they found out that their own son is not as religious as they believed, they'll be devastated. And that's why I keep it from them. Because I don't want to make them sad. Even if they found out, though, they'd never kill me."

"Or me?"

She says this with complete seriousness, and I feel a sudden urge to hit her across face, to slap that pale white cheek and leave a red mark across it, to rattle those brown eyes from their narrow world view. I've never felt anything like it before, and it leaves me shaken. I stare up at the spinning fan, which sounds like distant thunder.

"They're not going to kill you either," I say. "They're no different from your parents."

I can see in Anna eyes that she doesn't believe me.

"I'll just feel more comfortable if it's not on Facebook," she says. "Please?"

We are standing, thought I don't remember us doing so. The half-eaten calzones lie in their cardboard containers on the coffee table. Anna's large eyes are open wide, still afraid, but also pleading, almost sorrowful.

"Fine," I say. "Fine."

Yet inside, I don't feel fine. I shake with rage and sorrow, like Othello, and I watch, helpless, as the fan's blades circle overhead and across the dirty ceiling.

꒦

I sit on the leather couch at another of Justin's parties. Anna has left early, and after her tepid kiss goodbye, I find myself alone, chugging beers and listening to the buzz of conversation around me. The beige carpeting and off-white walls, once the dimensions of a comforting bubble, now seem constricting and limited, the space they enclose just an echo chamber where the same liberal views circulate upon the wine-scented air, while outside, beyond the balcony and out in the city, in restaurants and upper-middle class suburbs, the actual views that shape our culture drift across the world like some invisible biological weapon.

The white guy next to me is talking about politics. "My parents say that because European welfare states like France give their citizens everything, from healthcare to unemployment insurance to free museums, they have the right to demand assimilation, to tell their Muslim citizens to put away the veils and the Korans."

The girl across from him responds. "That's bullshit. European colonialism destroyed the Muslim world, creating persistent economic and cultural inequalities. So it's hypocritical for French people whose country was built off the exploitation of North African Muslims too complain about a few hijabs."

I stare at her. She has wavy black hair and large brown eyes, and her skin color is the same as mine. I never learn her name, but we make out on the balcony and then walk down Shattuck to my apartment. Before we have sex, she pauses at the postcard above my desk, and her fingers brush over the white dome.

"It's beautiful," she says, with reverence.

But afterwards, lying beside her on my twin bed, all I can do is stare at the spot where Anna stood and compare the darkness of this girl's slumbering skin to Anna's, haloed in white.

༓

Anna and I break up the next day, in her apartment. I can't keep what happened a secret and so end up telling her. There is a lot of yelling and crying, but mostly on her part, a torrent of emotion circulating on the warm air. I feel above it all, perched on the edge of one of the fan's dust-covered blades, a spectator watching two actors reciting prewritten lines, the swirling scene beneath me tragic yet inevitable.

༓

Many years later, I'm working in Oakland at a non-profit that tracks anti-Muslim hate crimes when I see Facebook photos of her wedding. She removed me shortly after our breakup, but a mutual friend of ours went and is tagged in the album. The wedding is at a church, and the groom is as white as the flower arrangement, a Scandinavian-looking guy with a Viking's build and big bushy beard that is attractive on him but would probably get me stopped by the TSA. Anna is smiling in every picture, and in one I see her parents, smiling too. I try to imagine myself in the groom's place in each photo, standing beside Anna at the altar, laughing with her at some offscreen joke, her head leaning against my shoulder as she smiles wistfully. But the images in my head feel utterly impossible.

One of the photos I click to is of Anna leaning towards her Viking-groom, about to eat a piece of chocolate he's holding out to her, and it calls to mind a memory that I've long since buried, from a month or two before everything with her fell apart. I was determined to get her to like Indian food, so I told her I'd cook a recipe, a spicy variation of Chicken Korma that my dad always made when I was little. She was resistant at first but ultimately agreed. She sat at my kitchen table, studying for a political science test, while I worked diligently, pulling the marinated chicken pieces from the fridge, sautéing the onions and the garlic and the ginger, chopping the tomatoes and the chilis, slowly decreasing the heat and adding the cumin and coriander and turmeric and cinnamon and cloves and, of course, red chili powder—and as the mixture cooked, all these varied aromas filled the tiny kitchen with a spiciness that hung in the very air, like an enchanting mist enveloping us both.

When it was finished, I dipped my finger in the red-orange masala and held it out for her to taste. Tentatively, she did so. The feel of her lips against my skin gave me a sudden jolt, a feeling more powerful than if I'd ingested the spiciest of chilis.

"It's good, no?" I asked, watching her eyes.

"Yeah," she said, smiling. "Yeah, it is."

ALICIA RAZVI

The Hands of Fate

I reach for my plastic cup of ginger ale. My eyes linger on my ragged nails and stained fingers. The flight attendant sees them too. I chew my lip.

"Do you need hand sanitizer, Miss?" he asks.

"Yes please." I say. I washed my hands just minutes before boarding the plane, hand sanitizer isn't going to help. I stare down at my hands and worry over them. Nails cut short to the quick, stained and dirty looking, rough in places, my thumb nail covered with a fraying bandage. Should I cover them with polish? Get a manicure when I land in DC?

My heartbeat assures me, "No. You have earned these hands." But my vanity tugs at me.

Surely the politicians in Washington would notice as we shake hands and accept business cards. They might recoil. They would judge.

Bargaining with myself, I reason, "But, I am a farmer. I am allowed working hands." And then waffle, "Would the talking heads in Washington listen to me harder if I looked more polished?" I was summoned to DC by the National Farmers Union to lobby, to share our stories. Not just my farming story, but of hundreds of Wisconsin farmers. I was there to be heard.

My hands; small, but wide and strong. Thumb through middle finger stained an inky dull purple black. Wedding ring that turns freely on the finger but is nearly impossible to remove. Blister on my left inner thumb, peeling a bit on the knuckles and older looking than the rest of me. Callous on my left ring finger, rough skin leaning towards metal plated on each inner pointer. A small splatter burn, old scars on my left pointer and right thumb and a bit of mehndi design remaining on my right middle finger.

Just last week, my nails were unstained. My hands were fancy, pampered, adorned for a family wedding of my husband's side. From India originally, he has a very large extended family and one of his myriad cousins got married. In some ways, Indian weddings are the same as the weddings I grew up attending in my white mid-western Catholic family. There is a bride, a groom, some attendants, a wedding cake, and flowers. The couple ends up married at the end. This is where the similarities die down.

In the weddings of my upbringing, the bride wears white, the groom, black, the young woman is walked in by her father, down a long row of pews dressed in starchy satin bows, through a vast, echoing church with high ceilings and the heavy handed organist plays Canon in D or Ave Maria. Children might be invited. Then again, they might not.

"Kids should be seen but not heard," my family says with a smile and a wink. They are probably kidding, I think. The weddings begin in early afternoon, run under an hour then the crowd is ushered into an adjoining fellowship hall where coffee with fried chicken and mashed potatoes or ham sandwiches with coleslaw are served. Then comes the beer and the band. Dancing to "Twist and Shout," the "Chicken Dance" and a little Elvis ensues. We are all ushered into the evening, back to our lives no later than 10 p.m.

Indian weddings, on the other hand, are loud, colorful affairs that go on for days. The events generally dictate that certain colors should be worn, and other colors avoided, and that certain styles of dress are more suited to some nights than others. They begin late in the evening and never start on time and end with sleeping children, sore feet staggering home in the wee hours of the morning with your babies in your arms. Last week, my hands sewed last minute adjustments to several outfits to be worn by my family. Letting out, taking in, stitching up rips and changing hems. Last week, my hands were iced like cakes, with intricate mehndi designs. Each hand done by a different cousin-in-law as we caught up on each other's lives. And each night, my wrists were encircled with several bangles on top of shiny lovely outfits fancier than anything my childhood dress-up day fantasies might have dreamt. These nights, my hands slipped my three children into their outfits. Buttoned and bow-tied, pressed and zipped. Each child, looking as perfect and done up as a gift for just a moment, until the heat of evening or the thrill of play tugged at them too hard and they became unraveled and disheveled. Each night, for four nights, the events would feel the same with the dressing up, the late start, the noise, but would appear to be different in color, in purpose and in venue. Mercifully the festivities come to an end after just under a week. And then, my hands and the hands of my husband, share the wheel on our sixteen-hour drive home through the night. We cruise through the traffic and back to our quiet life in Wisconsin.

Our lives have been so loud these last few days, nobody talks as we jettison our family away. Shabbar drives one handed, letting his free hand feel the air of the night as we whip past cities and farm fields. My hands, in the more predictable "ten and two" wheel position allow me perceived control on the road and generally in life. As I drive through the night, I reminisce about our own union, seventeen years earlier. It was so different from the celebration we just finished.

Our wedding was a quiet and quick affair held on a snowy January afternoon. That day contained a dress I did not choose, a handful of unsuspecting community members who came to mosque to pray that day and stayed for the free meal, and tight faced family members. I cannot bear to think back to the day of our wedding without bitterness rising in my throat. Our union was not welcomed. It was rallied against. It was boycotted. It was, at the time, a blemish on my mother-in-law's devout faith, strict parenting, and obedient family. Mostly, and always outwardly, I keep a brave face and laugh about our small little wedding. But in the dark with just my thoughts and exhaustion looming, I feel sad and beat up. My mother-in-law and I have never gotten over that divide between us. It began with her disappointment in all that I was not. She should have been able to choose her son's wife. Inwardly, I know she would never have chosen a blond with wild curls and blue eyes, who was left-handed and older than her son. Since I could not possibly change my shortcomings to fit the perceived mold of a "perfect daughter-in-law," I never even tried. I ignored the breach and let the chasm deepen.

But my husband and I, we have loved one another for eighteen years. Maybe longer even. I swallow down regret. I flex my grip on the steering wheel, and I force myself to remember our truest beginning. Not the wedding, but the courtship.

In our earliest days together, our time was spent hand in hand, walking and talking and planning. Shabbar was raised with a strict no dating expectation and his faith is deep and devout. As I made my feelings openly known to him, we took great long walks through our small college town hashing out the details of a hypothetical relationship. Could we marry? In a culture of arrangement, it would be tough. Where might we live? He never considered having his own mind in the matter, he'd go where his parents told him to go. Or he'd go where he got a job offer. It was simple. I complicated things. I knew that I was a small-town girl who'd shrivel in the anonymity of big city life. Living near his family in Chicago, for that reason alone, would be ruled out. To be fair to both sides, living near my parents, would be ruled out as well. Those many miles, slowly walking into the sun, our conversations were full of the perceived veil of control. We chose our path. We forged our destiny. On those walks, my hand in his, we could do all the things. I would find an Islamic tutor, for he could not be my sole source of faith. I would convert and the choice to cover with hijab would be mine alone. We would start telling his parents about me straight away. We would marry. We would live in the small town where we went to college. He would get work in computer engineering and sponsorship for a green from a businessman who wanted to take a chance on him. I would teach at a nearby school. We'd have three kids, two cats, and a little house with a garden. We would live happily ever after.

Drawn back to the drive, I crack a window in the minivan. The turnpike stretches straight and smooth, my thoughts quicken and my hands itch as we draw nearer home. Most of those early dreams came true. But roads and life get bumpy, take detours, and change destination. Three kids, two cats, and a job in computer engineering exist. And so does a micro-farm, a change in career path for me and an unanticipated gratitude for life's direction.

It is late summer in Wisconsin. High harvest. Everything is growing, including the weeds. The bangles have come off, the mehndi will fade and my hands will look themselves again within moments of my arrival home. I eagerly await the eggs I will gather and wash, the turkeys I will feed, the lawn I will mow. As soon as we pull into the driveway, my hands are at work once again.

Two weeks later, these hands I see on the plane reflect life of a diversified farmer in late August. The stains came from the two five-gallon buckets of concord grapes I picked, plucked, and peeled to yield my family and our CSA, the forty half-pints of grape jam we will sell at markets and spread with our peanut butter this school year. The cut came from fixing the apple slicing machine used to rotate endless piles of apples and create perfectly uniform slices for the dehydrator. Just yesterday, these hands plucked enough kale, cut enough broccoli, pulled enough squash, snipped enough sage, and baked enough caramel apple pies to fill thirteen CSA bags. And a similar weekly harvest is expected every Sunday until mid-October.

The peeling skin on my knuckle comes from the bucket of bleach water I used to clean all my surfaces over and again with our most recent chicken harvest. The blister comes from wielding a butcher knife on Saturday to process seventeen chickens. These birds, hand raised from chicks, walked right into my arms on their last day so that I could prepare them for butcher. My eyes get wet thinking of these chickens. Baby chicks are not automatically drawn to water. The first and most important action in chicken raising is dipping their little beaks into the waterer. Without attention to this detail, they can easily die of thirst just steps from the water source. My hands, ungloved and assured, have handled these birds from their first meal and first drink of water until their last, from the little balls of yellow fluff to the 6 lb white feathered, clucking, pecking animals of the present. They are offered water, spoken to softly and with gratitude in their final moments. My husband's hands, strong and true performed the kill-cut as his lips utter the words, *"Bismillah Ar Rahman, Nir Rahim, Allah hu Akbar"* in the name of God, the merciful the compassionate, God is Great. These birds, these Halal birds, will nourish our family with weekly meals of roast chicken this winter. A bubble of pride forms in my chest as I fill my freezer after a sweaty day of hard work.

In life, gratitude and humility are my True North, and that pride bubble is quickly pricked as I remember, the limits of my hands. The reason every beat of joy and success is equally measured with anxiety and worry. There are limits to hands, no matter how strong.

Nine years into our marriage, my hands did not feel capable. They did not concern themselves with filling the freezer, packing school lunches or baking pies for customers. That winter, my hands were consumed with caregiving. I had just given birth to our third child, making me the mother of a six-year-old, a two-year old, and a newborn. Even in the delivery room, Shabbar was sick. I dared not wake him with my post-uterine cramps, he felt crummy, so I paged the nurse who sat with me while the advil kicked in and eased my discomfort. After three months of feeling unwell, my husband was diagnosed with leukemia. Cancer, in a thirty-one-year old man. In those early days, my hands needed washing. They could carry infection into the room and leave it there for his non-existent immune system to be powerless over. Hot water, anti-microbial soap, and a two-minute scrub. This needed repeating every time I left and re-entered his hospital room. My hands would touch the cool of the window and then squelch the terrible heat that poured out of him while his temperature climbed to 105 degrees. My hands would rub lotion on his legs and arms to heal the dry skin of hospitals and the deep red-purple pigment that stained the areas that his clothing touched. This stain that was left as his red cells died off and rose to his skin's surface. My hands would shave his head when he began pulling out whiskers in great clumps.

But my hands could not stop the fear from creeping into my heart. My hands could not procure a medicine that could save him. He'd need a stem cell transplant to survive. He might never be the same, we were told. With this cure, came a compromised immune system and handfuls upon handfuls of pills. Chemotherapy. Radiation. He'd need to spend months in isolation from our children, from the great unwashed public, from life as we knew it. Confined to a small hospital room from January through mid-April having only a view of the cemetery to re-assure him and then in a bedroom at his parent's house from mid-April through July, my hands could do very little.

Helpless hands. Empty hands. Useless hands. I could not comfort all the people all the time because we could never occupy the same space. I could not keep house because my kids and I were nomadic for the one-hundred days from the stem cell transplant until the day we once again lived together. My hands could not heal. No amount of love that I could visualize transferring from my hand to his back as I rubbed it, could cure the cancer. I could neither be everything to my children nor be everything to my husband. And it felt wrong to be anything for myself in that moment. I never did find balance between the two. I could only focus my gaze in one direction or the other. As my strength waned and my resolve dimmed, anxiety and fear began to seep into me.

I did have prayer. As a convert Muslim, I prayed with head and hands flat on the ground. Pressed into the rug or the grass, trying to extract calm of the earth. Pulling strength from the firmament into my hands. And as a former Catholic, I also prayed hands held up, face turned up. Pleading, crying, hoping to catch the blessings and miracles as they fell from the sky. And I did feel the blessings as they landed. I felt the release as I unburdened my shoulders each night from the weight of it all. And I felt the shift in energy as the miracles tumbled into our path.

That is when I discovered how important were the hands of others. Other hands lifted in prayer as my husband fought for his life. Muslim hands, Christian hands, Buddhist hands, Atheist hands. All hands, folded, up turned, planted into the earth, shoved in pockets, touching emblems of faith. They all lifted our family.

There were both hands of intention and hands of deed. There were the hands of the young family, Dad, Mama, pregnant with baby number two and toddler who'd come and shovel my snowy driveway with each winter storm. There were the hands of the no nonsense co-worker who took care of my grocery shopping and helped raise nearly 3,000 dollars for medical and incidental expenses as we endured. There were the anonymous hands that created meals to leave on my doorstep. There were the hands of my cousins-in-law and in-blood, who wrote to me from India, from Maryland, from Atlanta offering me glimpses into their lives, chatty bits to get my mind off life, and healing assurances that whatever happened, we would be okay. There were the hands of the babysitters that I left my babies in each moment I spent with my husband in the hospital. And the hands of the nurses I left my husband in each night as I went home to my children.

Restoratively, the hands of my mother-in-law, who'd just finished her last radiation treatment to beat breast cancer, prepared a space of recovery for her son. For the hundred days after the stem cell transplant, we couldn't not all occupy the same space. In this moment, my mother-in-law opened her home. Gave up her bed and cared for everyone in her path. Lunches and lessons for kids if I was at the hospital, meals, and a clean quiet home for Shabbar when I was sleeping on a couch with my kids somewhere else. The care she gave her son and her grandchildren shifted the gaping wound of our relationship to that of a scar. Still visible and sometimes aching but cobbled over with a tougher tissue than that which holds everything unwounded together.

Most gratefully, the raised hands of my husband's siblings who volunteered to be tested as stem cell donors. His brother, who seemed so opposite Shabbar in personality, was a perfect match in genetics. He, who endured the appointments, the shots, the surgery for the central line and the extraction of stem cells, without one backward glance. Needles, illness, recovery time. He quietly saved my husband's life.

The hands of my husband and my babies themselves, my balm. At the hospital, Shabbar's hand was my greatest physical contact. Our hands anchored us to one another as we watched the chemo drip into his central line, as he was put on metabolic food bags because eating was too painful. As he recovered between treatments and we would walk around the block. He held my hand, I held his. We shared what strength we had with one another.

The hands that make me cry these eight years later, are the hands of my children. They held mine with utter trust that I could make things better. I needed that. I needed to believe that I could help, make brave, and create safety for someone. My kids gave me that. At night, when the anxiety threatened to overtake me, I would pile my children around me on whatever full-size mattress we were afforded wherever we were staying and soak them in, hold their hands, rub their backs, nurse the baby, and smell their heads. Their hands refueled my courage.

Eventually, weariness overtook fear, and I forgot that I felt undeserving of my own healing. This exhaustion allowed my own hands to save me. At the end of July, seven months after the whole cancer nightmare began, we were dropped back into our lives. My husband was cured. My family was reunited. We went through all the motions. Life was starting back up again for us. But I was worse off. I was so scared, so anxious, in a place so dark that I could only pretend to live. On one of those bad nights, when I gleaned strength from my children as they slept, I awoke pooled in sweat and shaking around 3 a.m. After many deep breaths and prayers for calm, I saw, in my mind's eye, my hand holding a seed. And I watched that seed sprout and grow into a plant right in my palm. A spark of hope burned in my belly and relief warmed my chest. In a moment that was so out of my control, I saw that I could control the life of a plant. I could take a seed, provide it love and care and create something beautiful or nutritious or wholesome from it. Further, I was in control of that life. I could grab that plant, that life, by the roots and move it, place it, provide it the best living conditions, and feed my family with it.

That year, we moved to our micro-farm. We put in a big garden. We tapped maple trees. We grew food and flowers. My hands worked out my worry by weeding a row of radish. They solved back burner problems by feeding the laying hens and standing with them for a few moments. They taught me gratitude for the abundance I was surrounded by as I picked the food planted before I lived there, but provided perennially, the apples, raspberries, and grapes. I learned that my hands had the ability to control some things like removal of the Colorado Potato Beetle to ensure a potato bounty that winter and how my hands had no effect on other things, like their inability to stop a thirty-inch snowfall in April that would collapse our greenhouse.

With each new year on the micro-farm, we discovered a new love. First came chickens for eggs, and meat, then a CSA was created, now I bake pies and can chutney for farmers markets and bakeries as well. The new skills my hands have afforded us astounds me.

With all this learning, I found a community of fellow farmers. Support, encouragement, and a desire for change endeared me to this hardworking bunch. In sharing our successes and failures, I realized that we all have a life story worth knowing. Raising the voice of the fellow farmer became another trajectory of life Shabbar and I could not have anticipated.

With thoughts returning to the flight attendant and Washington, I cast off notions of manicures and judgment rendered on a life I love. I trust in these hands of mine as I gaze forward to Washington and beyond. True, yesterday they skinned a five-gallon bucket of grapes for jam, and the day before, they filled a freezer with farm raised chicken but today my hands share this story as I fly across the country. Tomorrow, I will shake the hands of our country's lawmakers and tell them the stories of these hands and the hands of the farmers in my state. I will tell them of the hands that milk cows, grow grain, butcher lamb, chicken, and turkey, and yet need to leave the farm for more employment or hold out that hand for assistance because they cannot fully provide for their families. And the days after that, these hands will be back home incubating chicks, washing potatoes and gathering firewood for maple sugar fires.

These hands. My beautiful, ugly, strong, small, dinged up, working hands. They are my badge of honor. I know I will not paint my nails or buff away the stains. I will not cover up the scars or hide my cracked knuckles. Nor will I apologize for their appearance. These hands are my strength. They are my proof of living a life I love.

BUSHRA REHMAN

Rapunzel's Mother or a Pakistani Woman
Newly Arrived in America

And with a cabbage, a box of eggs so clean she could easily forget
the source of their existence, my mother filled her silver cart
and moved in line to make her purchase.

The cashier turned a sharp glance at the small brown woman
with the pierced nose and covered head. She didn't fit
into this, an American supermarket.

"And what?" asked the cashier, "are you willing to pay for this?"
She held the head of lettuce in the air. It reflected
off her rhinestone glasses and the hairspray in her hair.

"But this," said my mother, "is America. I thought there was no barter here."

"Hmmmph," said the cashier. "There's give and take all over the world.
What made you think it would be different here?"
She shook her head and her plastic hair.

"But I have money." My mother tried to act like she didn't care.
Her English broke all over her and fell apart in the air.

But the cashier cackled, "No, no, no, my dear, what I want is here."
She jabbed a nail, silver-painted and crooked, at my young mother's stomach
which I had just begun to share.

"That is the price you'll have to pay, my dear, for this fresh lettuce.
Each egg that erupts into a new-blown head will be the property
of this here supermarket, country, and nation.

"And don't even think of running because we've got the goods on you.
Along with every other immigrant, we've got your passport
your foreign passport right here."

She made to reach into her too tight jeans, but my mother, she ran out of there.
The shopping girl openly laughed behind her, and the lines and lines
of customers just stood there with their stupid grins.

My mother ran, the door opened by itself.
My mother ran, but she still found herself
in a foreign land, far away from home.

Ammi's Cassettes

The other day, I found my mother's cassettes from the Eighties
They were full of love songs from Indian movies
Ammi used to tape them from the TV
while she cleaned

And I thought back to the orange carpets
the sofas with their plastic
the way everything was dusted and perfect

I tried to fill the memory with her music
to come up with something peaceful
something splendid
but the tapes, they just didn't play that way

You see, they caught all the background noise:
the sound of babies crying
children fighting
fire engines going
and then the sound of a child being hit

The children wouldn't stop making noise
until my mother's own voice would break
then there would be nothing
but the sound of her crying
and the sound of music
in a language
my mother was dying to hear

And I thought back to the orange carpets
the way I would press my face against them
and against the plastic sofas
until the perspiration would make it stick
and listen to the sound of her crying
and all the love songs of longing

They promised everything
missing in our house
with its orange carpets
everything missing in the plastic
everything she ever recorded

Masjid

The minar and dome of our masjid
took longer to grow than trees
Our fathers bought the land, then tilled it
Before that, it was a parking lot
for our neighbors the Jehovah's Witness
They sold it when the door to door
wasn't bringing in enough donations

Our fathers sowed the seeds
Qurans and janamazes. In all my years
from when I was four to sixteen
the walls went up, and then the dome grew
the same pace my breasts did

The minar too, grew to reach
the heights of the Queen's sky
push up past the telephone lines
let itself poke up, respectful still
of the Episcopalian church steeple next to it
the flat brick surface of the kingdom
of the Jehovah's Witness

It was fine real estate for religion
on National street, a church
a kingdom and a masjid
crammed next to each other
wall to wall, skin to skin

And if you crossed the street
there was a Catholic store
selling crucifixes and paintings
of women and men in hell burning

The sinners looked like all of us
but I always thought that all of us
in our agony looked like Jesus

MARINA REZA

Lashes

The woman who commits zina and the man who commits zina,
lash each of them one hundred lashes.
Do not let pity deter you in a matter ordered by God,
if you believe in God and the Last Day
—Qur'an 24.2, Muhammad Assad translation

Women have an Islamic right to exemption from
criminalization or punishment for consensual adult intercourse.
—Asra Nomani, "Islamic Bill of Rights for Women in the Bedroom," 2005

Ryan

Ryan doesn't mind the patch of sun gracing his face as he sleeps. I tell him he must have one of the prettiest sunrises to look at in this area. There were no sheets on the bed last time, but there are some now. He sleeps and sleeps and sleeps. The night before, we drank too much and nibbled on pizza. He interviewed me about sex and boys, Mimi, Mimi and Islam, me and Islam, and I told him everything in that interview, and we slept together, and then it's quite possible I told him too much.

Dhaka, Bangladesh: Lake Circus, Kalabagan

Yusuf, the Arabic teacher, ran away with one of the three female house cleaners. She didn't have a torn ear and wasn't mute like the third. The second one had thin lips and was forgettable. Mimi was suspicious of him, always, and asked my grandmother to sit in the room while he taught me and my sister how to read Arabic. Finishing the Qur'an meant stuffing the face of those around you with sweets and never knowing exactly what it was that you read.

Woodside, New York: Apt #F5

My tutor was in the seventh grade when I was in the third. She was named Niti, and she would talk about periods and said sex was the moment the tip of the man's penis touched the tip of the woman's nipple. I believed it. Nothing told me otherwise, anyway.

I would turn my head away as she changed her clothes but would watch her fight with her brother Rishabh and then stare as he sat on her stomach when she lay down on her back, and he pretended to squeeze her breasts and defy her as she pleaded, weepy, that he go to hell.

I didn't learn what sex was until I opened up the Oxford dictionary at ten years old, sitting under the mosquito net over my bed one afternoon in Dhaka. Merriam-Webster was never as explicit.

Techniques of Fiction

A portion from a short story I wrote before I ever had sex:

"In twelve nights, Benny will be in Daria's body. He will march his fingers around Daria's chunky neck, and when she flinches, strands of whole-wheat hair will shift and folds of her stomach will shift, and Daria will suck her stomach in and become a taut little thing. She is like one of those cherubic Botticelli cupids, legs like Courbet painted them—immovable trunks waiting to be pressed. Benny will map out her ear with his tongue. *Clack clack clack clack clack clack.* Benny thinks of the verb to describe this sound in case your idea of clack and mine are different and can only agree when Benny uses the verb 'to lap.'"

A classmate remarks, "This sex scene is done very well. Very visual. One of the best I've ever read."

Where did I come up with this shit.

The Movies

Bonnie Hunt is trying to explain sex to her daughter in *Now and Then*. Mimi is asking why I am only eight, saying that it is inappropriate. Mimi calls sex scenes "scenes." A "scene" could also be a kiss. A softer "scene," to me, was one in which we didn't have to necessarily whiplash our heads away or cover our eyes; the tenderness in the kiss might mask the sexual quality of it, is how I've come to rationalize it. Tongues swirling and clacking up against one another would be inappropriate.

I heard about the movie where the female has sex through a hole in the sheet, and I assumed that would also be the case with Islam, thinking it could make sense given the Muslim conservatism I grew up with.

The sound of paper crinkling: dirty. Crinkling sheets, the sheets crumpling through your fingers. At any moment on any day, the sudden small sounds of a chair being nudged or someone sighing are not unlike sex sounds.

Each time my parents went out and my sister was not home, I turned to a cable network and flipped through channels to find a sex scene, or a kiss at the least, and looked forward to the chance to see it alone, to make up for the massive censorship of my childhood. For a few years, the search always meant fast-forwarding through Bollywood's *1942 Love Story* on a video cassette. In Dhaka, it was Sonique's music video for "It Feels So Good" on MTV.

Looking for sex, or a love scene.

But how can you rub against the furniture when written prayers and images of mosques are all around the house?

Showers

When Mimi said true Muslims only listen to instrumental music, my sister and I laughed.

When Mimi told me why she still bathes with a bucket and pail, I could not stop thinking about it.

She runs soap and shampoo all over her body so the *shayatin*—devil-esque beings said to emerge when people are at their most vulnerable—cannot get a glimpse. "Haven't I told you and your sister to shower with your panties on and remove them quickly to wash toward the end and then quickly change into your clothes?"

I think of Mimi bathing, her bottom grazing the bathtub. I think of the image on the cover of Annie Ernaux's *Shame*.

What belongs to religion? What belongs to Mimi's personal paranoia?

Family secrets are secreted and then secreting.

Look at how different the characters in the same nursery rhyme looked in different books.

How can you separate the stories from the superstitions from the secrets from the sound?

My fourteen-year-old cousin running away with a man she met on the internet.

The dish running away with the spoon.

Dietary Habits

When Mimi started embracing halal meat, my sister and I didn't think much of it.

Halal permissible. *Haram*: forbidden. Both words can describe various aspects of a Muslim's life, but also poultry.

Halal food was temporarily served at the university cafeteria, but was quickly discontinued after few students showed interest. The leftovers were swiftly given away.

Haram substances, according to the Qur'an: pork and all its products, animals improperly slaughtered or slaughtered in the name of anyone except Allah, alcoholic drinks (including intoxicants), carcasses of dead animals, blood.

To kill an animal in a *halal* manner is to do it almost invisibly, so the animal loses consciousness quickly, so its fears don't kick in, before any emotions get involved.

Ryan

I woke up next to Ryan after he had an episode of sleep paralysis, and his account of it was eerily similar to that of mine a year ago. You feel strapped down to your bed, unable to move, and there are black shadow-like spirits—or *shayatin*, as Mimi might say—in the room flying around the room.

Ryan does not have xylophone ribs. No hard, wooden sounds when I lightly tap that area. Many instruments fill his room. Mascara is wrapped around my lashes in clumps and I am self-conscious that twisting and turning has made my eyes puffy, smeared the kohl. He couldn't find his keys the next morning and let me take a can of pomegranate seltzer water from the fridge. Jethro, the backyard chicken, was no longer there.

It will be better next time. My stomach will be flatter then.

Ch 4: Prohibited Acts and Forbidden Partners: Illicit Sex in Islamic Jurisprudence

"Sex is, paradoxically, both the most private, intimate act humans can undertake and a profoundly social activity."[1]

Zina

Halal and *haram* can also refer to the sort of activities one engages in.

Zina: extramarital or premarital sex.

My sister and I found Pakistani porn on my father's laptop.

Look at the marital people we know doing non-marital things.

Here is the chasing.

Look at the non-marital people we know doing marital things.

The running.

Was it licit or illicit?

Where have Papa's hands been?

I don't think about his hands years later at college, where I am too busy numbing out every weekend, and pretty soon, every other day.

Walking home at 2 a.m. from the library, feeling intensely alone. *This is it? College?*

Before it ever happened, I remember thinking, *This is it? Sex?*

And how reductive the baseball metaphors inching up to it.

When it was announced that our PE class would be baseball or softball that quarter, my stomach sank.

A Visit

Sam and Anthony are sitting on my sheets smirking and they are frank about what they've done and what they'll do later. I take pride in the fact that I introduced them to one another at a fraternity. I ask them if they have ever had sex with more than one person at once? Sam replies that once, there were four in total and he was the only boy. Anthony smirks and I have no idea what he is thinking. I leave my room pretending I will do something else, to give them space, to see if anything will happen besides the obvious movement of their hands over the surface of each others' clothing. At least I could say right then and there that I gave them the chance.

Class

In Bharatnatyam II, my South Indian dance class, Hari is teaching us the mime portion, the part of the dance where we are taking clean, minimal steps forward and focusing on our hand gestures, trying to match our facial expressions to the movements. "Try not to be sloppy," he says. For the gesture in which both our pointer fingers come downward to meet each other, he says, "Be intentional and look into the audience with a coy look or a come-hither glance—whatever, you do, make it intense!" I try to sear the imaginary audience in front of me.

Robert Henri in *The Art Spirit*: "Do what you do intensely."

We are talking about colonialism, orientalism, exoticism, and the professor shows us a book of photographs of nude women with veils covering their faces.

My boss at the university press is explaining what a money shot is as she picks up a book by Rae Armantrout. So much to be getting away with in poetry.

Blood

All we know is reenactment.

"Ritualized compulsive comfort-seeking (what traditionalists call 'addiction') is a *normal* response to the adversity experienced in childhood, just like bleeding is a normal response to being stabbed."[2]

Balance is God but there is always some new high.

Mornings listening to covers of "Disorder" by Joy Division.

What is the nightly ritual you return to? Intellectualize and glamorize the shit out of it.

"We must note whether he plucks his hair, picks at his skin, or weeps."[3]

I dig and peel. Little pearls of blood. Little lobster eyes, sans lashes.

"When a dog keeps licking one spot until its fur comes off, we don't wonder whether it was unloved as a puppy. We know it just doesn't seem to have an off switch for a common behavior."[4]

Where have Papa's hands been?

Nesha: under the influence.

Mimi and Papa pray five times a day but I could only move through the motions.

When I'm bloody, I am told to stay away from the prayer rug.

I am considered impure. Haram.

When skin breaks during a fast, the fast is broken, too.

Baudelaire told me to stay drunk, so I did.

All we know is reenactment.

Will You Love, or Be Arranged?

Wake up before 12 p.m. or else the shayatin will rule your day. There is no future for you, Mimi says, when you arise after 12 p.m.

Well, was it love or wasn't it?

Mimi never says.

Hold

When the handle is depressed, could I flush my compulsions, too?

Intergenerational transmission. How to give it back.

Happy birthday Mimi. You made it. I made it too. I peeled all these scabs for you.

The flush valve opens. Scrubbing and flushing. I'm blushing. Hushing my inner kids. Babes. Young and sensitive. They keep me up, run me late, demand things.

Does anything ever, does anything ever, does anything ever leave the body?

When I was seven, Gayoun Lee stepped down from a chair onto a parakeet we had taken out of its cage. We watched a flattened body and scattered plumage. A leaky beak. We were babes: young and sensitive.

How moments run in you long after they've run out.

How every sexual encounter leaves a deposit.

The plumbing is old and sensitive.

Please flush gently and hold.

---

1. Kecia Ali, *Sexual Ethics and Islam: Feminist Reflections on Qur'an, Hadith, and Jurisprudence* (London: OneWorld Publications, 2006), 56.
2. Stevens Jane. 2017. "Substance-abuse doc says: Stop chasing the drug! Focus on ACEs," *ACES Connection*, May 1, 2017. https://www.acesconnection.com/blog/substance-abuse-doc-says-stop-chasing-the-drug-and-focus-on-the-aces.
3. Hippocrates, *Epidemics* 1
4. Demelo, June. "How I Overcame My Skin Picking Addiction." *O the Oprah Magazine*, May 2017. http://www.oprah.com/inspiration/psychological-reason-behind-addiction-to-picking-skin

ZOHRA SAED

Aqua Net Days

It is Sunday in Brooklyn, 1988. The *dukhtarha*, or the girls, from Avenue Y come over, sneak Aqua Net hairspray into my bathroom to give me a make-over. At 11-years-old, I am introduced to the tall magenta bottle with a fishnet pattern. The packaging itself is a promise to turn my hair into luscious windswept waves that look touchable yet retain its stiff form.

Not one of three sisters think to open the window, focused as they are on turning my pin straight hair into waves. It's not easy to look like a teen *Lisa Lisa*—especially without the *Cult Jam* backing me up. When I choke on the spray and my nostrils burn, "Be a big girl!" is all they say as they tease up my *extreme-Uzbeki* hair nudging me on the shoulder for me to thank them for their patience. "*Tashakur.*"

"Your Farsi is stiffer than my hair. Tush Tush to you too." They lean on each other's shoulders and giggle. They catch reflections of themselves in the bathroom mirror and frost their lips first then mine with *Wet n' Wild* tangerine lip gloss.

These girls, with fluffy feathered hair and banana clips with faux-hawks, are the ideal Afghan girls, dukhtar-i-Kabuli. They listen to Ahmad Zahir and Freestyle, dance to both in the same swivel hips and arms way. Every chance to look at a mirror is another dab at lip gloss, or blue eyeliner and another eruption of hairspray. Their names are assimilable, a benefit of having modern Kabuli parents: Donna, Anjila (now spelled Angela), and Hel'en'ā—the stresses on the wrong letters, so they still sound "exotic" says their teacher with the moustache and the roaming eyes.

Their apartment is better, they say, it overlooks Avenue Y on the corner just above the Russian delicatessen. Even if it is smaller and has only three rooms besides the bathroom. The living room, also now their parents' bedroom, with a tushak, a foam mattress covered in rich burgundy and gold tinseled velvet. For their son, a medium sized couch. The three sisters share one queen sized bed covered in the lush blanket with floral patterns that they brought from Kabul. A few of the small things they were able to transport. They sleep in a row, "Traditional is better," they say.

Khala, to me, and madar, to them, floats in an air of melancholia and rose water. At home, she occupies this cushion most of the time, and when she comes over, she sits in father's arm chair, the arraam chair—"Did you know it is not about arms? But about resting, it is from the Farsi word, *arraam*, rest?" She teaches us like she used to back in Kabul. Khala with a long face the color of ivory and a beauty mark just to the right of her nose. She is the ideal Afghan beauty with jet-black hair, "*Ey buut'eh beh rahim*," a statue without emotions is her stoic expression and the title of her favorite Ahmad Zahir song. But it isn't because she put on airs, it is her heart that is the statue, or the mechanical part of her.

Khala, an early heart transplant patient, had blood filter in and out of her through a tube. When she lifted her opaque black silk veil then you'd see where her heart was cut out and the plastic mechanic box in its place.

At fifteen, Anjila is the closest to me in age but she is shokh, mischievous. When we go to the *Madajo's Video Rental Shop* on Avenue Z, she flirts with the pimply check out boy and gets early copies of the latest teen films. This is how we find awkward films that end with jocks chasing cheerleaders, somehow only in towels. The sisters giggle incessantly. Take notes on make up, hair clips, and imitate the way the actresses stretch the words till the last syllable of words lilt up like smiles. And they learn to overuse the word "like." Sometimes they lean down and generously whisper a joke or a secret into my hair, but my eager ears never catch the thread. Sadah, simple, they cluck their tongues like old aunties and shake their heads. I am hopeless.

The *dukhtar-i-Kabuli* are Texans really who miss the dry heat and twang of Austen and hate New York winters. Three sisters, an unemployed father who proclaimed to be a distant relative of the former king (but aren't all Afghan exiles?), a heart-patient mother, and an elder brother who works three part-time jobs to support the entire family.

One night, Anjila asks for my mother's earrings over the phone, "Like Zolay, why don't you like bring me khala's earrings? Come tonight, and I have a gift for you . . . from Texas!" and that is all it takes to get me to sneak the yellow shringari out from madar's jewelry box. Anjila plots further with me, "Say that you are buying milk!" and so I say I need milk desperately and smuggle out my mother's yellow rhinestone-studded teardrops. At the door of their third-floor walk-up, the smell of cold cuts and pickles from downstairs are strong, Anjila greets me with a hug that turns me into a limp doll. She whispers in the dark kitchen so that her parents don't know I am there. She speaks, I listen—privileged to be privy to a fourteen-year-old's dramas.

"These earrings are the perfect with my magenta sweater dress and yellow stirrup pants! His heart will be water in my hands! Don't you think so?"

"I do," I say, "Of course, it has to work!"

In her galley kitchen, the exhaust fan is filled with a light, yellow grease from cooking qormas and palaws. She stares just over my shoulder and talks to her own reflection in the toaster oven on the counter. It is Anjila in front of me and the silver reflection of Anjila's face behind me, I sit patiently chilled by the opened window and listen to her daydream about being the most beautiful girl in a school crowded with heavily made up Italian girls.

She weighs the earrings in her hand as if they are currency. Warm breath, stifled giggles, and a cookie in my palm. I am back on my way down the narrow steep stairwell.

The earrings belong to madar, and I will have to answer to her. But this walk alone at 11 p.m., running such a grown girl errand, and sneaking like water to and from my apartment at night is all mine.

OMAR SARWAR

Origami Butterfly

On the way out of the apartment complex, Aamir tightened his fingers around the upper straps of his backpack, easing the load of the oversize lunchbox and spiral-bound workbooks on his spine. The only child of a Pakistani expatriate couple, he was a wisp of a boy, much littler than his peers in the second grade, with a solid vermilion T-shirt, a brown button nose, and ears as prominent as those of a baby François' langur. The spoonful of cod-liver oil he'd been fed at home a few moments earlier made his gorge rise, so to dull the taste of the ocean, he popped a pebble of *ume* plum candy into his mouth, hoping that he wouldn't have to swallow it before his eleventh day at school had begun. The walk from Homat Viceroy to Azabu International School clocked in at just under twenty minutes, which was an agreeable commute for an elementary schoolchild traversing the quietest streets of central Tokyo. It was a still, hazy Monday morning in mid-September. The cicadas had formed a sonic kaleidoscope of treble and impassioned buzzing, churring, and crackling that appeared to invert creation itself, as if to declare to the world: "Man has no dominion over the creeping things that creep upon the earth."

Aamir knew the way to school by heart, but not two stop signs into his journey he had an urge to take a shortcut, a narrow stone path that snaked through a nest of aging low-rise folk houses, each with the translucent screens of its sliding *shōji* doors half-punctured, each seemingly uninhabited by any children. Today, though, he spotted a surprisingly small number of desiccated insect husks strewing the length of the passage. This failed to stop a resident adolescent Japanese girl from sweeping them aside with her thick dun-colored wooden sandals, as though the creatures hadn't had any business coming out in the first place. He tilted his buzz-cut head down and squinted, partly to be able to see through the plumes of steam pouring out of kitchen windows but also to avoid meeting her eyes. For the preceding Thursday, she'd frowned at him slightly as he passed by her, and he felt instinctively that it was better to proceed without giving her a customary greeting. The sudden barking of a dog nearby jounced his diminutive frame, sending him sprinting off the path and onto a thin peel of asphalt that stretched all the way to Azabu's main entrance.

It was in this gentlest part of the walk that Aamir's shoulders usually started to unknot. Since kindergarten he'd daydreamed of things like piloting an All Nippon Airways jumbo jet from Haneda Airport, crossing over the Shiodome skyscrapers which, from the clouds, might have resembled a set of misaligned but still earthquake-proof dominoes. *Would he see Homat Viceroy in Roppongi from the cockpit or at least Arisugawa Park in nearby Hirō?* Occasionally he fancied himself a captain rocketing a massive submarine with the head of a shinkansen and the tail of a helicopter all the way to Maui's Wailea Beach in under an hour. *Easy peasy. Shoot up to get some air, park on the sand, steal a hotel pool wristband, get past the lifeguard, then go whooshing down that giant white waterslide!*

This week, however, he didn't need to conjure much; he could experience the real thing. He carried a letter from his mother asking the school to excuse his absence next Friday, when his aunt's family in Pakistan had been scheduled to visit Tokyo. Although his parents had not yet decided what they planned to do, his mother, whom he affectionately called Ammi and with whom he spoke strictly in their mother tongue, had proposed a few ideas last night.

First, a short drive to Tokyo Tower to view Mt. Fuji, which from that distance had always appeared to Aamir as a blue gemstone under an upside-down cone of sugar. *But Mt. Fuji was where they had a safari park without cages for its animals and roads for cars to go through it. Last year when his family drove into the safari, a huge tiger raised its leg and peed all over the Toyota Corolla's windshield. It was craaazy!*

Ammi had also mentioned a tour of Ginza, with its glittering department stores and flashy pachinko parlors whose ringing and dinging sounded no different to Aamir than a high-powered Nintendo game. *He didn't like the pachinko places. The whole place just sounded like machines playing sounds from Mario World 3, like the sound of Mario's flying raccoon tail hitting the Koopa Paratroopas and Para-Goombas. Plus everyone was old. Boring.*

The third idea was a day at Aamir's most treasured Kōrakuen Amusement Park, which had live-action performances by the famous 1990 television superheroes, Fiveman. His lips made a slim crescent as he pictured the latter possibility—a chance to see his idol, Five Black, the only warrior on the team who boasted a side-snap kick and communicated in different languages, even with aliens. Aamir recalled a commercial about the entertainment show. A real-life version of Super Five Robo, Galactic Silver Imperial *Chōjū* Super Beasts, and Vulgyre the villain himself—only Kōrakuen had these wonders. *One, two, three, four, five, Faibu Man! But he had to remind Ammi not to pack kebab sandwiches, or watery dal, or keema mattar like she did before every trip. And not to play the tape of Nusrat Fateh Something Something in the car because he always sounded like Humpty Dumpty under an evil spell!*

Aamir snapped to attention as an unexpected gust of air threatened to topple him. Nearing the crest of the road to school, he suddenly felt something flash before his eyes, an image of someone he'd seen the previous week—someone he hoped to see again—etched in the most delicate fretwork of his mind. It was the boy in blue he'd caught a glimpse of last Wednesday while maundering by the edge of the playground, a tall Japanese lad with a short-sleeve V-neck, jeans, and sneakers—all blue. He'd been standing in the schoolyard right at the end of recess with an easel, a brush, and a snowy white canvas that dwarfed little Aamir. On a table adjacent to the easel had been a vinyl-sized palette splashed in a rainbow. He had dewy cheekbones, tousled hair as black as the tip of an ibis' wing, and kind brown eyes that glinted in the sun. Aamir's own eyes had grown wide, too, resembling a pair of castella *dorayaki* patties. That the boy had been alone puzzled Aamir; normally, students painted in a group setting, supervised by the school art teacher, Yamanaka Sensei, who had been absent that day. He was curious to see what the boy had been crafting. The indigo, tan, cerulean, and maroon fluid dripping from the boundary of his palette must have meant that he'd been bringing the sand, cement, and drabness of Azabu to life. Aamir had a wish to ask the boy in blue what exactly he'd been creating that day, but by then the recess whistle had been blown.

A lump lodged itself in Aamir's throat as he imprinted in his memory this discovery from last week. The road to Azabu tapered as he descended to the campus, which usually bustled with kids who arrived at 8 a.m., cherishing the twenty minutes they had to play before homeroom. Students of every grade—from kindergarten to sixth—flitted about a circular playground stocked with tetherballs, jungle gyms, jump ropes, and an enormous russet sandbox at its center, like the pit of a nectarine. The ash-gray buildings that ringed the playing field towered over a shifting mosaic of young wayfarers whose families' professional commitments precluded putting down roots in Japan, and whose ancestries lay in a constellation of cities, everywhere from Juneau to Jakarta, but who typically had at least one Japanese parent.

Aamir ingested the lentil's worth of candy left on his tongue. As he went past the front gate, he turned abruptly to the right toward a hidden clearing between the faculty house and the gymnasium, crouching beside a rough-hewn fence, where he intended to remain until 8:20 a.m.. He feared his classmate, Mamoru, had been roaming the playground, and the thought of being anywhere close to him put Aamir's nerves on edge. For last Thursday, in the sandbox, as he was molding dirt into the shape of a wigwam, he had sat motionless on his haunches as Mamoru and his squadron of goons took turns flattening the mound.

"You can't dig or make anything here, *Ameeru-kun*" Mamoru had said, tapping his left palm with a black shovel.

"Why not?" Aamir had asked, his voice quavering.

"Cuz you look like shit, *Mimi-Mimi-Meeru*," Mamoru had replied, using the Japanese word for ears in onomatopoeic fashion to ridicule Aamir's appearance.

"What?"

"Your skin looks like a piece of shit!"

A snicker cascaded over the arena. The sidekicks had by then created an arc around their quarry but with just enough space between themselves for the other kids to stare at the brownest second-grader at Azabu.

The memory of this confrontation sent chills rippling up Aamir's back. He remembered feeling his stomach fold in on itself, trying to resist the humiliation of being witnessed on the verge of tears by coliseum spectators, then dashing to sanctuary in the shadowy crevices that separated vast concrete columns of dimly lit classrooms.

Realizing he only had eight minutes till homeroom, he tiptoed out of his hiding place, ambling over to the attendance office in the faculty house to deposit his mother's letter. Just as he turned around to exit the building, he caught sight of the boy in blue down the hall heading straight in his direction. He felt himself stiffen. It had been one thing to admire a handsome boy at some remove from that chaotic amoeba of a schoolyard. It was quite another to be standing right in front of him, frozen like a stargazer eyeing a pearlfish. He was even taller and more dashing than Aamir had first observed! Today the boy wore a two-button blazer, matching navy trousers, and a crisp white shirt with a cutaway collar barely containing the golf ball protruding from his throat. His hair, now lacquered and wavelike, draped his right eye, causing him to clear his vision by swinging his head rightward and backward periodically. His satchel, fastened loosely by two gold-colored buckles and bulging with a sheaf of bent papers, suggested that he'd left home in somewhat of a hurry. Yet his gait remained measured in a manner that defied the brute awkwardness of adolescence. The heavy clacking of his dress shoes was like a carpenter knocking his mallet into a slack wooden joint. But at last! A name in English emblazoned across the pocket of his jacket. Takuzō.

Although his eyes were downcast as he passed by, Takuzō offered Aamir a gracious glance, followed by a charming simper that said he already considered the two of them close. There was a quickening in Aamir that thrilled and terrified him at once, elation swelling his breast, shame roiling his belly. He felt his head unshackle itself—painlessly—from his torso, floating above his body, buoyed by something powerful and electrifying. And though he was inside a dreary building, he looked up and saw the vast sweep of sky and inhaled it with all his might, storing the wind in his lower back. Yet, for a few seconds, it felt as if he had no need to exhale, and something warm and clear and bright near his crown had set him down as tenderly as a sculptor placing a porcelain figurine on display.

Aamir stood rapt as Takuzō climbed the stairs leading up from the entrance hall to the chambers where it had been rumored that the older kids gazed at odd ivory boxes while pecking a slab of plastic squares with their fingers. The creaking of the entrance door startled him, and when he turned around, he was struck by the aura of the ordinarily radiant, cheerful head librarian, Chiba-san, looking at him as though he didn't belong there. Not knowing whether to say anything to her, he made his way to homeroom.

Takuzō. He liked that name. It was just . . . pretty. He liked Takuzō because he seemed nice. He wanted to talk to him but didn't know if he could do it in Japanese. He only knew how to say his name (Ameeru), ohayō gozaimasu, konnichiwa, and some vegetables—like carrots (ninjin), potatoes (jagaimo) and cucumbers (kyūri). What if he told Takuzō that he could say hello to him in Urdu, and he could learn how to say hello back? Maybe he'd like that!

"*Assalam Alaikum, Takuzō-kun.*"

"*Wa alaikum assalam, Ameeru-kun.*"

"*That's how you say hello in Pakistan. I say it at home to my mom and dad.*"

"*Do you?*"

"*Yeah, it's the same as saying 'ohayō gozaimasu,' but there's no word like 'konnichiwa' because you say 'Assalam Alaikum' to grown-ups all day long.*"

"*Cool!*"

He hoped that Takuzō would shake his hand or hold it. And maybe after they said hello to each other, Takuzō could make a painting for him. Or he could give him the brush and show him how to make a big gingko tree with the two of them standing underneath it. Then they could give each other a nice long hug!

On Tuesday afternoon, a whistle issued from the direction of the art studio, which had already drawn a freshet of second graders arranged in a crooked line, waiting for their teacher to open his door. There was no sign of Takuzō. A twinge of disappointment came over Aamir as he wound his way to art class. Inside the studio, everyone sat at a large rectangular table on which Yamanaka Sensei, a mad genius with horn-rimmed glasses and flecks of sawdust in his mustache, set the materials for the project of the day. He'd brought out a co-lossal oval glass container with neatly stacked decks of origami paper—yellow, orange, white, then pink, like the petal of a plumeria flower. Today's project was butterflies, and the students had the option of treating the butterflies as friend-ly gifts with notes on them.

Aamir had done a fine job of fashioning frogs, hats, and pinwheels out of paper in first grade, and felt confident about the present task. He plucked an orange square from the container and got to work, crease by crease, layer by layer. Most of the students had decided to write messages on their inventions, giggling as their eyes darted across the room, guessing what things others might be writing in secret. Aamir adjusted the edges of his butterfly as he thought about what to write; some minutes later, he raised his hand to get the attention of Yamanaka Sensei's apprentice, a Japanese photographer. As she leaned over his shoulder, he asked her in the faintest whisper how to write "I love you" in Japanese. "Ai shiteru," she said, beaming. He pressed down on the outer wing, mimicking her Japanese script, adding his name as written in *katakana*, taking pains not to let the ink smudge. The apprentice nodded approvingly and asked who the message was for. Aamir's face reddened; he sat silent for a minute, un-sure of how to respond. Then tears welled in his eyes.

On the way out of school, he held the butterfly in his hands so as not to damage it. He chose the long way home, taking a street where his favorite candy shop was located. The atmosphere had become tranquil, and the once noisy cicadas in the trees played the last shrill notes of their summertime tymbals before hurtling into the dust below, relieving all of Honshū of its misery. At that moment he saw a figure on the road pacing himself gingerly, dressed in cyan blue, swathed in sunlight. Takuzō! Aamir followed hesitantly at a safe distance. Around the last bend of the road, he saw Takuzō walk into the old-fashioned candy shop from which Aamir purchased all of his sweets—a place that, in spite of its decay, featured a delightful array of confections, from watermelon pastilles to vanilla-coated breadsticks to cola-flavored gummies. He peered at the store from behind a brick wall, trying to guess what treats this special visitor might have been considering inside. Several minutes later, he emerged with merchandise in hand; Aamir determined from the shape and color of what Takuzō was holding that it was soda candy. *Wow! Takuzō* liked Guriko soda candy too?! Maybe he came to this shop a lot too on his way home!

The five o'clock chime reverberated throughout Minato Ward as Takuzō traveled in a direction far away from Homat Viceroy. Aamir knew it was time to go home but had an idea. Sneaking into the store through a back door that the owner used to leave ajar, he treaded stealthily on a rutted plank of wood to the section farthest from the cash register, right where all the soda candies were kept. A space between the soda candy boxes took form where Takuzō must have made his selection; Aamir carefully nestled his butterfly in that gap. *He hoped Takuzō* would come back tomorrow for more soda candy and find his gift and message. Yes! *Takuzō would wonder who 'Ameeru' is and try to find him at school, and play tetherball with him, sing silly Japanese B.B.Queens songs with him, hold him close.*

Each day the rest of that week, Aamir identified new viewing spots around the school during recess, searching for Takuzō, his chest aching, but never saw him again. He imagined that Takuzō had taken the orange butterfly somewhere far away, and that after he read the message, it had turned into a real one before his eyes. And perhaps that butterfly was still on a journey back to Aamir, carrying a message from Takuzō, saying to him: one day, my friend.

Sharia Love, Sort Of

The first time I told Steve I loved him was the night of the 2016 presidential election. As the final state counts came, I felt I was running out of time. Steve and I had moved in together that spring, and I still had not uttered the words that mattered. We were even married, sort of.

I had spent the campaign swallowing unchartered fear. I am a Muslim, a writer, and mother to a seventeen-year-old Afghan-American son. Steve's sister is gay. His daughter was living Mexico with her boyfriend who grew up undocumented in New York City. Trump's campaign rhetoric targeted all of the above (and more): Muslim, queer, immigrants, undocumented.

I am also chubby, or fluffy, as my son says. Trump doesn't like fat women, either. He doesn't seem to like women at all.

I'm white. I have that going for me.

As the results came in on election night, the state of my broke, fat ass—the journey to find my authentic self (the existential crisis that consumed my daily habits)—seemed so First World. Steve and I huddled close with limbs heavy and numb. We were too shocked to do much else. America had become untamed and unsafe for people we loved.

"I guess I need tell you something," I said.

"What do you need to tell me?" He chuckled. I sounded so serious.

I took a deep breath.

"I love you. I need to tell you this before it is too late, before the world ends tomorrow." Steve started laughing. "You tell me now, after all this time?"

"I had to tell you before they come get me." I started laughing, too. It was one of those moments. Nothing was funny. Everything was funny.

I didn't know who *they* were exactly, but I felt vulnerable and uncertain. In a matter of a few hours, America had transformed into dangerous frontier territory. I had to confess my secrets now. I didn't know what later might bring.

ॐ

Steve's entrance into my world signaled a shift in a personal compass. Since becoming Muslim almost half a life ago, I had been so good, because white girls are *so good*. We have to be. Everyone is watching. No drinking! No sex! No gratuitous showing of the body!

Now, I was changing into an unrecognizable shape and questioning the color of my soul as my country was questioning the color of hers. It's one thing to let go of stuff when you're twenty-five years old. It is another experience when you're in your forties. There's so much life on the bones now. The scale is heavier on sad days because sadness and doubt carry a certain density. I didn't know much about my new self when I met Steve except that I no longer understood how to be Muslim—or American—in seclusion from the wonders of the world.

There was more to it, of course.

It was a month into dating Steve when I saw it: a red Turkish prayer rug, a *ja-e-namaz*, demurely rolled up in the corner of his apartment, the inexpensive kind found by the dozens at bazaars throughout the Muslim world. The rug was a relic from the 1990s when Steve had lived in a rural West Virginia spiritual community. He had taken care of the cows and dervished with Sufis. He had studied with Thich Nhat Hahn. He had his past lives. I had mine. By my self-centered calculations, my past demanded reconciliation. I had more shit to clear, like a twelve-year marriage I had left, in part because I wanted to have a relationship with my faith that wasn't dictated by someone else.

"No man should ever tell a woman how to talk to God," my Southern Baptist grandma said to me back when I swung on tire swings under North Florida oak trees. Women took me to church while the men stayed home spread wide on the recliners. When I became Muslim at nineteen years old—years before marriage—there wasn't a man in sight. I forgot about her words when I married. I forgot about this when I agreed to become the kind of Muslim woman I wasn't. In the twelfth year of marriage, I remembered I was wild and beautiful and that I found God in strange places.

Later, in my fourth year as a divorcee and in early my forties, I lost all interest in being good. I roamed feral because the heart isn't any use if it can't expand in unpredictable ways. Indeed, the Qu'ran tells readers the heart expands or constricts when longing (or when rejecting) the Divine I questioned what the performance of faith meant if that particular performance didn't stir the soul, didn't quicken the pulse. Certainly, to be with a non-Muslim man wasn't for good Muslim women. I was thick with wonder and longing, so I placed a wager that I'd discover a little bit of God in this new relationship.

Steve's bookshelves included books by Rumi and other Islamic philosophers. He told me that at one point in his life, his meditation was *Bismillah Ar-Rahman*

Ar-Rahim, in the name of God, the most Merciful, most Compassionate. He had never mentioned the prayer rug. I unfolded the *ja-e-namaz* and admired the soft pelt. It was almost like new, and orange-red like Revlon lipstick. Prayer Rug Rouge.

The literal translation of *ja-e-namaz* is Persian for "place of prayer." I looked at the rug and rejoiced. Maybe it was a sign. Maybe a relationship with Steve held a place for all of my parts, for my spiritual wildness. This romance could blossom into *jai-e-qalb*, a brave place of the heart.

᧽

Steve agreed to a *nikkah*, an Islamic wedding, before we moved in together. Few imams conduct marriages between a Muslim woman and a non-Muslim man. However, the *nikkah* can be performed with witnesses. The marriage would be a religious formality, a component of shariah law. Shariah literally means a path, or a way, to righteousness. In the absence of tradition, I opted for a righteous path with a feminist twist. I wanted the partnership with Steve to be within the parameters of my faith even if he wasn't Muslim. We gathered witnesses under a gazebo in North Carolina. We read through the *nikkah* and signed our names. I edited the document to alleviate Steve from all the Allah parts. Those parts where mine alone. I cried a little. It was terribly informal and sweet. We wore jeans. I believe that most of us might have been barefoot. This was in the spring, back when the world felt more certain.

᧽

I did not tell Steve that I loved him the day of *nikkah*.

I did not tell him a few months after we started dating when I came down with a severe case of Norovirus. I was at an event at a bookstore when the virus took hold. Steve lived a block away. I couldn't drive home. He set my Ibrahim up on his couch. For two days, he made sure he got fed and to school and back. Steve worked at that bookstore, and he came home during the day to check on me. He gave me wet washcloths and glasses of ice water. The prayer rug in the corner kept me company, its presence looming larger. That sheath, that place of prostration, is where the heart collides with her secrets. Yet, I didn't tell Steve about my secret as he nursed me back to health.

Several months later, Steve asked: "Hey, if Hillary Clinton had won, would you have told me that you love me?"

"Probably not." I admitted. "That's one good thing about the election, I guess. It got me to let go of my secrets."

There was more to it than that, of course.

November 8th was the day I finally said it. I worried that America had come undone. I wasn't sure I could make it on my own. I needed more than promises of thoughts and prayers. This moment demanded something beautiful, something brave, something fierce.

Someone once told me to chase what is beautiful in Islam. Chasing beauty can send a woman to uncharted places. The signs of God show up in the strangest ways, if I'm eager to see. I believe in chasing what is beautiful about America, too. America made me wild with thick legs that can carry me far. The America that I know told me to think beyond my borders. She insisted on it. *We don't make small women here*, she said, *so don't fold yourself to fit in tight places*. Because she knew of my ferocious heart and vigorous limbs, America gave me Islam. In return, Islam tethered me to the world. I am a homegrown, radical creation.

I have to go on faith that beauty exists beyond the current ugliness; that prayer and love are excellent places to start if one is brave enough to go wild. The red prayer rug is now jagged on the edges, like a gap-toothed grin. It is big enough for the all of me and remains completely still when I prostrate, when my forehead communes with this hallowed, precious earth.

TARIQ SHAH

untitled

10. —and where is the pure and holy mosque now—and where are the blubbering uncles soaking their snot slick beards in holy vows—and who protects the nurse from her doctor's frivolous malpractice suits—and what dawns as her parents endure five open heart surgeries between them—and to whom do the black-clad ciotka wail—and what becomes of daughters who convert and speak wonder bread arabic and insist upon christmas trees—and who sees when grandma shah's thanksgiving fit pulls her son from his hot soup to mount and bash her shape back into dutiful invisible silence—and who is bob besides a widower plumber semi retiree—and what happens to his glasses she means to plant like a bulb along the silk road someday once the weather cooperates—and what happens after the earthquake gobbles up my thirty thousand blood relatives—and what happens when forward backward side to side demand I march in circles—and how to call glottal throat gurgled calls to prayer songs—and where go those months of fasting saved up like stacks of cash cooling in the heavenbank—and who lifted his prayer beads, his prayers—and has anyone told his first wife the cousin wife arranged without consent—and what do we do with these miscarriages—and where does his name go after leaving our lips for the last time—and what happens to the buttermilk now that no one drinks it—and what is left to return to—and what does his daughter recall of her father on eid al adha—and what sprouts up from the ring of baby teeth she interred in the soil of the house that rots where it stands——and what happens to the spectacled man I mistook for the archangel jibril when I learn he is just a janitor—and who needs ninety-nine names—and what is this doing to us all—and why has no one come—and what will return his normal color—and what comes to surahs recited by children who speak the tongue but cannot swallow it—and what won't we all fall for—and please can you spell that—and is that not his lucky undershirt worn thin as gauze across the sky—and what to call this what is this other   than   the   afterlife—

and what about the benz who drives the dead home from the optometrist—and what happens once the pipes freeze again—and what on earth is making that smell—and will they wait while I purge this thumbtack balloon—and how can the kinks be haram how can baseball how can standing on a chair be punishment—and how did anyone get through those holidays liquor free—and when will bush return dad's checks—and I wonder what would father's father find within me—and in which direction is mecca—and one of the good ones—and is anything easier than apostasy—and what to serve up this cold hole to make it shut its trap—and how do I fold my love in a meat locker—and who is that in the corner in the cloak in my dream—and when will the coast be clear—and is he able to think now that we have all skipped town—and to what depth must I dig to hit good clay—and where do my first fifteen years belong—and how long can I keep his final breath before it spoils—and whose turn is it to mop the sink water puddles after wudu—and could I get the requirements for pakistani citizenship quick before I change my mind—and last time it's pak as in glock and stan as in swan and I like me in between—and but where did dad learn to love blazing saddles—and what melody is it in his head in the shower behind the wheel after supper—and how will he ever manage to stone all my new friends to death—and does anyone else find his smile like a scimitar—and do his friends remember him did he make them laugh did they soften him—and is he scared of that knife above—and who murmurs suicide to my brother—and how much bad news must I break—and how many debts can mom assume—and how long until we pull the plug—and what will next year's summer feel like—and are we dogs—and would you believe they can not halt the spread of the fires—and thank god we all died when we did—and what—and O how cruel is this pretty sunset.

DEEMA SHEHABI

Ghazal: A Lover's Quarrel with the World

History gallops over the margins of your page, what's a story, but its
    plural all over the world?
Arabic lulls ageless in your ears, but to you, what most matters is temporal
    in this world.

The Sheikh with a gold pen in his pocket, the girl lathering her father's
    head with musk,
and you—pearling over Whitman's poems—all have a lover's quarrel
    with the world.

A riddle of childhood loss soaks the rearview mirror in an Arizona desert,
and you drive past the unsaid but ignite nothing immoral in this world.

When you put your head down to grass to gaze at the fallen sparrow,
your eyes met rest in its body and what's silent became oral in the world.

The child, splintered with too many voices, hears only yours,
and her paths, dismantled of sound, light up murals of this world.

A sweet theft, a heavy hour of grief, and a ghazal posturing for friendships
that never fade, vine-leafed gardens in which we hide against the perils
    of this world.

Her face is a balm against fracture; the light on her moon is a cheek you
    return to,
and you say time has no stride against her flushed lips, flickering corals
    of this world.

How else to bundle this dark where pillow meets dream,
and the one acquainted with the night rises like an immortal of this
    world?

Robert Frost at the Alumnae Garden

October's stealth light
leavens the skin
then molts into Nuttall Oaks.

No preamble to a scream
interrupts the glistening rub
of downward wings

except for the hum
of poets acquainted with one another.
The one made of bronze

cools the day's fire from their breaths,
so that news of faraway
places lifts briefly,

and in this afternoon
there are no bodies scraped
from deformed fans in Kashmir

nor children gushing out
of cemented pipes in Gaza.
For a small wrinkle,

the women of Tahrir
caress dragonflies with their fingertips
and flood the tank's long arm

with bracelets of jasmine.
The fluted fountain
in the courtyard

is only an ode
to timelessness,
but not shadows

as we elide
over an inscription
with a watchman in it.

ADEEBA TALUKDER

Ghazal
—after Javaid Quraishi

beloved, light
of the gathering:

you know your beauty.

set him free,
he of tired wings,
        of lonely song.

In the *mehfil*, spare him
your glances; think once

of his house,
how the walls tremble

with each storm.

again he lights
his floors with

the flame of you:
he turns, like smoke,
into himself,

kneels
at your door again

to meet your glance
with his.

search him:
he is a wasteland.

for his heart,
    sift the ash.

January 9th, 2008

What they call mania
is a mind
brilliant in darkness.

In you, Manhattan blinks.

No one hears your terror
at the East River,
how it beats

its head upon the rocks.

When you dethroned God
you saw the world

too vast, too heavy
to hold, and to learn this

was to learn wrath.
In these white rooms,

no one comes
to mourn your death,

then rebirth.

God, awake all   night:
rest, rest.

You are weary,
and the world turns without you.

FATIMA VAN HATTUM

5.11.18

The tiger orchid on the bathtub ledge bloomed today
and I finished the first year of my PhD
what use are theories of decoloniality feminism critical race

when everything falls
apart?

a concept remains a concept
a theory just
        a theory

better to care for orchids
just so, the light, the moisture, just so
bring things into balance

my first year PhD taught me about the online etymology dictionary
but I'd rather make up the roots of words
according to my mood, for example,
how "silence" comes from torment because
it begins with a sigh
and ends with a hiss

        I thought if I loved hard, hard, hard

there is mold in the bathtub grout
I'm convinced we brought it all the way from London
where everything eventually rots

even the right conditions for the orchid
can still just
        be wrong

Rocks and Fiction

Rocks weigh in her sweater
pockets, wool sagging misshapen.

One grasshopper leg
torn askew between magazine
and plastic cup
he'll die tonight, irrelevant

at the mercy of something
immense like, one million
refugees on a Jordanian plain
a limb askew, a death tonight.

Are you Muslim

or something?

I know it's off topic, but
what's with the blue headscarf?

You   creator of fictions
weighed down by rocks.

The thing about belonging
is that
          it's mostly just longing.

RABÍA VAN HATTUM

End of Ramadan

The absolute calls:
Stop wandering in the labyrinth of the relative
and return.
This month inverted time
prayers opened realms of space
and the people gathered
singing, singing.
Our human existence
a pool spreading wider, deeper
diluting our selves
into indigo ecstasy of ink
written or not
we cannot know.

Most everything can contain the sacred,
even the shape of a rock,
so prayer belongs most everywhere.
We have a direction and our prayers go there
But also towards a destination
within, their origin.
And the ink draws that map together
at both ends, one point.

If you forget, how will you know peace?
If you forget, how will you share food?
Don't lose this balance,
spend your entire span
learning what medicine really means.
And be courteous to the world
so it will depart from you easily.

Notes from Lefke

I have a suitcase held together in one place by a diaper pin.
Scents of Jerusalem souk spices
emerge from folds of Turkish embroidered scarves.
Some dirty laundry softens spaces for ceramic calligraphy tiles.

Everywhere in Lefke oranges litter the streets.
Oranges appear spilled in sharp curved ditches of a mountain road
where the lorry turned too quickly.
Each one tasting unique

The prayers are like that
each with taste
scattered, quickly passed
turmoil of color and language in constant motion, distracting

Until the voice of passion lifts above it
Calling and responding to the magnificent revelation.
My entire body vibrates
blood circulating to divine melody.
My mind tries to define words that I have learned,
poetry of guidance.

We follow, molded into compatible configuration,
But we can only rule ourselves.
And it takes a long time,
a life time.

SEEMA YASMIN

Dhosa

To make these dhosa, first you have to soak two kinds of lentils.

Why is that?

Because only lazy women use one lentil type.

And then what do you do?

You soak the black lentils with the yellow lentils plus the methi seeds. Soak them at night and bind that thick fabric belt I gave you really tightly around your lower belly. Keeps the skin firm and helps the baby weight shrink faster.

Does that really work though?

Yes, it does. Don't say stupid things. Bind the belt very tight. Go to sleep. Wake up in the morning and wash your face with a cup of warm water that has half a lemon squeezed into it.

That will keep your skin nice and pale. I will teach you the thing for your in between place later.

What's that?

Bunches of herbs we soak in a bucket of hot water and you squat over it. Spread your sari skirt over the bucket. The steam heals everything in between.

Sounds like something Gwyneth Paltrow would recommend.

I don't know who that is. Does she make dhosa? I bet she doesn't make dhosa like mine. Now listen. Soak the rice separately and then mix everything together with just a little bit of water. In the winter you must add some salt. In the summer, you don't need salt. Grind it all in a Breville blender, I think your cousin gave you one for your wedding. Make a paste, not too thick, not too thin. Leave it in a warm place to ferment. When it's bubbly, heat the tawa and ladle the mixture onto there. Just a thin layer. It will crisp up like a giant, perfect, pancake. Then put in the fillings and the chutneys.

Oh my God, my mouth is watering.

That is the thing with your generation. You are the Kings of Eating, not the Kings of Making. What will you do when I die? These recipes will die with me. What will I do in my grave? Make dhosa? No. That is why you have to stop asking things and listen. Are you writing this down?

No, I'm filming it. I'm going to make a YouTube video. How many cups of water did you put in the blender?

Too much questions. Not enough watch and listen. You can see with your eyes how much water is the correct amount of water. Your eyes tell you when something is wrong.

But my followers will want to know how many cups of water they should add.

Can they not see? Can they not hear? You can tell what is correct. Incorrect amount makes incorrect dhosa. Now peel a pound of potatoes, dice the potatoes and leave them to the side for one minute.

I read that a lot of the nutrients in potatoes are either in the skin or very close to the skin so it's better not to peel them. Plus you get more fiber that way.

Do you want fiber or do you want correct recipe? Fry this much mustard seeds in hot ghee with a curry leaf. I gave you some last Sunday in a Ziploc bag after the sermon. I hope you put them in the fridge. Do you still have that magnet on the fridge, the one with the prayer for plenty of boy children?

I have the curry leaves and the prayer magnet.

Don't tell me any of this one-child nonsense. Even though you have a boy, you should have more.

We are thinking of adopting when Saleem is a few years old.

I think that is haraam. You should ask the imam. He is very sick but ask him. He will tell you. When the seeds start to make *futt futt futt* sound, add minced garlic, ginger, green chili, and a little sprinkle of turmeric. Then, add the diced potatoes. So easy this recipe, betah. You could make it every week for your girlfriends when they come to watch films. Do you still talk to that Nazneen girl? I heard she cut her hair very short.

I haven't seen her in years. The potatoes are amazing. So, you put that in the middle of the dhosa, pour over the dhal, which, I already know how to make that, and then the chutneys? I was thinking of buying them frozen. It's a lot of effort to make so many different chutneys.

Yes, you can use frozen chutneys. And then you can use frozen potatoes and frozen rice and frozen dhosa. Why not eat frozen everything? Why learn anything? You children will give me a heart problem. That is what happened to the imam. He had to listen to too many questions. Betah, if you start eating frozen everything—I heard that's what Nazneen does—I beg you, please don't cut your hair short like that harlot. Leave this old woman with just a little bit of dignity.

Ma, you're only fifty-four.

I know. Don't put that last bit in your YouYou video, ok?

Contributors' Notes

Hina Ahmed is from Binghamton, New York. She has a BA in history and an MA in teaching from Binghamton University. Her published work has appeared in *Archer Magazine*, NYU's *Aftab Literary Magazine*, *Turkish Literature and Art*, *Adelaide Literary Magazine*, *EastLit Journal*, and *FemAsia Magazine*, among others. She was also a short story finalist in the Adelaide Literary Competition of 2018. In addition to writing short stories, poetry, and essays, her novel, *The Dance of the Firefly* is forthcoming.

Tanzila "Taz" Ahmed is a political activist, storyteller, poet, and artist based in Los Angeles. She creates at the intersection of counternarratives and culture-shifting as a South Asian American Muslim second-gen woman. She's turned out over 500,000 Asian American voters, recorded her #GoodMuslimBadMuslim podcast at the White House, and makes #MuslimVDay cards annually. Her essays are published in the anthologies Pretty Bitches, Shades of Prejudice, Good Girls Marry Doctors, Love Inshallah, and numerous online publications.

Kaveh Akbar is the author of *Pilgrim Bell* (Graywolf 2021).

Sarah Ghazal Ali is a Pakistani-American poet with roots in California. She is currently an MFA candidate at the University of Massachusetts, Amherst, where she also teaches creative writing and English composition. Her poems have appeared in or are forthcoming from Homonym Journal and others. Find her at twitter.com/sarwwaa.

Threa Almontaser is an Arab-American writer from New York City. She is the recipient of scholarships from the Tin House Writers' Workshop, Community of Writers at Squaw Valley, The Kerouac House in Orlando, among others. Nominated for the Pushcart Prize, Best of the Net, and Best New Poets, her work is published in or forthcoming from The Offing, Nimrod, Tinderbox, Adroit, and elsewhere. She teaches English to immigrants and refugees in Raleigh. For more, please visit threawrites.com.

Hala Alyan is a Palestinian American writer and clinical psychologist whose work has appeared in *The New York Times*, *Guernica*, and elsewhere. Her poetry collections have won the Arab American Book Award and the Crab Orchard Series. Her debut novel, SALT HOUSES, was published by Houghton Mifflin Harcourt in 2017 and was the winner of the Arab American Book Award and the Dayton Literary Peace Prize.

Barrak Alzaid (@barrakstar) is a writer, artist, and curator. His work in progress, *Fabulous at Five*, is a memoir relating his queer coming of age in Kuwait. It is a story of family fracture, reconciliation, and finding true love. He is a founding member of the artist collective GCC, which examines the Arab Gulf region's transformations and shifting systems of power. He was a 2018 Lambda Literary Retreat fellow.

Ruth Awad is the Lebanese-American author of *Set to Music a Wildfire* (Southern Indiana Review Press, 2017), which won the 2016 Michael Waters Poetry Prize and the 2018 Ohioana Book Award for Poetry. She received the 2016 Ohio Arts Council Individual Excellence Award and won the 2013 and 2012 Dorothy Sargent Rosenberg Poetry Prize and the 2011 Copper Nickel Poetry Contest. Her work appears in *Poetry*, *Poem-a-Day*, *The Believer*, *The New Republic*, and elsewhere.

a. azad is a New York City-based activist, writer, and educator. They are invested in imagining queer and trans Muslim liberation and community care.

Ayeh Bandeh-Ahmadi's forthcoming memoir-in-stories, *Ayat*, was a finalist for the Chautauqua Foundation's Janus Prize, recognizing an emerging writer's work for daring innovations that reorder literary conventions and readers' imaginations. Her writing has been recognized by *PANK*, *Entropy* magazine's Top 25 of 2019, and the Bread Loaf Katharine Bakeless Nason Scholarship. She teaches personal essay to Washington DC high school students for PEN/Faulkner. Find her online at www.heyayeh.com.

Mariam Bazeed is a nonbinary Egyptian immigrant, writer, and performance artist living in a rent-stabilized apartment in Brooklyn. An alliteration-leaning writer of prose, poetry, plays, and personal essays, they have an MFA from Hunter College and are—sometimes hard, sometimes hardly—at work on a novel. To procrastinate from facing the blank page, Mariam curates a monthly(ish) world-music salon and open mic in Brooklyn and is a slow student of Arabic music.

Aaliyah Bilal is a fiction and non-fiction writer based in Shanghai, China. A graduate of Oberlin College and the School of Oriental and African Studies (University of London), she's finishing a graphic novel and a short story collection centered on the lives of Black American Muslims.

Dr. Mandy Brauer, an American child psychologist, visited Northern Pakistan with her children, discovering Islam and learning about the Palestinian/Israeli conflict there. That trip changed her life. Later she went to Gaza and afterwards to Egypt, where she taught at A.U.C. and Cairo University Medical School. She's published many *bibliotherapy* books for children in Arabic and English. Currently, she's writing stories for teens about Egypt. She and her husband spend much of their time in Egypt and Indonesia.

Hayan Charara is the author of three poetry books—*The Alchemist's Diary, The Sadness of Others,* and *Something Sinister*—and a children's book, *The Three Lucys.* He also edited Inclined to Speak, an anthology of contemporary Arab American poetry, and with Fady Joudah edits the Etel Adnan Poetry Series. He teaches in the creative writing program and the Honors College at the University of Houston.

Leila Chatti is a Tunisian-American poet and author of *Deluge* (Copper Canyon Press) and the chapbooks *Ebb* and *Tunsiya/Amrikiya.* She is the recipient of fellowships from the Fine Arts Work Center in Provincetown, the Wisconsin Institute for Creative Writing, and Cleveland State University, where she is the inaugural Anisfield-Wolf Fellow in Publishing and Writing. Her work appears in *Ploughshares, Tin House, American Poetry Review,* and elsewhere.

Zara Chowdhary has an MFA in Creative Writing and Environment from Iowa State University. She has served as Visual Arts Editor for the literary journal Flyway. She has also worked as a screenwriter in Mumbai and produced for films and advertising for ten years. She enjoys working at the intersection of environmental and political equity through her fiction, nonfiction, and occasional dabbling in poetry.

Mahdi Chowdhury is a Toronto-based artist, writer, and historian.

Aslan Demir is a writer from Turkey, born in Van, an eastern Kurdish city. He grew up in his grandfather's village. After completing his higher education in Kayseri, he went to Pakistan, where he completed his bachelor's as a double major in English Literature and the Urdu Language. Living in Islamabad for six years, he went to Mongolia, where he taught English for four years. He is currently working towards his MFA in Creative Writing at Lindenwood University Saint Charles, USA. His works have been published in several magazines, most of which are on injustice and ordeal his kin, Kurds been going through

Ramy El-Etreby: I am a queer Muslim and Arab American theater artist, writer, poet, and performer from Los Angeles, California. I am a contributing writer to the groundbreaking 2014 anthology, Salaam, Love: American Muslim Men on Love, Sex and Intimacy. My writing has appeared online in the *Huffington Post*, *KCET*, *Queerty*, and the award-winning blog *Love Inshallah*. My theater work operates at the intersection of arts and social justice as I work in collaboration with communities with stories that are rarely told. I have participated in theater projects in prisons, museums, places of worship, schools, community centers, forests, and riverbanks. I have written and performed my own memoir-based solo show titled "The Ride: A Solo Journey" sharing dramatic stories from my life that have shaped me, including coming out publicly in the L.A. Times as well as healing from the tragic loss of my first love. This submission is my first attempt at writing a piece of dramatic fiction.

Hazem Fahmy is a Pushcart-nominated poet and critic from Cairo. He is currently pursuing his MA in Middle Eastern Studies and Film Studies from the University of Texas at Austin. His debut chapbook, "Red//Jild//Prayer" won the 2017 Diode Editions Contest. A Kundiman Fellow, his poetry has appeared or is forthcoming in *Apogee*, *AAWW*, the *Boston Review*, and *The Offing*. He is a reader for the *Shade Journal*, and a contributing writer to *Film Inquiry*.

Tarfia Faizullah is the author of *Registers of Illuminated Villages* (Graywolf 2018) and *Seam* (SIU 2014). Tarfia's poems appear widely in magazines and anthologies in the United States and abroad and have been translated into Bengali, Spanish, Farsi, and Chinese. The recipient of a Fulbright fellowship, three Pushcart Prizes, and many other honors, Tarfia presents work at institutions and organizations worldwide. In 2016, Harvard Law School named her as one of 50 Women Inspiring Change. Tarfia was born to Bangladeshi immigrants in Brooklyn, NY, and grew up in Texas.

Yahya Frederickson's poetry collections include *In a Homeland Not Far: New & Selected Poems* (Press 53, 2017), *The Gold Shop of Ba-'Ali* (Lost Horse Press, 2014), and four chapbooks, most recently *The Birds of al-Merjeh Square: Poems from Syria* (Finishing Line Press, 2014). A former Peace Corps Volunteer in Yemen and Fulbright Scholar in Syria, Saudi Arabia, and Kyrgyzstan, he is a professor of English at Minnesota State University Moorhead.

Farah Ghafoor's poems are forthcoming or published in *Room, Ninth Letter, Big Lucks, Halal if You Hear Me* (Haymarket Books, 2019), and elsewhere. Her work has been nominated for Best New Poets and Best of the Net. She is the editor-in-chief of Sugar Rascals Magazine and attends the University of Toronto.

Lamya H is a queer Muslim writer living in New York City. Her work has appeared in the LA Review of Books, VICE, Salon, Vox, and others. She was a Lambda Literary Fellow in 2015 and a Queer Arts Mentorship Fellow in 2017. Find her on Twitter: @lamyaisangry.

Samina Hadi-Tabassum is an associate professor at Erikson Institute in Chicago. Her first book of poems, *Muslim Melancholia* (2017), was published by Red Mountain Press. She has published poems in *East Lit Journal, Soul-Lit, Journal of Postcolonial Literature, Papercuts, Indian Review, Classical Poets, Mosaic, Main Street Rag, Tin House*, and *riksha*. This is her first published short story.

Umar Hanif grew up in Savoy, Illinois, near the University of Illinois at Urbana-Champaign. Umar is currently an undergraduate at Washington University in St. Louis pursuing majors in History and English with a concentration in Creative Writing. Umar's parents immigrated from Indonesia and raised their family Sunni Muslim. Umar spends free time watching cooking shows with roommates Lou and Amelia.

Shadab Zeest Hashmi is the author of poetry collections *Kohl and Chalk* and *Baker of Tarifa*. Her latest work, *Ghazal Cosmopolitan*, is a book of essays and poems exploring the culture and craft of the ghazal form. Winner of the San Diego Book Award for poetry, the Nazim Hikmet Prize, and multiple Pushcart nominations, Zeest Hashmi's poetry has been translated into Spanish and Urdu and has appeared in anthologies and journals worldwide, most recently in McSweeney's *In the Shape of a Human Body I am Visiting the Earth*. She has taught in the MFA program at San Diego State University as a writer-in-residence, and her work has been included in the Language Arts curriculum for grades 7–12 (Asian American and Pacific Islander women poets) as well as college courses in Creative Writing and the Humanities.

Noor Hindi (she/her) is a Palestinian-American poet who is currently pursuing her MFA in poetry through the NEOMFA program. Her poems have appeared or are forthcoming in The Rumpus, Winter Tangerine, Tinderbox Poetry, and Cosmonauts Avenue. Her essays have appeared in or are forthcoming in Literary Hub and American Poetry Review. Hindi is a Senior Reporter for The Devil Strip Magazine. Follow her on Twitter @MyNrhindi, or visit her website at noorhindi.com.

Mahin Ibrahim is a writer. Her writing has appeared in the anthology *Halal If You Hear Me, Narratively*, and *Amaliah*. She started her career in tech, where she last produced digital video. She has a fondness for hiking trails and seahorses. Connect with her @mahinsays on Twitter or at mahinibrahim.com.

Hilal Isler's writing has appeared in the *Paris Review, Literary Hub*, the *Los Angeles Review of Books* online, and elsewhere. She teaches college social justice.

Mohja Kahf is a professor of comparative literature and Middle Eastern studies at the University of Arkansas since 1995, Mohja Kahf is the author of *E-mails from Scheherazad, The Girl in the Tangerine Scarf*, and *Hagar Poems*. She is the winner of the Press 53 Award for Poetry for her 2020 book *My Lover Feeds Me Grapefruit*.

Seelai Karzai is a poet, community organizer, and chocolate enthusiast who hails from New York City. She is currently an MFA student at the University of Oregon. Seelai received a master's degree in women, gender and sexuality studies, and religion from Harvard University, and a B.A. in English Literature and Classics from Hunter College in New York City. Her writing has appeared in the *Fragmented Futures* exhibit zine, *Newtown Literary Journal*, and *DASH Literary Journal*.

Saba Keramati is a multiracial writer from the San Francisco Bay Area. She is currently an MFA candidate at the University of California – Davis studying English Literature and Creative Writing (Poetry). Her work has appeared in *re:asian* and *Michigan Quarterly Review*. She was a 2019 Kenyon Review Writer's Workshop scholarship recipient.

Uzma Aslam Khan is an award-winning author of five novels that include *Trespassing*, nominated for a 2003 Commonwealth Prize; *The Geometry of God*, one of *Kirkus Review*'s Best Books of 2009, and winner of the Bronze award at the Independent Book Publishers Awards; *Thinner Than Skin*, longlisted for the Man Asian Literary Prize and the DSC Prize for South Asian Literature, and winner of the inaugural French Embassy Prize for Best Fiction at the Karachi Literature Festival 2014. Khan's fifth novel, *The Miraculous True History of Nomi Ali*, set in the Japanese-occupied British penal colony of the Andaman Islands during WW2, was released as a lead title by Context/Westland Books in 2019. It has been shortlisted for the Tata Literature Live! Best Book of the Year Award for Fiction 2019.

Khan's work has appeared in *Granta*, *The Massachusetts Review*, *Guardian*, *Nimrod International Journal*, *Counterpunch*, *Drawbridge*, *Dawn*, *Herald*, among other periodicals and journals, and is forthcoming in *Calyx* journal. Follow her on Instagram @uzmaaslamkhan_writer or visit http://uzmaaslamkhan.blogspot.com

Naaz Khan is a writer based in Chicago, IL. A prolific writer, she has contributed to over 50 media outlets internationally, including the *Chicago Tribune*, *NPR*, *Public Radio International*, and more. Her writing has been translated into French, Arabic, Hebrew, Urdu, Tagalog, and Bahasa. She loves good food and Bollywood movies.

Nashwa Lina Khan is an interdisciplinary community-based facilitator, instructor, and researcher. She holds a Masters of Environmental Studies from York University. Her graduate work uses decolonial methodologies to make sense of the impacts of family law on sex workers, HIV positive women, Refugee women, and unwed mothers in Morocco accessing healthcare services. She is currently working on a small chapbook of poems she never thought she would share. You can find her tweeting @nashwakay.

Shamima Khan: My mother once found me telling stories to a crowd of people when I was just a toddler, so technically, I have over three decades of storytelling experience. I published my first poem at the age of seven and won the City of Ottawa's youth poetry award. I have been published in both print magazines and online, for example, on the *CBC Canada* site.

Since 2007 I've been performing my pieces as part of the annual Expressions of Muslim Women showcase as well as at various other events in Ontario. Because the media, society and pop culture often depict Muslims, especially Muslim women, in a certain way that determines the perceptions of us, it is important for me as a Muslimah to strive for Muslim women to have a voice, to speak up and be able to tell our own stories ourselves. So I write to connect, to make sense of this world, and to let my soul transcend the confines of my skin. I believe stories are magical, spiritual, and powerful.

Serena W. Lin believes writing is a political act of connection and cuts her teeth on monsters, myth, and magic. Serena writes fiction, poetry, blogs, essays, plays, reviews. Her works have appeared in *The Rumpus, Drunken Boat/Anomaly, cream city review, Hyphen, Bitch, Hyperallergic,* among other outlets. Serena is a community lawyer and former public defender. She's an alum of VONA and Rutgers-Newark. Website: www.SerenaWLin.com

Tariq Luthun is a data consultant, community organizer, and poet from Detroit, MI. The son of Palestinian immigrants, he earned his MFA in Poetry from the Program for Writers at Warren Wilson College and currently serves as Editor of the Micro Department at The Offing. Luthun's writing has earned him an Emmy Award and the honor of Best of the Net. His work has appeared in *Vinyl Poetry, Lit Hub, Mizna, Winter Tangerine Review,* and *Button Poetry,* among others.

Tara Mesalik MacMahon: A graduate of Pomona College and Harvard University, I am an emerging poet working on my first collection of poems—*Even the Sky Bleeds.* My work has appeared or is forthcoming in *Nimrod International Journal, Cold Mountain Review, Duende, Passager,* among others. I was a finalist for the Francine Ringold Award for New Writers and the Patricia Dobler Poetry Award. Spanish appears frequently in my poems as I have spent a considerable amount of my life with family in both Southern California and Mexico, where I became a bilingual speaker. I currently reside in the San Juan Islands with my husband Paul and our rescue dog Heck.

Haroon Moghul is a Fellow at the Shalom Hartman Institute. He's been published widely, including by the *New York Times, Washington Post, CNN,* and *Foreign Policy,* and contributed original content to NPR's *Fresh Air.* In 2016, he was honored with the Religion News Writer's Awards for Religion Reporting Excellence. Haroon is the author of three books, including *How to be a Muslim: An American Story,* which the Washington Post called "an extraordinary gift," and "an authentic portrayal of a vastly misunderstood community." Previously, he was a Fellow at Fordham Law School's Center on National Security and with the National Security Studies Program at New America Foundation.

Haroon is a member of the Advisory Committee on Cultural Engagement at the Metropolitan Museum of Art in New York City. He played a critical role in the development of the Islamic Center at New York University and continues to advise Muslim community institutions and organizations. He graduated from Columbia University with an M.A. in Middle Eastern, South Asian, and African Studies. He once designed and led heritage tours of Spain, Turkey, and Bosnia, which was some of the coolest work he's ever done. His next book brings together theology, autobiography, and a little bit of comedy to introduce Islam to a mainstream audience. It is scheduled for a Spring 2021 publication date.

Faisal Mohyuddin: I am also the author of the chapbook, "The Riddle of Longing" (Backbone, 2017). The child of immigrants from Pakistan, I teach English at Highland Park High School in Illinois, serve as an educator adviser to the global not-for-profit Narrative 4, and live with my family in Chicago.

Nour Naas is a Libyan writer from Vallejo, California. She is a VONA/Voices and Winter Tangerine fellow whose work has previously appeared or is forthcoming in *Catapult, The Establishment, Huffington Post, SBS Australia,* and *New Moons: Contemporary Writing by North American Muslims Anthology.*
She is currently at work on a collection of essays exploring her grief in the aftermath of her mother's death and the Libyan revolution.

Leila C. Nadir is an interspecies kin-maker, creative-critical researcher, undisciplined storyteller, and eccentric educator. She is also Assistant Professor and Founding Director of the Environmental Humanities Program at a university in New York State. Her work has been supported by the National Endowment for the Arts, New York Foundation for the Arts, and the New York Council on the Arts. She is currently finishing a memoir about growing up in an Afghan-American Muslim-Catholic family during the Cold War.

Noor Ibn Najam is a poet who teases, challenges, breaks, and creates language. She's a fellow of Callaloo, The Watering Hole, and The Vermont Studio Center with poems published by the Academy of American Poets, The Rumpus, and others. Her chapbook, Praise to Lesser Gods of Love, was published by Glass poetry press in 2019 and contemplates the ever-shifting role of love in the human experience and how best to worship such a multitudinous deity.

Samina Najmi teaches multiethnic US literature at California State University, Fresno. A Hedgebrook alumna, her creative nonfiction has appeared in *World Literature Today*, *The Massachusetts Review*, *The Rumpus*, and other journals. Her essay "Abdul" won *Map Literary's* 2012 nonfiction prize. Daughter of multigenerational migrations, Samina grew up in Pakistan and England. She believes in everyone's three feet of influence and the power of literature to extend our reach beyond it.

Sham-e-Ali Nayeem is an Indian American poet and artist of Hyderabadi descent. She is the author of the book *City of Pearls* (2019, UpSet Press) and the recipient of the Loft Literary Center's Spoken Word Immersion Fellowship.

Zeeshan Pathan is the author of *The Minister of Disturbances* (Diode Editions, 2020). He attended Washington University in Saint Louis, where he studied poetry with acclaimed poets, including Mary Jo Bang and Carl Phillips. At Columbia University, he received a Fellowship to study poetry at the graduate level, and he completed his M.F.A. under the late Lucie Brock-Broido. His poetry has been featured in *Tarpaulin Sky Press Magazine* and in *Poetry Northwest*.

Hana Qwfan is a Muslim Yemeni American writer. She has her bachelor's degree in Sociology and English Literature from CSUB. Hana formerly worked as a nonfiction editor for *Synaesthesia Magazine*, as well as a writer for UC Berkeley's *threads*, a magazine run by and for Muslim college students. You can find her previous work at threadsatcal.org, or see her Twitter @itsaplatesworld. Her writing is usually inspired by her religion and by her father, Ali.

Anisa Rahim is a writer and lawyer. Her poetry has appeared in *BlazeVOX*, *Tiny Seed Literary Journal*, *Red Eft Review*, *OJAL: Open Journal of Arts and Letters*, and elsewhere. She has an MFA in Creative Writing from Rutgers-Newark. See more of her work at anisarahim.com.

Duaa Randhawa is a writer and sociologist born and raised in Queens, New York. Her writing is a combination of creative non-fiction and prose-poetry, which meets at the juncture of experience, identity, and community. This poem is part of a larger collection titled "Bouts." "Bouts" is an exploration of self, identity, and history and all the nuances and confusions that come along with such an exploration.

Sehrish Ranjha's stories have appeared or are forthcoming in West Branch, The Malahat Review, and elsewhere. She divides her time between Los Angeles and Lahore, Pakistan.

Aatif Rashid is the author of the novel *Portrait of Sebastian Khan*. He's published stories in *The Massachusetts Review*, *Arcturus*, *Barrelhouse*, and *Triangle House*, and nonfiction in *The Los Angeles Review of Books*, *Lit Hub*, and other places. He currently writes regularly for The Kenyon Review blog.

Alicia Razvi is a farmer, a baker, and a writer. She gratefully owns a sustainable micro-farm in Wisconsin with her husband and three kids. She is living a dream life of growing, raising, producing, and advocating for local food. Alicia became the first Muslim chapter president of Farmers Union in 2016 and is active in the role still today. She is very new in her writing journey with just one other publication to date.

Bushra Rehman is author of the poetry collection *Marianna's Beauty Salon* and *Corona*, a dark comedy about being Desi-American. She co-edited the anthology *Colonize This! Young Women of Color on Today's Feminism*, one of Ms. Magazine's "100 Best Non-fiction Books of All Time." Rehman's first YA novel, *Corona: Stories of a Queens Girlhood*, is forthcoming from Tor/Macmillan. She is creator of the community-based writing workshop 'Two Truths and a Lie: Writing Memoir and Autobiographical Fiction."

Marina Reza was born in Dhaka, Bangladesh, to Muslim parents who brought her to New York City at one-year-old. She received a B.A. in English from Wesleyan University with certificates in Creative Writing and South Asian Studies. Her writing has appeared in *Bone Bouquet, Having A Whiskey Coke With You, and First Times: A Collection of Stories Gathered by Max Bevilacqua.* A certified trauma-conscious yoga teacher, Marina can be found clacking away on her typewriter and working on her recovery from substance abuse and childhood trauma.

Omar Sarwar was born in New York City. He has trekked to Mt. Everest's base, sung with the Singapore Philharmonic Chamber Choir and spent his early childhood in the heart of Tokyo. Omar has written for publications like *Huff-Post* and *The Advocate* on religion and sexuality. When not writing, he enjoys bhangra, metaphysics, and giving people dating advice he never follows. The enclosed story is derived from his experiences as a young boy living in Japan as a Pakistani expatriate.

Zohra Saed is a Brooklyn based Afghan-American poet. She is the co-editor of *One Story, Thirty Stories: An Anthology of Contemporary Afghan American Literature* (University of Arkansas Press), editor of *Langston Hughes: Poems, Photos, and Notebooks from Turkestan* (Lost & Found, The CUNY Poetics Documents Initiative); and *Woman. Hand/Pen.* (Belladonna Chaplet). Her essays on the Central Asian diaspora have appeared in *Eating Asian America* (NYU Press) and *The Asian American Literary Review.* She co-founded UpSet Press, a Brooklyn-based nonprofit indie press, with poet Robert Booras. Aqua Net Days was an Honorable Mention in the Glimmer Train Very Short Story Contest (Summer 2018).

Deonna Kelli Sayed is an author and performer based in Greensboro, North Carolina. She is a collector of experiences, from working with a French Chef to organizing Greensboro Bound: A Literary Festival. Her work is featured in *Love, Inshallah: The Secret Love Lives of American Muslim Women* and in *Everywhere Stories: Short Fiction From a Global Planet.* She represents PEN

America as the NC Piedmont Representative and works for the North Carolina Writers' Network.

Tariq Shah writes fiction and poetry and was born and raised in Illinois. His work appears or is forthcoming in No, Dear Magazine, Anomaly (fka Drunken Boat), Gravel, King Kong Magazine, BlazeVox, and other publications. He holds an MFA in Creative Writing from St. Joseph's College in Brooklyn, where he now lives.

Deema Shehabi is the author of *Thirteen Departures from the Moon* and co-editor with Beau Beausolcil of *Al-Mutanabbi Street Starts Here*, for which she received the Northern California Book Award's NCBR Recognition Award. She is also co-author of *Diaspo/Renga* with Marilyn Hacker and the winner of the Nazim Hikmet poetry competition in 2018. Deema's work has appeared in literary magazines and anthologies, including *Literary Imagination, the Kenyon Review, Literary Hub, Poetry London,* and *Crab Orchard*, to name a few. Her work has been translated into French, Farsi, and Arabic, and she has been nominated for the Pushcart Prize several times.

Adeeba Shahid Talukder is a Pakistani-American poet, singer, and translator of Urdu and Persian poetry. She is the author of *What Is Not Beautiful* (Glass Poetry Press, 2018), and her book *Shahr-e-jaanaan: The City of the Beloved*, forthcoming through Tupelo Press, is a winner of the Kundiman Poetry Prize. Adeeba holds an MFA in Creative Writing from the University of Michigan and is a Poets House 2017 Emerging Poets Fellow.

Fatima van Hattum is from New Mexico, is Muslim, eats most things with chile, and has a large wonderful family and confusing background. She often writes because she is uncomfortable. She is a PhD student in Language, Literacy, and Sociocultural Studies and works at NewMexicoWomen.Org. Her work has been published in *CALYX Journal, Critical Inquiry in Language Studies, Intersections, Chicana/Latina Studies, openDemocracy,* and *Poetry of the People*, the zine of Alas de Agua art collective.

Rabía van Hattum is grateful to be a Muslima living most of her life in the mountains of northern New Mexico. Her greatest education has been learning to read the Qur'an, mingling with the human family in many lands of the world, and raising five extraordinary children. She especially thanks Allah every day for her husband, her greatest treasure.

Seema Yasmin is an Emmy Award-winning journalist, medical doctor, poet, professor, and author of three books, including *Muslim Women Are Everything* (HarperCollins). Yasmin was a finalist for the Pulitzer prize in 2017 for breaking news reporting. Her poetry collection, *For Filthy Women Who Worry About Disappointing God*, was winner of the Diode Editions poetry chapbook contest. Yasmin is director of the Stanford Center for Health Communication and clinical assistant professor at Stanford University School of Medicine.